The Trial of the Cursed Wanderer

Book Three of The Scale Seekers

By A.R. Cook

Also from Author A.R. Cook

The Scholar and the Sphinx Series
The Scholar, the Sphinx and the Shades of Nyx
The Scholar, the Sphinx and the Fang of Fenrir
The Scholar, the Sphinx and the Threads of Fate

Short Stories
"The Saintly Stew" from *The Kress Project*
"Necromancing Over Coffee" from *Women of the Woods*
"Demons in the Pages" and "The Last Quest of the Drunken Wizard"
from *Chronicles of Mirstone*
"The Dark Lord and the God Machine" from *Magic of Mirstone*
"The Hunt for the Wandering Mystic" from *Quests of Mirstone*
"Wanted: One Dragonrider for a Persnickety Princess"
from *Dragon Riders of Mirstone*

The Scale Seekers Series
The Secrets of the Moonstone Heir
The Legend of the Lightscale
The Trial of the Cursed Wanderer

Cover Artwork by Trisha Stadel
www.miraculux.de

I dedicate this novel to all those who don't give up on the journey; the stars are always within reach to those who believe.

PROLOGUE

The Goddess peered through the Hollow Eye.

All Luuva Gros was in the palm of her hand. Vast untouched plains raced by in a blur beneath her, and all the greens and yellows of the grass blended into one flowing sea. She caught glimpses of the tall stone Towers of the Knighthood that lined the borders between the Noblelands and the stretch of dreaded wilderness, the Inbetween, that separated the North and South. The goddess did not like looking at the Inbetween. It was a cacophony of the muggy expulsions of dark magic from the Court of Darkscale's sorcerers, and from the Court of Bloodburn's great ash-smeared engines that belched noxious fumes into the sky. The horrid Malaise Cloud hung over the entire stretch of forbidden land, and the Goddess knew it was deadlier than the dark magic or machines that produced it. Such a realm of doom was impossible for anyone in the South or the North to travel through it by foot or mount, so the two remained isolated except for the occasional brave sailors who skirted around the Inbetween by ship along the coast. She turned the Hollow Eye away from it, looking for more pleasant surroundings.

The Goddess's world was not as large as one might think a deity would have. She had been asleep for the longest time—how much time had passed, she was not sure, but she noticed there were no more Hij-Urawran, more simplistically called the Salamandrian Sages, so she figured a good deal of time must have passed. She had awakened in her modest sleeping quarters, the marble and pearl fireplace now cold and lifeless. She remembered the sparkling fire that had once inhabited the fireplace, and how its warmth had lulled her to sleep.

She could not leave her room—they told her she was not ready yet. Once she could leave her room, she would not be able to leave the museum she dwelled within. At least she was not completely alone; her keepers waited on her hand and foot. They did not talk much, however. She was left to her special artifacts and to muse about the world outside and its fragile, funny peoples. The Goddess sighed in her loneliness.

She wanted to find the Wretched who had caused all the trouble in the South. Having not been awake long, she did not know much about him, but she heard whispered words from her keepers. They spoke in hushed tones of a horrid beast that could alter things at the slightest touch. The Goddess did not approve of evil creatures, but they intrigued her, in the same way she was intrigued by "heroes" who lived and died by the code of virtue. She wanted to be fully knowledgeable about all things happening in the world. She did, after all, have a lot of catching up to do.

There were some things she knew for certain. Or perhaps it was gut instinct, or something inscribed so deep in her psyche that she knew it could not just be fancy or her imagination. Someone was coming. Someone who would help her understand. Someone who would make everything all right.

"Mother..." the goddess whispered to herself. The very word filled her with warmth and comfort. She had never had a mother, or father, and her keepers were hardly the kind of family she had witnessed so often through the Hollow Eye. She used to hope the man who protected the Taigalands, the Hijn of Frost, might be like a father to her. He was somewhere in the museum, but the keepers hid him from her. They were unhappy with him – deep down, she knew why, but it did not seem right. Hopefully, Mother would come before anything bad happened to him…

Suddenly, something happened through the Hollow Eye that took her by surprise. The images in the Eye flickered by rapidly, like someone flipping the pages of a book with one flourish. It showed her disfiguring dark magic spreading like wildfire over the plains, the forests, the mountains, and even the sea. Even the Inbetween became more gruesome, a writhing mass of gnarled tendrils, jagged shards and bleeding earth, as that twisted force rippled over it like a flood. It was a vision, the Hollow Eye revealing to her a fleeting glimpse of what was to be – what *could* be. All living beings, every creature of flesh, feather, scale or leaf, were altered into distorted abominations she had only dreamt about in her deepest, most frightening nightmares – and for a goddess, whose imagination far surpassed those of mortals, such nightmares could shatter a sound mind.

In that horrible, twisted design, she saw *him*. His eyes were roiling with rage and hatred, his malicious smile beckoning those to madness. The Twisted One, the Distortionist, a shifting contortion of insanity and mayhem made flesh, had consumed everything.

The Goddess was stunned and, for the first time in ages, terrified. She put down the artifact and settled back against the feather pillows and silken quilts of her bed.

She's coming, she tried to console herself as she

shivered. *Mother's coming, and she'll make everything okay…*

CHAPTER ONE
Awakening

"Don'tcrowd'im! Give'imsomeair!"

Gabriel awoke to faces staring down at him.

"*Bwyhwonuwihu*," one of the faces said, in a distinct, bubbly dialect.

Gabriel blinked his eyes and groaned softly. Already the past was flowing back into his drowsy consciousness. He had been on a ramshackle merchant ship, sailing up the coast, when he and his crew had been attacked. Not by pirates — if it had been pirates, he would have been able to handle the ambush easily. He had been attacked with magic, such powerful magic that it had destroyed the ship. There had been two of them, two Hijn — one of them had tried to kidnap Gabriel and his crew, the other had tried to save them...but then *she* intervened...

Gabriel sat up slowly, the foreign faces edging away to allow him space. He held his head, trying to get a grasp of all the conflicting thoughts in his waterlogged brain. He looked around the small room, and at first, he thought it was painted in green stripes. Then he saw that the walls and floor were constructed of poles of bamboo so tightly lashed together that they were seamless. He was lying on a simple bed, the frame made from the same bamboo as the walls with a fish-skin mattress — only now did he acknowledge the smell. He could hear the rumble of the ocean, lapping rhythmically. The room bounced to this rhythm, so Gabriel deduced that he was in a ship's cabin. His tattered, muddy-brown clothing was dry after his long sleep. His wide-brimmed hat sat snuggly on his head, but he wondered if these Coast People had studied him when they pulled him out of the water. Had they removed his hat and seen the scars, blood-red blotches edged in charred skin, that plagued his forehead and down his right cheek? If they had, they were disgusted enough to put his hat back on.

"*Bwynahem hywi?*" said another Coast Person.

Gabriel shifted his eyes to the crowd around him. There were seven of them, speckled-skinned people with webbed hands and feet, and they splayed bony dorsal fins out from their spines. They were a tribe of people who called themselves Bwryji-hunoro-hemi-bryhem, but most referred to them as the Coast People. They had dark blue skin speckled in translucent green, amber and orange spots, and eyes that were wine red, amethyst, or rose pink. They dressed in sleeveless tunics and skirts, decorated with fish scales, shells, and the feathers of sea birds. The seven Coast People gazed at Gabriel with concern, but also glanced at one another and shrugged, not sure what to do with the human male.

"You'reawake!" came a piping voice, his rapid use of the Mutual Language barely understandable. A little pearl-toned face appeared at Gabriel's bedside. It was a Yopeis-Gichen, one of the people native to the Ring of Springs, but he was unique for his species. He had most of the same traits as his kind, including his four-foot-tall height and long glide-fins above his ears, and when the fins were folded in, they trailed down to his lower back. The four white illicia on his face, his fleshy "whiskers", twitched, sensitive to the air around him. This Yopeis had the distinctive scale color of buttercream yellow that coated his scalp and his back, while other Yopeis-Gichen were commonly green, gray or silver. This odd coloring was one of the physical aspects that signified that he was also a Hijn—the heir of the Wind Dragon—and he was the Hijn who had saved Gabriel and his crew.

"YouwereoutforalongtimeIcantellyou," the Yopeis rattled on, nudging Gabriel with his gloved hand. "IwassomixedupafterthatfightwithMerrosandIdon'tkno wwhatwasgoingonwiththatshinylightbuttheshipblewupa ndthatwasexcitingbutI—"

"Woasim!" Gabriel cut off the Yopeis to gather his thoughts. The man sighed. "Woasim, what's going on? And say it *slowly*."

Woasim twitched his whiskers, two of which stemmed from his eyebrows, and the other two stemmed from each side of his nose. It was said that the pearl-drop bulbs on the tips of each whisker could sense the four winds. He smoothed out these whiskers, and then he cleared his voice and tried his best to speak slower. "Right before that bright light blew up the boat, I got out my lucky bar of soap." He produced the object, which was a small round disc that smelled of milk, honey and rose petals. "I used my soap to make a protective bubble around me, and that explosion knocked me out. When I came to, I was floating on the ocean in my bubble. Thanks to my lucky soap, I didn't drown." Woasim gave his lucky soap a kiss, and then spat from the taste.

"You used a bubble as a shield?" Gabriel asked, his eyebrow raised.

"Age-old secret. Mix your soap with some Wuta bean gum, and the bubbles are super strong and unpoppable! I'll give you the recipe later. Anyway, I rolled along in my bubble for the longest time to find all of you, and there you guys were, sleeping on that piece of driftwood. I thought you must be very cold, but I didn't want to wake you. So, I put each of you in a bubble and whisked you all here while you slept."

"And where is *here*?"

"A Bwryji fishing boat," Woasim replied, stuffing his soap back into his coat pocket. "Lucky thing it was out here. I didn't think I'd have enough energy to fly all of you all the way over to the Isles."

"All of…" The full reality seeped into Gabriel's mind. "Desert Rain! Where is — "

"Relax, she's right there," Woasim answered, pointing to the side.

Gabriel looked over and saw Desert Rain lying on another bamboo bed a few feet away from him. She was sleeping, her long dark hair in tangles around her peaceful face. The Coast People, from the looks of it, acted more wary of her than they did of Gabriel. Gabriel was clearly human, but it was not clear what Desert Rain was. Her skin was a golden-ochre hue, her clawed fingers and toes were elongated and slender, her soft doe-like ears extended down to her shoulders, and two periwinkle-blue moonstones marked her forehead. She, like Woasim, was a Hijn, having inherited her moonstone markings and other strange traits from the Moon Dragoness. One of the Coast People ventured to poke a finger at Desert Rain's feet, which were prehensile, like a second pair of hands. Desert Rain twitched slightly at this, but did not awaken.

Gabriel watched her, remembering how he had been with her on that piece of driftwood bobbing helplessly on the ocean. She had been the true cause of the ship exploding, she and that sword of hers. What sort of magical powers that sword or Desert Rain had, it was clear she could not control them. Frankly, after all he had been through as of late, Gabriel was fed up with magic.

"Did you bring the others here as well?" Gabriel asked.

"IfoundtheQuetzalinandthered-headedguy —" Woasim paused and took a deep breath. "They're in the next cabin. But I couldn't find Merros anywhere, or those other three guys that were on the boat with you. Maybe Merros took them somewhere. Oh, and I picked up a few things from the wreckage. You want me to show you?"

"In a minute." Gabriel stretched, cracking a few stiff joints. A Coast Person brought over a large bowl-shaped shell full of fresh water to Gabriel, offering it to him. Gabriel took the shell and drank deeply before he returned it with a nod of thanks.

"I would like some time alone, if you don't mind," he said to his hosts.

The Coast People did not understand at first, but Woasim said something to them in rapid Bwryji. They nodded in acknowledgement and scuttled out of the room.

Woasim bounced up next to Gabriel on the bed, staring intently into his eyes. "You remind me of someone," the Wind Hijn said, sniffing at the man, who stared back at him icily. Ultimately, Woasim shrugged, and sat down on the edge of the bed, swinging his booted feet like a bored child. "So, how do you know Desert Rain? I didn't think she had many friends. Then again, I didn't think I'd ever see her on a boat, so far from her home. I could never figure out why she liked to spend all her time in that desert, by herself. Me, I like to go everywhere, riding the wind currents. I could never stay in any one place *that* long." He looked over at Gabriel, who grimaced at Woasim's ramblings. "But it's a good thing I was hanging around the oceanside the last few days, isn't it? 'Cause then I wouldn't have been able to help you guys!"

Gabriel slowly stood up, shaking on his weary legs. "How *did* you happened to be in the right place at the right time?"

"There'saverygoodstorytoexplainthat—"

"Save it." Gabriel made his way into an adjoining cabin, where he found his other two companions. The Quetzalin, Chiriku, was sitting on her bed, pecking at a plate-sized shell full of raw fish. The other one, the red-haired merchant Mac, was snoring, a trail of drool escaping down the side of his cheek. His scaly tail hung off the edge of the bed like a languid snake. The truth was, Mac was a lizard, one of the scorned Bayou Folk that was considered a lesser race, a "Lejenous." This one, for some reason, had the ability to change his upper half to look human, but he claimed to have no direct control over this. Why Desert Rain let this pseudo-reptile follow her around, Gabriel could not understand.

"Hey, you're up." Chiriku put down her food. Her feathers were scruffy and a mousy brown, washed clean of her royal blue dye. Feather-dying was a common practice of the Quetzalin, the female bird people who mainly resided in Syphurius. Their male counterparts, the Falcolin, were not quite so fussy about appearances, but they were just as stubborn. Chiriku was in the uncomfortable situation of being half Quetzalin, half human, and half-breeds in Quetzalin and Falcolin society were detested. It was no wonder Chiriku wore a permanent scowl on her short beak, and was about as welcoming as a wounded bear.

"He's managed well, I trust?" Gabriel asked, gesturing to the snoring Mac.

The corner of Chiriku's beak twisted up into a smirk. "What a stupid bum. We almost die, but he's taking it easy like it's a holiday. Is Donkey Ears still out?"

"Donkey Ears" was the ungracious nickname that Chiriku had bestowed on Desert Rain. Gabriel nodded.

Woasim bounded into the room after Gabriel, his brown eyes smiling. "Here we are, all nice and cozy." He removed one of his oversized leather boots, and wriggled his little pink toes. He tipped his boot upside down, and a trickle of water dribbled onto the sandy floor, followed by a thumb-sized fish. "I knew I had something in there," he said.

"So, what's with you anyway, Wing-head?" Chiriku asked.

Woasim cocked his head to the side curiously. "*Wing*-head? These are specialized fins, thank you very much. Not wings." He expanded out the two fins on each side of his head, which were about as long as his body, and folded them back. "Fin-head would be more apropos. And what do you mean, 'what's with me'?"

"I mean, what's with you flying in out of nowhere and fighting that water wizard? Kind of convenient, don't you think?"

Woasim wrinkled his nose. "I wouldn't say 'convenient.' It really wasn't convenient for me at all. That water titan that Merros conjured up almost drowned me!"

"She means, it was convenient for *us* that you showed up to help," Gabriel clarified.

"Well, as I was about to say, there's a very

interesting story behind that." Woasim scratched his chin and tapped his foot. There was a length of silence.

Gabriel sighed. "Which is...?"

Woasim snapped his head towards him, as if he had forgotten Gabriel was there. "Hmm? Oh, sorry, she was just telling me...anyway, you told me to 'save' my story. Honestly, you should make up your mind about these things. Hey, look who's awake!"

Everyone turned their heads to see Desert Rain standing in the doorway. She rubbed her left eye and blinked perplexedly. Her eyes were yet another item on the list of her odd physical traits—they were mismatched, the left one being hazelnut brown, the right being a dazzling sea green.

"I'm afraid I've left you all waiting," she said groggily.

"Nah, we're still waiting for Scale-butt to come to," Chiriku said, glancing over at Mac. She picked up one of her empty plates and tossed it at the lizard, and it landed smack on Mac's stomach. He awoke with a start, but when he saw the empty shell-plate, he sniffed it, and looked up at Chiriku.

"Could you toss-ssck me one with a bit of food on it-tkk, if you don't-tkk mind?" he asked in his Bayou dialect.

Desert Rain walked over to Woasim, bending down to be more eye-level with him. "Woasim, did you bring us here?"

"Isuredid, Isuredid! DoyouwanttoseewhatelseIbroughtbackfromtheshipwreckIgot lotsandlotsofstuff—"

"Before you get too caught up in that sentence," Desert Rain said, "I just want to thank you, for coming to

our aid. I don't know what would have happened if…"
She trailed off, as she glanced around the room again.
"Woasim, where are the Vermin brothers?"

Woasim pursed his lips in puzzlement. "The who?"

"Goude, Gimch and Gank, the other three who were with us on the boat. Did you find them too?"

The Wind Hijn scratched his chin, and then his eyes opened wide as he remembered. "Oh, the three Lejenous. Yeah, I remember them. Didn't look especially sea-worthy to me. But then again, I don't know how sea-worthy dog-faced people can be. I've never really seen a dog-faced person before, now that I think of it—"

"Where are they?" Desert Rain reiterated.

Woasim's cheerful countenance faltered. "I… I couldn't find them."

Desert Rain's ears drooped. She closed her eyes, as if she did not want anyone to see the apprehension in them. "Guerda-Shalyr, those poor boys…"

"The Vermin boys can handle themselves," Gabriel said. "They probably found something to float on and the tide took them towards the mainland."

"Or maybe Merros rescued them," Woasim suggested.

Desert Rain shook her head. "Not rescued. Kidnapped. That's what Merros was planning to do with all of us. But he had no control over what he was doing." She paused. "This wouldn't have happened if I hadn't convinced those boys to let us use their boat."

"Don't start up on the whole 'self-pity' routine again," Chiriku sighed irritably.

"But you're right, Merros wasn't himself," Woasim agreed. "Why was he acting so strange?"

Desert Rain's face crumpled, and she could not answer. She was troubled, and Gabriel knew it was more than having been ambushed by Merros. Something had happened when she tried to reason with Merros, when she tried to get him to tell her why he was attacking them. She had figured out that the Ocean Hijn was possessed by some force, some other entity. She had even known the name of it…she called it "Katawa"…

"Desert Rain," Gabriel said gruffly, putting a hand on her shoulder. "There are important things you have yet to explain to me, about where we're going and what you're trying to find."

Desert Rain sighed. "I wouldn't even know where to begin, Gabriel."

Mac stuffed his mouth with the food Chiriku gave him, although they were the food items she was too disgusted to eat. He chewed on what looked like a sea slug when he said, "Let Gila Gul have more time to wake-kk up, will you? She ain't even eaten yet-tkk. Hey Gila, do you want-tkk this? Don't know what it is-ssck, but it's fresh!"

Desert Rain smiled and declined with a gesture.

Woasim tugged at Gabriel's pant leg. The little Hijn was bounding up and down like a happy rabbit. "YouguyswanttoseewhatIpickedupfromtheshipwreck? Igotlotsofgreatbooty!" He paused, and then made a sheepish grin. "Hee hee hee… Booty," he chuckled.

*   *   *

Barrels, clothing, ropes, pots and pans, two wooden chests, and a variety of small random items from Woasim's pillaging littered the deck of the fishing boat.

The Coast fishermen did not look happy about having this clutter, since it reduced their space to work.

"*You* picked up all this?" Chiriku asked the Yopeis skeptically.

"Yep! Took a trip or two," Woasim said, already rummaging through one of the barrels — it was full of uncooked, watery rice. "But everything I found is in pretty good shape. It's almost like something was protecting all this stuff when the boat blew up."

Desert Rain shuffled among the barrels and piles of junk, scanning furiously among the contents. Mac was picking at the items too, stuffing any intact knick-knacks into his pockets, anything that he could possibly resell. Chiriku kicked at things, her arms crossed. Gabriel walked among the items patiently, silently contemplating if any of the items were still usable, or if they could trade any of these things for new supplies.

"Woasim…" Desert Rain turned to the small Hijn. "Did you find a sword in the wreckage? A long sword with sapphires in the hilt?"

Woasim scratched his head. "A sword? Oh, you mean that glowing sword that made the ship go kaboom?"

Desert Rain nodded with hope in her eyes.

"Nope. It probably sunk like a rock," the Wind Hijn said matter-of-factly.

The desert Hijn plopped down onto one of the chests, holding her head in her hands.

Mac came over and patted her on the back. "There there, Dez. It's-ssck only a sword. Just-tkk a material thing, that's-ssck all."

"You don't understand, Mac. It was Silverheart! It was a promise." She ran her long fingers through her flowing hair, and she took a deep breath. "I promised I would take responsibility for this madness. I promised I'd take up the fight..."

"You didn't know how to use that thing," Gabriel said.

Desert Rain looked straight at Gabriel, her frown radiating hurt and anger. There was a momentary flash in her green eye, like the spark of a fire. Then her countenance softened. She looked away. "I didn't mean to destroy the ship," she murmured.

Chiriku rolled her eyes. "Look, the stupid boat blew up. End of story. Anyway, we've got all the protection we need right here." She pointed to the sheath on her back that held her beloved warhammer. Granted, the warhammer had been a burden when she was pedaling out in the open ocean, but she would have rather drowned with it before letting it go. It was a gift from her deceased grandfather, and she carried the weight with pride.

"Don't be sad, Desert Rain," Woasim cooed, patting her knee. "Here, I found something. Once it dries out, it'll make a nice purse." He dug into several of his coat pockets until he found what he was looking for. What he pulled out looked like a wadded-up bunch of black fabric, but when he smoothed it out, it was a velvet pouch. "Women like purses, right? I mean, I guess not all women might...maybe you prefer a travel pack?"

Desert Rain perked up at the familiar pouch. "Gothart's bag!" She took it from Woasim. "How did you find this?"

Woasim smiled at seeing Desert Rain lighten up. "It was floating inside an empty barrel. I thought it might be something worth saving, being such a nice bag."

"Can we never get rid of that thing?" Chiriku sneered. "Don't tell me, that obnoxious goat is still hiding inside it."

"A goat? In the bag?" Woasim scooted closer to Desert Rain, his eyes wide with anticipation. "Is it a magical goat? Let me see!"

Desert Rain's hand tightened around the pouch. No, Gothart Grandwitt, the Trickster, was not in there. She was fine with that—in fact, if he had been in the pouch, the first thing she would have done was throw it back into the ocean. This whole mess was Gothart's fault. He was the one that had brought Katawa into her life in the first place, leaving the demon half-dead in her house. And when he could have used his tricks to help save them from Merros, he abandoned her to save himself. The one nice thing he had ever done for her was give her Silverheart, but that was after he had stolen it from its rightful owner. The goat had reasoned that he could take it since Swordmaster Skyhan was dead, but that hardly made his actions justifiable.

"No, he's not in here," she said. "He's gone, back to wherever it was he crawled out of. But maybe he left something in this pouch that we can use."

"I doubt the bag is magical anymore, with Gothart gone," Gabriel noted. "After all, Tricksters can't place permanent spells on objects. Their tricks are short-lived illusions."

Desert Rain drew the drawstring and opened the pouch, nonetheless. It appeared empty, a small space of blackness. But that was how the pouch always seemed, even when Gothart had been inside it. She reached her hand into the pouch, hoping that maybe something would mysteriously appear. Her fingers felt the soft bottom of the bag, and its finely-sewn seam. She turned the bag inside out, to see if she may have missed something small. Nothing.

"Good," Chiriku huffed. "I hated that stupid goat anyway."

"Aww," Woasim moaned. "I would've liked to see a magical goat. I once saw a magical chicken, but I've never seen a magical goat."

Desert Rain couldn't help but feel disappointed. Anything could have been helpful at this point, even a bag that could have held enough supplies to fill a house. She jabbed her hand to turn the bag outside-in, and her fist tore through the bottom of the pouch. Everyone saw, however, that despite the tearing sound — and the fact that her arm was into the pouch up to her elbow — that on the outside, the bag had not torn at all. Her arm had simply vanished into the pouch.

Woasim's jaw dropped. "How are you doing that?" he asked.

Desert Rain shook her head. "I don't know. I must've torn through some secret hole." She reached in deeper, sinking her arm up to the shoulder, while Woasim stared in child-like wonder at her magic trick. A few of the Coast fishermen stopped what they were doing and watched the desert Hijn and her pouch with fascination.

Finally, Desert Rain's fingertips brushed against something — something cool and smooth to the touch. Her long, slender fingers wrapped around the object, and out of the bag she drew the shining, gem-studded Silverheart. Waves of silvery light flowed across the perfect blade, and fire shimmered in the sword's blue sapphires.

"My word," Mac gasped. "That sword found its way back-kk to you!"

Woasim clapped his hands. "Now pull out a rabbit! No, wait, you can pull *me* out of the bag! Just let me hop in there first…"

CHAPTER TWO
The Vermin Brothers and the Ocean Rider

It was dark inside the jug. Gank Vermin did not
know what was happening, other than that he had been
stuffed into this grimy vessel, and that he was cold, wet,
and his toes squished in something that felt like mashed-
up maggots. There was no room to move his arms or
legs, not even enough room to shake the icy water out of
his fur. He felt a rhythmic bouncing, an occasional jolt, as
he was carried. There were a few holes in the lid of his
tight prison, barely enough for air. Once or twice the lid
lifted, just enough to slip in a scrap of stale fish or raw
meat, which Gank gobbled up despite the fact his
stomach was churning in fear. Dark visions spun in his
brain, of what those distorted monsters or their leader,
that red-eyed sea wizard, may be doing to his brothers,
or what they may have done already. The little Vermin
feared that the wizard had fed Goude and Gimch to
those beasts, and that Gank would be a snack later. Or
worse…

After enduring the confines of the jar for so long —
two days, five days, weeks, who knew — Gank broke his
terrified silence and howled in fervent demand to be let
out to relieve himself. Just when he could no longer
contain himself, he felt the jug hit the ground with a
heavy thump. An overcast sky greeted his sight as the lid
of his prison was yanked off. Gank bolted out of the jar,
scrambled over to the first form of shrubbery he could
make out and went about his very-much-needed-to-be-

done business. When he finished, his brain returned to the situation at hand, and he turned back to meet the malformed faces of his captors.

The skins of the Distorted were an unsettling purple-green in color, molded and wrenched around muscle and bone in unnatural stretches and tears like mangled clay. Appendages ended in claws or bloated hooves, bodies were adorned with quills, scales or protruding bone, and faces were warped beyond verbal description. Some may have once been human, may have once been animal, it was too difficult to tell them apart now. The eyes, however, were still of mortal men, and they were full of pain and pleading. Such eyes were penetrating enough to make one forget their nightmarish features.

Gank froze, too frightened to run. Perhaps it was not only fear that rooted him to the spot; he would not abandon his brothers. He had to find them and wait for a chance for all three of them to escape together. That was why he put up little struggle when one of the Distorted grabbed him by the scruff of his neck and plopped him back inside the jar, yet it did not reseal it with the lid. Gank cowered inside the jug for a few minutes, imagining what kinds of spices were going to be dumped on him before he was placed, jar and all, over a cooking fire. When nothing happened, he summoned up what little courage he had and snuck a quick glance over the rim of his jug.

The landscape around him was saturated in gray from one horizon to the other, and off to the west were foreboding clouds of smoky blackness. Green lightning pulsed inside the bowels of the clouds, and the soft grumble of their thunder echoed across the plains of desolate rock and gravel. Meager thorn bushes sparsely dotted the plains, and one could catch the quick panicked scurry of a beetle from one rock to another. A hazy orange glow emanated from a small campfire that the Distorted huddled around. They had two nets full of rotting fish, and the Distorted gnawed at the food with an unquenchable appetite. One figure who did not eat was sitting patiently on a rock on the opposite side of the fire from where Gank was watching. It was the red-eyed wizard, a lanky man with skin as blue as the depths of the ocean, with hair as white as sea foam, and webbed fingers like those of the Coast People. Shells and treasures of the sea decorated his clothing, yet his attire was ragged and faded, as if he had weathered through more than his fair share of storms.

Gank was more terrified of the wizard than any of the Distorted. The Distorted were strong and vicious, but the wizard had magic and could probably turn Gank into a toad or a turnip if he so desired. Yet there was something different about the wizard now than before. The first time Gank had seen him on the ship, the wizard had an enraged look in his eyes, a malicious look, like that of a rabid wolf. Now, the wizard seemed composed, reserved, peaceful. He stared off into the distance, towards the threatening clouds, his arms crossed over his chest. Gank thought that perhaps the wizard had forgotten about him. Maybe now was a good time to find his brothers and get out of this horrible place.

Gank looked around, trying to make out any familiar faces amidst the contorted ones of the Distorted. Then he spotted two shaggy shapes sitting behind the wizard, the light of the campfire barely illuminating the brown fur of his burly brother Goude, or the black fur of his spindly brother, Gimch. Something snaked out from where his brothers were sitting, along the ground and around the rock that the wizard was seated upon. Gank could make out what it was—a rusty chain. His brothers were chained, wrists and ankles shackled.

A scheme immediately began weaving together in Gank's head. He would wait until everyone fell asleep, then he would sneak over, unchain his brothers and—

"Come here, little one."

Gank instantly ducked back inside his jar. *I'm not here, I'm not here, I'm not here,* he repeated silently to himself, hoping that if he believed it enough that it might come true. But he did not disappear, and soon he worried that the wizard might get mad if he did not come out. He nervously raised his head out of the jar. The wizard was staring at him, his crimson eyes set ablaze by the reflection of the campfire, yet there was comfort in that doleful gaze. He said nothing, only waited as Gank stared back, terrified. A tiny bit of hope urged Gank out of the jar, for perhaps the wizard would not put a curse on him after all, and was going to be nice enough to let him see his brothers before feeding him to the monsters. Gank awkwardly spilled out of the jar, and made his way cautiously around the campfire, past the Distorted, who gave him anguished glances as he crept by. The little Vermin brother finally slinked up to the wizard, nervously wringing his hands.

The wizard sighed, his face stricken with sadness. He raised a hand towards Gank, who instinctively shuddered away from it, but the hand came to rest gently on Gank's head, patting him reassuringly. "You have nothing to fear from me," the wizard said.

Goude and Gimch turned their weary heads to

look at Gank. They had not had the luxury of being carried all this way like their little brother. Their feet were swollen and raw from the endless walk, their wrists sore from the iron cuffs that bound them, and their snouts rubbed red from the crude rope muzzles that silenced them.

"You may untie their mouths," the wizard said to Gank. "I would have done so myself, but I fear your brothers may cost me my fingers if I did."

It took Gank a minute or two, but he was able to wrestle the ropes off his brothers' muzzles. Goude and Gimch stretched their jaws, displaying the sharp canine teeth that the wizard had worried about. Goude immediately snarled and gnashed his teeth at their captor, who did not make any reaction.

"No no no, don't make him angry!" Gank pleaded, clamping his little hands over Goude's mouth. "He'll turn you into snail!"

The wizard shook his head. "No, my young friend. I have no power here. I am a prisoner, as you are."

All three Vermin brothers glanced at one another, unsure.

"A short time ago, I held great power," the wizard continued. "I was Merros, the Ocean Rider, the Heir of the Sage Waterweaver. But I no longer command the currents, for the power has been siphoned by another. I have become the instrument through which a malevolent force manipulates my gifts for his own despicable purposes."

Gank tilted his head to the side. "Huh?"

"I think he said he's being used," Gimch explained.

"And I think he's a blue-faced liar," Goude growled. "We all saw what he did! Smashed our boat into pieces!"

Merros sighed. "That was not my will. The same force that compelled me to do those terrible acts is the same force that has reduced these poor souls to their misshapen state." He gestured towards the Distorted, who were watching the foursome warily.

Gank, needing something to cling to for comfort, gripped the hem of Merros's tattered robe. "Wha…who did that to them?"

"He will come for us," Merros replied. "He will come from the cursed land, where he hides. He will come to reclaim his hold on me, and he will work his evil on you."

"THEN LET'S RUN AWAY!" Gank squealed, but instantly the Distorted advanced closer, huddling around them and cutting off any path of escape.

The hair bristled on Goude's backside. He looked at the wizard. "If you're really not as bad as you say, then tell those things to move aside and let us go."

Merros regarded the brothers with patience. "I have no control over the Distorted. They are *his* creations, driven by the muddled belief that their obedience to him will lessen their pain and release them from his curse. They cannot go home, cannot go back to the way they were, so they have lost hope, and without hope, they are broken and afraid."

Gimch shifted uncomfortably. "If you aren't controlled by, whoever it is, then why don't *you* escape? You can use your magic, can't you?"

The Water Hijn pursed his lips in thought. "It's strange, how I slipped out of the Wretched's control. It had something to do with that light, I believe. It came from Desert Rain's sword. It was as if it banished the cloud of shadow from my mind. But it did not banish this." He rolled up the sleeves of his robe, to reveal blotches of muddy purple, shaped like smudged handprints, infecting his arms and hands. "As long as these marks are on me, they block my ability to willingly use my magic. Although, perhaps the light nullified their effect..."

Merros held up his hands, each tattooed with a spiraling sea serpent on the palm, and he closed his eyes. He began to silently chant a mantra, in words the Vermin brothers could not understand, for it was in the lost language of Dragontongue. A soft blue glow started to radiate from Merros's palms, and then suddenly the dark splotches sent their oozing color through his veins, burning in his blood. He clenched his teeth, stifled a groan and retracted his hands. He nearly keeled over, but he recovered as the dark ooze slipped out of his veins and back into the handprints. He hung his head. "My magic cannot help us," he sadly confirmed.

"Forget the magic!" Goude bared his teeth, readying his muscles even though he was still handcuffed. "I'll take 'em all on! They're a bunch of pip squeaks!"

"Don't be so brash, my friend," Merros advised. "The Distorted are in constant pain, to the point of forgetting what life was like without it, so anything you would do would barely faze them. Even one as large as you cannot take on a whole group of them. But I will make you three a promise. As long as I am free of this demon's mental bondage, I will do all I can to keep you from suffering the same fate as the Distorted."

Gank looked imploringly up at Merros. "You promise?"

Merros patted Gank's head. "This is a time when we must all unite, young one. We must all try to protect one another."

"So, a Noble like you wants to protect us 'lesser ones'?" Gimch asked.

Merros turned a stern glance towards Gimch. "I confess, I haven't always been tolerant of those who were not considered Nobles, but I've been given the chance to rethink my beliefs. I would rather we be brethren than become lost to the Distortion."

Goude snorted a laugh. "You say that now, since you don't have your fancy magic. I bet you're thinking about trading us to that demon so he'll give you your magic powers back."

The red tinge of Merros's eyes suddenly flickered with anger. "I have *not* been so corrupted as to use innocent lives to attain my own desires! And it is not the loss of my powers that I must remain here!"

"What is it, then?" Gimch asked.

The fire in Merros's eyes dwindled. He clasped his hands together tightly. His body shrunk inwards, as if something inside of him was on the verge of breaking.

"That Wretched has my wife," he whispered.

As if to confirm this miserable truth, the Distorted around them started to shift restlessly and bay mournfully in cacophonous chorus. The Vermin brothers shrunk away from them, their heartbeats quickening as the Distorted grew more agitated and started to close in towards them. Then the chorus lifted their faces up, moaning their cries to the sky. Merros began to grow pale, and the blotch markings on his body burned, causing him to shudder. Turning his face towards that gray, tombstone sky, he saw the approach of a twisting cloud in the distance. The cloud slithered through the air with the distinctive shape of a storm wyrm, a leviathan body of rain, ice and lightning.

A small part of Merros felt a twinge of relief, for he knew this storm wyrm was his wife's work, as she was V'Tanna, the Mistress of Storms. It meant she was still alive, and for the most part, unharmed. But that same part of Merros also knew of the curse placed upon her, the same one placed upon him, although her mind was more far gone than his due to the Distortionist's severe hold on her. It made Merros's blood boil, and yet he knew he did not wield the power to free her, or the others, of the Twisted One.

"What's making them do that??" Gank whined, tugging at Merros's robe. "Why are they making all that noise?"

Merros sighed, clasping his hands together tightly. He hung his head. "They are heralding the arrival of the Distortionist."

CHAPTER THREE
Arriving in Wayfarer's Thumb;
A Heated Talk in the Hot Spring

"I'll tell you how I got here," Woasim announced as he and the four adventurers sat in one of the cabins below deck. He stood up on a chair, poising himself in a presentational manner. "For a long time, the Yopeis-Gichen of the Ring of Springs have been trying to form their own regiment for the Knighthood of Luuva. We decided that they would show the Knighthood that we should be considered to become knights too, by going on a mission. As the local Hijn and Know-Everything-Person, I oversaw finding a good mission. I figured that since Yopeis are small and can hide well, that maybe we could do a spy mission. I spent months scouting around all Luuva Gros, and then the winds sent me a rumor that the Bloodburn clan had constructed a new engine. I thought this would be a great spy mission for the Yopeis to find out if the rumor was true and maybe sabotage it. I went back home to tell them, and found that V'Tanna had sent me one of her enchanted paper cranes weeks ago. I always like getting a paper crane from V'Tanna, they make great pets since you don't have to feed them or anything—"

Gabriel cleared his throat loudly.

Woasim paused, as if expecting Gabriel to say something, but then realized what the throat-clearing was for. "Oh, right, focus. Anyway, the crane had a message from the Hijn Council, and they told me to go to

Vaes Galahar. I went there, and this old dwarf told me that a Wretched had stolen away most of the Hijn, but Desert Rain and Clova Flor were on the way to see the Ahshi Elves in the Forestlands, so I went *there*, and I found Clova but she told me you had gone to go find something up north, and I figured you must be going north by ship since no one goes on foot through the Inbetween, so I searched around the coast and then the winds told me that Merros was nearby, *soooooo* I thought I'd go talk to him about what in Luuva was going on, but then he attacked me and we got into that big fight and, well, you know the rest since you were there and all." He took a deep breath as he finished his monologue.

Mac applauded. "My, you've got-tkk yourself a marvelous set of windpipes-ssck," he commented.

"How is Clova?" Desert Rain asked. She still felt terrible that she had left her dear friend behind when Clova was sick. Leaving her in Juka Basin, not knowing if Katawa might go there next…

Woasim shrugged. "It was hard to tell. She looked happy to see me, then sad, then angry, then said something about gathering a whole bunch of elk and elves and lots and lots of seeds…she was kind of distracted, I think."

Elk and elves? And seeds? Desert Rain knew seeds were Clova's primary ingredient to her flora-spawning magic. What was she planning?

"Bwyhika hwy suum fwedahin," one of the Coast men shouted on the deck above.

"Ah, he said he sees our destination on the horizon," Woasim chirped merrily. "We'll be docking soon."

"It's about time," Chiriku sighed, stretching her

arms. "I can't wait to get back on solid ground."

"Clearly you ain't-ttk a water fowl," Mac said with a smirk, for which he received a punch in the arm from the Quetzalin.

The port they arrived at was not a glamorous one; even the port which they had sailed out of in the Bayou had been more typical variety than this one. This was a dock built on a small cape jetting out of the coastline like a thumb—thus why the area had been dubbed the Wayfarer's Thumb. It vaguely hinted at what the grand ports of the Coast People's native home, the Bwonuwihu Islands, looked like. The islands' wharfs were full of bronze and emerald sea turtles, its infamous coral labyrinths that swirled up and around into multi-colored pillars, or the lush bamboo forests that were home to the giant green Wonu crabs and the onyx kingfishers with beaks curved like scimitars. The islands were a thriving ecosystem, the Coast People living among neighbors of tortoises, scuttling shellfish, and seabirds.

While the docks of Wayfarer's Thumb were simple, a series of wooden plank walkways, it more than made up for this in its boat capacity. The harbor was littered with boats, vessels of every shape and size, although their fishing ship was by far the largest type. Beyond the port was a small village nestled among the cattails and long grasses, of modest homes molded from clay and shaped to reflect Nautilus shells, a homage to the beloved oceans surrounding them.

Mac watched a Wonu crab waddling along the shoreline, and thought how he would give anything for a pot of hot water and some butter right now.

Gabriel made his selections among the salvaged bits that Woasim had recovered for either keeping or trading, and gathered them up into one of the chests. Chiriku jumped onto the dock as soon as the ship came within reach, and as the others made their way down to the walkway with their belongings, she paced back and forth along the port, squawking, "Move it, already! I need to find a dye shop, now!"

Woasim, always the helpful one, gladly directed Chiriku to an ink collector, who operated out of a shell-house a short ways down the beach. To her dismay, the Coast People Isles did not have access to the high-quality feather dyes that Syphurius had, nor did she have the correct currency (honestly, what kind of people bartered with shells and pearls instead of using money?). But she made do with a small bottle of blue-tinted squid ink that the vendor let her have in exchange for a small pink pearl that Woasim plucked out of his right ear.

"You've heard of 'pearls of wisdom,' yes?" Woasim explained. "And Hijn are supposed to be the wisest of all. I figure if I keep a pearl or two in my ear, eventually I'll have that wisdom leak into my brain."

Chiriku smirked. "If you got any spare pearls in there, let me have a couple for safekeeping."

Gabriel scouted around Wayfarer's Thumb, trying to find vendors for better supplies and hoping someone might know the Mutual Language well enough for him to trade. Woasim knew of a highly regarded hot spring house nearby, and suggested Gabriel meet the rest of them there when he was done, so the group could relax and recuperate. Desert Rain, despite feeling soaked from their journey by sea, did want familiar warmth on her skin before venturing on towards the chilling northern Taigalands.

Mac was never one to reject a nice spa, and as

soon as the group arrived at the Spring House, he settled himself right into the inviting pool of frothy water and ritualistic sea salts. He didn't mind he had to keep on his trousers—for decency's sake, even though they did get their own private room—and he felt a little more at home since the Coast People did not seem to mind his reptilian aspects, or at least they made no indication of it. Perhaps being fish people, they did not mind those of a scaly nature. Chiriku refused to set foot in any more water, so she sat near the edge of the pool and meticulously went about dying her feathers as best as she could with the sticky squid ink.

"You need some help there, Chi?" Mac asked as he watched the Quetzalin grow increasingly frustrated as the ink dripped down onto her clothes. "You're starting to look-kk like a spotted toad."

"I'm fine," Chiriku protested, shaking the excess ink off her arm to splatter onto Mac's face. "And if anyone around here looks like a fat bottom-feeding toad—"

"Honestly," Desert Rain sighed to herself as she rested her feet in the hot spring, flexing her finger-like toes, "Those two never stop bickering unless we're being attacked by something. I wish they would give it a rest for a while."

Woasim, on the other hand, smiled at Mac and Chiriku as he bobbed playfully in the hot spring, and he turned his head towards Desert Rain at her comment. "Why do you want them to stop? Granted, it's a rather unusual courtship, but I think it's wonderful."

Mac and Chiriku's argument stopped dead, and they stared wide-eyed at the Yopeis-Gichen. Mac stifled a laugh, biting his lips to keep from smiling.

"I am *not* courting anyone!" Chiriku cawed. "Especially not *him*! As if I could ever have feelings like that towards a…a…" She fished for the correct word but instead snapped her gaze at Mac. "Isn't what Fin-head said completely idiotic?"

Mac scratched the side of his nose. "I don't-ttk know, Chi. You're kind of cute-ttk when you get all flustered like-kk that."

Chiriku gawked at him, but then her face scrunched up in indignation and she punched Mac in the shoulder again. It made Mac laugh, so Chiriku got up and walked to the corner of the room, before sitting down and returning to her primping.

Desert Rain rolled up her sleeves to feel the steam on her arms, and as she did so, she looked at the blue marble bracelet lined in gold on her wrist. She was grateful that this trinket had helped them escape from Merros, but it also reminded her that she was running out of time. The desert shaman had gifted it to her, to protect what was left of her soul after Katawa had fractured it and taken a piece of it with him. *When a soul is broken, you'll become feral*, the demon mocked her. What would become of her if she didn't get the stolen piece of her essence back? How long did it take for a soul to unravel? How long would the magic in this bracelet work? Strangely enough, she did not find this as urgent as she initially had all those weeks ago, which felt like a lifetime had passed since then. There was more at stake than just herself. If she did end up becoming feral, and she was aware of it, she would do what she had to do, even if that meant…

Gabriel returned in a short amount of time, having efficiently sold what he could in exchange for the Coast

People's currency, palm-sized white shells, so they could afford lodging for the night. He also had traded for better provisions, although none of the vendors of Wayfarer's Thumb sold the items that he ideally would have wanted for their journey ahead. He acquired a couple of skinning knives, a fishing net, three canteens, and a cheap sail that he figured he could convert into a tent. He also got a pair of shark-skin boots with thick soles, which he plopped down by Desert Rain's side.

"You need better shoes for going up north," he said, pointing at Desert Rain's meager foot wrappings.

Desert Rain felt humbled that Gabriel thought of her wellbeing with all the other things on his mind, but as she looked over the boots, and her odd feet, she reluctantly replied, "But my toes are too long to fit these. That's why I don't wear shoes."

With an irritated sigh, Gabriel sat down beside her, pulled her feet out of the water and began unwrapping them. Desert Rain's breath stopped inside her chest, and she wasn't sure why. Perhaps it was the intimacy of this action, when she had known Gabriel for such a short time. Maybe it was because, even though he had denied it several times, part of her still ached for Gabriel to be Swordmaster Skyhan returned from the Eternal Deep. Gabriel's silver-blue eyes made it impossible for her to not think of Skyhan. When he gently curled in her toes, making a fist with her foot, she felt her face flush. Gabriel appeared not to notice any of this as he wrapped her feet up again. With her toes curled in, Desert Rain's foot was close to the length of a regular foot, although it felt a tad uncomfortable to her when she slid on the boot to see if it fit.

When she told him this, Gabriel said, "Would you

rather be a little uncomfortable, or lose your feet to frostbite?"

At this, Desert Rain remained silent. She did not know what frostbite was like, never having lived in a cold climate, but its name made it sound painful. She looked away from Gabriel and gave him a soft, "Thank you."

Gabriel continued about his business, filling the canteens with water from a large clam-shell basin the Spring House provided. He paused for a moment, his brow wrinkled in thought. "Desert Rain, may I speak to you in private?"

Desert Rain waded out of the spring and walked over to the basin, testing her new boots on wobbly feet. "What is it?"

"There's something we need to get straight right now. You've been acting strangely toward me since our encounter with the Distorted. That needs to stop."

She stared at him with a perplexed expression. "I don't understand."

"You treat me differently when you see me as I really am, rather than this other person who you insist I must be. Who is this person you believe me to be? Tell me, so I can explain to you why you're mistaken." He looked straight into her eyes, locking on them and holding her gaze.

Desert Rain tugged on her left ear, tightening her lips. "I'm sorry I bother you with my silliness. I won't bring it up again. If you are who you say you are, then I believe you." She turned to go back to the pool, but Gabriel took hold of her arm.

"Tell me," he insisted, not allowing her to evade the question that easily.

Her green eye flared again. She clenched her hands into fists and shifted her gaze away from him. "He was a Knight. There are some parts of you that remind me of him. But it's foolishness that I confuse you for him...because I watched him die."

Gabriel released her. His voice was low and somber. "I'm sorry for your loss. I'm sure he died with dignity and honor, as all true Knights do. Grieve for now if you must, but you have a hard journey ahead of you and you cannot be haunted by ghosts."

The Hijn looked sternly at him, finding his practical observation callous. She managed to keep her voice steady. "Have you ever lost anyone close to you, Gabriel? Or worse, were you ever responsible for the death of a loved one? Are you so stone-hearted that tragedy doesn't affect you?"

The drifter narrowed his eyes. "When one's life is constant tragedy, you grow immune to its sting."

"Constant tragedy?" Desert Rain would have laughed if she were not so angry. "First of all, I have lived three, maybe four times longer than you have, so you have barely begun to live. Second, what makes your life 'constant tragedy'? Because you have those blemishes? Because you had a family that cared about you, and you left them behind to come with us? You keep running away from your life. Sir Skyhan fought not only for his life, but for others as well. You're right. You're not *him*!"

Gabriel froze, stunned. Desert Rain thought that her words had affected him, until he said, with a soft, shaking voice, "Sir Skyhan? He's the one you were talking about? He's dead?"

His sudden change in disposition surprised her.

She nodded.

The drifter looked as if someone had knocked the wind out of him. He steadied himself with both hands on the basin, staring down into the cool water. After several seconds of contemplation, he turned to Desert Rain with a hard look on his face.

"How?" he demanded, his voice tense. "How did he die?"

By now, their conversation had drawn the attention of Woasim, Mac and Chiriku. The three stopped what they were doing to watch the scene with unbreakable interest. Woasim's large eyes widened even larger, and his lip quivered. "Did she say, Skyhan? No, not Master Skyhan…oh, poor Miss Mage, how sad she must be…"

Desert Rain was speechless as Gabriel's crystalline eyes bore into her with a hot intensity. The memory of Skyhan's death was as clear for her now as it was when she witnessed it. She could have told him in detail, how Skyhan had summoned his sacred magic of Purelight to overcome Katawa, how the Wretched had countered it with his dreadful Distortion, how the sword Silverheart had unleashed an extraordinary burst of power that filled the entire sky with blazing light, but Katawa had somehow survived it — and only Silverheart remained, the last piece of the Swordmaster to be found. But all Desert Rain could say was, "Katawa killed him."

Gabriel took a deep, sharp breath. His face was contorted with confusion, disbelief, and dismay. After a minute of looking like he might strangle the closest thing — which made Desert Rain step back from him — he walked out of the room and out of the Spring House, without another word.

Desert Rain pursued Gabriel from a safe distance. "Gabriel, hold on! What are you talking about? Did you know Skyhan? Where are you going?"

"Leave me be," he ordered, quickening his pace down the path.

"So, you're going to abandon us too?" Desert Rain hollered after him.

Gabriel didn't turn around. He stopped, however, when Woasim dropped down in front of him, having ridden a breeze to surpass him.

"Yes, it is sad to lose someone," the Yopeis said, his eyes misty. "I can see you are upset. But let us comfort you in this hard time—"

Gabriel shoved the small Hijn to the ground. Woasim was stunned, not to mention hurt, and sat up and wiped his teary eyes. Desert Rain was so infuriated by this, she picked up a small stone out of the grass and threw it right at Gabriel's head. It bounced off the brim of his hat, but it was enough to halt Gabriel in his tracks and look back at her. She picked up another, larger stone, and raised it over her shoulder to throw it.

"What is the point of this?" Gabriel hollered at her, as he raised his arms to protect himself from the potential stoning.

"It's like when the Zi'Gax attacked us," she replied. "You pay attention when there's a fight. I'll start a fight if that's what gets you back over here."

By now, Mac and Chiriku had followed from the Spring House and caught up to them. Chiriku's eyebrows rose, and she jogged over with a bemused smile. "Now that's the kind of logic I like," she remarked.

Gabriel tightened his lips and lowered his arms. "Desert Rain, I'm not your enemy."

Desert Rain lowered her arm. "How did you know Skyhan? Were you a…a squire in the Knighthood? A stableboy, what?"

"What does it matter?" he spat. "He's gone. The great hero, dead. What hope do any of us have against that demon? What hope can any of us have ever again?"

Desert Rain dropped the stone to the ground. She bore her gaze into Gabriel. "What do you propose we do? Give up? You can if you want to, Gabriel. You don't want to talk to me, you want to run away every time something goes wrong, so quit. But I *can't* quit. I'm scared, I'm tired, I'm placing my life and all of Luuva Gros in the hands of a legend that may not even exist…you ask me what hope can we have? Hope's *all* I have. That's my armor. That's my weapon. What's yours?"

Gabriel was quiet. Everyone was quiet.

"I'm going north," Desert Rain said. She walked over to Woasim and helped him to his feet, wiping away his tears with her hand. She gave him a sad smile. "You can join me, or you can stay here. This place is as safe as any, which means not very. But you've all chosen to come this far. I'm not letting Sir Skyhan die in vain. But that's my burden, not yours."

"Gila…" Mac placed a hand on Desert Rain's shoulder.

Gabriel looked up at the sky, letting out a long breath. "Give me time," he murmured. "I will let you know my decision." He slowly walked away towards a nearby bamboo hut, which displayed a sign written with Bwryji letters and a picture of a red blowfish. Judging from the steam and smells coming from it, it must be a restaurant.

Chiriku crossed her arms and made a clicking sound with her beak. "Do we really want that load of crazy tagging along with us?"

Desert Rain watched as Gabriel walked into the hut. Would he really come back? Or would he slip off while they weren't looking?

Mac squeezed her shoulder. "Don't-tkk you fret-tkk, Gila Gul. He'll realize soon enough that-tkk he'd be missing something an awful lot-tkk if he ran off." He gave her a wink and a grin.

Woasim wiped away one last tear with his ear-fin, and beamed a genuine smile. "That's right, the Wretched-Whippers stay together!"

CHAPTER FOUR
Gabriel's Decision; Woasim on the Team

Gabriel slapped a few shell coins on the counter where a young Coast girl was serving drinks, grabbed a bottle of what looked like a passable liquor and sat down at a table in the corner of the restaurant. He took a swig, which was a wine with the slightest hint of fish flavor, and pulled his hat further down over his eyes.

It was a tempting thought to go after this Katawa. What did he need that empty-headed Hijn and her annoying friends for? They would just get in the way. On the other hand, he had no idea how to find him. Whatever Desert Rain's quest was — he still wasn't sure, other than to find the Elfë Taigas in the north — it meant she had some plan to track down Katawa and fight him. Did she really plan to fight the Wretched herself? Ruling out the possibility that she had a death wish, she clearly had no idea what she was up against. It seemed that there was a mutual benefit here: she could lead him to Katawa, and he could do the bloody work.

He took another gulp of his wine. Then again, why should he get caught up in all of this? Yes, Katawa killed Skyhan, but Skyhan was the Swordmaster. He was bound to be eliminated by some evil creature eventually. There was a cruel irony to it all — for all the nonsense Skyhan had spouted about how honor and virtue was what made one strong, *he* was the one dead, and Gabriel, for all his tainted corruption that supposedly made him "weak," was alive and well. Maybe this touch of wickedness inside of him would serve him better than all the goodness that he had tried to do to redeem himself.

You are not like them, Skyhan had told him. *The Wretched are beyond salvation. They chose their path a long time ago, with no wish to come back to the light. But you have a choice to change, to become pure and good. Do not lose your way. When you know you have smothered out that seed of evil within you, come to me, and you will be whole again...*

Gabriel slammed his bottle down on the table. How could he be saved now? Who would help him? He had a few options. He could disappear into the wilderness, waste away and be trapped in his misery for the rest of his life. Or, he could keep drifting from town to town to help random, nameless people with their petty troubles, and gradually his blotchy scars would — might — diminish. Or, he could stay with Desert Rain and her gaggle, protect her on her quest and fight this demon, a truly honorable act that might solidify his freedom forever.

Gabriel sighed and leaned back in his chair. He had to admit, there was one thing Desert Rain had given him, something he hadn't had in a long time, not in the real sense of the word. Now he had a purpose.

*   *   *

The Spring House was built onto the side of a modest inn, where Desert Rain and the others chose to spend the night before heading out in the morning. Naturally, she assumed Woasim would be heading home for the Ring of Springs, since he already had his own "secret mission", but as they made themselves comfortable in their room, Woasim said, "So, why are we going to the Taigalands? You haven't told me yet."

Desert Rain paused. "Oh…I didn't think you'd want to come with us. Didn't you have that spy mission you were working on?"

"That can wait," he replied, as he sat and bounced on one of the beds. "After all, if there's a big evil thing out there that made poor Swordmaster Skyhan go away…" He couldn't quite bring himself to say *killed*, and he did his best to hide his sorrow, "…and you're going someplace to find others than can help stop it, then I'm on board. If we're going to the Taigalands, are we going to see Kidran? I like him, he's like a brother, a snow brother—"

Chiriku kicked the bed that Woasim was bouncing on. "What Donkey Ears is saying, is that you *should* go back home to your little mission. Right?"

Desert Rain bit her lip as Woasim looked over at her with those big brown eyes. Before she could formulate a response, the Yopeis bounded off the bed and jumped over to her. "Can I come? Can I come? Can I come? Please please pleeeeeease?"

It wasn't a bad idea. Woasim knew the layout of northern Luuva Gros as well as he knew his whiskers, and he had been to the Taigalands before. Even though Desert Rain had the Darkscale compass to detect the Hijn magic that Kidran would (hopefully) be signaling them with, Woasim would have a better idea of where to go. The problem was, she was trying to keep too many people from getting involved with this, particularly since the item she was seeking, the Lightscale, was supposed to be a heavily guarded secret. Mac and Chiriku were already privy to the information, and not that Woasim couldn't be trusted with the knowledge of the

Lightscale…well, actually, he probably couldn't. He may have been good natured, but he was a notorious gossiper.

"I mean, if you really don't want me along, that's all right," Woasim said with a pouted lower lip for dramatic effect. "But I can do a lot of things to help! I mean, I do want to become the first Yopeis-Gichen Knight Commander, after all, and my wind magic would help in case we run into something yucky. And the winds can tell me the right way to go. And Mum says that…" He trailed off momentarily, as he furrowed his brow, as if concentrating. After a long pause, he nodded. "Oh…right! Talking too much again. Mum's the word." He put his finger to his lips in a *hush* gesture.

Desert Rain narrowed her eyes. "*Mum* says?"

Mac, lying back on a chair across the room, shrugged nonchalantly. "He's got-ttk some good points-ssck, Gila. Wouldn't-ttk hurt to have him along."

Desert Rain thought on it. "All right," she decided. "We do need your help. And yes, we are trying to find Kidran, but we really need to find the Elfë Taigas' home."

"The snow elves?" Woasim scratched his head. "Do they know we're coming?"

"It's complicated. Kidran should be able to help us find them."

Woasim sat back on the bed, his interest renewed. "Do they have some magic spell that will freeze the bad guy? Or a giant iceberg they can drop on him? Or a special snow monster that will eat him?"

Desert Rain's ears were twitching, as she tried to decide whether to lie about the Lightscale or just leave it, when Chiriku interrupted. "That's on a need-to-know basis. Now settle down before you get on my nerves, okay?"

The Wind Hijn saw the razor-sharp glint in the Quetzalin's eye and instantly sat still.

"Donkey Ears and I will share this bed," Chiriku confirmed. "Mac, you and the fishboy can have that one."

Mac smirked, unable to resist himself. "Now that's-ssck a shame. And here I thought-tkk maybe you and I could finally continue with the whole courtship that the little guy was talking about-ttk…"

He immediately received a swift kick to the shins.

Woasim stifled a giggle, thinking to himself how he'd like to be in love like that someday.

* * *

Chiriku awoke in the early hours, finding the room still dark. It sounded like everyone else was still asleep—Mac's snoring could best a boar, and Desert Rain mumbled something in her sleep. Deciding the slumbering symphony was too much, Chiriku slipped out of bed to find a scrap of breakfast.

She shuffled her way out of the inn and found that the denizens of Wayfarer's Thumb were already going about the day, fisherman preparing to cast off from the docks. She groaned in irritation—even Syphurius, for the busy city that it was, at least had official work hours; this was far too early for anyone to work. She smoothed back her head feathers, realizing she felt a bit grimy, and contemplated a trip to the bath house before breakfast.

"Morningmorningmorning!" she heard, and it set the teeth in her beak on edge. She turned and looked over at Woasim, who was awake, bright, and annoyingly chipper. *Who could possibly be this lucid this early?* Chiriku thought to herself.

Woasim was not only lucid but was working on something beside the inn. As she shambled over, she could see it was a large plank of wood that Woasim was affixing with runners on the bottom. He had a set of tools on the ground next to him, and he was currently holding a hammer with both his little hands, trying to drive a crooked nail into the wood. A heap of planks and discarded boat debris was piled beside him.

"What are you up to?" Chiriku asked with a yawn.

"I'm building us a sled!" Woasim chirped.

The bird girl blinked in confusion at him. "Why?"

Woasim put down the hammer, looking over his work. "We're going to the Taigalands, right? A sled would help us through the snow faster than going on foot. And once I get the sail attached, our sled can be wind-powered. See how I think ahead? That's a good thing for a Knight to do, right?"

The corner of Chiriku's beak pulled up into a half-grin. "Uh, how are we supposed to get this thing to the Taigalands? This won't slide too well on dry land, and it's a long way to get to the Taigalands from here. I don't think wind alone can push a sled with four...maybe five people, if Moody Boy hasn't already ditched us."

"Moody Boy? Oh, Gabriel. Yes, I see. You like to give people funny names." Woasim put his hands on his hips and huffed at the sled. "What would you suggest?"

Chiriku raised her eyebrows in interest. "Me? I guess... you flew us all to the boat before, right? Can't you just fly us all to the Taigalands with bubbles, or whatever?"

Woasim tapped a finger on his chin. "Hmmm… Too hard for me to corral everyone in bubbles, you may all float off in different directions. I guess I could take one person at a time, but that would take a while. Like, weeks, months."

"What if you just made one big bubble we could all float inside?"

Woasim ruminated. "I could try making a bubble that big, but it's harder to reinforce a bubble that size to keep from popping. And five people inside would weigh it down. We'd only get a few inches off the ground. Might as well walk at that rate."

Chiriku scratched her head. "What if we added heat? Heat rises, like the time my grandpa made a floating lantern for me. He put a candle inside that made the lantern rise into the air. Can we do something like that?"

"Something like that…" Woasim eyes widened in awe. "That's brilliant! And here they say Quetzalin and Falcolin are bird-brained, ha! But then again…" He cocked his head to the side, giving her a puzzled look. "You're a little different, aren't you?"

Chiriku frowned. "Yeah, I'm not purebred. So what?"

Woasim was suddenly quiet, staring at the ground. He then nodded and closed his eyes, smiling. "Yes, I know you said that. You're right, Mum. Human, you think? Hmm hmm. Yes, the legs, right."

Chiriku glared at Woasim, wondering if he was having a mental breakdown. "You okay?"

Woasim opened his eyes. "Oh, sorrysorrysorry. It's just, she told me there was something special about you. She's very perceptive."

"Who's *she*?"

"Zephyrsong."

Chiriku was not sure if this was a game he was playing. "Who's Zephyrsong?"

Woasim gawked at Chiriku, and then broke out laughing. "Who's...did you hear that? Who's Zephyrsong, she says! As if...Oh, well, I suppose. She's young, I guess she might not remember all the Sages' names...that's true, even I don't remember the Sage who chose Sir Skyhan. Oh, how tragic! Poor Sir Skyhan!"

"Sages?" Chiriku knotted her eyebrows. "What's that got to do with anything?"

"Zephyrsong's a Sage, of course."

"Wait, what? As in, one of the dragons? And you're...talking to it? Right now?"

Woasim nodded vigorously.

Chiriku shook her head. "That's impossible. The Salamandrian Sages have been gone for...I mean, no one's seen them in forever."

"Not out *there*," Woasim said, gesturing around himself. "It's funny, I've never seen the other Hijn talking to their Sages. But I talk to mine all the time. She's in here, with me." He pointed to his chest, his heart.

"O...kay," Chiriku replied, wondering if she should go tell the others that Woasim was a nutcase. "Zephyrsong is...a dragon. Inside you."

"Queen Dragon of the Winds," he confirmed with a nod. He winced. "Oh, right, she says I don't have to include the queen part. She prefers 'mother.' I call her Mum. Would you like to meet her?"

"Uh...inside you? I don't think I can fit in there."

Woasim was quiet again, and then he grinned. "She says it's all right. There's a time and place for everything. She says you must be hungry and should go get some breakfast." He reached into his ear and popped out another pearl, handing it to her. "I need to go find some rope. And more soap. Rope and soap, rope and soap..."

He scampered off, while Chiriku left to hunt down a food vendor. *Great, everyone is turning into a sack of insanity*, she thought.

She spotted the hut with the red blowfish sign, deciding that was as good a place as any to find some food. She walked in and spotted Gabriel in the corner, passed out at his table beside a couple empty wine bottles. He had clearly been there all night long. Chiriku guessed the staff, which appeared to be one Coast girl from the looks of it, had been unable to wake him to get him to leave.

Chiriku approached the sleeping man, glancing at the bottles. "Only two? What a light weight." She nudged him hard, to no effect. She placed a hand on his hat, but barely shifted it before he quickly grasped the brim, keeping her from removing it. He snapped his gaze up at her, glaring at her with exhaustion and ire.

"Pleasant dreams, Moody?" the Quetzalin asked with a smirk. "You know, clinging to that stupid hat doesn't make you 'mysterious'. You just look childish."

Gabriel leaned back in his chair, placing his feet up on the table. "Ironic, you of all people saying someone else is acting childish."

"I'm Quetzalin. We're notoriously goose-tempered. What's your excuse?"

The man let out a low growl of tired irritation, wiping a hand over his mouth. He squeezed his eyes closed, as if only now was the hangover kicking in.

"Would you leave me alone, kid?"

Chiriku clicked her beak. "I don't care whether you come with us or not. But I think Donkey...Dez does. And if we're going to fight that bastard – I mean, I can hold my own, but Mac's useless, Dez isn't a fighter, and the Fin-head...well, he might be nuts. So, why not join the freak show? Be the ringleader?"

Gabriel scowled at her. "Was that supposed to be a pep talk?"

"Give me a break, it's early."

"Don't talk to me like I'm one of you," the man grumbled. "You don't know what I've been through. You don't know what it's like to be —"

"There it is, the whole 'no one understands me' bit. Sure, I don't understand what it's like to want to hide your messed-up parts, right." Chiriku lifted her knee up high. "Like I can even *walk* without people pointing out that I have legs that bend the wrong way for a Quetzalin. Or Mac doesn't have to pretend to be human just to make a living. Or Dez – I mean, 'nough said. So no, nobody in this rag-tag group of weirdos could possibly understand what you're dealing with, you and your weird skin condition that you can cover with a hat. Get over yourself." With that, she walked over to the Coast girl at the front counter and started pantomiming that she wanted food. The Coast girl guided Chiriku to her own table and then disappeared to a room in the back, from where a cloud of steam and the scents of boiling fish wafted out.

Gabriel mentally chewed on Chiriku's words for a while. Funny, he really had not thought about anyone else's unusual appearances. There were all types in Luuva Gros – who could really set the bar for what would be considered normal? But Chiriku was right; who was he to moan about his scars when everyone had them, on the outside or not? And she did have a point. If he did not take the role of "ringleader," and she put it, how would any of them get to the north to find this…whatever it was? Desert Rain was not prepared for this, not alone and not with that lazy lizard, snippy bird girl, or scatterbrained Yopeis.

Well, there it was then. To the quest. To his redemption. If they survived.

*   *   *

Desert Rain, meanwhile, was having an unusual dream.

She walked down a sandy path dusted with rosy petals, bordered on both sides by blossoming trees of light pink flowers. Cherry blossom trees…Desert Rain could not remember the last time she had seen those. She could not even place where this many cherry trees grew in Luuva Gros; where was she?

Ahead, she saw the path open into a wide arena of sorts, or a garden of sand and statues. It was peaceful, *meditative*, as Clova Flor might say. Desert Rain wiggled her toes in the sand, an aching reminder of home, although this sand felt cool to the touch. The statues of the garden were ancient, weathered by time and wind. They represented men and women of all races, all wearing armor and holding weapons. They reminded her of the statues that had been in the Council Hall in Vaes Galahar, but smaller, truer to the size of their once living counterparts. Knights of old. Knights that Desert Rain was not familiar with, not that she had memorized every knight in Luuva's history despite all her reading. But these statues felt particularly archaic. Lost to time.

At the far end of the garden was a striking marble statue, twice as tall as the others; a creature covered in pewter-hued scales, with a long equine face, a serpentine neck, a body like a lion and a tail that curled around its feet in coils. It, too, was decked in armor, glistening in the sunlight like liquid silver trimmed with gold, with a helmet that accommodated its curling horns and impressive crest. A pair of chrome wings were folded neatly on its back, each wing tipped with golden blades. An armored dragon.

Desert Rain puzzled over this statue. She had never read about or heard of an armored Sage. Sages did not even wear clothes, unless shifted into a Noble form. What need did a Sage, in true form, have for armor? She approached the statue reverently, wondering if there was a plaque or something to give her insight into its creation. As she came closer, she marveled over the well-carved features, the carefully molded face, the vibrant cobalt-blue eyes. Made from sapphires, perhaps? Like the ones in Silverheart's pommel and guard…

Oh. *Oooooooh.* Was this…could this be…?

It then dawned on Desert Rain that the eyes were looking at her. The chest plate of the statue was slowly, steadily, rising and falling. The statue, which was not a statue, was breathing.

Desert Rain's mind scrambled for words, as she had not addressed a Sage directly in a long, long time.

"H…Hello," was all she could come up with.

The dragon blinked slowly. "Greetings, heir of Bellaluna," he replied in a voice as deep as a gorge, as resonant as a church bell, as stirring as a war cry.

Desert Rain mustered an awkward smile. "You knew Bellaluna?"

"All Salamandrian Sages are brethren, but she and I are both celestial dragons. We knew each other quite well." The dragon rose to its feet, planting its taloned feet firmly. "It is time that we spoke. You possess Silverheart. It must be wielded. I will teach you to do this." He stepped forwards into the arena, his tail swishing behind him.

Desert Rain blinked, startled, feeling his words press on her with unimaginable weight. "But… wait, hold on a second! You are… were… Swordmaster Skyhan's dragon."

The dragon paused. "That is correct," he said.

"I saw you. When he fought Katawa in Syphurius. I thought it was just Purelight, but that thing I saw come from Silverheart… that was you."

"Also correct."

Desert Rain's heart was thumping hard in her chest. "Wha…what happened? Where is Skyan? What did the Purelight do? What were you doing? How could Katawa survive that? What—"

"Still yourself." The dragon's command was stern but gentle. "All you must know is Skyhan can no longer wield the sword. As the heir of a celestial dragon, you must inherit this task."

The small spring of hope that had surfaced in Desert Rain's heart quickly dried up. "So, Skyhan really is…"

"The Swordmaster sacrificed himself to the Purelight to give it his strength. He is gone." There was no tone of regret in the dragon's tone, only confirmation.

Desert Rain lowered her gaze. Deep down, she

knew Skyhan was not coming back. She knew she had to let go of any hope she had that a part of him might remain. It was not any easier to accept this answer. She lifted her head to the dragon. "Wouldn't... another Knight, another Hijn, be a better choice..."

"No. You possess Silverheart. You must wield it."

There was instantly something in Desert Rain's hand. She looked down to see she was holding Silverheart, although her grip on it was difficult due to her elongated fingers. "Wait, you're going to train me? In my dream?" She had been aware she was in a dream from the moment it started; she had felt a sense of peace and safety she had not felt in weeks, so figured it could not be reality.

"For starters," the dragon replied. He walked to the center of the arena and turned to face her. Then, the dragon shrank, its neck shortening, its tail retracting into its body, its horns and crest receding. He stood on two legs, having taken on the appearance of a knight, with a dragon-faced mask connected to the helmet. His resemblance to Skyhan sent an invisible arrow through Desert Rain's stomach, and she stifled her desire to weep.

"I...I don't even know your name," she admitted, embarrassed that she did not know a Sage's title.

The knight placed a hand over his heart. "I was once called Veritas Lucen, the Star of Virtue and Honor. If it suits you, you may call me Sir Luce."

Desert Rain held up the sword, and felt the cool metal subtly shift in her hands. The handle adjusted its width to suit her grip, and even the sword's weight lightened for easier handling. This was just like what happened when she had fought the Zi'Gax, the sword modifying itself to be a weapon suitable for her. Or perhaps she needed to be suitable for the weapon.

"Was it you who possessed me before? When I was fighting those goblins in the forest?" she asked.

"You were unprepared. I deemed it necessary to assist."

"Um, thank you for that," Desert Rain said as she bowed her head. "But, if I may ask, if you can take over any time I hold the sword, why then train me? Can't you just 'assist' whenever I need you? Don't misunderstand, I'm honored by your offer, but it takes years to become a decent swordfighter, and I don't have time —"

Before she could finish her sentence, she was suddenly on her knees, facing the ground, her arm twisted back behind her, and a gnarl of pain shot through her arm and back. She dropped Silverheart as the knight bent her arm back, leaving her defenseless. She yelped, having not even seen Sir Luce move, but he was over her, holding her in his iron grip so she could not get away.

"You will not always have others to fight your battles," he thundered, twisting her arm tighter. "You will not always have me. You will not always have the sword. You must learn to defend yourself and defend others. This is not negotiable. Am I clear?"

"Yes!" Desert Rain blurted, and she gasped as the knight released her. She rubbed her shoulder, regaining her composure. This dragon meant business. She recovered Silverheart, folding her fingers around the grip. "How do we begin?"

The knight stood tall over her, and offered her his hand to help her stand up. "You are right. There is little time, and much to learn. That is why you will train awake and asleep. Not one moment shall be wasted. Above all else, you must keep this in your heart: always fight to protect those who need you. Do not use your strength to dominate or belittle the innocent. Be the guiding star for the lost, the wellspring for the desperate, the promise for the hopeless. Only by living the path of honor will Silverheart reveal its secrets to you, and you can overcome your enemy. To be a knight is also to be a shepherd, and the first thing you need to do is get your troop in line. They are undisciplined, unruly. Be patient, be mindful, but be firm. Be a Knight of Luuva, Desert Rain."

She opened her eyes. The arena, the trees, and Sir Luce were gone. She lied on her bed at the inn, as dawn crept in through the window. She sighed, somewhat disappointed that the dream was over, since she had rather liked it despite the residual pain in her arm. What a dream, to have such an effect on her...

That was when she realized she was holding Silverheart, its hilt on her chest, the blade pointing toward her feet, with her fingers tight around the grip. Had she retrieved it in her sleep? Was Sir Luce inside it right now, and could he possess her again? The realization that he could make her push the sword to the floor, where it clattered loudly enough to wake Mac from his slumber.

"Awww, is it-tkk morning already?" he yawned. "Sleep is good, but breakfast-tkk is better."

CHAPTER FIVE
Desert Rain Takes Charge; Woasim's Marvelous Sky Boat

"Ta da!" Woasim threw up his hands in a flourish as he stood beside a rickety wooden boat, about thirty feet long, with the large sail splayed across the top like a tarp and cumbersome knots of rope lining the edges. Desert Rain, Gabriel, Chiriku and Mac looked it over, perplexed.

Chiriku put her hands on her hips. "Ta-da, what? You bought a fishing boat and tied a sail to it the wrong way?"

Woasim laughed. "No, no, not a fishing boat. A sky boat! Much better than the sled I was making. Look, when the sail gets filled with hot air from the underside, it'll go up, just like those floating lanterns you were talking about. If my calculations are right, it should be able to hold enough air to lift the boat with us and supplies in it. And the boat's big enough to fit all of us and our supplies. It'll be easier for my winds to steer us all together in one vessel, see?"

Gabriel did not look impressed, but he came over to the boat and tested the rope knots. "And how do you plan to fill this sail with hot air?"

"Just-tkk have Chi talk-kk," Mac mumbled with a smirk.

Chiriku's feathers ruffled as she glared at Mac. "Do you want to lose an eye? Because that's how you lose an eye."

"This is the best part," Woasim said, chuckling as

he ran a short way off and brought over a bucket of water and a lit oil lamp. He took out his piece of soap hanging from his neck and lathered up his hands in the bucket. Forming his thumb and index finger into an O shape, he blew a bubble about the size of a pumpkin and held it in his hand.

"Desert Rain, would you mind lifting that lamp and holding the flame next to my bubble?" he asked. "You're going to love this!"

Desert Rain did as he asked, picking up the oil lamp and holding it next to the bubble. She assumed the bubble would pop from the heat, but instead Woasim placed the bubble around the flame and then lifted the flame away. The result was a hovering flame inside the bubble, and instantly the bubble rose high above his head. Desert Rain caught the bubble before it flew away, surprised that the bubble felt only a little warm, and that the flame inside was not going out despite being inside an enclosed space.

"Neat, right? I figure a couple hundred of those should lift the boat. And those are about the right size - any bigger and the bubble gets less stable, and the flame won't lift it." Woasim clapped his hands at his own magic trick.

"And how long until those flames go out?" Gabriel asked.

Woasim scratched his head. "Not sure, but if we bring the oil lamp with us, we can always make new flames to put in any bubbles where it might go out. But I think they should last a good while, long enough for us to get to the Ring of Springs."

"Well, ain't-ttk that nifty," Mac said. "Fire bubbles! You'll have to show me how to do that-tkk, would be a fine thing to sell at festivals."

"I wouldn't try to profiteer on magic, if I were you," Desert Rain warned, handing the bubble to Woasim. "We've seen what it can do in the wrong hands."

"So, let me get this straight," Chiriku said, looking cock-eyed at the boat. "You want me to get into that moldy old boat, which we're lifting with bubbles, to be steered by a guy who talks to his imaginary friend? No offense, but I'd rather walk the whole way on hot coals."

Gabriel narrowed his eyes on her, then turned to Desert Rain. "Perhaps it would be prudent to leave those who don't wish to accompany us here for the time being."

"I'm sorry, did I ask you to make my decisions for me?" the bird girl retorted.

"Now Chi, don't-tkk get all feisty–" Mac started.

"I'll get good and feisty if I want, you scaly-backsided bum!"

Woasim pouted, putting his hands on his hips. "You're not a very nice person sometimes, you know?"

Chiriku's feathers fluffed out so much, it looked like she might explode. "Now the Fin-head wants to get on my case? You all know Donkey Ears would be dead without me–"

"Don't call Desert Rain Donkey Ears! It's not cute, it's mean!"

Desert Rain blinked tiredly as the argument ensued between the wind Hijn, bird girl and lizard, while Gabriel rubbed his sinuses with his fingers. This would not do. She could not have them all bickering all the way up north; she needed everyone to unite. Sir Luce's words echoed in her thoughts: *Get your troop in line. They are undisciplined, unruly. Be patient, be mindful, but be firm.*

Firm…Desert Rain could be firm. But she was also miffed, and she felt a searing pain around her green eye. A deep growl bubbled up from her throat, followed by an exasperated, "Shut up!"

Everyone snapped their eyes at her. Even the townsfolk walking nearby stopped what they were doing to see what the commotion was.

Desert Rain took a deep - stalling-time-to-think-what-to-say-next deep – breath before crossing her arms and giving the group a good, hard look. "I won't tolerate this anymore. No more bickering. No more juvenile behavior. No back talk. We have a mission, and by the Sages, we're going to do it as a united front. We have to find the Lightscale. We have to stop Katawa, or we all, everyone in Luuva Gros, will fall to ruin. And I'm not going to let that happen. If you are going to follow, you need to listen to me and follow my orders to the letter. Understood?"

Her orders were met with silence and surprised gawks. Even Chiriku had nothing to say.

Desert Rain felt pretty good, but she was wary to let her stern demeanor drop yet. "Okay, to start with, I'm assigning everyone jobs. Everyone will pull their weight. Mac, you will oversee supplies, keeping stock of what we need and knowing exactly where everything is. Chiriku, you'll be our scout. Help Woasim keep an eye out for anything that might come after us while we're in the air."

A funny grin curled at the corner of Chiriku's mouth. "And if I spot a Distorted first, do I get to bash it with my hammer?"

"Depends. But that leads me to say…" She turned to Gabriel. "You know combat. I saw you fight the

Zi'Gax. So, I'm putting you in charge of combat training. Everyone here will need to know how to properly defend themselves."

Gabriel gave her an even, stoic look. "Do you really think that's a good idea? Putting weapons in the hands of people who don't have a single warrior's bone in their body?"

"Hey, I know how to fight!" Chiriku retorted. "This hammer saved Dez's life, you know."

Desert Rain remained firm. "Sometimes, I'm concerned by what you think you know. Look, we'll all need training, which apparently I'll be doing day and night, whether I like it or not."

Gabriel raised an eyebrow. "What does that mean?"

Desert Rain bit her lip, wondering if she should keep her dream a secret. But then, keeping secrets had been what started this whole mess. If Sir Luce didn't want her to tell, he would have said something. "Have you ever heard the name Veritas Lucen?"

The man's eyes bulged and his breath caught in his throat. Desert Rain had not seen him look this petrified since the time she tried to get him to wield Silverheart. After a long moment, he exhaled, his expression hardening.

"He spoke to you?" he asked in a low voice, almost a growl.

"In a...manner of speaking," Desert Rain replied. "I don't suppose you could tell me who—"

"I'll train these people, under one condition," he said coldly, cutting her off. "You never ask me what I know about Skyhan, or anything to do with him, *ever*. And don't talk to your new...*friend* about him. Or me."

Well, that opens up a whole new box of curiosity, Desert Rain thought, but she nodded.

"Oooh, I like this new 'take charge' you," Woasim giggled. "So, what will I be?"

"Pilot and, um, aeronaut," Desert Rain said. "And, until the Knighthood makes it official, you will be our troop's guardian knight."

Woasim's eyes dilated, and his cheeks flushed pink as a huge smile brightened his face. "Really? You'll hire *me* to be a knight? Oh, you're wonderful, Dez!" He gave her a big hug, his arms wrapping around her waist.

She awkwardly stooped to hug him back, her arms embracing him around the shoulders. "Now, we need to get moving. Mac, get our provisions ready and in the boat. Chiriku, you and I will help Woasim fill up the sail. Gabriel, help tie the boat down until we're ready to take off."

*   *   *

"Woooooo weeeeeeeee!" Woasim cried, as the wind whipped around his face and ears. "Who would've guessed we'd make the first ever sky boat!"

Desert Rain was surprised that the invention worked so well. Not only worked, but managed to rise to a decent height and reach a good speed - not a neck-breaking pace, but a brisk float-along as the ground whisked by below. Woasim's control of the wind helped with speed and staying on course, and it was a pretty sight to see the cluster of flame-bubbles hovering above their heads, captured securely in the sail.

Chiriku took to her scouting duties quickly, her eye glued to the wooden telescope that Gabriel had bought with the other supplies. She scanned the sky, the ground, the horizon as she stood at the starboard of the boat. Desert Rain wondered if she was so attentive because she was trying to avoid chatting with anyone else after their last group quarrel. Mac was taking it easy portside, naturally, resting against the fish-leather flasks of water and the packs of Wuta beans, roasted seaweed, and dried fish they had secured before leaving Wayfarer's Thumb. Gabriel was being his usual stoic self, seated at the stern, while Woasim stood at the bow, conducting the winds with his hands like an orchestral maestro.

He glanced over his shoulder back at Desert Rain, who was seated dead smack in the center of the boat. "We're setting a good pace. We should reach the Ring of Springs by tomorrow's sunset. But if anyone needs a break to stretch their legs, if you start to get air sick, or to..." He lowered his voice, as if saying something he should not. "To do your *business*, let me know. I can bring the boat down." He knitted his eyebrows in concern. "Are you feeling all right, Dez? I know the sky's not really your, uh, comfort zone."

Desert Rain smiled; it was sweet of Woasim to think of her, but that was his nature. "If I can ride Clova's eagle and not lose my lunch, I can handle this fine."

"Good. I bet riding on one of her birds is loads of fun! When we get back from all this, we should have a race!"

Thank the Divine Beasts that Katawa didn't capture him, Desert Rain thought. *Or Clova. I pray the others are still alive. I wish I knew what Katawa was doing right now, if what I'm doing is the right course of action. Next time I sleep, I'll have to ask Sir Luce what he might know about the*

Darkscale. He must know something...

Her thoughts were interrupted by Chiriku's long moan of "Boooooooriiiiiiing." The bird girl collapsed the small telescope and walked over to where Woasim was standing. "So, how's your 'mum' doing today?" she asked sardonically.

"Oh, just fine, just fine! She loves flying," Woasim replied, clearly not picking up on the sarcasm. "She also says it's good you're helping Desert Rain. You're both good for each other."

"Yeah? How so?"

Woasim's paused a moment. "Well, she says...people need people. And you both don't have many people, because you both think you don't deserve to have people. But you do. I think you're both scared to be yourselves because of how people have treated you. But you should always be you, because no one else can be. And that's pretty special."

Desert Rain frowned at Woasim's words. *He puts things far too simply. If only he understood what mistakes I've made, who I've hurt. He'd be scared too... But it's good for Chiriku to hear this.*

Chiriku, however, also scowled. "Does Mum always speak in platitudes?"

"Sometimes. But just because something is said often, doesn't mean it doesn't bear importance. It's good to be reminded of things, because we forget really easily, especially when we're hurting." Woasim grinned at her. "I really wish you could talk to Mum directly. I think she could make you feel better."

"I'm fine." Chiriku could not hide the bitter tone, or maybe she was not trying to.

"Of course." Woasim lowered his hands from

conducting and turned to face her. "But, you know, if you're never *not* fine, you can tell us, right? You can talk to me about it, if you want. I'm very good at keeping secrets, or singing…uh, plaid tunes, as you said? Ooh, I know lots of tunes! I don't know how a plaid one goes, though. You may have to hum a few bars."

Chiriku let a small grin crack her beak. "You know what a platitude is."

Woasim nodded. "Yeah, but I was trying to make you smile. I was close, I got a little something riiiiight there."

"You're weird."

"Why, thank you! I work at it," Woasim chuckled.

You certainly do, Desert Rain thought, but she found herself smiling too.

*   *   *

That night, Desert Rain was back in the cherry tree orchard.

Sir Luce stood in the arena, in his armored human shape. His mask glinted like an abalone shell in the sunlight. "You fare well?" he asked.

Desert Rain let out a long breath, still feeling the weariness of the trek. "As fair as I can be. Are we training?"

"Of course." He unsheathed a sword from his scabbard, a simple wooden waster.

The Hijn tilted her head. "Um, this *is* a dream, right? I mean, does it matter whether you use a wooden sword or a steel one? We won't get hurt either way?"

Sir Luce narrowed his eyes. "What good is training if you don't experience the consequences of poor defense?"

"Fair enough. But, I mean, that won't affect 'real' me, will it?"

"The mind and the body are linked. What happens here can have effects on your physical form."

Desert Rain tightened her lips. "And how do I explain to everyone if I'm a beaten, bruised mess when I wake up?"

Sir Luce gave her an irritated glare. "They're your troop. Figure it out."

Again, Silverheart materialized in Desert Rain's hands. "And what if I accidentally hurt you?"

She thought she saw a funny squint in Sir Luce's eyes, like he was grinning. "Don't concern yourself with that."

You mean, no possibility of that happening, she thought.

"I wasn't going to be so blunt, but yes," the dragon replied.

Desert Rain blanched. "You can read my thoughts?"

"We're in your dreamscape. All things here are your thoughts. With time, you will learn to control this dreamscape, and in turn, you'll learn to control the real world around you."

"What do you mean?"

"Let's not put the tail before the maw. Focus."

Desert Rain did not like that she could not hide anything from Sir Luce *–Try not to think of anything too personal, just focus on the training*—but she trusted a Sage to not be too invasive.

"We'll start with the basics." Sir Luce shifted into a fight stance, one foot in front of the other. "Strike me."

Desert Rain hesitated, as her mind raced. *I can't strike him — but he's reading my thoughts, he'll know I'm panicking! Now I'm stalling, and he could hit me back before I know it... just swing!*

She swung, bringing the sword up over her shoulder and hurling it down towards the knight. It was a sloppy strike, of course, which Sir Luce deflected with barely any effort. He followed it up with a quick whack to her left side, which was wide open. She stumbled, grasping her side as pain shot through her every nerve.

"Guerda-Shalyr, that was awful," Desert Rain gasped.

"Yes," Sir Luce stated plainly. "Never leave yourself open and keep your focus on where you're striking." He paused, giving her a pointed stare. "Where did you learn that name?"

"What name? Oh, Guerda-Shalyr? That's just...a saying. People out in the Gold Dragon Desert say that all the time. I don't really know what it means."

Sir Luce looked at her oddly for a moment. "And you've never met anyone by that name?"

Desert Rain raised an eyebrow. "N...no. Should I have?"

"There lies your problem. You know so much more than you realize. Buried knowledge that could do you so much good. But let us return to our lesson, which I now understand will require much more patience than I thought..."

*   *   *

"Uh, guys?" Chiriku stood up straight as she looked through her telescope. "I think I see something...

not right?"

Desert Rain, in her weary daze, perked up her ears at Chiriku's voice. It was the second day of traveling, and the morning sun had cleared the horizon a short time ago. She had hoped they would be in the Ring of Springs before nightfall, but Woasim only kept promising they were making good time with no precise answer as to how close they were. She had spent most of the trip trying not to move much — she had told everyone she had not slept well, but really, she was so sore from Sir Luce's training, she could barely move.

She had not counted on the training affecting her body so drastically, given that it had all occurred in her sleep. She had, in fact, been training with Sir Luce for what she thought had been days, weeks, learning different stances, techniques, offences, defenses, doing her best to wrap her mind around all the rapid-fire lessons the Sage taught her. But each morning when she awoke, she realized time in her mind passed differently than in the waking world. In two nights' sleep, she had trained for what she estimated to about three months of training. And her muscles felt every — second — of — it. Thankfully, things like cuts and mild stab wounds — yes, she had received plenty of those in her training — did not translate into her flesh except as dark bruises, and her clothing covered those. She'd rather no one saw them anyway.

Gabriel got up from his seat at the stern, which had been his designated spot the last two days, and came over to Chiriku. He took the spyglass from her and looked through it in the direction she had been viewing. "Hmm…that is definitely 'not right'."

"What isn't?" Woasim asked, coming over to

them.

"Those are conifers. They shouldn't change that color, even in colder weather," Gabriel replied.

"Let me see! Let me see!" Woasim gestured for the telescope, taking it and looking through it.

"What color?" Desert Rain asked. "You're talking about the trees?"

Woasim lowered the spyglass, his eyes huge. "Red...bright, blood red." His breathing suddenly became unsteady, and he dropped the telescope.

Desert Rain strained to see ahead, making out a streak of crimson in the otherwise green canopy. It was unnatural, as if the forest had started to bleed.

"Hey, nothin' wrong with red, right-ttk?" Mac said, yawning and flicking his tail. "What's got-ttk you so spooked?"

"I've seen this before. Those trees are poisoned. Runoff from the blood-crude that powers the...I'll take a closer look. You all wait here." Before anyone could argue, he expanded his head-fins and took off on a gust of wind, speeding towards the trees far ahead.

"That airhead!" Gabriel growled. "We can't control this ship without him! We could be blown off course."

Desert Rain took a deep, calming breath. "I'm sure he won't be gone long. He's just scouting ahead. As long as the wind stays even, we should be fine for a few minutes."

Mac stood up, stretching his arms and legs. "Or maybe we should just-ttk land this thing until he gets back-kk. I personally don't-ttk like being in a ship without-ttk a pilot-ttk. But we saw what-ttk he had to do to get us to land for the night-ttk. We can do that-ttk ourselves."

Desert Rain looked up at the flame bubbles overhead. "Well, I suppose all he did was release a few of these bubbles. It was an easy descent after that."

"But it's *his* magic," Gabriel pointed out. "He knows how those bubbles work. I wouldn't start messing with a Hijn's magic without him here."

Mac chuckled. "Oh, come on! It's tossin' bubbles away, nothin' is easier. Even little tadpoles could do it-ttk." He reached up towards one of the flame bubbles.

"Mac, hold it—"

The lizard took hold of one, pulling it down out of the bunch. "See? Sim said these things are unpoppable. We'll just-ttk pitch-ch a few overboard and we'll float-ttk down gent-tkle as a leaf..."

The bubble popped between Mac's hands. The flame inside, however, did not go out; instead, it drifted directly up and alighted on the sail, rapidly consuming the fabric with a tongue of fire.

Mac stared wide-eyed at the expanding fire. "I must-ttk not know my own strength," he said with a croak.

Gabriel scrambled for the flasks of water, but it would not have helped. As the fire spread, the heat caused more of the bubbles to pop, sending more flames up into the sail, plaguing it like a colony of fire ants. The ship was starting to descend, but at a much faster pace than intended and tipping backward quickly as all the supplies and passengers slid towards the stern.

Chiriku squawked in panic. "Mac, if we survive this, I'm going to kill you!"

"Everyone, get to the bow!" Gabriel ordered. "We need to balance out the boat!"

"Does that really matter?!" Desert Rain shouted, watching the canopy below approaching faster and faster.

"I'd rather we land with the boat under us than on top of us," Gabriel retorted. He scanned the ground ahead, spotting a break in the trees. "I think we can make it to that pond if we can keep this steady!"

Everyone crowded to the bow, as their packs of food slipped off the back of the ship. This permitted some balance, as they all clung white-knuckled to the ropes of the sail. The flaming vessel began to pitch into a nose-dive, and Desert Rain held her breath and clamped her eyes shut as the boat skimmed the top of the canopy and barreled towards the small body of water below.

Desert Rain's thoughts rang clear. *Bellaluna...Sir Luce...Divine Beasts, don't let us die! Protect my friends! Give me hope!*

"Dez? Hey, Gila Gul! Breathe! Open your eyes."

She slowly, cautiously, cracked open one eyelid. Had she blacked out? She did not remember the boat landing, as it now floated on the surface of a grimy, muddy pond. The sail was gone, burned away to a few charred scraps that drifted on the water around them. The boat itself seemed no worse for wear, but they were oarless and sail-less, so they bobbed on the pond's surface with no means to go anywhere.

Mac, Chiriku, and Gabriel were all looking at her, as she continued to cling to the side of the boat. Mac patted her shoulder. "There now, Gila. You can let-ttk go now. We're all safe."

"That's debatable," Gabriel said, looking about. "We're sitting ducks out here."

"Speak for yourself," Chiriku said, patting the

head of her warhammer over her shoulder. "How'd we even survive that?"

"I don't know," Gabriel replied. "It must've had something to do with that blue fire."

"Blue fire?" Desert Rain steadied herself, looking around the boat. "What blue fire?"

Mac scratched his chin. "It-ttk must've been a side effect of Sim's magic-kk. The fire turned bright-ttk blue, and I could feel our descent-ttk slow down. Like-kk it was keeping us aloft-ttk. You didn't see that-ttk?"

Desert Rain felt her face flush in embarrassment. "My...eyes were closed."

"But how does wind magic turn fire blue?" Chiriku asked. "And Woasim isn't even here."

Gabriel stared at Desert Rain with what she thought was a grimace, but maybe that was his default look. It reminded her of how Sir Luce looked at her, when he thought she knew more than she was letting on. She wished she did know more; she was starting to hate inexplicable things happening, whether good or bad. Gabriel did not think she had something to do with this, did he? Blue fire was certainly not in her wheelhouse. If Fierno the Fire Hijn was here, he would be laughing himself silly at the very notion that Desert Rain could control fire of any sort.

"Well, the important thing is we're alive," she replied. "Woasim must be nearby. Do we have anything we can paddle with?"

"Your hands," Gabriel answered dryly.

Chiriku groaned, running her hands against her pants as if she could already feel the griminess of the water. "I hate getting wet."

Mac smirked and uncoiled his scaly tail. "I don't-ttk mind dippin' into some muddy water. Feels like-kk home."

Desert Rain wrinkled her nose at the sludgy water. Paddling by hand would take hours with a boat this size, on a lake this large. She would rather have a good strong wind push them to shore. She stood up, cupping her hands around her mouth. "Woasim! Where are—"

Gabriel grabbed her roughly, shoving her back down into her seat and slapping his hand over her mouth. "Are you crazy?" he spat at her in a low voice. "We're stuck out here, and you want to attract attention?"

Desert Rain pulled his hand away from her lips. "Attention from what?"

"Look at this lake."

She did, observing the muddy water closer. No, it was not mud—oil. Dark, slimy oil. She cautiously dipped her fingers in, rubbing the nasty substance between them. "Woasim said something about blood-crude …what is it?"

"If that's what this is, then we are in more danger than you—"

Desert Rain's ears caught a strange metallic sound, but she did not have enough time to process what it could be before something large and heavy slammed into the bow of the boat. Everyone jumped back from the black, rusty hook that had punched through the wood, and snagged onto the floor of the boat. The hook was attached to a long stretch of thick, iron chain that extended to the shore and into the trees beyond, to wherever it had been cast from. Just as quickly as it had caught them, the hook yanked back and the boat surged forwards as the chain retracted, reeling them in like a fish.

Everyone was thrown off balance, falling backward against the floor and grasping onto anything that would keep them from being flung from the vessel. The spray of oily water misted them as the lake rushed by them, and then an abrupt bump indicated they were being dragged against ground, as the lake was replaced by a blur of trees on both sides.

"Bail out!" Gabriel called out, grabbing Desert Rain around the waist. "Everybody, jump now!"

"Wait—" Desert Rain started, but then she was suddenly mid-air as Gabriel leapt from the boat with her in his arms. Thankfully, they did not collide into any trees, but they hit the forest floor hard and tumbled for several yards before coming to a stop. Desert Rain craned her head to look up, but the boat, hook and chain had already vanished past the trees.

"Why did you do that??" she yelled, pushing Gabriel away and sitting up. "You left Mac and Chiriku back there! We all should have jumped together!"

Gabriel sat up, dusting off his coat sleeves. "I told them to jump. Should I have gathered everyone up like a bundle of sticks, or trusted they're smart enough to jump on their own?"

"But...you jumped with me..."

"That's different. You would've made sure everyone else jumped first before you did, and by then, you'd be dead."

Desert Rain narrowed her eyes. "Oh, so I should be thanking you, because I'm too stupid to save myself?"

Gabriel took a deep breath and gave her a glare. "Now is not the time to talk. We need to find the others."

Desert Rain stood and glanced around at the layer

of blood-red pine needles coating the forest floor. Everything around them was awash in scarlet; even the gray tree trunks of the conifers were lined with streaks of dark red. The smell in the air was not of fresh pine, as one might expect – it reeked of decay, rot, and sulfur. There was not a soul in sight, not a sound from above. All life had fled from here, leaving a hushed hinterland of crimson corpses.

"Maybe now, you can tell me what's caused all this?" she asked in a whisper.

The whispering turned out to be pointless, since several tall, imposing shapes suddenly stepped out from behind the trees. They greeted her with eyes of rust orange, their lower faces masked by tarnished chainmail veils. Their skin was soaked deep burgundy as wine, and their bulky bodies were swathed in soot-stained armor and blackened leather. All of them wore gauntlets with loaded wristbows, aimed at her and Gabriel.

"Bloodburn," Gabriel sighed, raising his hands over his head.

CHAPTER SIX
The Grand Imperial Battle Train (G.I.B.T. for short)

Any of the Three Courts of the Wretched could strike paralyzing fear into the hearts of the bravest warriors, but the Court of Bloodburn were known as nightmare savages of the most bloodthirsty degree. They were not dull-witted, however; over the centuries, they had developed technological marvels beyond that of the Noble Races, great mechanizations of iron, steel, and smoke. The most impressive of these now loomed ahead of Desert Rain and Gabriel, as they were marched along by their Bloodburn captors: a mile-long, smog-belching, segmented metal serpent, with iron spikes on the front that looked like a row of fangs, and just above that, a red lantern that glowed with a hellish flame. Desert Rain swore it was following them, a horrid otherworld eye.

She had never seen such a machine before, given that the Noble Races had banned this kind of equipment due to its pollutive and destructive nature. As they approached, she observed that this metal serpent did not slide on its belly, but it had wheels, eight on each segment of the body. On each side, the wheels were connected by steel plates on a continuous track that looped around them, which Desert Rain imagined they could crush anything unfortunate enough to be in their way into a flat pulp. Lights illuminated all along the metal serpent from round windows – *Are these all caravans on wheels, that move without horses or elk?* Desert Rain thought. She thought back to what Woasim has said, about the rumors that the Bloodburn had constructed some new kind of engine – how she wished those had only been rumors. No wonder even the Knights of Luuva broke into a terrified sweat at the mention of Bloodburn, if this was the kind of technology they could produce.

Smoke hung heavy in the air, making it difficult for Desert Rain or Gabriel to breathe. The Bloodburn were unfazed by it, and hundreds of them were crawling everywhere, either adjusting and fixing various parts of the great machine, or standing guard with polished halberds. They paused as the captives walked by, grinning nasty smiles and whispering to one another. Desert Rain was not even sure if the Bloodburn spoke the Mutual Language, but she thought she heard some words like, "fresh" and "meat." Maybe she misheard... she hoped she misheard.

They marched along to one of the caravans near to the front of the line, where there was a large, arched door. This was clearly the finest of the cars, polished free of ash and given some wrought iron detail work, shapes like spears and thorned vines along the sides. It had a dark beauty to it, although it was lost on Desert Rain, who felt a massive lump in her stomach. She hesitated, but a jab in her back from one of the Bloodburn guards' wristbows urged her through the door and into the caravan.

Inside was a room of gaudy luxury that rivaled even the wealthiest of Syphurius, but this was an icy, militaristic kind of luxury rather than a plush, aristocratic one. Iron furniture with reptile-hide cushions, floor candelabras that twisted like gnarled tree branches, and walls covered in torturous weaponry gave the impression of an executioner's lair. Tables of cooked and raw meats flanked a wide, gray-marbled throne, each arm carved into a snarling, horned dog head. What sat upon that throne was the most frightening thing of all, and Desert Rain instinctively grabbed Gabriel's arm as her eyes went wide with panic.

A large Bloodburn glared at her with his three sets of eyes, set in three separate heads on his broad, muscled shoulders. The center head, and the rest of the body, was burgundy-skinned like the other Bloodburns, although his maw was squarer, with a short tusk protruding up from the bottom lip. His orange gaze poured into Desert Rain and Gabriel like liquid fire, and his bald head was raked with old white scars. The head to the right was metallic golden skin, shinier than Desert Rain's light umber flesh, with equally golden curly locks and bright, blue eyes akin to lapis lazuli. It was a thinner face than the thick, brutish middle one, and seemed to stare at Desert Rain with a mildly annoyed scrutiny. The third head, there was little to say about it, for it had a burlap sack placed over it, with no more than one hole for its left eye to peak through, a cataract-white orb in the otherwise indiscernible visage. The body of the three-headed monstrosity was covered in a scaly leather tunic and boots trimmed with wolf fur, and a black-steeled breastplate with an icon smithed into it: a blood droplet, with two flames on each side of it, held within a four-clawed hand.

Desert Rain's hand slowly inched towards the pouch hanging from her belt, the one holding the concealed Silverheart. But Gabriel made a quick "tssk" sound, giving her a quick look of warning. She bit her lip, relaxing her arm, even though she was ready to vomit in fear. Whipping out a Wretched-slaying weapon to a three-headed Bloodburn might be a bad idea.

The middle head ground his teeth and spoke in a deep, rumbling voice. "What pathetic whelps are these, that you bother me with?"

"We found them on the lake, after they fell out of the sky, my lord," one of the Bloodburn captors replied.

"Fell out of the sky? What rot is that?" the middle head snarled.

The captor paled, his body stiff as a tree. "I…uh, we think they were with the Yopies-Gichen. The Hijn."

Desert Rain could not stop herself. "Woasim? You haven't hurt him, have you?"

The middle head snapped his gaze at her, baring his teeth. "You will speak when spoken to, wench!" His anger abruptly dwindled, as he took a good, hard look at her. "What kind of Wretched are you?"

Desert Rain cringed at his assessment. It was not the first time she had been accused of being a Wretched. Even now, she heard the cries of her family, those she had once held dear as a child, spitting the word at her when they saw what she had transformed into after her so-called "blessing." Although maybe she could use this to her advantage. "I'm…uh…"

"Oh, don't be ludicrous," said the golden head, rolling its eyes. "She's as much a Wretched as I am a toad. Certainly not Darkscale, far too delicate and doesn't reek of malaise. Not Secret Sacroth, look at those exotic eyes! Dear lady, do approach. Don't be shy."

Don't be shy? This guy's crazy! Desert Rain thought. She did not get a choice, however, as another sharp jab to her back shoved her forwards towards the Bloodburn monstrocity. Something about the golden head reminded her a lot of Anthron of the Ahshi Elves, an erudite with an elegant way of speaking. The golden head pursed his lips, rubbing his chin with the right hand of the body, which was gold-skinned as well. "Hmm…human features, although some are exaggerated. And…oh, look at that!" He pointed a finger at her moonstone markings. "A dragon's mark! Oh, how fortuitous for us! Two Hijn on the same day! You know, if we keep having Hijn falling into our laps like this, we might have some good bargaining chips for…you know who."

"Bah! I will never bargain with that misshapen freak," the burgundy head roared. "The Distortionist can rot in the Eternal Deep, for all I care!"

Guerda-Shalyr, even the Bloodburn know about Katawa! Desert Rain's troubled thoughts were interrupted when she noticed the third head, the one with the burlap sack, was staring at her with his one, milky eye. He tilted his head at her, and she sensed something about him…as if, he was trying to place her…

"Don't look at him!" the middle head ordered, raising his body's red left hand, which he seemed to control. With a swift swipe, he shifted the third head's sack so the eye was covered. "Useless. I should just cut it off and be done with it!"

"Now now, you know you can't do that," the golden head said, and then he looked back to Desert Rain. "But where are our manners? I am Strategist Veni-Primum, and this is our good General Vidi-Etiam-Sero the Strongbred. The third…well, it's of little importance. Now, you and your friend have been brought aboard our Grand Imperial Battle Train–the G.I.B.T. for short–and are officially property of the Bloodburn Court. If you prove to be useful, you shall live. I don't think it's necessary to explain what happens if you're *not* useful."

Desert Rain's eyes shifted to the tables of meat beside the throne.

"Exactly," Veni said with a smile. "Now, Hijn, what kind of magic do you do?"

Desert Rain took a deep breath, steadying her nerves. "I am the heir of the Moon Dragoness. I can be of service to you, and will pledge my magic to the Bloodburn if you release my friend and the other Hijn you found."

"Dez!" Gabriel hissed.

The two heads broke out into uproarious laughter, while the shrouded one slumped to the side. The Bloodburn general slapped a hand to his forehead as he hacked a pungent, noxious guffaw. "You are in no position to bargain!" he barked through his laughter. "You all belong to Bloodburn now! And if the Distortionist can command so many of you weak-willed Hijn to his desires, then I can command you! What makes you think you can tell me what to do?"

Something hot stung in Desert Rain's green eye. She should have been scared; but instead, she heard that new voice in her head again. The one saying, *You are a Knight of Luuva. You must do what Skyhan can no longer do. What would he do in this situation?*

Whether it was her voice, or Sir Luce's, it jolted her to action. She reached into her pouch and withdrew Silverheart, shining with silvery glory. She pointed the blade at General Vidi's face, feeling satisfaction as his smug countenance snapped into aghast alarm.

"I am Desert Rain, and this is Silverheart, which once belonged to the Swordmaster," she announced, gripping the hilt in both hands. "And *this* is the reason you should let me and my friends go. I don't think it's necessary to explain what happens if you don't."

Veni blanched, jerking his head back as far as he could from the fearsome blade. "Silverheart...the untouchable sword! Kill her! Kill her now!"

Desert Rain heard the guards shifting position, and she turned to see them all pointing their wristbows at her. *Divine Beasts, this was a stupid move.*

"Hold your fire!" General Vidi stood up from his throne, giving Desert Rain such a dark, hateful stare, she thought he was going to crush her himself with his massive fist. He reached out towards the sword, but it crackled with blue-white energy, biting at his fingers with rippling lightning. He pulled his hand back, growling at Desert Rain with the resonance of thunder, but she held her ground. She knew he could not take it from her. This was like with the Zi'Gax; no one of a dark nature could touch Silverheart.

After a moment, General Vidi chuckled, a wry grin on his face. "You want me to release you, the human and the little Yopies? Fine, I'm ready to bargain. You can go, if you give me that sword."

Desert Rain paused, wondering why General Vidi stopped the guards from killing her. Did he know something she did not? It was a moot point; what could he do with a sword he could not touch?

"I can't do that," she managed to squeak out.

"She's right," Veni said. "It's not enough for the wielder of Silverheart to bequeath the sword to a new owner and it still retain its magnificent powers. Especially not to a Wretched."

Ah, so that was it. General Vidi must believe she could willingly gift Silverheart to him, and killing her before then would render the sword useless. Veni seemed to know better.

"However, there might be another way," Veni continued, with a devious grin. "If she becomes more to you than just a prisoner, if she is bound to you in body, mind and soul, then what belongs to her would then also, legally, belong to you."

"Legally?" Desert Rain did not like where this was going.

"What are you blathering about?" General Vidi was equally confused.

"You know, legally. As in, marriage," Veni explained.

OOOOOOOH NOOOOOOO. The voice was loud and slow in Desert Rain's mind. This had to be a joke, right?

"And having a Bloodburn Hijn would be prestigious," Veni added, whispering into Vidi's ear like a literal devil on his shoulder. "Imagine, rubbing this in the faces of that pompous Darkscale Court, that *we* can control *our* dragon blessed. And it never hurts to have some ancient magic at our disposal."

Desert Rain raised the sword in front of her, in a fighting stance. "You are INSANE if you think I would ever, EVER marry you, you disgusting —"

Veni gestured for her to turn around. Desert Rain turned her head to see all the guards aiming their wristbows at Gabriel's throat and chest. He looked back at her with a hard look, a silent plea: *Don't do it. I'll be fine.*

But it was not a choice. Gabriel, Woasim, and wherever Mac and Chiriku had ended up, they were all in danger. If Swordmaster Skyhan were here, no doubt he could slice the head off every Wretched in the room before a single one could pull the trigger on their wristbow. But she barely had a handle on the basics of swordplay – would Sir Luce possess the sword again? He must know she needed his help! But after waiting several eternal seconds, hoping for the sensation of Silverheart's magic to kick in, there was nothing. Sir Luce was not responding. With a heavy sigh, Desert Rain lowered her sword, and her gaze, to the floor.

*　　*　　*

"What're you thinking, Mac?"

The lizard and the Quetzalin watched the two Bloodburn scouts from a good distance, hiding high in one of the tall pine trees. Thanks to being dampened by the mist from the lake, Mac had slipped into his natural, reptilian state, covered head to tail-tip in cardinal red scales that blended well with the toxic pine needles around him. Chiriku, while not blending in with her surroundings, was light and agile, even with her warhammer on her back, so she positioned herself on a tree branch perfectly still with hardly a rustle. They had managed to jump from the boat and scramble up the tree before the Bloodburn found them, and from the looks of it, the demons had no idea if, or where, any other intruders might be found.

Mac scanned the area below, marveling at the great Bloodburn battle train. He whispered close to Chiriku's ear. "I be thinkin'…we need to slip past-ttk those nasties-ss down there, find Dez, Gabe, and Sim in that machine, get-ttk them out-ttk, and then run faster than frogs in fryin' pans."

Chiriku rolled her eyes. "Oh, how simple."

"Now, don't-ttk you worry about-ttk the sneakin'. I'll handle that-ttk." Mac gave her a sly grin and started to remove his tunic.

Chiriku instantly turned her eyes away. "What're you doing??"

"Oh, don't-ttk be so modest-ttk."

"*Me* be modest? *You're* the one who needs some modesty!"

Mac responded by handing her his vest, tunic, trousers, and shoes. "Now don't-ttk lose anythin' out-ttk of my pockets-ssk."

Chiriku continued to look away from him as she accepted the clothes, which were heavy due to all the knick-knacks he stored in his plethora of pockets. She listened as he climbed down the tree. *That scale-brain is nuts! I could just go down there and clobber those ugly, leech-faced —*

When she glanced back down to find Mac, he was nowhere to be seen. How had he vanished so quickly? She searched the forest floor, blanketed in bright red pine needles, but she could see no one except the two Bloodburn up ahead. She held her breath, staying perfectly still, as the two scouts walked under her tree. She could hear them conversing in a hushed, guttural speech, but it was muffled behind their chainmail masks.

One of the scouts let out a gurgled gasp as a long tail snaked up from the ground and wrapped around his neck. The tail slammed him into the tree trunk several times before the Bloodburn went limp, sliding to the ground. The other Bloodburn, baffled by what he just saw, aimed his wristbow at the base of the tree, snarling a command. Only now could he see there was a scaly creature hiding among the red pine needles, a chameleon humanoid that neither of the scouts had detected. Before the scout could fire off a shot, he was trampled from above, as Chiriku leapt down and landed squarely on top of him. A quick thwack of her hammer to his face sent the chainmail mask flying, along with a gush of blood out of his nose, and the Bloodburn lied still.

"Nice, Chi," Mac said, as he stood up. "I'll take-kk my akk-oo-ter-mens back-kk, thanks."

"I think you mean accoutre…never mind. Good attempt at a big word for you." Chiriku, in her jump down from the tree, had spilled Mac's clothes on the ground, so she fetched them and handed them back to him. She again averted her gaze while he dressed, but she could hear Mac was doing something near one of the unconscious Bloodburn. "What are you doing now?"

"Gotta blend in," he replied, and a few minutes later, he was also dressed in the Bloodburn's outer apparel and armor. It was a close enough fit, although the chainmail mask protruded out due to his lizard snout. "Come on, Chi, get-ttk changed."

Chiriku looked down at the second Bloodburn. "Mac, it works for you because your scales are the same color as their skin. I'll stick out, even with a disguise on."

"Well, you do love dyin' your feathers," Mac said. He pointed to the one Bloodburn who was still bleeding out of his nose.

"Mac, that's disgusting! How do I even know demon blood isn't acidic or something? It could burn my feathers clean off!"

Mac reached down towards the Bloodburn's face and swiped up some of the blood with his fingers. "Doesn't—tkk seem to be. Now come on, you want-ttk to find our friends or not-ttk?"

Chiriku took a deep breath. "Fine. But you owe me a spa day after this. These guys came from that direction, so that's where we need to go, right?"

Mac opened his mouth to answer, but his reply was cut short by a thunderous, blasting horn, a roar like that of an infernal whale somewhere not so far away. The ground shook, a ripping quake that something heavy and monstrous was making its move through the otherwise serene forest. Mac and Chiriku looked up, above the trees, to see a plume of black smoke winding its way upwards, the breath of a ravenous, ash-spitting furnace.

"That-ttk would be the way," Mac replied, gulping hard. "And if that-tkk thing's anythin' like my old cart-tkk, I'd say it's gettin' ready to be on the move. Best-ttk go now, before we miss our ride!"

*   *   *

Desert Rain was thrown into a dark room, the door slamming and locking behind her. She did not know which train car she was in; the guards had dragged her so quickly through so many of the cars, she had lost count. Not that she had been counting anyway – her mind scrambled as she had watched Gabriel torn from her, whisked away to somewhere else in this train of terror for whatever the Bloodburns planned to do with him. Her mind screamed for Sir Luce, although he would be of little help now since General Vidi ordered her to leave Silverheart on one of his weapon racks. It was little solace that he, nor any of the Bloodburns, would be able to pick up the sword to use it. It hung on his wall like a prize, and maybe that was good enough for Vidi, for now. Suddenly, she could also feel the floor beneath her shaking, and her body swayed as she felt the room lurch forwards. Dear dragons, were they moving? The train was leaving! Where were they going? Wherever the Bloodburn clan went, poison and decay spread. And if they were headed back to the Inbetween, there would be no hope left. She would never get to the Elfë Taigas, never find the Lightscale, never save her friends...

Her friends! What of Mac and Chiriku? They had probably been captured too, and were panicking like she was, held in another part of this train. Desert Rain stared at the locked door for a long minute, as if some tiny piece of the universe might pity her and magically unlock it for her. Of course not. She leaned her back against the wall, and slid down to sit on the cold, musty floor. She could not see anything, as the room possessed no light source except through the thin bars of the tiny window of the door. She pulled in her knees and burrowed her face into them, expecting tears to flow but found her eyes dry as a bone, empty. She was too exhausted, too defeated to cry. She had lost everything. Gabriel, Silverheart, Mac, Chiriku, Woasim...

"Dez?" came a small, familiar voice from the other side of the room.

Desert Rain snapped her head up as a familiar figure toddled out from the shadows into view. "Woasim! Oh, Guerda-Shayler! Thank the Sages you're all right!"

Woasim smiled, and he extended his arms out to her, but he could not lift his arms out far. His hands were imprisoned inside iron casings, like two thumbless mittens, and those casings were chained to the wall with inch-thick links. The weight of them were clearly a strain on him, for he winced as he tried to move. "I'm sorry, Dez. I'd give you a hug, but I'm a little stuck."

Desert Rain stood up, rushing to him as the horror of Woasim's situation shook her. She took his imprisoned hands in hers, looking the casings over. "Why did they do this to you?"

"Eh, they must've figured out my Hijn magic is gesticular," he answered. "Good thing it isn't verbal like the other Hijn, otherwise they might've welded my mouth shut! These mittens are rather tight, though. I'd rather they have given me some wool ones."

Rage burbled in Desert Rain's chest, but she remained calm. "Don't worry, I...I can try to break you out. Then we can get out of here, find the others, and escape."

Woasim grinned tiredly at her. Even in the darkness of the room, Desert Rain could tell he was out of energy, weak and hungry. But his eyes still shined with hope. "Yes, yes, Dez! They didn't give you any bindings. You have moon magic! Uh...remind me what that does?"

Honestly, Desert Rain wished she could tell him what the Blueshine was *supposed* to do, what Grandma Luna had always intended her to use it for. However, she could only use it for what she knew she could do with it. She could shatter Woasim's casings with it, maybe shatter the door too, if she could focus well enough to not botch it. She took Woasim's casings, one in each hand, and closed her eyes. She heard the soft voice in her mind.

Now, just enough magic to cover the casings. They should break apart, just like glass. Not too much Blueshine, though, otherwise you might get some on Woasim...oh, Divine Beasts, if you mess up, you might shatter Woasim! What if you push too much energy? What if he moves ever so slightly? What if I end up shattering his arms clean off? Why am I so bad at this? Why can't I just do my magic right like everyone else...

Desert Rain dropped his hands, pulling her arms into her chest. "I...I can't. If I mess up, I could kill you by accident."

Woasim was quiet, regarding her with concern, but then he flashed her a big smile. "That's okay. Thank you for not wanting to risk me. But what if you try doing whatever you were planning on the chains? That would at least free me from the wall. Then we can worry about getting these mittens off later."

Desert Rain thought on that for a moment. "Yes, maybe I can do that. That at least doesn't put you directly in harm's way."

The light coming from the door was abruptly blocked. Desert Rain saw the golden face of Veni looking through the bars at her.

"Oh, gracious, I told the General you don't belong in here! See, Vidi? Is this the kind of accommodation you want your future queen to be in?" Veni chided.

Veni's face moved aside as Vidi's horrible, snarling one looked into the room. He grumbled softly. "Do what you want, Veni. You do all the planning."

"Of course, I'm the strategist." Veni's face came back into view. "Now, we'll have a nice room made up for you, my dear. Trust me, I'm as ashamed as anyone to put you in there like some common prisoner. But don't fret. In a few days, we should be in Haven's End, and once we conquer that city, we can have a lovely little wedding party. I'll even design and have one of our tailors make you a suitable gown, all the frills and jewels you could want! Doesn't that sound nice?"

"Wedding? I love weddings!" Woasim chirped up. "Who's getting married?"

Desert Rain side-eyed Woasim with a frown. "They want me to marry the general, Sim."

Woasim's smile instantly crashed into an open-mouthed horror. He turned to look at Veni, furrowing his brow and trying to raise his iron-laden hands. "She doesn't look happy about it! She doesn't want to marry him! Do you, Dez?"

"It's hardly about what she *wants*," Veni replied dryly. "It's an appropriate union. Transactionally beneficial. Besides, she already consented. Didn't you, Miss Hijn?"

Desert Rain sighed, but then gave Veni a sharp look. "Where's Gabriel?"

"Hmm? Oh, your human escort. He's a strong specimen, so we'll put him to good use. Can always use more grunts around here. We'll make sure he attends to your every need, once you're queen. You'll need some servants of your own, after all."

Desert Rain wanted nothing more in that moment but to punch both Veni and Vidi in their smug, ugly faces. But something the strategist had said struck her. "Wait, you said we're headed to Haven's End? Kidran mentioned that town once. That's far north of here. Why are you heading so far from the Inbetween?"

Veni chuckled, showing his sharp teeth in a horrid smile. "There's no reason to stay trapped in that wasteland anymore. That Distortionist fellow and his minions have the Knighthood scrambling for reinforcements, and all the border guard troops have fled. The Courts of the Wretched will reign once again in

the Noblelands! Best the Bloodburn gain as much
territory as we can, before those Darkscale or Secret
Sacroth start snatching up land. And for all we conquer,
you will be queen of it! Lucky girl, you!"

Desert Rain swallowed back the acid taste of
vomit. How was Katawa literally destroying everything
so quickly? His crimes were bleeding throughout Luuva
Gros, allowing other Wretched clans to gain a foothold in
the Noblelands. And if the Courts were scrambling to
acquire as much territory as possible, there would be war
everywhere. So many innocent lives would be lost.

"Queen? But...you're not a king," Woasim
pointed out.

Veni glared at him with pure venom, but replied
with a cold, soft voice. "Royal blood runs in our veins.
And as far as you're concerned, we own you and
everything on this train."

Desert Rain glowered at Veni, curling her lip.
"You realize that whatever you conquer, Katawa is
simply going to steal it from you?"

Veni tilted his head at her. "Who?"

"For Luuva's sake...the Distortionist! He's
planning to twist everything to his image with his
powers, including you!"

Veni's face was literally pushed out of the way by
Vidi's hand, who came into frame again. "I do not fear
that Darkscale fool! He came to us just a few weeks ago,
trying to forge an alliance with the Bloodburn. I told him
we didn't need him, or his measly forces, to conquer
what we want! And he just slunk away, the coward. He
knew better than to challenge me!"

Desert Rain opened her mouth to reply, but
nothing came out in her shocked state. Why would

Katawa try to make an alliance with Bloodburn? Surely, he was powerful enough to get whatever he wanted, without having to play nice. He had overpowered nearly all the Hijn, after all. Couldn't he just overtake the Bloodburn, who were without defensive magic, or magic of any kind? What would he need them for, anyway?

"Enough chit chat for now," Veni said, peeking through the bars again. "Just be patient, and we'll get everything arranged for you. And if you're good, we'll even improve accommodations for your...little steward, I suppose?" he asked, pointing at Woasim. "And none of your escorts will come to harm, if you do what we say." Then he and the general were gone, as Desert Rain listened as their plodding footsteps faded away.

Desert Rain buried her face in her hands. "Oh, Woasim, what am I going to do?"

Woasim tried his best to get his arms around her waist in a hug. "Don't worry, Dez. We'll figure this out together. We'll be okay."

A snicker in the corner of the room caught Desert Rain's ears. She looked over to see a tall shadow, with glowing eyes of yellow in the dark.

"I wouldn't be too sure about that," Katawa said.

CHAPTER SEVEN
Gabriel Gets a New Crew

Gabriel was seething, but he kept it contained behind his dark glare. He was shoved forwards at the end of a spiky cudgel, held by a Bloodburn warden who was a foot taller than he was and ten times as gruesome. The demon reeked of oil and a body odor Gabriel could only compare to burning refuse. The warden forced Gabriel out of General Vidi's car, across a short platform and into the next car, which was lined with Bloodburn guards along the walls. They continued through several more cars, up towards the very front of the entire mechanism where a smokestack belched out foul fumes. The great engine.

Gabriel did his best not to look at the other Bloodburn guards as he passed them. He could hear them snickering, jeering at him with curses and mockery. It had been bad enough to watch them tear Desert Rain away, taking her wherever they had, but as soon as she was gone, they had descended on him like jackals. They stripped him of just about everything except his trousers; he had attempted to lash out when one of them snatched the hat from his head, but a punch to his face had been the result. Then they bound his wrists with barbed wire, and it jabbed into his skin with dozens of metal teeth. He felt so exposed, so vulnerable. There was no where he could turn his face without one of those devils seeing it, and this warden had a delightful time mocking him: "Oh, you're not a pretty one, are you? Diseased? Or fought someone out of your league? Or maybe you're just unlucky. See, just as well you work for us now. Who else would want damaged trash like you?"

Damaged. If only this bastard really knew.

Gabriel was pushed forwards up the steps into a sweltering, muggy car that made it hard to breathe between the heat and the toxic smell. Before him was a boiler room unlike any he had ever seen, with a firebox as tall as two men with a burning mouth that could swallow a bull in one gulp. It was a deep room, piled with loads of firewood and some kind of glassy obsidian rocks speckled with red flecks. Feeding these items into the firebox was a line of eight Yopeis-Gichen, cuffed at the ankles with iron and connected by a long rusty chain. They looked at Gabriel and the warden as they entered, but the Yopeis could only stare glassy-eyed.

Gabriel's body tensed as he saw the prisoners were soot-stained and shriveled in the boiler heat. "These are Yopeis...they're amphibious, they'll dehydrate in this heat with no water—"

"They get their water ration, if they do good work," the Bloodburn warden barked. "As will you. And good timing too, looks like we have another meat sack to replace."

He gestured to the front of the chain gang, the Yopeis nearest to the firebox. Or, who had been nearest, as the Yopeis was lying on the floor motionless, his tender skin reddened to a crisp. He was not breathing.

"Eh, these critters are useless. Can't wait until we can get more human grunts. They last longer." The warden shoved Gabriel over to the dead Yopeis, took out his keys, knelt to undo the deceased's cuff, and strapped it onto Gabriel's ankle. A Yopeis is much smaller than a human, so the cuff pinched tight against Gabriel's skin, but he did not react to it. Only once he was secured did the warden unwind the wire from Gabriel's wrists, where tiny drops of blood speckled his skin. The warden grabbed the dead Yopeis by his fin-ears and started to drag him away out of the boiler room.

"Now get to feeding the boiler!" the Bloodburn growled as he departed. "If this train slows down even the slightest bit, it's a lashing for all of you!" He then exited, slamming the cumbersome door behind him. The rusty scrape of a long iron drawbar sliding across the door confirmed they were locked in.

As soon as the Bloodburn was gone, the Yopeis-Gichens all turned to Gabriel with sad eyes. But they said nothing, and kept passing the wood from calloused hand to hand along to Gabriel.

Gabriel let out a long breath, taking the wood and tossing it into the firebox. Already, his skin was in pain, and he was sure he would blister in no time. *Maybe this is what I deserve*, he thought. *Penance. And that Wretched was right, what else is a damaged soul like me good for? Skyhan would have had everyone saved by now. I'm...nothing.*

Damn that Skyhan. Had to go and die. What is that saying, only the good die young? Yeah, explains why I'm still alive. And after all his bluster, all that fine, noble talk about saving myself. Saving us. It was all for nothing. Now I'll never be complete. I'll never be —

"Sir?"

Gabriel heard the small voice behind him. A young hunter-green Yopeis, no doubt put near the front of the chain gang because of his youth, looked up at him while handing him another wood log. "Sorry they caught you. We have a system, so you know. We go through a stack of the wood, and then we burn some of the blood crude-stones. But you want to add that stuff sparingly, it can pack a punch."

Gabriel took the wood and knelt to be eye-level with the Yopeis. "How did you all get here?"

"The Bloodburn invaded the Ring of Springs. They took all of us," the young one replied. "We were waiting for our Hijn to come back with a report, but he never came. We fear the worst."

Gabriel put a hand on the Yopeis's shoulder. "Your Hijn is alive," he said, "and we're going to make sure he's all right. We need to help him, and my friend."

All the Yopeis glanced at each other, confused and scared. But the young one's eyes widened in interest. "How are we going to do that?"

Gabriel glanced back towards the door. "When will that warden come back?"

"He'll come to bring us our water rations, which won't be before the end of the day. And we get food rations in the morning. If the boiler's fed enough, maybe we can rest for an hour."

Gabriel glanced at the door, thinking. "What's your name?"

The Yopeis stood up as straight as he could. "Dunmore. But you can call me Dun."

"Okay, Dun, I have a plan, but you're going to have to help me..."

*   *   *

"This was the dumbest plan of all time!" Chiriku called over the rush of the wind. She clung tight to the vertical railing on the back end of the final train car, struggling to keep her feet above the ground. Mac hung onto the same railing beside her, as there was no place else to secure a grip. There was no door into this final car – it was most likely a cargo hold only accessible from the adjoining car – so while there was no risk of a Bloodburn spotting them from there, there was also no easy way to get into the moving train.

"Hey, at least-ttk we were able to get-ttk here with no one bein' the wiser," Mac replied. "But I wasn't-ttk about to get-ttk on board shoulder to shoulder with those nasty fellows."

Chiriku had to agree. Even though Mac could have passed well enough as a Bloodburn with his disguise on, and she had slicked down all of her head and face feathers in blood so may have gone unnoticed for a while, it would have been risking it to board with so many Bloodburn. Someone might have realized they were unfamiliar faces. They had managed to hide under the train until all the others got on board, and then as the machine started to move, they slipped out and hid on the back end.

"So, we're just going to hang here until our arms fall off?" Chiriku retorted.

Mac shook his head. "Ye of little faith. You forget-ttk, I have sticky fingers." He reached up with one hand, as small pads formed on the tips of his fingers. He pressed his fingers into the wall, and when he felt secure, he released the railing altogether and started to scale the car, climbing up to the top.

"Mac, we'll get blown off this thing from up there!" Chiriku called.

"Just-ttk hang onto my tail, and we'll crawl along until we find a safe way in," Mac replied.

He extended his tail down to her, and she grabbed

on, although not confident in this plan. But how else would they find Desert Rain and Gabriel? Mac pulled her up, and then quietly and cautiously, on hands and feet, began to make his way across the top of the car. Chiriku followed behind, the wind whipping against her whole body, watching the world flash by her like she was flying.

We better find Donkey Ears and Moody Boy fast, she thought, *before this whole plan blows up in our faces!*

*   *   *

"Dez? Dez! What's wrong?" Woasim strained against his chains to try and reach Desert Rain, who had backed against the far wall and was staring with terrified eyes at something.

"GO AWAY!" she screamed, grasping her head and curling up in a defensive ball. "How did you even get in here? Leave us alone!"

Woasim turned around to where she was looking, and then he turned back to her, his brow knitted in worry. "Dez, who are you talking to? Me?"

Desert Rain lifted her head to him, disbelief on her face. "What? No, it's Katawa! He's right there!"

"Um...I don't see anyone," Woasim replied.

Desert Rain's heart thudded so hard, it was all she could hear. How could Woasim not see him? Was she losing her mind? She looked again, and Katawa stood right there, a few feet from Woasim. He was as she remembered him, a strange blend of her features and his own, a long-eared Hijn with light lavender skin and storm-blue hair down to his shoulders. His yellow eyes locked on her, his pupils narrow feline slits. The

Distortionist gave her a mocking little wave of his fingers, grinning at her.

"But...I...why can he not see you?" she rasped.

Katawa raised his eyebrows. "The better question is, how can *you* see me?"

Woasim bit his lip, but then took a breath and gave Desert Rain a determined look. "I believe you." He turned around, holding his arms out as best he could, facing whatever was scaring his friend. "You are not welcomed here, whatever you are! If Dez wants you to leave, then be gone!"

Katawa regarded the little Yopeis, smirking. "Annoying little thing, isn't he?" He then proceeded to step forward, and stepped straight *through* Woasim, approaching Desert Rain.

"Wha...you're...not really here," she realized, her voice barely a whisper.

"Well, no, not in the flesh. This is just a trick left over from my benefactor. I never found much use of it before. I'm not the spying kind, as you know...well, except when I used to spy on my brother. Before he had me killed." Katawa's grin soured, as a malicious glint flickered in his eye. "But anyway, it has its uses. I didn't expect you would be able to see me. Although, I shouldn't be surprised."

Desert Rain, knowing now that Katawa was not physically there, sat up straight and looked him in the eye. "Why's that?"

"You're the Moon Hijn! The moon is tied to the night, and night is the portal to shadows, spirits, all that otherworldly mess. I guess my ghost form is part of all that." He gave her a dubious look. "You can't tell me this is the first time you've seen a ghost."

Desert Rain thought back to her spiritual encounter with the deceased elf Sir Valdrase, when the desert shaman had summoned him to give her a message. She had not considered that summoning had only worked because she had an ability to see spirits. "I don't exactly go looking for ghosts," she replied.

"Ghosts? Is that what you're talking to?" Woasim asked, as his ears shivered. "But if he's a ghost, then he's dead, right? That's how it works?"

"Not exactly," Desert Rain replied. "But what kind of benefactor gave you the ability to walk about as a spirit? The Lifescourge?"

Katawa stifled a laugh. "Ah, yes, I remember your Hijn Council calling him that. 'That evil creature could mean disaster for all of us!' A bit dramatic, I say. Time distorts history, without my help at all. Poor old Balthazin would be so disappointed to know how he's been remembered, as some life-sucking, world-decaying entity. Then again, I suppose he's indirectly responsible for what this world will become."

Balthazin? Why did that name sound familiar? It was something Desert Rain had once read, in one of her books at home. Now that she recalled, she had written a play about someone with that name, long ago. *The Solemn Soliloquy of Balthazin the...* "Balthazin the Death Walker?"

Woasim froze when she said that. His ears flattened against his sides, and he scooted back, muttering something so rapidly, she could not tell what it was. His voice was quiet and monotone, and she thought it might be some protective prayer. She managed to make out his words, "Save us from the Eternal Deep."

Katawa watched Woasim with mild amusement. "Remind me to collect him when I get here. But yes, I keep forgetting how clever you are, Desert Rain. So studious. Now we know every secret about one another. Heirs to the Moon Dragoness and the Keeper of the Eternal Deep. What a pair we make."

Desert Rain had missed most of what Katawa had said, fixating on one thing. "You're coming here? In person?"

"I have to, don't I? I was keeping an eye on the Bloodburn, after their dismissal of my offer of alliance. But now that you're here, I'll have to save you before I make these ungrateful dolts see the error of their ways. Speaking of which, what was that nonsense that pompous idiot was talking about? Something about you being queen?"

Desert Rain felt a funny feeling in her chest, almost like she wanted to laugh. She stood up, giving Katawa a cheeky grin. "General Vidi wants to exploit a loophole that he can own me and whatever I possess by marrying me. Want to be the best man?"

Katawa's grinning face morphed into something Desert Rain could not remember ever seeing from him before: a dismayed frown of betrayal. His eyes blazed with furious intensity, his lips pulling back to bare his fanged teeth, and his voice warped into the sound of an organist slamming his hands on all the keys. "I'LL TEAR THE EYES OUT OFF THAT BASTARD AND SHOVE THEM STRAIGHT UP HIS—" He cut himself off, taking a deep breath and smoothing back his hair. His voice returned to its cool confidence. "But here I am, making this all about me, when you must be mortified. My poor, golden girl." He reached forwards to caress her cheek, but his hand went through her and she could not feel anything. She was thankful for that.

"Anyway, I best go for now," Katawa said casually. "My body is vulnerable for however long I go about like this. But now that I know this train is heading north, that will give me some time to refresh myself, catch up with you, and retrieve you right after I slaughter these Bloodburn fools. Sleep well, my love." He blew her a kiss, and then he vanished like he had never been there.

Desert Rain ran straight for the door, pounding on it with her fist. "Can anyone hear me? Katawa is coming back! He's going to attack all of us! For Divine Beasts' sake, someone listen to me!"

"Dez, I don't think they'll listen," Woasim said, coming back over to her. "But that Veni guy said they were going to move you to a nicer room. Maybe when he comes back, you can warn him. Is the ghost gone?"

Desert Rain took a deep breath, resting her hands against the door. "Yes, he's gone. But he'll be back." She grunted and tugged down on her ears. "I'm such an idiot! I got us trapped, I don't have the sword, who knows what they've done with Gabriel—"

"Hey, hey," Woasim said in a calming voice, "there's no point in beating yourself up. And you didn't get us trapped. I should've stayed with you guys, made sure you got to safety before I did any investigating. But I'm going to do everything I can to make things right. And you will too, right?"

Desert Rain looked back at him, smiling weakly. "Right. Let's try the Blueshine. Maybe I can free you from the chains."

She went over and took hold of Woasim's chains, putting about three feet of distance between herself and him. She wrapped her fingers tight around the cold metal, closing her eyes and softly murmuring the words of dragon-tongue to summon the magic from within. She could feel the sensation bubble up inside of her, the cool wash of a midnight stream, of dreams and moonlight and dancing stars across the night sky. It flowed through her like a song, and for a second, all the world melted away, and there was only peace and quiet music in her mind.

But then she felt a pinch in her fingers, tiny cold needles prickling her hands. She opened her eyes to see the chains morphing into sea-blue glass, crusting over fingers with a stinging frost. This was okay, this always happened when she summoned Blueshine. She was doing good. Maybe that was enough—but the Blueshine kept going. The chain continued to turn to glass, crawling along the links, crawling closer and closer to Woasim's encasings. He did not seem scared of her magic; his eyes were glued to the chain, watching the transformation with wonder.

"Ooooh, Dez! How beautiful!" he cooed. "I never knew you could do that!"

His words were encouraging. Maybe she could like the magic flow a little longer, enough to enchant his encasings so she could break them off too.

Break them off…

Break his arms off…

The thought sent shocks of panic through her. Desert Rain jerked her hands back, and this one small movement caused the chain to shatter into hundreds of splinter-thin shards. The magic had not quite reached the casings, but Woasim was able to jump back from the obliterated chain, freed from the wall.

"Wow! Would you look at that! You did it!" Woasim cheered, able to lift his arms a little higher without the weight of the chain. "I didn't know moon magic was so neat!"

Desert Rain shivered, rubbing her hands together to scrub off the glassy frost. "I'm sorry, I thought I could do your mitts too. But I panicked, I'm sorry."

"Sorry? Why? You were amazing! I don't understand why you're so scared of your magic. You're so capable, Dez. Is it because Fierno isn't nice to you? I never liked the way he treats you. He's just a…a hot head! If all the other Hijn knew what you could do…Dez?"

Desert Rain had turned away from him. She hugged herself, gripping her sleeves. "I'm a screw-up, Sim. I'm not capable at all. I thought I could be, but…I can't even control one simple spell long enough without ruining it. I can't go anywhere without stumbling into danger and putting everyone at risk. I wish I was like you. I wish…I was somebody else. Because anyone else would be better."

After a moment, she felt two short arms wrap around her waist, even with the iron casings making it hard to do so. "I don't want you to be anybody else. I like Desert Rain. I wish you would, too. Because Desert Rain is the best."

And there it was. Tears cascaded down Desert Rain's face, a dam finally burst. She still did not believe it, not totally, but it was nice to hear him say it. It was nice to imagine it might be true, for a moment. She turned around and knelt, hugging Woasim in return. Oh, how foolish she had been, to be alone in that desert for so long! To have shunned Woasim, and Clova, people who had reached out to her and she had been too scared to take their hands.

"You're too good, Sim," she said through her sniffling.

"I like to think I'm the right amount of good," he said, smiling. "Now how about we get out of here? Do you think you're up to it?"

Desert Rain looked over at the door. "I think I could shatter the door, but what do we do then? If they catch us, they'll just lock us up again. And there's no getting off this train while it's moving. I mean, if we can get your mitts off, then you could summon some wind, maybe use it to slow down this machine."

Woasim thought on this. "I bet if we can get something to cut through the locks on these mittens... hey, where's Silverheart?"

Silverheart! Of course! They had to get the sword back. It could break the casings without hurting Woasim. Silverheart would never harm the innocent. "General Vidi's got it in his chambers. But how do we get from here to there? There's got to be guards everywhere, and Vidi isn't going to let us stroll in there and take Silverheart back. We don't have anything to protect ourselves."

The Wind Hijn tapped his foot as he contemplated. Then he smiled, but not his usual cheerful one; this was a sneaky, mischievous grin. "We're going to have to get a little crafty..."

*   *   *

The guard groused as he entered the prison car. It was sunset, and the train had been on the move all day without stopping. He hated being trapped on this machine about as much as he hated food duty, and he shrugged the bag of stale bread slung over his shoulder. The engine would need to cool down soon, so he looked forward to a short stop and rest for the night.

He grabbed fistfuls of bread, tossing them into the windows of the cell doors without much thought. Grubby little Yopies-Gichens. They didn't seem worth wasting food on, but at least they got the scraps while the Bloodburn got the meat. It was tempting to open one of these cells and sneak out one of these fish people, have some private meat for himself. But the general would not have it.

As he approached the cell door in the middle of the car, he noticed something odd. The door, normally a dark iron, was glistening like ice. A foggy, blue sheen covered the door and its frame. He paused, trying to figure out what was going on. Oh, right, this was the cell with those magic people. He set down his sack and withdrew his cudgel, advancing slowly. He stood in front of the door, looking it over. He was about to tap it lightly with his cudgel when a yellow Yopeis crashed straight through the door and slugged him hard over the head with two iron casings. The guard was out cold, keeling over with a thump on the floor.

"I guess that was crafty," Desert Rain said, stepping out through the doorway.

Woasim laughed, shaking the glassy shards off his clothes. "See, these mittens did come in handy! And they were supposed to keep me from attacking them. I do love irony."

Desert Rain picked up the cudgel that the guard had dropped. She cautiously checked him over for anything else useful, and she found a ring of keys. "These must be keys for different cars. Okay, so we have to find our way around without being—"

"Hey Dez? Can you stuff some of that bread in my mouth? I'm starving," Woasim said.

Desert Rain's stomach growled, since neither of them had eaten all day. She did as Woasim asked, and his mouth opened like a gaping fish when she offered him some bread. They both ate a few chunks, and while it was not the most appealing food, it was enough to give them some strength back.

"Okay, now let's free the others." Woasim lifted his hands towards the other cells.

Desert Rain paused. "Of course, Sim, but where are they going to go? The train's still moving. They'll still be trapped here."

Woasim nodded. "I see your point. Then the first thing we need to do is stop this train."

"And I suppose you know how to do that?"

"Sure. We'll just ask whoever is driving."

Desert Rain crossed her arms. "You have a way of oversimplifying everything, Sim."

"I rather think of it as un-complicating things." He grinned and started walking towards the exit door to the car.

Desert Rain grabbed his shoulder to stop him. "Then what is your 'un-complicated' way of getting through all these cars, past all the Bloodburn, past General Vidi and Veni, finding the driver, and somehow convincing him to stop the train?"

Woasim winked at her. "You just said it beautifully."

"No, you're not understand—"

The door at the opposite end of the car creaked open. Desert Rain and Woasim stopped short as they saw two Bloodburn slip into the car. The two guards halted when they saw them, and one of them shouted in a familiar female squawk: "Guys! Oh shoot, you already knocked that guard out. I was hoping to do that."

Desert Rain exhaled the breath she had been holding. "Chi! What on earth happened to you? Why are you—"

"Smothered in blood, wearing this ridiculous getup? Ask the lizard," Chiriku replied, pointing her thumb at the guard with the reptilian eyes beside her.

"Mac! Thank the Sages." Desert Rain walked over to them, embracing them each. "How did you escape?"

"Never got-ttk caught-ttk. Too slippery for 'em," Mac bragged. "But by pure luck-kk, we were able to pick-kk a lock-kk and hide out-ttk in a storage car for the last-ttk few hours. Until that-ttk fellow came to get-ttk some bread, and he forgot-ttk to lock-kk the doors behind 'im."

"Wow, I really didn't recognize either of you when you came in." Desert Rain scratched her cheek in thought. "Actually, this might be useful for what we need to do."

CHAPTER EIGHT
Rebellion!

The warden slid the drawbar aside and slammed the door to the boiler room open with a clang. He carried a leather flask in hand, and he sneered at the seven Yopeis with a curled lip.

"Water rations," he growled. "Not that the lot of you deserve it."

The Yopeis laid down their logs and picked up small wooden cups they had set aside nearby. The warden began sloshing muddy water into each cup, spilling more of it on the floor than getting it into the vessels.

"A few more hours and then I'll switch you lot out with the others," the warden said, but when he came to Gabriel, who had no cup, he laughed. "'Cept you. You can go all night, I wager. Oh, did I forget to give you a cup? Guess you'll be drinking from your hands, then."

Dun extended his cup out to Gabriel. "You can borrow mine—"

The warden slapped the cup from Dun's hand onto the floor. "You mind your business," he snarled. "You lose your cup, you don't get any water."

Gabriel was too thirsty to care how he got the water. He cupped his hands and drank quickly as the sludgy water filled them. It was putrid, but at least it was cool. As the warden turned to leave, Gabriel shot Dun a pointed look. Dun took a deep breath and then collapsed onto the floor. He coughed and convulsed for a few moments, and then lay still.

The warden whipped his head back around. "Ugh, another one? I swear, I spend more time replacing these blighters than having any time to myself." He came back over and grabbed Dun around the ankle. He took out his keys and undid the cuff, which clinked onto the floor.

This left a good length of chain between Gabriel and the next Yopeis. Which was all Gabriel needed.

As the warden turned back toward the door, Gabriel grabbed the chain, lunged forwards, and got it over the Bloodburn's head. He wrapped the rusty metal links around the demon's neck and tightened it with all his might. The warden gagged, dropping Dun and clawing at the chain in a frenzy. Dun, upon being released, sprang back to life and got up on his feet. He hesitated, trying to remember what Gabriel had told him to do, and then he saw the keys dangling from the warden's belt. He ran forth, grasping for the keys, but the warden kicked him away.

"Gaaah...Fools!" the warden rasped, and he brought his arm with his wristbow over his shoulder. He tried to shoot Gabriel in the face, but the man jerked away from the bolt just in time, although the bolt managed to nick his cheek. Gabriel continued to pull with every ounce of strength, but after a long day of toil, his energy was fading fast. The Bloodburn pivoted, leaning over to throw Gabriel off him. Gabriel continued to hang on, but his vision was getting dark, his chest tightening. He did not know how much longer he could do this.

The warden let out a strangled scream as Dun rushed over, clamped into his leg, and sank his teeth through the trousers into his hamstrings. The Bloodburn buckled, which allowed Gabriel to plant a foot on the warden's back and push while pulling the chain. The warden fell belly-first to the floor, scrambling to get up, but Dun and the other six Yopeis piled on top of him. After a few long, excruciating minutes of gurgling and wheezing, the warden finally stopped struggling. His whole body went limp, and his now purple face relaxed into a blank expression.

"Oh my..." Dun poked at the warden carefully. "I didn't know if these demons could really die."

Gabriel yanked the keys and the cudgel from the dead warden's belt and unlocked his ankle cuff. He tossed the keys to Dun. "Free them." He then hefted the cudgel on his shoulder. "Then find wherever they're keeping the others."

"What are you going to do?" Dun asked.

"Bash some Bloodburn skulls."

Dun went down the line of chain, unlocking the cuffs from his brethren. "That sounds all well and good, but we can be more helpful to you, you know."

"How so?"

"Well, the Bloodburn are an army." Dun grinned, gesturing to the others. "And if you help us free the rest of our village, then we'll be one too. We just need a general."

Gabriel scanned the group of dirty, half-starved Yopeis. How were these people, who by nature were pacifists, supposed to fight against the most brutal barbarians in Luuva Gros? Yet there was something different in the air. Even the most docile of creatures could be pushed to their limit, and he could see a new fire in the eyes of these prisoners. They did not want to flee. They wanted payback.

"No, you need weapons," Gabriel replied. "And I know exactly where to get them."

*   *   *

Desert Rain held her breath as she and Woasim were escorted through several cars, with Mac and Chiriku holding them by their arms. The possibility of a real Bloodburn seeing through their ruse felt inevitable, but for every guard they passed, no one batted an eye. The sentinels designated at the doorways of certain train cars appeared to be in a daze; Desert Rain surmised they had ridiculously long shifts, and figured no one on board seemed threatening enough for them to remain on high alert.

They passed through a car lined with cots stacked upon one another, with Bloodburns sleeping, playing cards, or mauling the flesh off meat bones. Again, no one paid them mind, although some of them gave her derisive glances. Desert Rain figured they were not doing anything worse to her because they must have already heard that they were going to have a new "queen" soon, and harassing her in any way would result in punishment. She heard snickering, whispers, maybe someone saying, "General's lost his mind, who'd want that?" She held her head high, ignoring the mockery and stares. Yet, she noticed something odd that she had not before. Now that these Bloodburn were not in uniform–that was, their veiled masks were off–she could see they were all uniquely different. Some were bald-flesh like she had assumed they all were, but some were a bit scaly, some a bit feathery, some with a light layer of thin fur. A couple were even beak-nosed, or snouted. It was as if, despite them all being the same wine-red color, they were not all the same species. No wonder no one questioned Mac or Chiriku's slightly off appearance; some of these Bloodburn looked exactly like them.

They passed through a dozen cars of Bloodburn soldiers before walking into a car full of the spoils of conquerors. Baskets of pearls and aragonite, the currency of those who lived in the Rings of Springs, were heaped on one side of the room, along with piles of sea silk fabric, coral furniture, jars of various salts, tufa and limestone statues and artworks, water vases–anything that could be pilfered from Yopeis-Gichen homes and marketplaces. Desert Rain's heart ached to think what ruin the Ring of Springs had fallen to. She had never seen it herself, but it was well known throughout Luuva Gros what a mystical place of refreshing waters, crystalline coves and luxurious lagoons it was. Would there be anything left for Woasim and his people to return home to?

Woasim looked upon the spoils, his eyes brimming with tears. "Oh my…they took everything…I shouldn't have left home. I should have been there to stop them…"

"You couldn't have known. The Knighthood had kept the Bloodburn confined to the Inbetween. No one could have predicted what they'd do once the Knights were scattered." Desert Rain sighed.

Woasim inhaled deeply, steadying himself. "We can rebuild everything once we rescue all the Yopeis and make sure these Wretched can never come back to do this again."

"How much farther do we have to go?" Chiriku asked, scratching her scalp and ruffling some of her red-stained feathers. "This machine is so darn looooong."

"I think our holding cell was about ten of these caravans from the front," Desert Rain said, "but we're going to have to pass through General Vidi's quarters to get to the engine. We'll have to improvise. Mac can lead me in, and I'll say I demand a private meeting. Then maybe you can all slip past while I have him distracted."

"But he's got three heads. I think one of them is bound to notice us," Woasim pointed out.

The room suddenly jolted forwards, and there was a loud burst from somewhere nearby. A deep rumbling and grinding resounded from ahead.

"What was that?" Chiriku squawked.

Mac sniffed the air. "Well, if that-ttk was anythin' like-kk when my old cart-ttk used to get-ttk the hiccups, and judgin' by the smell, I'd say this thing's engine just-ttk blew like a flame put-ttk to swamp gas."

*   *   *

The Grand Imperial Battle Train's engineer, a short, stocky Bloodburn who would have made a Stonebreaker Dwarf feel tall, nearly fell out of his seat as the train rattled and shook with a loud BOOM from below him. His station at the train's controls were directly above the boiler engine, and panic gripped his heart as he already surmised something in the boiler had exploded.

"Oh no no no no no no no," he whimpered, and he grasped the controls so hard his knuckles turned white. He would have to veer the train steady, but he knew pulling the brakes right now would not do much good–if the boiler was overloaded, then the engine would need to cool down first before the brakes would work properly. The good news was, they were driving on a long stretch of valley that posed no obstacles or hindrances for hundreds of miles. The bad news was, with the boiler at maximum heat, the train was speeding along much faster than it was designed to. He could feel sweat soaking through his overalls and hat, and he readjusted his thick goggles. He hoped he could quickly remedy whatever the problem was without arousing the anger of–

An unintelligible roar resounded from the direction of General Vidi's car.

The engineer was already forming in his mind what to say. *It was those damned Yopeis-Gichen! Must've thrown too much fuel in the boiler. I thought the warden told them how much to put in at a time! I just drive the train, you can't blame me!*

There was a guardsmen sleep car and three fuel cars between General Vidi's car and the boiler room, and the irate Bloodburn leader clomped his way through them in an undeterred beeline. "Who's fouled up this time?" he bellowed, awaking the six sleeping guardsmen. They promptly gathered themselves and followed him.

They plowed through the fuel cars, one full of freshly chopped wood, the other two packed with blood-crude stones stacked in piles. Vidi threw open the door exiting the fuel car, seeing that the door to the boiler room was wide open. Through the door, he could see the boiler raging, fire licking through the grates and filling the room with dense smoke.

"Vidi, I would suggest–" Veni started, but the general barreled ahead into the boiler room, with his guardsmen in tow. Vidi wanted nothing more than to throttle these worthless Yopeis, but as he fumbled around in the smoke, he realized none of his newly acquired slaves were in there. Only their chains remained.

Perhaps, if he and his guards had not been so quick to pass through the fuel cars, he might have noticed all the small figures hiding behind the piles of crude stones. Possibly, they might have seen a hint of the one human male hanging off the side of the engine car. Because they had not, and were now blinded by the smoke, no one was fast enough to see the human swing his way back on the gangway connection, slam the door to the engine room shut, and then slide the thick iron bolt across with a heavy *thunk* to lock them in.

"CURSE THOSE FOOLS! THEY'RE ALL DEAD!" General Vidi howled. "Break that door down, NOW!"

Gabriel hoped that maybe the Bloodburn would asphyxiate from the smoke or overheat before they could break down the door, but there was a vent to the smokestack, so the smoke would waft out. Those blood-crude stones really did "pack a punch" as Dun had warned him. Having overloaded the boiler with them had the desired effect, and that would keep those Bloodburn busy for a while.

He ran back into the first fuel car. "Okay, looks like the general brought all his personal guards with him. Should be a straight shot from here to his room. Grab whatever weapons you can and let's–"

He heard someone clamber into the car behind him. Turning around, he saw a short Bloodburn wearing overalls, goggles, and a hat, who froze upon seeing him. The Bloodburn engineer looked around at the dozen Yopeis, this tall human, and then he looked behind him as he heard the banging against the boiler room door.

"Um...the general and his men are all in there?" the engineer asked.

Gabriel shot him a look of murderous contempt. That was enough to convince the engineer to spin around, run to the gangway connection, and leap clean off the train.

"We might need to move faster than I thought," Gabriel said, surmising if the Bloodburn were now leaping from the train, they could be careening towards disaster. He and the Yopeis dashed through the cars, clearing each gangway connection as the wind rushed around them, until they arrived in General Vidi's vacant car.

"Oh my," Dun said, looking around at the array of weaponry. "I don't even know what half of these things are. They do look like fun though, don't they?" He had a funny little smirk in the corner of his lips.

Each Yopeis selected a weapon, at least the lighter ones they could handle, and Gabriel was about to select a spiked mace when he spotted the shining, silver sword on the wall. Silverheart. His heart stirred, a mixture of temptation and terror. He could not leave the sword here. But what would happen if he tried to take it? He knew Silverheart could not be touched by the impure—after all, he had tried to handle it once...

He approached the sword with slow, cautious reverence. His fingers twitched, already screaming, as he lifted his hand towards the hilt. He could feel a heat pulsating from the sword, and fear strangled his heart. Could he bear it if the sword shocked him? What would it mean if it did? That all these years of strife, of going out into the world to remove these stains of wickedness from his soul, would be all for nothing?

He pulled away from Silverheart. The sword had not chosen him. He had seen it before; it had chosen Desert Rain. He needed to free her, to bring her to the sword. He hated feeling so helpless, unable to even deliver the sword to her, but she was the one, not him.

A door from behind General Vidi's throne opened, sliding aside as four figures entered the room. They peeked out from behind the throne. "Gabriel?"

Gabriel looked over to see Desert Rain and Woasim, followed by two Bloodburn who looked a little odd. He then recognized their eyes, not the orange of a true Bloodburn. He grinned. "Took you long enough."

"Oh, Gabe! You're burnt all over!" Desert Rain ran over to him, looking over his boiler-heated skin. "I'm sorry, I don't have anything to heal this..."

"Don't worry about that, it'll peel off," he replied. He found it funny she was so concerned with that; it was not even that bad. His skin was only a bit red. She certainly had not had that reaction the first time she saw his scars.

"My brothers!" Woasim cried, opening his arms to them. "Thank the Sages, you're safe! I promise, I shan't leave you defenseless again!"

"Shan't? Who says 'shan't'?" muttered Chiriku.

The Yopeis crowded around him, embracing him in a group hug. Woasim noticed their weapons. "Oh, dear, you don't plan to–"

"Revolt!" Dun cried, and the others cheered in response, raising their daggers, short swords, maces, and clubs. "You may be our protector, Woasim of the Winds, but our general has taught us we must be able to defend ourselves!"

"I told you all, I'm not your general," Gabriel said.

"And if we're going to face all the other Bloodburn on this train, we're going to have to have a plan, not just leap head-first into a brawl–"

Screaming erupted from somewhere nearby. It was farther back on the train, and it was not only cries of battle, but hellish, piercing screams of agony. Desert Rain felt her blood run cold as she also heard blasting thunder, and the hammering sound of rain on the roof of the car.

Gabriel ran to the door, stepping out onto the connection and leaning out as far as he could to see around the sides of the train cars. He darted back inside the car, his hair wet and his eyes wide. He threw the door shut behind him. "Okay, so that whole thing about a plan, we're going to have to throw that out the window."

Before anyone could ask what he was talking about, something of substantial weight dropped onto the roof of the car–that was, several *somethings* landed on top of the car. Everyone inside could hear painful screeching and the scraping of claws against the roof, and a few moments later, that scraping could be heard against the train car doors.

Gabriel went to the wall and lifted a mace from one of the hooks. "Our Distorted friends are back."

"What? But…how did they get here so fast?" Desert Rain already surmised *how* they got here; given the weather and that they had seemingly dropped out of the sky, the Distorted had been transported in one of V'Tanna's storm-cloud wyrms, which could cover distance faster than even this train. Even so, between the time that Katawa had appeared to her and now, this was a quickly arranged assault. Unless…he had never really left that area after his last encounter with the Bloodburn. He and the Distorted must have stayed hidden in the nearby forest and followed the train all this distance, biding his time until he could get revenge for General Vidi's dismissal of him. *Oh, Guerda-Shalyr...*

"Wait, did you know they were coming?" Chiriku asked.

"Well, I mean...it's a long story. We have to get the Yopeis off this train, now!" Desert Rain shivered as she thought of a fate worse than these poor Yopeis being enslaved grunts–if Katawa got his hands on them, they would be forced to join his legions after their bodies and spirits would be literally twisted to his desires.

"But the other holding cells are all the way at the back of the train! We'll need to go through the Bloodburn and the Distorted to reach them!" Dun said, his face blanching.

Woasim mulled this over and then made a resolute nod. "Right! Everyone, you must jump off this train! Use your ears like I do to glide, it'll slow your fall. Desert Rain and I'll go free the others."

"You're not-ttk doin' this by yourselves!" Mac argued.

"No, I've got Mum too. If I can just use my wind magic..." He turned to Desert Rain, eyes pleading. "Dez, I know you're worried, but you've got to try your magic again. You have to break these mittens off me."

Desert Rain shook her head. "No, wait...we've got Silverheart now! I'll use it to break the locks!"

She dashed to where Silverheart hung on the wall, grabbing the hilt. The back door of the train car was suddenly torn off its hinges, and three mangle-faced Distorted of unusual size stuck their faces inside, shrieking with such virulence that it would have sent vengeful souls of the damned running back to their graves.

"Out, out now!" Woasim ordered, throwing his arms towards the fuel cars. "Get in the fuel car and lock the doors!"

Dun and the other Yopeis were frozen in fear. "But…but they're everywhere! And those Bloodburn are still locked in the boiler room!"

Woasim gave Dun a reassuring look. "I will come for you, I promise! Gabriel, please protect them. Once I'm free, I can use the winds to get us all out of here."

Chiriku tore off her disguise, grabbing for her warhammer across her back. An excited glint sparkled in her eye. "Come on, Mac, let's smack some nightmares!"

Mac, shaking and turning a pale shade of pink, gripped his cudgel tightly. "Ooooooo….kaaaaaaay…."

As one of the Distorted crawled into the car, Chiriku ran over and swung upwards with her warhammer in a wide swoop, colliding it with the Distorted's jaw. The monster reeled back into the other two behind him, who looked at Chiriku with wild, beastly mania. Gabriel went to Vidi's throne, pushing it backwards with all his might, despite its massive size and density. Mac picked up on the plan, and joined Gabriel, shoving against the burdensome, iron chair. It began to slide backwards towards the door.

"Keep 'em back-kk just a little longer, Chi!" Mac hollered, as he and Gabriel slowly pushed the throne across the floor. The Yopeis, swallowing their fear, scampered over and helped, yanking the throne in unison. Chiriku swung again at the Distorted, forcing them back out the door, and she managed to slide out of the way just in time as the throne slammed against the doorframe, shutting the Distorted out. It would not be a long-term solution, as the twisted claws were already scratching their way around the edges of the throne, but it would buy them a little time.

The Yopeis hightailed it out the other door, leaping to the next train car. Gabriel followed them, with Chiriku and Mac tailing behind. Desert Rain and Woasim ran towards the connection, ready to jump, when another Distorted leapt down from above, blocking their way.

"Lock the door!" she called, bringing Silverheart in front of her in a defensive stance. She could see past the Distorted to the next car, where the others were looking back at her, panic in their eyes. Chiriku and Gabriel were already coming back, weapons at the ready to help her.

The Distorted are just going to keep coming. I've got to give the others a chance to get away. If this train could go faster…with less cars…

She swung Silverheart low towards the Distorted's legs. The Distorted lashed out for the sword to swat it from her hands, but Silverheart's electric ward shocked its fingers and raced up its arm. Taken aback, the beast spun away from the sword, losing its footing on the narrow connection, and tumbled off the train. But the Distorted was not what Desert Rain had been aiming for; with the white lightning heating the blade, Silverheart sliced into the connection between the two cars with a blazing energy that cut through like warm butter.

"Dez, no!" Gabriel called, but his side of the train, now disconnected from so many cars, pulled ahead so fast, he had no time to jump back to her. Desert Rain watched as the others rolled away, seeing there were no Distorted on the roof of their cars. She could already feel her car slowing down, with no engine to pull it. She shut the door, locking herself and Woasim in.

Woasim tightened his lips, his mind racing. "Okay, they should be fine for a few minutes. But we'll need to act quickly, if you can break my mittens now."

Desert Rain turned to him as he lifted his encasings towards her. She eyed the locks on his bindings, focusing. Silverheart would not hurt him, she was sure of it. She positioned herself, set the blade against the locks of one encasing to judge the right angle, then raised the sword and brought it down with a strong swing. There was a bright, blue spark that popped, and then the locks to the encasing clattered onto the floor.

"You did it! Fantastic!" Woasim cheered, and he shook the encasing off. It clattered on the floor, his hand freed. "Now, the other one–"

Two raptor claws, as long as sabers, pierced through the roof. They sliced through the metal like paper, cutting a three-foot diameter hole, and the circular piece of ceiling crashed into the floor. Desert Rain and Woasim looked up to see someone descending into the car, two long clawed fingers extending from his back like deformed wings. Dressed in crimson and gold, looking ironically regal and refined, the Distortionist dropped down into the car with ease, grinning from ear to ear.

"There you are, my dear," he said as he wrung rainwater from his jacket. "You do like to make things a challenge, don't you?"

Desert Rain, paralyzed, shifted her eyes to Woasim, wondering if he was seeing what she was seeing, or if Katawa was in ghost form again. Judging from the fact that Woasim was staring with stunned bewilderment, his ears flattened against his head, it was clear that Katawa was there in the flesh.

CHAPTER NINE

A Vengeful Wind Rises; The Last Stand of the Three-Headed Bloodburn

"Sorry for my being so unkempt," Katawa went on, retracting his finger-tendrils into his back. "Storm clouds are a convenient way to travel, but not a dry one."

Desert Rain swallowed the knot in her chest and held Silverheart in both hands in a longpoint guard stance, the blade aimed toward his face. She braced herself, keeping her breathing steady. *Remember what Sir Luce taught you. You can do a strong thrust or a quick cut from this position.*

The Distortionist looked at Silverheart, pursing his lips. "Oh, so that's where that went. And here I am, having so quickly packed up my army and rushed here to see you, and you greet me like this. I didn't expect a warm reunion, but I don't even get a 'hello'? How have you been? How's complete domination going? Nothing?"

Desert Rain gripped the sword tighter, hoping any second Sir Luce would take over, but knew to be prepared to fight if he did not.

Katawa chuckled in amusement. "Look at you, more confident than when I left you in that hole in the desert. It's kind of...alluring." He casually approached her, stopping a mere inch from the tip of Silverheart's blade. "My instincts were right about you. You and I are going to do so many marvels together. I know you may hate me for it, at first. But you'll come around."

Desert Rain did not like how he was so in control

of the situation. She knew that Silverheart could, at the very least, shock him even if she could not deliver a solid blow. So, why couldn't she do it? He was right there, unflinching. Just one thrust forward, into his throat. She could end him, end his spread of Distortion right now. Why couldn't she move?

Katawa stepped forward again, sliding the side of his neck near the blade. "My head's right here. Aren't you going to make good on your threat? After all, it's not the first time you've impaled my neck," he said, his sinister smile souring. "But we both know you're not going to do it. And you know why not."

Woasim, restraining his urge to speak, quietly began gesturing with his one free hand, although without both hands, his magic would be limited. He moved his fingers in a circular motion, as a small rope tornado slowly swirled into being. He could summon up just enough single handedly to push this fiend back out through the hole he came in—

Katawa moved so quickly, neither Desert Rain nor Woasim comprehended it. In a blink, the Distortionist had snatched the Yopeis by his free arm and hoisted him clean off the floor. A loud snap in Woasim's wrist killed the wind magic, and he howled in pain.

"STOP!" Desert Rain lunged forth, and the tip of Silverheart stabbed an inch into a spot on the left side of Katawa's chest, near his arm pit. He looked down at the impalement but did not move, not even a twitch. Desert Rain's confidence vanished as she watched Katawa's bemused expression morph into demonic glee. *Wh…why isn't Silverheart hurting him? Do something!!*

Katawa held up a finger towards her, waiving it in an "uh uh" gesture. "I've endured more pain in my life than you can imagine. I could joke about barely feeling your little 'poke,' but that would be low brow," he said. He pinched the blade between two fingers and tugged it out of his bleeding flesh, which oozed with blackness. He then pressed the wound shut, as his flesh molded like clay into a thin scar. "Besides, what good is this little show? You know I'm heir to the Death Walker. I didn't die when your pathetic boyfriend tried to kill me. I didn't die when my insolent brother tried. And you...you could have struck me in a vital place just now. I don't even know what would happen if you were to, say, cut off my head. I'm almost curious enough for you to try it. But you don't have it in you to do it."

"Because Dez isn't a cold-blooded murderer!" Woasim retorted through his pain. "She has a good heart! She has a good soul!"

"Soul?" Katawa leaned close to him, smirking with sharp teeth. "She didn't tell you, did she? I own her soul! Besides, killing me won't undo what I've done. The Distortion survives without me. And she wants to see all your Hijn friends again. She actually cares about you lot, for some insipid reason. That's why she won't kill. But trust me, I can find the right motivation for her."

"You...you're the ghost that scared Dez," Woasim said, taking a swing at Katawa's side with his iron-bound hand, but he could not get enough force behind it to make any impact. "You're the one she said possessed my friend Merros! You've been wicked to the people I care about! Leave us alone!"

Katawa looked at Woasim as if he were a buzzing gnat. "Not much to you. Still, one more Hijn to add to my collection."

"NO! Not him!" She brought her sword around to

Katawa's exposed wrist, as if she would lop off the hand holding Woasim. She knew her voice was unsteady, desperate, but she locked eyes with Katawa and tightened her grip on her sword. "Not this one. I'll go with you, right now, I'll do whatever you want. Just don't distort him! Let him go!"

Katawa rolled his eyes, grimacing. "Back to this martyred pleading. Not that I mind the pleading, but I expected better from you. Very well, how can I say no to those beautiful eyes?" He dropped Woasim, who collapsed onto the floor, wincing from his broken wrist.

Desert Rain allowed Silverheart to drop to the floor beside her as she knelt beside Woasim, embracing him close. She carefully helped him onto his feet. "Sim, I'm sorry, I'm so sorry…"

Woasim looked into Desert Rain's eyes. He softened his voice. "Mum says…it's okay, Dez. It's going to be okay."

He gasped as one of Katawa's clawed finger-tendrils drove deep into his back, between his shoulder blades.

Desert Rain's heart seized as Woasim fell forwards, limp, into her arms. She saw the stain of crimson blossoming across the back of his vest. She pressed her hand hard against the wounds, trying to stop the bleeding, but it pooled between her fingers. She shut her eyes, hot tears seeping through her eyelids. "No, no!! Please, someone, anyone, please help him! Take my life, save him!"

She cradled him in her arms, feeling the strength leaving his body. He looked up at her with tired, lightless eyes, and yet, he still managed a weak smile. "Never stop being you, Desert Rain. Always be you…" His final exhale was quiet, like a prayer, as his eyes closed for the last time.

Desert Rain wanted to scream. She wanted to break the sky with her anguish. But her voice was little more than a soft, vile hiss at her enemy. "I *hate* you."

Katawa narrowed his eyes on her, his finger-tendril slithering back into his skin. "I already gave you one Hijn for free, did you expect me to just keep giving you what you want, without a price? Besides, you get all sentimental and weak when you feel the need to protect these insects. You're much more useful when they're no longer an issue. Now, if you're done crying over that corpse, we can be on our — "

Desert Rain roared — a brazen, unbridled, world-shaking roar — as her right eye radiated like a jade sun, filled with the burning of her hatred, her agony, her fury. Dropping Woasim, she flung both hands at Katawa and an explosion of glacial blue light filled the room. A deafening crackle filled her ears, and for a moment, she thought both of her arms had burst into fire and blood. But all of that was momentary, as the light and the roar and the burning suddenly ceased as if abruptly waking from a nightmare. Her eyes felt like lava had been poured over them. She was blinded for a few seconds, but as she blinked to summon cool tears, her vision slowly restored.

Frosted blue glass plastered everything before and around her. The floor, the walls, the furniture, the weaponry, were coated in a sea frozen in time. Katawa was enveloped in glass, his face and body in a posture of terrified surprise. His mouth agape, his eyes petrified wide open, he looked like someone staring into the maws of death. He had become no more than a glass sculpture, fitted in a shimmering, smooth coffin.

Was this real? Desert Rain could not believe it, but as she slowly lowered her arms, she realized what had happened. She had done it. She had finally killed him.

Her relief was short-lived, as she felt the presence of something else in the room. Turning her head, she saw Woasim was suspended above the floor, caught within a swirling ball of air that held him like a gentle hand. He was cradled by the wind like he was on a bed, his eyes were closed, and his arms crossed over his chest. He looked at peace.

"Sim?" Desert Rain held her breath, hoping this was a sign of life.

Slowly, his body lifted forwards, until he was fully facing her. His eyes shot open, two white-glowing orbs that held none of the warmth she knew of him. These were eyes of another world, another time...another being.

"**Be not afraid, chosen of Bellaluna**," a deep, female voice emitted from Woasim's mouth. "**The winds demand retribution!**"

Desert Rain's jaw dropped. "M....Mum?"

An unearthly moan poured from Woasim, as his mouth opened wide and a strange, pale steam escaped from it. The wind bubble around him expanded, rushing faster and stronger, forming into a cyclone that sent cracks through the surrounding glass. The pale steam began to take shape: a white, gossamer body like that of a swan crossed with a horse, but each foot had long, eagle talons on the ends. It bristled with soft feathers all over, four ivory wings extended from its back, and a tail like a bundle of ribbons whipped about behind it. It shrieked a hurricane wail, and then burst out through the back wall of the car, shattering the glass into millions of snowflake shards.

The winds howled in cacophonous chorus, and Desert Rain lost her footing as the force of it knocked her over. She spotted Silverheart, which had also evaded being concealed in glass, and it slid across the smooth floor towards the back of the car, the winds drawing it out. She dove for it, snatching the sword by the hilt before it fell off the train, and slid it quickly into its pouch. Woasim remained suspended in place until the entirety of the pale steam had left his mouth, and then his eyes shut and his limp body was caught in the current of the gale. Just as he was about to be flung from the train car, Desert Rain pushed herself up and caught him mid-air, wrapping her arms around him as the two of them were flown high, clear off the train, clear off the earth. She struggled to breathe against the crushing winds, but she hung on tightly to Woasim, squeezing her eyes shut.

No. I'm not letting go. If the winds must punish me too, so be it.

Open your eyes, chosen of Bellaluna. Be witness to my wrath.

Despite her instinct to keep her eyes closed, Desert Rain forced them open. She and Woasim were floating high above, and she saw beneath them was that strange white creature, wings enveloping them. Ahead of them was the gray storm-cloud wyrm, rolling in a spiral coil toward them, lightning like teeth in its maw. The wind creature propelled itself towards it with arrow swiftness, and the winds created a funnel that blasted into the storm cloud like a hammer from the heavens. The clouds were blown apart, the storm wyrm dissipated. Far below, the Distorted continued to tear into the train cars as infuriated Bloodburn tried to fight them off, wristbows firing and weapons flailing. Desert Rain hugged Woasim close as the wind dragoness's spirit plummeted down, a nose-dive towards the line of train cars, and proceeded to rip through each one with the ease of shredding paper.

Metal crunched as the caravans split open or fell onto their sides, wheels and treads rolling in the air. The Distorted howled and the Bloodburn screamed as the winds blew them away, dispersing them like drifting dandelion seeds. They seemed weightless against the power of the gale, two armies laid to instant waste and tossed into the sky, out of sight. The dragon spirit lifted itself as it approached the last stretch of cars, its talons ripping off the roofs. Desert Rain looked down to see those were prisoner cars, where all the remaining Yopeis-Gichen were being held, shivering in their cells. The poor creatures cowered amid the raging winds, but the winds' fury was not for them. Gentle zephyrs scooped each of them from their cells, lifting them from the train and setting them down on the soft grasses of the valley. The Yopeis watched on in wonder as the spirit swirled about them, being ridden by a strange golden-skinned woman who was holding their beloved Wind Hijn.

Desert Rain wept. For Woasim, for these Yopeis who lost their Hijn, for so much pain and suffering in the world. What could she tell them that would bring comfort? What could she do for a people whose lives had been upended?

Do not weep. We must finish this.

The dragon spirit veered around, its tail streaming behind as sunlight caught it and painted it as a rainbow, and took off back the way it came, heading towards the rumbling engine still on the move.

*   *   *

"Why did she do that?" Chiriku squawked, tugging off her veil.

Gabriel watched as the train cars receded, and Desert Rain shut the door behind her. How much he wished he could smack some sense into the woman. "She was keeping the Distorted from reaching us. We must go back. We need to turn this machine around!"

"Excuse me?" Mac said in high-pitched disbelief. "Not-ttk to argue, but-ttk does anyone here know how to drive this-ss contraption?"

"And there are a lot of mad Bloodburn that could break out of the boiler room any second!" Dun reminded them.

"Then stay here. Mac, Chi, come with me." Gripping tight to his battle mace, Gabriel led the two through the train cars, past the boiler room door, which was now severely dented and bulging outwards as loud clangs continued against it. They climbed a short ladder up and above the boiler room, into the control room. Before them was a large panel of levers, buttons, and switches, and a large window showing the stretch of land ahead.

"Mac, you've driven machine carts before," Chiriku said. "You're the only one who understands machines."

Mac's jaw hung open at the complicated panel. "Yeah, I drive a merchant-ttk cart-ttk. A tiny, two-lever cart-ttk. I ain't-ttk driven nothin' like-kk this!"

"Well, that's two levers more than any of us have experience with," Gabriel said. "Try to figure out how to maneuver this thing and turn it around. Chi and I'll handle the general."

The bird girl smiled. "Can I bash the middle head? I'll leave you Goldy Locks, if you want."

Mac slowly sat down in the control chair, his eyes darting all over the panel. "Ooookay, oooookay. If this is anythin' like-kk my cart-ttk, then...this should be the brake-kk." He reached down to a long lever on the right side, clamping on the handle and pulling back. The lever would not budge. He took both hands to it, wrapping his tail around the middle of the handle, and yanked with all his might. In response, the lever snapped clean off.

"If that-ttk was the brake-kk, then it-ttk ain't-ttk anymore," Mac sighed. He grabbed what he assumed to be the steering mechanism and carefully turned it towards the right. The wheels responded, as the train drifted gradually in a wide turn. Out the window, he could see dry-grass plains all around, which gave him ample space to maneuver, but he jumped with every loud pound that came from the boiler room below.

Gabriel left him to it, as he and Chiriku descended back down the ladder to the landing outside the boiler room. Dun and the other Yopeis stood in the fuel car, looking at the boiler room door, which became more dented outward with each blow.

"We'll barricade the door," Gabriel said as he approached them. "We'll grab the heaviest logs from–"

"We don't want to do that," Dun replied, giving Gabriel a hard look.

Gabriel paused, casting his gaze over the irate Yopeis, each gripping their acquired weapons. He had an inkling what they were thinking. "You're not serious–"

Dun held up his hatchet above his head. "It's like I said. We want our revolution! It's not enough to flee this train. It's not enough to keep hiding. We Yopeis-Gichen have been peaceful all our lives, but that didn't prevent war from coming upon us."

"But the Bloodburn are trained soldiers!"

"And we are more than they are. When they break down that door, we'll be ready. Will you fight with us, General?"

Gabriel tightened his lips, furrowing his brow. He had to give them credit, they were brave for being so small. He looked at Chiriku, who shouldered her warhammer. She grinned. "Hey, if they're game, I don't want to sit on the sidelines," she said.

The Yopeis hollered a unified war cry. Gabriel lifted his mace, testing its weight in his hand. "All right, then. Steel yourselves."

The drawbar across the door was almost broken out of its slots as another forceful pound slammed against the door. Gabriel calculated in his head the odds–if he and Chiriku could take Vidi and Veni, then maybe the Yopeis stood a chance against the six guards. The Yopeis were not trained, but they were quick and maybe could dodge the wristbow bolts. This was their decision to fight, and maybe there was no other way. If they all ran away now, General Vidi would just come back for them or continue to conquer more villages in the Noblelands. They had to try and stand up to him, right here, right now.

The pounding suddenly ceased. The boiler room became quiet.

Gabriel's muscles were wound tight, and the sudden lack of noise put him more on edge. Had the Bloodburn finally passed out from the smoke? Was this a trap? What could the Bloodburn possibly do if not break down the door?

The Yopeis looked at one another, their confidence waning. Chiriku narrowed her eyes on the door. "You think they gave up?" she whispered to Gabriel.

Gabriel shook his head. "They probably heard we're ready with an ambush for them. But it's not like they have anything in there to get the jump on us." He turned to Dun. "There isn't some secret hatch or another door out of the boiler room, is there?"

Dun scratched his head. "Not that I could see. And if there were, I don't think they would have kept trying to knock down the door. No, all that would be in there are the chains, the firewood, and a few piles of those crude stones."

Gabriel sucked in a quick breath as his realization clicked. "Everyone, clear the way!"

He barely had enough time to usher everyone back before the door blew open with a violent, inferno blast. Metal shards flew, pungent reddish smoke filled the air, and bits of burnt crude stone showered them like hundreds of falling stars. Gabriel cursed himself for not having thought of it sooner–the Bloodburn had been trapped in a room with a fire in the boiler, and enough crude stones to ignite as an explosive escape.

Through the smoke, the lumbering, loathsome shape of the three-headed Bloodburn leader loomed towards them. Veni coughed, looking worse for wear, while the bagged head shook soot and embers off his head. General Vidi, unfazed and undeterred, glowered at the group of rebels with pure, poisonous hate.

"I will rip the flesh off every last one of you!" he bellowed, raising his fists over his head and charging straight at Gabriel. Gabriel had enough space to dodge to the side, evading the general's powerful but slow pummel, and swung his mace up straight into Vidi's jaw. With a loud crack, Vidi's head snapped back, and he staggered a few feet before regaining his composure. "You...you did this!" he snarled, pointing a clawed finger at Gabriel.

Gabriel managed a quick look behind Vidi, to notice that none of the guards had come out of the boiler room. "Your men couldn't take the heat?" he taunted.

Veni laughed forcefully. "The blast from the crude stones was more volatile than we thought. No matter, we hardly need help to dispose of you and your fish fellows." He noticed Chiriku for the first time, and gave her a repulsed glare. "And what are you supposed to be, a giant chicken with a hammer?"

"I changed my mind," Chiriku said, readying her hammer. "This has your name on it, toad face."

The train car shook violently, and there was a soul-shivering howl from outside. General Vidi and Veni paused, sensing something was not right. Gabriel listened to the raging wind, bracing himself. Was it the storm, the one that had brought the Distorted? No, he sensed this was different. Even now, he could feel the chill of this wind, digging into his skin, and there was an overwhelming sensation of...sadness...

The back of the train car was blown wide open, as if two great hands had torn the back wall off and cast it away. Everyone froze as the hurricane winds thundered around them, and then something descended out of the cyclone and touched down on the floor of the car. Hair whipping around her face, Desert Rain stood there, holding a blood-soaked Woasim in her arms like a mother holding her child. Her eyes reflected mourning, heartbreak, but also resolve.

"General Vidi," she called over the roar of the winds. "Your army has been scattered. Your grand train is decimated, your plunder lost. The spirit of the wind dragoness has sought revenge for the death of her Hijn. I, my companions, and the Yopeis take leave of you, and should you attempt to halt our departure, the forces of nature will come down on your very heads."

Chiriku's eyes went wide as she looked at the motionless Woasim. "Death?"

Veni regarded Desert Rain, his frown tinged with apprehension. He leaned in as close to Vidi's ear as he could. "It would be prudent of us, given this Hijn's demonstration of her power, that we cut our losses and perhaps return to our realm to gather reinforces–"

General Vidi punched Veni straight in the mouth, to which the Strategist gasped as one of his perfect teeth was knocked loose. Vidi released a deep, low rumble, the declaration of a predator ready to kill. "I will not be dictated to by some wench! I don't care how powerful you think you are. If I cannot control you, then you must die!"

He charged forward, shoving Gabriel aside and slamming Chiriku into the wall. The Yopeis tried to stand their ground, but Vidi plowed through them, forcing them to scramble away from his crushing steps. Desert Rain did not move an inch as he advanced on her, raising his large, red fist high over his head, preparing to bring it down on her skull.

The fist froze in place. Vidi's head jerked, as he realized he could not move it. He strained, tensing every muscle in his arm, but the fist remained in the air. Veni blanched, his golden hand still held to his bleeding mouth, and he let out a small groan of realization. Vidi turned his gaze towards the other head, the one hooded in the sack, except for that one, milky eye that was locked on Vidi with raw, ferocious malice.

"What...are you...doing?" Vidi grunted, continuing to regain control of his arm. Slowly, like moss growing over a tree trunk, the burgundy skin on his arm shifted in hue, becoming a dark stone-gray, like an ember cooling. Vidi's jaw dropped, his eyes screaming panic. "NO, YOU GAVE ME CONTROL! YOU CAN'T TAKE IT BACK!"

A guttural, soft voice came from beneath the sack. "How dare you raise your fist to the Moon." The gray skin spread across the body, crossing over Vidi's chest and left leg, while the general bellowed curses to no avail. The gray hand reached down towards the floor, where a few hot cinders of crude stone lay at his feet. He curled his fingers around the cinders, and flames ignited around his fist, yet it did not seem to sear him. Standing up straight, he grasped Vidi's throat with his burning hand, squeezing tight as the fire burst with several pops and set Vidi's head aflame.

Vidi screeched a high, ringing squeal as the fire consumed his head. His wails dwindled into a viscous gurgle as the hand crushed his windpipe and charred his flesh while the fire flashed pure white. Vidi's face burned crisp into withered, fried skin, his eyes bulging in horror until they melted back into his skull, and a few seconds later, his head tumbled off and hit the floor with a spray of ash. The heat cauterized the stump of his neck, and not a drop of blood was spilled.

Veni stared, unbreathing and unblinking, at the smoking neck stump, and then turned his gaze to the sacked head. He gulped. "S....sire," he rasped.

The third head breathed deeply, and the gray hand removed the sack-mask. The face underneath was sharp-edged and solid as rock, the face of a hardened man. Cropped white locks framed his head, and a scraggly white beard matched it. His one cataract eye paired with a clear, emerald-green one, as dark as the Eternal Deep. The lines of his face told stories, songs of suffering and ballads of heavy bearing, and yet, there was patience in those weary eyes.

He and Veni looked down at Desert Rain, who stood petrified at the display of brutality she had just witnessed. Only now, that the horrible moment had passed, did she realize the wind had died down behind her, its fierce howling ceased. Perhaps the winds had finally been satisfied, finally felt justice was done. The gray head's voice was rough from years of silence, but it was still gentle. "I sympathize for your loss," he said.

Desert Rain could only nod.

"Since I first saw you, I knew who you were. You bear the mark of the moon," he continued. "Something my counterparts would not have recognized, or understood the weight it carries."

Desert Rain knit her eyebrows. "You are quite different from your 'counterparts.' A shame they wouldn't listen to reason."

"Reason seems to have left this land long ago," the gray face sighed, its lines deep with sorrow. "Does it stand to reason that a king would relinquish his power to those he believed would uphold our clan's survival, even if those he was giving his power to acted and *spoke* foolishly?" He snapped a sharp glance at Veni with his last two words.

The golden head held his tongue.

"A king, sir?" Desert Rain remembered Veni saying they had royal blood in their veins. She had not expected it to be quite so literal.

"Yes. Once I was a king. But my clan felt my leadership wasn't strong enough to help us rise above the Nobles or the other Courts of the Wretched. So, I silenced myself and left the leading to what I believed were my more 'persuasive' mouth pieces. But I could not stand by if my baser selves were going to do you harm."

Desert Rain bowed her head. "That's very kind of you, King V–"

"Ragnor."

Desert Rain twisted the corner of her mouth. "I kind of thought your name would be…something else. But why do you care who I am?"

King Ragnor gave her a sad smile. He turned, walking over to a stacked pile of logs and sat down. Everyone else in the room stood, unsure of this Bloodburn king, but they allowed themselves to be at ease. From the boiler room, several of the Bloodburn guards stumbled out, covered in soot and limping, having recovered from the earlier blast. They halted when they saw King Ragnor and Veni, with a scorched neck stump between them.

The king glared at them sternly. "Your general has been dismissed. Your strategist is being retitled to royal advisor, but only when I ask him for advice."

Veni emphatically nodded. "Yes, sire. Thank you, most gracious sire."

The guards glanced at one another, and back to their king. They immediately knelt, and then, whether it was through their own will or some involuntary reaction, their skins all shifted from burgundy to stone gray, their orange eyes altering to emerald green, a physical display of allegiance to their returned king.

"Now, where was I? Oh, yes, the Moon Dragoness. Please, come here." King Ragnor beckoned Desert Rain over. Still holding Woasim close, she walked over to him. The king could see the grief on her face, the weariness of her body. "I know you have been through much. I cannot alleviate your pain. But I remember a time, so long ago, before I grew these other heads. I knew Bellaluna. She and I spoke of many things. She nurtured my own wisdom, although I was too weak to live by it at the time."

Desert Rain was floored, struck speechless for a second. "You knew Bellaluna?"

"I was much younger then, of course," the king smiled wistfully. "It was during a time of great turmoil. We were all…changing. She was trying to help us. I think she planted a seed of light in my heart, to always guide me back from the darkness. Your coming here re-lit that seed. And if you are as she was, you can bring us all from the dark–"

As he spoke, the train came to a gradual, shaky halt. A few moments later, Mac came running into the car.

"Hey, I finally figured out-ttk which one was the brake-kk…" He paused when he looked around, seeing his companions, the Yopeis, the grayed Bloodburn guards, and a very large Bloodburn with two heads and a seared neck between them. He blinked, cocking an eyebrow. "You all, I can't-ttk walk-kk away for two minutes without-ttk somethin' happenin' that I clearly shouldn't-ttk have missed…"

Something landed heavily on the open end of the train car, having fallen from above. Desert Rain's heart leapt into her throat as she saw the figure, coated in shards of blue glass, his skin glittering with frozen specks, his breath clouding before his face as if he were standing in the midst of winter. His yellow eyes were dilated, and his lips curled into a wolf sneer.

"DESERT RAIN!" Katawa shivered in rage. "How DARE you use your powers on ME."

Desert Rain could not believe it, simply could not. How could he have survived the Blueshine? Could being the heir of the Death Walker truly keep him from ever being killed, by *anything*? Even if he had not been instantly killed, trying to break free of the glass should have shattered him into dust. Yet, even in her disbelief, she found her voice. "I'll use them again, and again, and again, until it ends you, Katawa."

King Ragnor stood up tall. "Distortionist, we told you to be gone, along with your creatures. If you won't listen to a general, you will listen to a king."

"Stay out of this, you decrepit fool," Katawa hissed. He tried to walk, but his legs were stiff and each step looked painful. His whole body was rigid, and Desert Rain realized that the Blueshine had, at least, infected his muscles enough that he could not shapeshift or grow his physical extensions. This, most likely, was what was enraging him more than anything, that this was one magic attack he was unable to immediately bounce back from.

Ragnor reached for the mace Gabriel was holding, and Gabriel handed it to him. The Bloodburn king came over to stand in front of Desert Rain, guarding her. "Guards, stand with your king. Do not let him pass." He looked over his shoulder. "Desert Rain, we will hold him off while you and the others leave. Head towards the northern mountains, you will find protection there."

Desert Rain could not believe she and her friends were being defended by Bloodburn, of all people. "I can't let you face him–"

"This is what we do. Fighting the Darkscale is not new to us, even if this one is formidable. Now go. We will buy you time."

Gabriel placed his hand on Desert Rain's shoulder. "Come on, while Katawa's weak. They may stand a chance."

"I AM NOT WEAK!" Katawa thundered, as his face began to morph, white tusks growing from his lips and black horns stabbing outwards from the sides of his head. "And I am done being polite. I am the Death Walker, and I am coming for you all."

Desert Rain was torn, but if her Blueshine could not kill him or even stop him, what else could she do? She could get everyone else to safety, that was what. She turned, still cradling Woasim as she ran, and Gabriel, Chiriku, Mac, and the Yopeis all dashed out the other door of the car. She watched to make sure all the Yopeis got off the train, hopping down from the connection onto the grass and sprinting as fast as they could across the valley.

Gabriel, Chiriku, and Mac stood below her, waiting "Dez, come on! Now!" Gabriel shouted.

Desert Rain gently passed the body of Woasim down to Chiriku, who took him in her arms. Just as she was about to jump from the train, she heard King Ragnor's voice boom, loud and illustrious: "Dragons speed, heir of Bellaluna, Mother of the Wretched!"

Desert Rain snapped her head back at those words. She did not get a chance to ask what in the name of Luuva he meant, when Gabriel reached up, grabbed her trouser leg, and pulled her down. Desert Rain tumbled down into his arms, her confusion forgotten. The four of them took off running, leaving her mystified about King Ragnor's final words.

CHAPTER TEN
Mourning a Fallen Friend; The Secret of Haven's End

The grave was not grand, or befitting of a Hijn, but it was dug with reverence and surrounded by those who loved the one entombed within. Despite the hard, frosted ground and lack of vegetation, the grave was decorated with what wildflowers the group could find, and circled with polished stones. There was little to mark the grave, but one of Woasim's red ribbons from his vest was tied to a sturdy stick and planted in the soil at the head of the burial mound. Beside that stick, several other sticks were planted, one for each Yopeis that had died on the train. Desert Rain hoped that Woasim would like this, without any pomp and circumstance, just those that loved him to bid him goodbye.

The seven Yopeis wept and lamented for their Hijn, even though the trek to distance themselves from what was left of the Imperial Train had left them exhausted. Gabriel had led everyone out of the valley and into a stretch of land dusted in hoarfrost, the borderland that led into the Taigalands beyond. It was a desolate and cold place, but not without resources. There was dry enough wood to burn for fire, sparse root vegetation if one knew how to spot it, and winter birds and rodents to trap for meat. He had pushed the group for hours, and only when they came upon a copse of crystal-tinged pine trees where there was plenty of cover, did he decide they could stop and rest for the night.

It was here that Desert Rain had chosen Woasim's

grave, a safe place where the ice crystals on the pine trees sparkled like a sky full of stars. She knew the Yopeis would deeply mourn him, but the one person she had not predicted would take it so hard was Chiriku. The teenager had carried his body the whole way, even when Desert Rain offered to carry him for a while. She had helped to dig the grave by hand, alongside the Yopeis. When Woasim was placed in the ground, she had plucked one of her cleanest feathers and set it between his fingers, laying his hand over his heart. It was a traditional Quetzalin and Falcolin farewell gesture, one usually reserved for family and close friends. Now she sat beside the grave in quiet contemplation, her feathers a dirt- and blood-crusted mess. Mac could not think of anything lighthearted to say to ease her sorrow, so he simply sat beside her as the chill in the air triggered his body for warm-bloodedness, and slowly he returned to his human appearance.

Gabriel went about building a firepit with stones and kindling from fallen branches, knowing this might be the only means they would have to survive the night. He wore the Bloodburn coat that Mac had used for disguise–thankfully it fit him well enough–but no one was properly attired for the cold. They had no real shelter to speak of, save the thick evergreen limbs above them that buffered them from the wind, although there was little wind blowing if at all. It was like the woods were frozen in time, nothing ruffling the trees or whispering in the night air. He hoped that whatever "protection" King Ragnor spoke of before they left would be in the direction they were headed. Hopefully, there would be a village or populated oasis nearby that would take in these Yopeis as refugees until they could get the means to return home.

"Do you need help?" he heard Desert Rain ask as she approached him. She looked like she was about to collapse, her hair in disarray and her clothing disheveled. She shivered, for they had lost all their snow gear back in the sky boat. Her boots were all she had, and at least those would stave off frostbite to her toes. Before he could even reply, she started gathering up firewood anyway, wherever she spotted fallen branches and twigs. He figured she wanted to keep busy, otherwise she would wallow in her sadness for Woasim.

"We're lucky we came upon this grove," he said. "We can gather pine nuts and maybe drain some sap from these trees. Not exactly tavern fare, but it'll feed everyone. There's probably places to find berries, maybe a stream to fish. I'll search for any sign of a nearby town once I've had a few hours' sleep."

Desert Rain tossed her armful of wood into the fire pit. "You shouldn't go by yourself. Chiriku can go with you. She seems to like her duty as scout."

"You should get some sleep."

"I will, once camp is set."

Gabriel could hear a steel resolve in her tone, something that had been developing since they landed in Wayfarer's Thumb. Or, perhaps more likely, since she started "dreaming" about her new friend. He remembered when he had started speaking differently too, all those years ago, after he met Veritas Lucen.

"I guess sleep wouldn't make you feel much rested. Not with your new mentor," he muttered.

Desert Rain gave him an even, steady gaze. "When will you tell me how you know Sir Luce? And Skyhan? If you want me to know, do it before Katawa kills me."

Gabriel sighed. Funny, she referred to Sir Luce by the same name he always had, where Skyhan had always used the more formal version. Rather than answer, he fished around in his coat pockets. He hoped he might find something useful in them, maybe something with which to help start a fire. He found a few things of interest, including some wristbow bolts, a whittling knife, a few coins that looked nothing like any currency he knew, and a small, wrapped package of something sticky, maybe tree resin. Mac whistled to him.

"Gabe, you need some flint?" He reached into one of his many pockets, extracting two small gray stones and tossing them to Gabriel. "Whenever you need something, check with the merchant. If you don't need that gum, I'll take it."

Gabriel tossed him the resin, which the lizard man broke off a piece to chew on, and gave pieces to a few Yopeis who asked for some. Gabriel knelt, tearing up a few patches of dry grass from the ground and placing them on top of the fire pit. He struck the flintstones against each other, encouraging small sparks.

"You used to train with Skyhan," Desert Rain said after he would not answer. "That's the only explanation how you knew them both. You were a Knight. Or maybe Skyhan's squire."

Gabriel paused, a curl in his lip. "The agreement was you wouldn't ask me about that."

"The agreement was I wouldn't ask you about that as long as you trained us in combat. Now, I realize we haven't exactly had that opportunity, but until you do, I feel like this agreement hasn't taken root."

"Fine, I'll start training tomorrow."

"Fine, then answer my question now. I'll stop asking once you start training."

The grass finally caught a small flame, and Gabriel gently blew on it to nurture its growth. "Why do you care? Skyhan's dead. And if your dream knight won't tell you, then you don't have to know. Focus on surviving rather than on me. Have a shred of sense in your head for once."

Desert Rain sat down beside him as the fire blossomed. "How's your skin?"

Gabriel paused, watching the flames dance. "The cold helps. It'll be fine in a few days. You're funny sometimes."

"How so?"

"You get all worried about my injuries, yet I don't recall you being so sympathetic when you saw my scars the first time. No 'oh dear, let's find you some salve' or nothing. But I get a little heat stroke, and you're all concerned."

Desert Rain wrapped her arms around her knees. "Well, I guess I never said anything about your scars because…they didn't seem like something that needed to be fixed."

The Yopeis wandered over to the fire, huddling around it for its much-needed warmth. Mac and Gabriel, being the tallest, climbed up the trees to shake down the pinecones, plenty to give everyone a decent ration of nuts. Gabriel was also able to use the knife in his coat to hack off the thick dark bark to reach the edible strips of pale inner bark, and while it was not delicious, it was quick and easy food. After the sufficient meal, and with the fire melting away some of the frost off the ground, the Yopeis huddled together and nodded off, unable to keep their eyes open any longer. Chiriku curled up under her Bloodburn coat to sleep, while Mac leaned back against a tree, curling his tail around his legs for warmth.

"I'll take first watch," Desert Rain said, feeding more sticks to the fire. "You get some sleep, and then you and Chi can scout in the morning."

Gabriel nodded, although from the way her head was swaying, he sensed Desert Rain might fall asleep any second. Daylight would come soon; if she did pass out, he was a light sleeper. After all, most of his nights for his whole life, he had to sleep with one eye open. He lied down, rolling over away from the campfire. Desert Rain tried to keep herself busy, braiding her long hair to keep it out of her face, tending the fire, listening for any strange noises. Every shadow cast by the firelight put her on edge. She imagined Katawa jumping out from behind any tree at any moment — she hoped King Ragnor and his guards might have been able to drive him off, but she feared the worst for them.

Somehow, even though these fears plagued her heart, her eyelids drooped and her breathing slowed, and for a single second, her eyes closed shut.

*   *   *

"Sometimes, survival is more important than a glorious victory," she heard a voice say. "Now, shall we continue our lessons?"

Desert Rain's eyes shot open. She was in the arena, with Sir Luce standing before her. Part of her knew she had to wake up, explain to her mentor that she was on watch, but the other part of her won out. That part coerced her to pick up a nearby stone and throw it hard at Sir Luce, and it bounced off his breastplate.

"You could have done something!" she screamed, tears forming in her eyes again. "You could have helped me! You should have taken control, have me overpower Katawa! You could have helped me save Woasim! Now he's dead!"

Sir Luce stared at her from the holes of his mask. "I warned you, I would not always be there to fight your battles."

"But you *are* here! Why did you do nothing? How *could* you do nothing? I wasn't ready, you know that!" She wheezed, trying to regain her breath, but heavy sobs racked her body.

The Knight was silent, but then he stepped towards her. "There was no possible way for you to win that fight. It was an unfortunate circumstance. I am sorry. But that is reality. Loss is as much a part of life as victory, perhaps even more so."

"But it's not fair. Woasim didn't deserve that."

"No, he did not. So, do not let his death be in vain."

Desert Rain wiped her eyes and stood up straight. "Then what am I to do? If Katawa has the powers of the Death Walker, then he can't be stopped! Even the Blueshine didn't break him. What hope is there?"

Sir Luce turned and walked over to a low, flat stone that materialized at the edge of the arena. It was six feet across, wide enough for two to sit upon, and when he approached the stone, his armor dissipated, except for his mask, leaving him in a dark-blue tunic and white breeches. He sat cross-legged upon the stone, resting his hands on his knees. "Sit with me."

Desert Rain released a long exhale. She dragged

herself over to the stone, sitting down beside him. She felt something cool around her ankles, and when she looked down, she saw her feet were bare, and the whole arena, the sand, the cherry orchard, the statues, had been replaced by pure blue ocean stretching to the horizon. It was like the stone that they sat on was floating above the water, a tiny island in the middle of azure endlessness.

"We Knights tend to focus greatly on the code that emphasizes the external. Defend those who cannot defend themselves. Always face the enemy. Be a champion of right against wrongdoing," Sir Luce said, closing his eyes. "Often, we forget we must focus inward as well. A tower cannot stand if built on weak foundations. Our foundation is our spirit. We cannot uphold peace if we cannot find it within."

"How exactly am I supposed to be at peace with–"

"You cannot face your enemy, or what you fear, if you do not know yourself. Peace will come when you accept all your failings, all your flaws, and know you can still stand strong. We are all born broken, Desert Rain, but when a bone is broken, the fracturing point can reheal stronger than before." Sir Luce's shoulders lowered, and he rested his hands in his lap. "I wish this was something your drifting companion understood better. I fear he never quite took to the lesson."

Desert Rain looked at him, furrowing her brow. "My drifting…oh, Gabriel. Now that you mention him, how is it you know each other? He won't tell me, but he clearly knew Skyhan, when he was alive. Or are you going to be all cryptic about it, too?"

Sir Luce stared out over the ocean, listening to the waves lapping. "It has been many years since Skyhan sent him off into the world, with the mission to do good deeds to erase the wickedness from his soul. A wickedness that he believed was manifested on his face. But scars do not stem from being evil. Often, they form from evil being done to us. This was long after Skyhan and I had already become bonded. I wish I could have explained, if there had been some way to make him listen..." He sighed, turning his gaze up to the fabricated sky. "That was Skyhan's one failing. Sometimes, the desire to be good, and see that goodness take root in others, overpowers our ability to accept we are not perfect."

Desert Rain thought on this. "Are you telling me, Skyhan told Gabriel he was evil? And that he had to rectify that? But...Gabriel isn't evil at all. A little aloof, perhaps, but I fail to believe that he could ever have been as bad as all that. And Skyhan is more perceptive than that, to simply dismiss someone as evil, especially someone he must have known well. Right?"

"How well he knew him...that is the root of the problem." Sir Luce turned his eyes to her. "I know you hurt. I know you feel broken. And that is why you will endure. Even though the enemy has stolen from you so much of your love, your heart, your soul, you are still here. And you are here as a testament of will. You are the part of those who have been lost that lingers on. You stand here for them. You stand here for you. Your enemy may seem invincible, but he stands for nothing. And those who stand for nothing will fall."

Desert Rain stared back into his eyes, feeling the power of his words fill her to the brim with boldness and even peace. Yet, the worm of doubt still wiggled in her mind. "But what if I can't do this? What if I can't find the Lightscale? How do I even know if the Lightscale, if it exists, will fix everything?"

"The Lightscale can't fix everything. It's *you* that will do that."

Desert Rain turned her gaze away. "I'm sorry. You just...remind me so much of him. How he saw something in me I didn't believe in. I miss him."

Sir Luce looked out to the ocean again. "He lives on because of you. As a Knight, you carry the code and virtues he did. And maybe, you can finish what he started."

"You mean, defeat Katawa?"

"I mean, you can help what is broken become whole again."

Desert Rain opened her eyes as a chill ran through her. She was back in the camp. The bonfire was waning, although there was still a soft orange glow beneath the remaining kindling. She looked around, and all appeared well–everyone was still asleep, safe and sound. She glanced at the slumbering Gabriel, whose back was still turned to her. A pang of sympathy stabbed her heart. How could Skyhan treat him that way, sending him off into the wilderness all alone, instead of guiding him in the ways of virtue? Why did he force Gabriel to figure it out by himself? What else didn't she know?

*   *   *

Chiriku jogged between the trees, out of breath as she approached the camp. "There's a trading post! Right over that way!"

The Yopeis and Mac turned their heads in her direction, their lips stained from the amber cloudberries they had found in the early morning while searching the nearby fields. The day was a little warmer, and the sunlight streaming through the evergreen branches was welcomed. Desert Rain had barely slept after her talk with Sir Luce, even after Gabriel had woken up and told her she could sleep. The drifter came wandering in behind Chiriku, less enthusiastically than the Quetzalin.

"A trading post? All the way out here?" Desert Rain rose from her seated position, and she groaned as every muscle ached.

"We must not be too far from Haven's End," Gabriel replied. "There's a river that runs nearby the trading post. It might be a passage that would take us to town."

"Have you ever been to Haven's End? How do you know of it?"

Gabriel gave her a tired grin. "You have no idea about all the places I've been. But no, never got quite as far north as Haven's End. I hear it's the only town of decent size in the Taigalands. And it's the last stop before you head into snow elf territory. Hopefully we can restock in town, and maybe someone can tell us the best direction to go. You know as well as I do, the Elfë Tiagas aren't exactly 'come on in, we baked you a cake' kind of people."

"I can't believe we're that close already. Guess the Imperial Train brought us a lot farther than I realized." Desert Rain's ears drooped, as she thought of all she had lost on that train, but she had to remain strong. The sooner they found the snow elves, and the Lightscale, the better. Her mind ruminated on the plan - resupply in Haven's End, head towards the mountains, use the compass in hopes it would detect Kidran's frost magic–

The compass! Desert Rain checked her pockets

frantically, but it already dawned on her. The Darkscale compass that she had taken from the Zi'Gax, the one that picked up on Hijn magic–she had not seen it since they had been on the Vermin Brothers' boat. It had not been among the things Woasim had salvaged from the wreck. How could she have forgotten such a crucial tool? Her heart sank, like an anchor dropping from her chest into her toes. "Gabriel...the Darkscale compass...I lost it."

Gabriel gave her an incredulous look and wiped his hand over his face. "You mean the thing we were relying on to help us locate the snow elves in this whole, wide, ludicrously massive Taigalands? That thing that narrowed our odds, however small, but now we literally have no odds of finding them? That compass?"

"It must've fallen out of my pocket when we fell into the ocean. I...I'm sorry."

"You have a magic bag that literally holds a whole sword, and you couldn't think to pop the compass in there?"

Desert Rain's mind raced for a solution. "Maybe... maybe someone in Haven's End will know where–"

"Even if someone in Haven's End has any inkling where the elves live, no one is stupid enough to guide us there. The snow elves make themselves difficult to find for a reason, and if we don't have anything that'll lock onto them–"

"Hey, hey, now," Mac said, abandoning what was left of his breakfast and coming over to them. "What's all this arguin' about-ttk?"

Desert Rain looked at Mac helplessly, throwing up her hands. "I lost the Darkscale compass. We have nothing to find the elves or Kidran with. I can't believe I came this far without realizing it. I'm such an idiot!" She tugged down hard on her ears, so angry at herself that she wanted to rip them off her head.

Mac gently put his hands on hers, coaxing her to release her ears. "Relax, Gila. This ain't-ttk no problem. We'll...uh...I..." He paused, a troubled arc in his eyebrows, but then he felt one of his pockets. He unsnapped a button on a back pocket, and drew out something round and familiar. "You see, I found it-ttk! I was hangin' onto it-ttk for you."

Desert Rain's heart leapt as she saw the compass in Mac's hand. The silver ball that acted as the orienting arrow hovered in the middle, showing that the compass still worked. "Guerda-Shalyr! Thank you, Mac! You're a lifesaver!"

"Why didn't you tell us you had it?" Gabriel asked, his tone sharp.

Mac scratched the nape of his neck. "Well, with all the goings on, and everyone needin' to, you know, think-kk about so much, I figured I'd bring it-ttk out-ttk when it-ttk was needed. Keep it-ttk safe in the meantime. Don't-ttk be sore with me, now."

"Oh, not at all!" Desert Rain hugged Mac. "You're wonderful!"

Mac grinned. "I know. So, no more of this-ss beatin' up on yourself."

Chiriku came over and gave Mac a light punch in the shoulder. "Way to give Dez a heart attack, Mac. Bet you were hoping to sell that thing when you had the chance."

"Hey! Give a lizard credit-ttk," he retorted. "We may be cold-blooded, but not cold-hearted."

"Um, Miss Dez?" Dun piped up, as all the Yopeis stood up. "If you have what you need, may we go now?

We're hoping someone in this town you're talking about can get us transport home. We'd really like to go home."

Desert Rain popped the compass into her pouch, tying the drawstring tight. "Of course. We should get moving. Chi, Gabe, lead the way."

*   *   *

The trading post was rustic and simple, somewhere between a shack and a barn, situated alongside a rushing but not deep river. The purveyor was a hearty-looking man, dressed in a sheepskin coat and hat, and appeared to have been weathered by many a winter. He bred a herd of Crescent Horn sheep, so his wares included anything and everything he could spin from their cream-colored wool. All of it looked so warm and comfortable–coats, hats, mittens, boots, and scarves– but the group had no money and little to trade. The purveyor was not a flint-hearted man; after hearing their tale of tribulation, he gifted some of his wares (even though his children-sized coats and hats still swallowed the Yopeis so they looked like unsheared sheep). He was also a ferryman in possession of a small fleet of riverboats, including one large enough to carry a dozen people. Since he had to make a delivery upriver to Haven's End anyway, he agreed to transport them all for the price of their company and assistance with the oars, two things he normally received little of.

As the boat floated lazily along the river, Chiriku snuggled into her coat and mittens, the first luxuries she had received since leaving Syphurius in what felt like ages ago. "This is soooooo nice," she cooed, but added with a sniff, "despite the smell."

"Chi, be polite," Desert Rain said, lowering her voice. "This kind man isn't asking anything from us for all this."

"What? I said it was nice," the Quetzalin replied with a shrug. "And it smells better than those sweaty Bloodburn."

Gabriel and Mac handled two of the rowing oars closer to the bow, while the sheepskin purveyor rowed from the stern. The Yopeis settled comfortably among the piles of wool, their faces rosier than they had been the last few days. About an hour later, the first signs of town life began to show up along the riverbanks: men in fishing boats catching salmon in nets, women driving sleighs pulled by caribou, and a wooden mill with a water wheel turning with the river's current. Soon, the first dwellings appeared along the river, modest turf huts made of stone with wooden roofs covered in moss. The farther they floated along, the more such huts showed up, crowding closer together, and more elaborate abodes with steeples painted in bright blues, reds, and greens rose up around them. Amidst the tall spruces and pines, Haven's End looked like a sprawling castle of so many spiraled towers, and with the snow-topped mountains behind them, it had all the whimsy of a fairytale dream.

Haven's End was populated with humans, and their clothing of choice was, quite unanimously, gray-spotted fur coats and light-blue woolen caps with white feathers. It struck Desert Rain as a peculiar fashion choice, and that everyone in town subscribed to it, but they seemed happy to see the sheepskin purveyor's boat slide up to the local dock. The strange visitors he had brought, however, were perplexing to them, and they stared at the flock of Yopeis that waddled off the boat.

Even Gabriel and Mac, who looked similar to the
Haven's End residents except for being dirty and
unkempt, received cautious looks. It was needless to say
they observed Desert Rain with gawks of confusion and
wariness.

"What, no one's seen a Quetzalin before?" Chiriku
muttered as she noticed the awkward stares. "I know
you people are remote, but give me a break."

One of the dockmen walked over to the purveyor,
whispering in his ear. Desert Rain's sensitive hearing
picked up the words, "Why did you bring these strangers
here?"

The purveyor smiled, patting the man on the
shoulder. "It's all right. The little ones need transport
home. I figured you could loan them some sleighs to
send them south to the next village. And the woman with
the moonstones needs your help."

Desert Rain's ears perked forwards at this. Why
was he pointing her out specifically? They all needed
help. Unless he meant...but how could he know?

The dockman glanced at Desert Rain, and his eyes
went wide. He ran off, while the other people near the
dock began to mumble among themselves. Desert Rain
sighed; wonderful, she had barely been here thirty
seconds, and everyone was treating her like she was a
freak already.

"Don't mind them," the purveyor said. "Would
you all mind helping me unload my bundles here? Wool
can be surprisingly heavy."

*   *   *

The local inn, the Twin Spindles, was a stone

longhouse with two cerulean steeples on top, where
Desert Rain and her group were directed to for lodging.
It was a simple but well-kept inn, and the moment they
were all through the front door, the scents of cooking
meat wafted to their noses. The innkeeper, a portly
elderly woman akin in shape to a teapot, served them a
lovely spread of salmon, trout, goose, various types of
berries and nuts, and teas made from orchid and
twinflower petals. Desert Rain hesitated at the
welcoming array, trying to think of how they would pay
for it all, but the innkeeper insisted that it was
complimentary to first-time guests.

That seems a little too good to be true, she thought,
*but the Yopeis and the others are so hungry. Surely, I can think
of something to repay for all this kindness.*

The innkeeper then guided them to rooms where
they could wash up with basins provided with goat-milk
soaps and heated water from the inn's kitchen hearth,
and rest on the softest, goose-down feather beds. Desert
Rain and Chiriku shared a room, while Mac and Gabriel
were guided to their own and the Yopeis to others. While
it was refreshing to wash off the dirt and grime, and
finally lay in a real bed again, Desert Rain could tell all of
this was not sitting well with Chiriku either.

"What kind of place gives away all this stuff for
free?" the Quetzalin said, rinsing off the lingering stains
from her feathers, returning to her clean russet brown
hue. "And is it weird we're the only guests in this inn?
Or this town? I seriously haven't seen anyone who looks
like they're not from around here."

Desert Rain laid back on her bed. "It does all feel a
bit strange. But we're not familiar with how things work
in the north. Maybe this is just how they treat visitors.

Besides, we won't stay long. If we don't abuse their hospitality, perhaps this is perfectly normal."

"Yeah, right." Chiriku dried off her head feathers with a woolen towel. She frowned as she looked at her arm feathers. "What are the odds this town has a proper dye salon?"

Desert Rain grinned. "You know, Chi, I think you look fine with your natural feather color. It's pretty."

"It's blah. Do you ever see brown Quetzalin in Syphurius? Falcolin, yeah, but they're gross." She walked over and sat down on her bed. "Blue is the hue for the real you. At least that's what the dye salespeople say."

Desert Rain fished the Darkscale compass from her pocket, looking it over. "I hope this will help us. If Kidran uses any magic, this should…" She paused, her brow furrowing. "That's odd."

Chiriku looked over. "What is?"

"The ball. It's…going all over the place."

The orienting ball inside the compass spun around the edges of the baseplate, going round and round as if it were chasing its own tail. No matter which way Desert Rain held it out, it continued to go in circles at a steady, constant pace.

"Is it broken?" Chiriku asked.

Desert Rain tapped at the compass glass. "I don't know. Seems like it wouldn't do anything if it were broken. As a matter of fact…it looks *too* flawless."

"Huh?"

"Well, Anthron repaired it, but it was still a bit dented and scratched. I remember this glass having a hairline crack. But this looks pristine. Brand new."

Chiriku scratched her head. "I don't know about that. I mean, that's the one we've had the whole time.

Maybe Anthron fixed it better than you remember."

Desert Rain frowned. "Either way, it's picking up on something. And whatever it is, the compass thinks it's everywhere."

"Sounds like a good reason to do some scouting," Chiriku said with a grin. "Find out what's going on in this town."

"If by 'scouting,' you mean 'spying,' I wouldn't," Desert Rain warned. "We don't want to do anything to offend anyone. And we want to keep as low a profile as possible. We shouldn't attract attention–any more attention, I mean."

"Hey, my profile's low. I'm practically invisible, when I want to be," the Quetzalin responded, flipping some of her head feathers with her hand. "But I'd like to know why everyone's got a dress code here, and not even a fashionable one. What if these Haven End's people are all cultists? All hail the Spotted Whats-its, or whatever?"

"That's an impressive leap you made, but I agree, something is unusual."

"Then let's do some scouting tonight," Chiriku whispered conspiratorially. "After the innkeeper and everyone's gone to bed."

"But what, exactly, are we looking for?"

"Dunno. Weird stuff. Magical stuff. I used to hear all the time about spellcasting students in Syphurius, they'd sneak out at night to do spells not sanctioned by the academy. Something about the witching hour, or midnight, being the best times for special secret spells. Those spellcasters were a bunch of creeps, sometimes."

Desert Rain sighed. "Okay, tonight we'll look around. But no invading anyone's privacy, understood?"

Chiriku groused. "Aww, then what's the point?"

*   *   *

Wake up! You're being entranced! Wake up, Desiree!
Desert Rain awoke with a start, as she felt an intense heat on her forehead. She sat up in bed, lightly touching her moonstone markings and found her whole head ached. What was that voice she heard? A dream? Yet the voice sounded so…the last time she had been called Desiree like that, her true name, was by…

"Grandma Luna?" Desert Rain looked around the dark room, but the only person there was Chiriku, sleeping soundly. She sighed; no, it must have been a dream. But why was it so urgent? She was about to lie down again when a sudden surge of panic ripped through her body. Something was wrong. Her moonstones flared again; they were telling her something, The Blueshine was telling her something.

"Chi? You awake?" Desert Rain got out of bed and went to her, shaking her gently. Chiriku was out completely, her breathing deep and slow. Desert Rain shook her harder, but the Quetzalin still did not wake. This was not normal sleep. Desert Rain pulled Chiriku up into a seated position, but still, she did not react. Desert Rain released her and the Quetzalin flopped back onto the bed, undisturbed.

Oh, Divine Beasts, has she been drugged? Desert Rain thought to the food the innkeeper had served them. But Desert Rain had eaten it too, although she had not eaten any of the meat. But if the innkeeper intended to drug them, why not put it in all the food? She carefully crept from her room, the hallway unlit and foreboding. She silently stalked down the hall to Gabriel and Mac's room, finding their door unlocked. She slunk in, seeing in the moonlight streaming through the window the two men sleeping as soundly as Chiriku.

"Gabriel? Mac? Get up, something's not right!" But no matter how she shook them, or raised her voice, both men slumbered on. When she yanked on Mac's tail, he tumbled from his bed and landed on the floor on a contorted position, but he continued to snore. The fact that Gabriel could not be roused, not even a mumble of consciousness, worried Desert Rain. He never slept this deeply. She left their room, checking on the Yopeis in the adjoining suites. They, too, had all the awareness of logs.

Okay, so everyone is in a deep sleep. And I'm not. Something's warning me, so I should trust my gut, she thought. She went back to her room and slipped into her wool coat and travel boots. She crept down the stairs to the main floor, finding it quiet and serene. Was the innkeeper here? How would Chiriku "scout" this situation?

She looked out the front window of the parlor room, finding all outside still except for a gentle snowfall of soft, thick flakes. Desert Rain felt a leap in her chest, as she had so often heard of snow, but had never seen it before. Back in her traveling caravan days, the family troupe never went as far north as this. But Kidran, decades ago when Desert Rain still attended Hijn Council meetings, had described it to her: like stardust trickling down from the sky. These snowflakes were more like goose down floating through the darkness, but it thrilled Desert Rain with such quiet beauty.

She opened the front door of the inn–strangely, not locked–and stepped out into the swirl of white, glittering in the moonbeams. It was cold, but there was no wind, so she barely noticed the chill. What a marvelous sight, something she had only read about in books, and she stood there as the flakes kissed her face. It was like an ivory desert around her, the streets and walkways coated in the glistening snow.

There were footprints in the snow near where she stood. Big, cat-like pawprints. Desert Rain stared for a long moment, trying to discern what animal they could have come from, when she realized several trails of these pawprints tracked through the snow, down the street. There was not just one large feline creature; there was a whole pack. She looked around, trying to spot where these creatures might be, but she saw nothing. Was this normal? Were these animals that typically roamed the area at night? If so, she wished someone in town might have warned her. Having to trek north with large wild cats in the vicinity would complicate matters.

Something compelled her to follow the tracks. She tightened her coat around herself and walked beside the pawprints, her ears perked forwards to anticipate any sounds. The farther she walked, the more pawprints she found, and it dawned on her that they were trailing out of stores, houses, and other buildings. More strangely, they were the only tracks–no human shoe or boot prints anywhere. If these animals were sneaking in and out of homes, no one had noticed or attempted to flee. Desert Rain's skin prickled in fear as she envisioned poor, mauled families in their beds. What if these animals hunted the people of this town? Should she go back to the inn, having left her friends vulnerable? Not yet; she had to know what was going on.

All the tracks converged before one building. It

was a one-story stone manor house, and a light cast a dull glow from a window. She stopped in front of the house, looking it up and down; still no sign of anyone or any animal. The pawprints led into the wide, open door ahead. Swallowing her anxiety, and patting her pouch at her side to make sure it was still there, she slipped up beside the door, peering in. She could hear voices inside, but they weren't close. She cautiously stepped through the doorway, observing the light in the window came from a lantern on a table, but there was little else in the front room.

Except it smelled ghastly, like wet fur, blood, and bad meat. That was when she noticed the buckets on the far side of the room, buckets full of dead mice, rats, and birds. *Guerda-Shalyr, what am I getting into?* she thought, covering her nose with the collar of her tunic. *If these are all for cat beasts, who's feeding them?*

The voices were coming from downstairs. There was a door leading down to what Desert Rain presumed was a cellar, and it was dark down there. She was tempted to run, but she reminded herself, *You've faced Bloodburn, the Zi' Gax, the Distorted, Katawa…whatever's down there can't be as bad as anything you've already faced.*

As best she could in her boots, she tiptoed slowly, softly, down the stairs, not making even a creak. The voices grew louder, and as she reached the bottom of the stairs, the floor of the cellar was dirt and the air smelled even worse. There was a broad curtain draped across a room ahead, and around the edges of the curtain, she could see light. She slipped towards the curtain, and without touching it, peeked through a slit between the curtain and the wall.

The room was full of gray-spotted, leopard-sized

cats. No, wait–not cats, for the heads were covered in white feathers with curved blue-gray beaks. White wings with black speckles were folded on their backs, and long, fluffy tails swiveled behind them. They lounged in every space of the room, which was shaped like a half-moon with a series of vaulted arches along the back wall. One of the larger creatures sat on a crate before the others, speaking in a firm voice, in intelligible Mutual Language.

"They all need to be sent away!" he said, the feathers on the top of his chest lifting in a crest. "I don't care what Cander said about the woman, no one can go farther than Haven's End!"

"Thunderpaw…" A smaller one of the creatures, short and round like a teapot, spoke up in a gentle, female voice.

"I told you, Yelloweye, to wait your turn!" the one called Thunderpaw retorted. "Now, I say we wipe the memories of the whole bunch. Make them think they got lost up the river and send them all in a sleigh to Thistledown."

"You can't wipe the mind of a Hijn!" argued one of the other creatures.

Thunderpaw rolled his eyes. "Just because Cander thinks that's what she is–"

"But what else can she be?" said Yelloweye. "I read her mind, and of all her companions at the inn. That's what she is, no doubt. How else can you explain why our Squobax doesn't work on her?"

Thunderpaw narrowed his eyes on her. "What do you mean, it doesn't work? You put her to sleep like the others, didn't you?"

"I did, but she didn't stay asleep. And she didn't stay in her room. She's standing right there." Yelloweye pointed a paw to where Desert Rain stood behind the curtain.

All the creatures turned and faced her.

Desert Rain's instinct was to turn and run, but before she could, one of the creatures closest to her swiped the curtain back with a clawed paw, exposing her to the entire room. She froze, glancing around at all the glowing eyed, sharp-beaked, claw-flexed creatures who glowered at her.

"Uh...hello," she squeaked.

CHAPTER ELEVEN
The Gryphons Guide the Way; Tension on the Trail

"What is the meaning of this?" Thunderpaw roared, his fur bristling. "It was your job to keep her asleep, Yelloweye!"

Yelloweye raised her beak up in a haughty sneer. "Well, just you try it, then. She's heiress to the Moon Dragoness. When the moon is full and high, our Squobax is weak to her."

Thunderpaw glared at Desert Rain, narrowing his eyes. Desert Rain could feel a strange sensation in her head, like her brain was a sponge, and she felt her eyelids getting heavy. Everything in the room began to morph, and for a second, she thought she saw a room full of humans in gray coats and white-feathered hats...

You stop this nonsense on my Desiree! She's done nothing to you!

The sensation stopped as Thunderpaw jerked his head back, his beak agape. He blinked rapidly and then ruffled his feathers. The other creatures in the room seemed to sense the same thing he had, and they shied away from Desert Rain, heads low to the ground.

"See?" Yelloweye smiled as she sauntered across the room to Desert Rain. "Now, you don't need to fear us. You remember me, don't you?"

"You...you're the innkeeper," Desert Rain replied in awe.

"Correct. I do apologize for the deception, but it's how we survive, and part of what we must do as guardians."

Desert Rain rubbed her head, clearing away the last bits of Thunderpaw's mental attack. "You're...you're all gryphons."

"Winter gryphons, to be precise," Yelloweye confirmed. "And proud of it."

"You all use...glamours? To disguise yourselves as humans?"

Thunderpaw chuckled. "Like your simple-minded spellcasters use? Nonsense. Our Squobax stems back to the ancient times, before the Great Manifestation, before your Sage Dragons tried to tame the wild magic. It has passed down through our tribe for generations. It is how we have survived this long, hidden from the eyes of the Noble races."

"Your...what?"

"Squobax, is what we call it. You might call it 'psychic magic'," Yelloweye said. "Although 'magic' is a loose term for it."

Psychic magic. Desert Rain had read about it in an old compendium of magic studies, and arguably Clova's Flightspeak magic could be classified as such, but it was very rare in Luuva Gros. They were powers that connected minds, allowing the caster to affect what others saw, heard, or even thought, but it could vary on who had the willpower to reject the suggestion. "But why the deception? What about the Noble people do you fear?"

"Oh, we don't fear them. It's simply part of our deal," Yelloweye replied.

"Yelloweye," Thunderpaw said, his voice stern with warning. "We don't know if we can trust her."

Yelloweye gave him an exasperated glare. "Like I

said, Thunder, I read her mind already. She's honest and true, perhaps a little naive-"

"I'm sure *she* thinks she's trustworthy. Her mission could be with good intentions, but that doesn't mean we can break our oath!"

"First of all," Desert Rain interjected, "I would appreciate it if you wouldn't read my mind, or my friends' minds, without our permission. Secondly, I'm not trying to put you in an awkward position with whatever your oath may be, or to whom. I really need to find the Elfë Taigas, and their Hijn Kidran. If you all know the Taigalands, would you be able to guide me and my friends to them? I realize they may not wish to be found, but the matter is urgent. The lives of everyone in Luuva Gros are at stake."

The winter gryphons cast glances at one another, grumbling among themselves. Thunderpaw narrowed his eyes on Desert Rain again. "And why should we comply? Many have come looking for the elves, but with selfish intent or desires of domination. We have promised to guard them, and this land, from those who would mean them ill. We cannot trust you simply because you're a Hijn. Not all dragons were of the altruistic sort."

Desert Rain wondered what he meant by that, but as she thought about it, the old tales said that Salamandrian Sages like Burning Talon, AshenClaw, Waterweaver, and Stormhowler could be as brutal as they were glorious. "I understand. But there is a terrible enemy out there. He calls himself the Distortionist. He's a Darkscale-"

"Yes, yes, we're all up to speed on that," Yelloweye said, tapping a claw to the side of her head.

"And I'm sorry for the ordeals you have been through. But this Lightscale you hope to find? You don't have a clear image in your mind of what that is, just a sketch you were shown. And we'd know of it, if the elves had it. Secrets are hard to keep from the winter gryphons."

"But not impossible, I bet." Desert Rain slowly paced the room, thinking. "The snow elves have their own brand of magic, don't they? Perhaps some that might block your Squobax. But that's beside the point. If you've read my mind and seen Katawa's horrible doings, then you must understand why finding the Lightscale is so important. Even if it doesn't exist, the snow elves must be our allies, as must you. Your abilities could help us stop Katawa. If we can't kill him, we can at least strike him where he's most vulnerable–his mind! He had his memories ripped out before, and you just said you could wipe minds."

The gryphons grumbled again.

"Yes, on the weak-willed," Thunderpaw admitted. "But this Katawa, it is clear he is warped in every way, even in mind. I fear trying to hold reign on that twisted psyche. Psychic magic can backfire on us, especially encountering the most depraved of minds."

Desert Rain threw her hands up in exasperation. "Then what must I do to convince you that my quest is just? Katawa scares you, as he does me. That's why you must stand with me! Imagine all Luuva Gros distorted to his will! Your homes, your land, your loved ones, all his to maim and maul. If your oath is to guard the elves, then you are oath-bound to lead me to them so I can protect them! Protect all of you!"

The gryphons grew silent. Yelloweye scratched herself behind her round, fluffy cat ear with her hind paw. "Protect us, how? With what will you protect us, if there is no Lightscale?"

Desert Rain reached into her pouch and withdrew Silverheart, holding it above her head. The gryphons' eyes dilated in the shimmering brilliance of the sword, and they were transfixed. One gryphon in the back let out a soft "Ooooooooooooh..."

"With my life!" Desert Rain shouted, although a small voice in her head said, *That was a bit corny, don't you think?*

Thunderpaw chuckled. "She sounds just like the Swordmaster, divine beasts bless him. Very well, Desert Rain, Hijn of the Moon Dragoness. You speak true, you speak bravely, just like a gryphon. We'll send your Yopeis-Gichen companions to Thistledown in the morning, and then we'll take you and your friends to the elves."

Desert Rain was struck dumb for a moment. "R...really? You will?"

"Yes, yes, now back to the inn with you before we change our minds," Yelloweye said, gently nudging Desert Rain out of the room. "We have much to discuss." She drew the curtain back, separating Desert Rain from the room.

Desert Rain slipped Silverheart back into the pouch. She turned and headed back up the stairs, back outside into the gently falling snow. Could she trust these gryphons? How did she know they weren't just telling her what she wanted to hear before wiping her thoughts and sending her away? Then again, if they were going to wipe her mind, why wait? And yet, something about their psychic powers, their Squobax, had already left some strange imprint on her mind...

It's all right, Desiree love. Best get some sleep now.

She looked around for the voice, although she knew she was alone.

No, she was never truly alone. She smiled.

*   *   *

By first daylight, all the Yopeis-Gichen were bundled up into a fine, red sleigh drawn by caribou in fine green harnesses with jingling bells, and a coachman dressed in a gray coat and feathered cap. They were off to Thistledown in better spirits, while Desert Rain and her crew saw them off at the carriage house of the Twin Spindles.

"Hopefully, all the other Yopeis who escaped the train will have found their way there," Desert Rain said. "Then they can all go home to the Rings of Springs together."

Chiriku shrugged. "Who knows? Anyway, who did you say offered to guide us to the mountains?"

"I didn't quite say, yet," Desert Rain replied. "We'll meet with them soon."

Mac stretched his arms wide, yawning. "All I know is-ss I got-ttk the best-ttk night's-ssk sleep in a long time. Slept-ttk like the dead."

Gabriel was quieter than usual, which was saying something. He had not said a thing all morning, not during breakfast and he barely got out a goodbye to the Yopeis, who had all hugged him before boarding the sleigh, lovingly calling him "general." Dunmore gave him an especially long hug, inviting Gabriel to tea anytime he was in the Rings of Springs. The man watched them head off out of town, the sleigh turning a corner before riding out of sight.

Desert Rain put a hand on his shoulder. "Gabriel? Are you going to be all right?"

Gabriel made a slight shrug. "Have to be."

"They'll make it home. They'll be fine."

"I know." He turned and started walking down the snow-dusted street. The others followed a few yards behind him at a casual pace.

Mac grinned. "He got-ttk attached. That's-ss cute."

Desert Rain furrowed her brow at him. "Caring for others is not 'cute,' Mac. I think Gabriel has tried not to care about others for a long time. Maybe because he's always had to leave others, or others have left him. He's learning to care again, and I'm sure it scares him, a little."

Mac's grin faltered. "Oh, I didn't-ttk mean that-ttk as, uh, der-ma-to-lo-gory or nothin'..."

Chiriku squinted at him. "As what?"

Mac shrugged. "You know, in a bad way."

"I think you mean, 'derogatory.' And I know you didn't, Mac." Desert Rain stuck her hands in her trouser pockets, feeling the compass in the right one. "By the way, I've been meaning to ask you about something–"

"You know, I've been thinking," Chiriku said, placing her hands behind her head in a relaxing gesture. "I kinda like this town. I know I was weirded out when we first got here, but something about these people, I kind of feel a connection, you know? Don't know why."

Desert Rain grinned. "Well, you have more in common with the people here than you might realize, Chi."

"Yeah? Why?"

Desert Rain wondered if she should tell her that Haven's End was populated with avian hybrids, much like Chiriku was. But maybe she should let the winter gryphons present themselves the way they thought best. "Because…they're wonderful. Like you."

Chiriku smirked and nudged her fist against Desert Rain's shoulder. "You're so weird, Dez."

They walked to the main square of town, where a group of ten villagers were waiting for them, including one tall, gray-bearded man holding a birch walking staff who, Desert Rain could tell, had Thunderpaw's piercing glare. The guide team was all prepared, including two sleds drawn by fluffy wolfdogs (*Were they truly dogs? Desert Rain wondered*), and bundles of supplies. The innkeeper–Desert Rain could now only visualize Yelloweye the gryphon, despite her human appearance–greeted them as they approached.

"The team is all set!" Yelloweye chirped, a smile linking her rosy cheeks. "Now, I think it's only fair to ask, are you sure this is what you want to do? It's dangerous out there, even for the most skilled of adventurers. The guide team will not be able to always guarantee your safety."

"Where are you guiding us to?" Gabriel asked, an edge to his tone. "Desert Rain says you can take us to the mountains, but what's there? Another village?"

Yelloweye gave him a sympathetic smile. "Everything you are searching for will be there. But it will be treacherous, and you must be prepared to face things you may not be ready for. Especially you."

Gabriel gave her a curious look. "Me? Why?"

Yelloweye took his hand and patted it gently. "Don't worry about it now. No point in carrying anxiety over the unavoidable."

Desert Rain looked to her friends, and then back to

Yelloweye. "Yes, we're ready." She leaned closely, whispering in Yelloweye's ear. "Can I tell my friends...you know?"

Yelloweye chuckled softly. "That's up to your friends to see the truth. People always want to see what they want to see, with or without the Squobax."

Desert Rain did not believe that was necessarily true–

"Oh, don't be so incredulous," Yelloweye said. "The Squobax works on a different level from what you're familiar with. You'll understand."

Desert Rain nodded, although she wished Yelloweye would stop speaking so cryptically–

"I'm not speaking cryptically. You just haven't comprehended it yet."

"Okay, you really need to stop doing that," Desert Rain said.

Yelloweye smiled sheepishly. "Sorry, old habit. Best of luck, dear." She gave Desert Rain a quick hug and then toddled off back towards the inn.

Mac scratched his head. "I've heard o' one-sided conversations before, but that-ttk was a bit-ttk spooky."

"Don't worry about it, Mac. Let's get going."

Gabriel looked over the two sleds. "These don't look big enough to carry all of us. I mean, each sled will need one of you guides to mush–"

Thunderpaw shook his head. "The dogs have made this run before. They don't need us to guide them. Two of you stand at the mushers' places, and two of you sit on the beds. The dogs will do the rest."

Gabriel frowned, clearly not satisfied with that explanation. "How are the rest of you going to travel?"

"We know this terrain well. We can keep up,"

Thunderpaw replied gruffly.

"On foot? Alongside running dogs?"

"Yes."

Gabriel crossed his arms, locking eyes with Thunderpaw as if he was waiting for the punchline to a joke. Eventually, he shook his head with a sigh. "You're the guides."

Chiriku walked alongside one of the sleds, looking at the line of gray, white, and black wolfdogs. "Hey, are these dogs nice? Can I pet them?"

"They're trained," Thunderpaw replied bluntly, securing a few bundles to the sled with rope.

Desert Rain really hoped the dogs were not more gryphons in disguise, as Chiriku playfully scratched one on the top of its head. It was written in the old books that gryphons were a proud tribe, and treating one like a pet would probably mortify it. The dog seemed to like the attention well enough, its long pink tongue lolling sideways from its mouth. Maybe these were all wild wolves that the gryphons were controlling with their psychic magic.

"All right, I'll take this sled," Chiriku decided. "This dog likes me. Coming, Mac?"

Mac's eyebrows lifted nearly clean off his forehead. "You want-ttk me to ride with you?"

"It's either you, Mr. Grumpy or the lady who thinks I'm 'wonderful,' so she must be crazy," the Quetzalin said. "No offense, Dez."

Desert Rain smiled. "Then I guess it's you and me, Gabe."

Gabriel shrugged. "Guess so."

*   *   *

"Are you going to tell me who, or what, these people really are?"

Desert Rain was seated on the cargo bed of the sled, right behind the supply bundles, while Gabriel stood at the back on the foot boards, gripping the handlebar. The snow was falling a bit harder as the flakes rushed past them, the dog team setting a good speed as they dashed through the snow. She turned back to look at him when he asked the question. "What do you mean?"

Gabriel did not look at her; his eyes were ahead, watching where they were going. Irritation was sketched into the corners of his mouth. "They don't have sleds of their own, yet every time we need to stop to let the dogs rest, they show up in a matter of minutes. These dogs know where to go without being given commands. I knew there was something off about these people the moment we stepped into that town, but it's clear you're not worried or suspicious about any of this. What do you know?"

Desert Rain knew if she lied, her ears would twitch twice, something she figured Gabriel had picked up on by now. So, she told the technical truth. "I know they won't harm us. They're our friends. They said they would bring us to the snow elves, and I believe them."

"What? They said they could take us directly to them?"

"Pretty much, or at least close."

Gabriel frowned. "How do they know the elves?"

Desert Rain paused. "They've known them…a long time. They're on friendly terms."

"And when did you find out all of this?"

"Last night, while you and the others were sleeping."

"Were you going to volunteer this information if I hadn't–"

"Gabe." Desert Rain reached up and put her hand on top of his on the handlebar. "Trust them. Trust me."

She half expected him to draw his hand away from hers, but he did not. Instead, he looked down at their hands, a strange, thoughtful expression on his face. It was Desert Rain who, after a few seconds, withdrew her hand and turned back to face front, praying her face was not flushing.

Gabriel looked forwards again, his expression hardening. "I would trust you better if you didn't keep secrets from me."

Desert Rain hunched into her coat, crossing her arms. "It wasn't a secret! I mean…okay, kind of. But it's not *my* secret, it's theirs, and for good reason. I'm not able to divulge it, unless they want me to. But I promise, they're helping us." She paused, but then turned around to face him again. "But look who's talking, about keeping secrets. Hiding that you knew Skyhan, not telling me why he sent you out into the world all alone–"

Gabriel slammed his heel down into the snow, causing the sled to drag. The guide dogs felt the sudden pull behind them, and they slowed to a stop. They looked back at their musher expectantly.

"Who told you *why* he sent me out?" Gabriel's voice was now tense, his grip on the handlebar tight enough to break it.

Desert Rain's ears flattened against her head, but she locked eyes with him. "Who do you think? But I find the reason ridiculous, as if you were inherently wicked and needed to be-"

"You don't know what you're talking about."

"Maybe not, but Sir Luce said-"

"You. Don't. Know. What. You're. Talking. About." Each word out of his mouth was like a needle, sharp and pointed.

Desert Rain straightened up in her seat. "Fine then. I keep giving you chances to tell me yourself, but you don't. Then you get angry when I find out in other ways. If you'd tell me yourself, then I'd have the clear picture. Then I wouldn't have to piece all the disjointed fragments together myself."

"I don't want you to piece it together! I don't want you to know!"

"Why not?"

"Because it's none of your damned business!"

"What are you afraid of?"

Gabriel stepped off the sled, coming around to stand in front of her. His hands were curled into tight fists. "I'm broken, don't you get it? And now that Skyhan's dead, I'm going to stay broken! I thought this ridiculous quest might save me. That's why I'm here, the only reason. But it's pointless. Even if we stop Katawa, even if we come out of this alive, it won't change who I am. I'm nothing! I'm a scarred, unwanted mistake that shouldn't be here at all. Skyhan was hoping I'd die out here, in the wilderness. He hoped I'd never come back. Then he'd be free of me, then he'd be..." He trailed off, the lines of his face drawn deep in anger, but then the lines disappeared, his expression stoic again. He groaned, wiping a hand over his forehead. "Forget it. Let's just go."

An intense, smothering sense of sadness

enveloped Desert Rain. Everything he said sounded so familiar to her. So many of those words, she had trapped inside her own mind for decades. Broken. Unwanted. Mistake. Never come back. She wanted to tell him it was all untrue, but how could she do that, when she believed all the same things about herself? And what would simply telling him do? Scars did not heal with words. Brokenness is a hard thing to escape from, when you are so used to believing that is what you are; how can you repair yourself when all you see every day are the pieces, and you don't even remember what the completed whole looks like anymore?

She slipped her long fingers underneath the sleeve of her coat, sliding them up her arm until she felt the cool, marble bracelet of protection. She wriggled it down her arm and pulled it off, holding it in her fingers. "Someone gave this to me, when I knew I had become broken," she said as reverently as a prayer. "I don't know how much magic might be left in it, but maybe it'll help hold you together." She held the bracelet out to him.

Gabriel looked at the bracelet uncertainly at first, but then he remembered. "Isn't that the thing you used to help Merros break free of Katawa's hold on him?" He glowered at it. "It repels evil."

"It protects. It drives away darkness in your soul and binds together your spirit. It won't hurt you."

Gabriel's hard expression softened. "Don't you need it?"

Desert Rain glanced at the bracelet, wondering if the shaman's magic had been holding her together, keeping her soul from fracturing further. But how much longer had Gabriel's spirit been breaking than hers? "I think I've had my share of it long enough."

Gabriel was hesitant, but eventually he reached out and touched the bracelet. It shimmered with a light, blue glow, but otherwise gave no reaction. He took the bracelet, eying it over, before he slipped it onto his arm under his sleeve. He paused, waiting for something–some delayed magic, some energy, some sensation–but seemed mildly relieved when nothing of note happened. "Thank you," he said.

Desert Rain smiled. "Well, I guess we should keep going. We don't have to talk anymore, if you don't want to."

Gabriel walked back to the rear of the sled, gripping the handlebar and placing his feet back on the foot boards. The dogs, seeing everyone was back in their places, started up again at a brisk pace, gradually breaking into a run again. Desert Rain squinted her eyes against the wind and snow in her face, wondering how close by the winter gryphons were, and hoping they were keeping their word and not leading them into disaster.

*   *   *

The two sleds met up after a few hours, as the dog teams came to stop alongside a lake to drink water and rest. In short time, the guides caught up with the four journeyers as they set up a quick camp with the supplies in the sleds. They made a small fire pit in which they used flint to ignite coals, and upon the hot coals they brewed a pot of tea in an iron kettle. The guides also provided dried strips of meat and bread, enough for everyone, including the dogs, to have a decent lunch.

The mountains were visible over the tops of the towering pine trees in the distance. They looked nothing like the mountains of Vaes Galahar in the South; these ivory summits, streaked with shadows of dark blue, looked like a line of jagged teeth.

"How far is it now?" Chiriku asked, glancing at the mountain range. "Looks pretty close, so it shouldn't be long, right?"

"Not as close as you think," Thunderpaw replied, chewing on dried meat. "We will keep moving until nightfall, and then we should reach them by tomorrow evening."

"Still that-ttk far?" Mac shivered. "Never been this-ss chilly in my life. Lizards-ssck don't-ttk do cold well."

Desert Rain took a spare blanket from her sled and brought it over to Mac. "As someone who's lived in the desert for most of her life, this is not exactly my terrain either. Just think warm thoughts for now."

"Mmmm…a good hot-ttk toddy would warm me right-ttk up," Mac said with a grin, wrapping himself in the blanket. "Hope those elves-ssck got-ttk some."

Desert Rain turned her gaze to Thunderpaw. "The Elfë Taigas will welcome us, won't they? They wouldn't turn us away, after how far we've come?"

Thunderpaw gave Desert Rain a stern look. "I guarantee nothing. We said we would take you to them. Whether they welcome you or turn you away is their choice."

Desert Rain took a deep breath, sitting down by the fire pit. If they could just get to Kidran, he would welcome them. He would convince the Elfë Taigas to help them, wouldn't he? Was he sending out magic signals, right now, in hopes they were coming? She knew it was not worth checking the Darkscale compass; the gryphons' psychic magic would throw off the compass's orientation. All she could do was pray this plan would work, that they were on their way to willing allies and not isolationists–or, worse, foes.

CHAPTER TWELVE
A Not-so-Warm Welcome; Bellaluna's Past Comes to Light

The glacier was an imposing wall of ivory ice, with jagged crystalline pillars jutting out all throughout its face. It stood at the base of the mountain in the center of a glassy, frozen lake, giving the impression of a castle surrounded by a moat. The ice shimmered with a cyan sheen, even though the sky was overcast and foggy. It was as if the glacier gleamed with a light all its own.

Thunderpaw grasped his walking stick tighter as he stared at the glacier for a long, silent moment. He then turned to his escorted company. "We promised you safe passage to the realm of the elves. We have kept our promise."

Desert Rain scanned all along the glacier, biting her lip. "This is…it? I don't see a door or any pathway from here. It's all ice over there."

Mac wrinkled his nose. "I don't-ttk suppose there's some sort-tkk of secret-tkk password we're supposed to give? Or should we have brought-ttk a peace offering? A basket-ttk of muffins?"

"If I have to smash some ice to find a door, I'm equipped for that," Chiriku said, patting her warhammer's head over her shoulder.

"No one's smashing anything." Gabriel took a deep breath. "I'm sure the elves already know we're here."

Thunderpaw nodded. "I advise you to be humble. If the elves will have you, do as they say. Do not question their customs or manners. Always speak respectfully and to the point. And..." He came close to Desert Rain, lowering his voice. "Do not let your eyes deceive you. What we gryphons are capable of, the Elfë Taigas can do tenfold."

Desert Rain furrowed her brow. "Would they use their abilities against us?"

Thunderpaw drew his lips into a straight line, and his eyes warned her. "I will wait here. If you do not return in an hour, I and my fellow guides will depart."

"But how will we get back, once we've spoken with the elves?"

Thunderpaw gave a strange, deep noise that Desert Rain thought might be a chuckle. "If the elves will have you, then that is truly the least of your concerns."

Desert Rain frowned. As usual, cryptic advice — although she figured Thunderpaw was choosing his words carefully, lest he say something of which the elves would disapprove. She gave the gryphon a nod of understanding, and then she turned towards the glacier. "All right, let's go."

Her party trudged through the snow towards the lake, the crunching of snow under their boots the only sound in the stark snow land. As they approached the edge of the water, which was such a deep, iridescent blue it almost seemed like liquid magic, they realized there was no bridge, no steppingstones, no boat — nothing to permit them to cross.

"If any of you are plannin' to go swimmin' across-ss, have fun freezin' your butts off," Mac said.

Gabriel scanned the lake. He tentatively stuck his foot out and tapped the water with the toe of his boot, which sent silver circles across the surface. "I'm guessing the lake has a magical ward or cantrip on it. Even if it's just to signal the elves of intruders."

"So, you touch it, of course," Chiriku said. "Good job springing the trap for us."

Desert Rain felt a sudden sharp sting in her forehead, and she scrunched her face and squeezed her eyes shut against the pain. She was about to attribute it to an abrupt migraine, when within the recesses of her mind —

No! You will not pry through her thoughts without her say so! I won't allow it!

Desert Rain opened her eyes. "Luna…?"

She looked over at the others, who had all fallen silent. They all stared straight ahead, not focused on anything, a blank expression on all their faces. Desert Rain waved a hand in front of Gabriel's eyes, but he made no reaction.

"Gabriel? Mac? Chi?" Desert Rain nudged each of them, but still, they made no response. "What's happening? Is this some kind of…"

You release my granddaughter's friends. You will have a mutual, open conversation with them like good hosts. This sort of invasion of privacy is rude!

"Grandma Luna? Who are you talking —"

The other three blinked, shaking their heads while whatever had bound them a second ago faded away.

"What in Luuva was that?" Chiriku asked, ruffling her head feathers.

"I heard Luna's voice," Desert Rain said. "She was telling someone to release us. As if someone was —"

"Enchanting us?" Gabriel grimaced. "I think the elves might have been trying to gain control of us with a spell."

"And we had no way of knowin'?" Mac said. "That's-ss some scary business."

Gabriel looked at Desert Rain. "Apparently, something about you convinced them to stop. What did you—"

The ripples on the lake spread farther, and farther, changing from gentle wrinkles into pulsing waves, steady as a heartbeat. From the glacier, strands of silver grew outwards across the water until they formed a glittering pathway that led from the shore to the glacier. The pathway solidified into a bridge, with guardrails that dripped glistening icicles along the sides.

Desert Rain carefully tested the bridge by tapping her toe on it, finding it solid. "I guess this is their way of saying we're allowed in," she said.

Gabriel furrowed his brow, skeptical, but he said nothing.

As they walked down the pathway, Chiriku nudged Desert Rain. "So, you can hear yours too, now?"

Desert Rain cocked her head at her. "My what?"

"You know, your dragon buddy. In your head. It talks to you, too?"

"Well, it only started yester—what do you mean, 'too'?"

Chiriku exhaled a long, solemn breath. "Woasim said he could talk to whoever his dragon was. Zippy-song, Zeffy-song, something like that. I thought he had some kind of imaginary friend, or he was nuts. But now you can hear yours too, unless you're just as crazy as he was."

Desert Rain thought about this. She believed what Woasim told Chiriku was true; he would have had no reason to lie or pretend. She felt a bit envious that

Woasim had had such a strong connection with his
dragon—Zephyrsong, that was what the Wind
Dragoness's name was—that he used to converse with
her regularly. If he were here now, maybe he could help
Desert Rain learn how to cultivate this ability better, so it
would not feel so sporadic when Bellaluna spoke in her
mind. She tried to quiet her mind, concentrating...*Hello?
Grandma Luna? Can you hear me? Oh, why is it that I can
hear you, but you won't speak to me?*

As they approached the glacier, the four scanned
the face of the towering ice formation before them, but it
was all an impenetrable wall. Chiriku walked up to the
ice and tapped on it with her knuckle. "So, how are we
supposed to get in?" she said. "Anyone see a door?"

"Maybe it's-ss around the back-kk," Mac
suggested.

"Or maybe I need to knock louder," the Quetzalin
said, starting to remove her warhammer from its sheath.

"Chi, I know you like to smash things, but this
isn't really—" Desert Rain went rigid, stopping mid-
sentence as she stared at the wall.

Chiriku paused, as she noticed Gabriel and Mac
were also staring oddly at the wall. When she looked, a
face in the ice caused her to jump back several feet in
surprise. The face slowly moved, passing through the
wall until, inexplicably, there was suddenly a full person
standing before them. The figure was an icicle of a
person, tall and slender, with skin so pale it was nearly
translucent. They wore a simple fitted gown of white
feathers, and a matching headwrap strung with beads
and crystals covered the figure's head down over their
eyes and ears, leaving only the sharp nose and thin,
bluish lips revealed. The figure folded their hands, each

adorned with silver rings connected by delicate chains, and stood with the statuesque stiffness of a sculpture.

"Um, hello?" Desert Rain offered, giving the stranger a slight wave, although she did not know if the person could see through the fabric of the headwrap. "We're—"

"Come," the figure, whose voice indicated she was a woman, replied in a calm, emotionless tone. She then turned and walked back through the wall. Only now did the four understand that there was, indeed, an opening in the wall, but it could only be seen at a certain angle; the way the ice was formed, it created the optical illusion of there being no opening at all.

"Well, that-ttk was a warm welcome," Mac muttered.

"I've never seen a snow elf before – other than Kidran, of course. She is…mesmerizing," Desert Rain said.

Gabriel raised an eyebrow at her. "Perhaps to some. It is said the Elfë Taigas are the most beautiful creatures in Luuva Gros. They hide their features because one look at their full beauty could enchant you permanently, and you'd never want to leave this place."

Desert Rain laughed lightly. "I don't think so. I mean, Kidran doesn't have that effect on anyone. He's handsome enough, I guess, but not overwhelmingly… then again, maybe he's like me and his Hijn transformation changed his appearance." She tried to remember what Kidran had looked like the last time she saw him, which was, granted, decades ago. Nothing about his features had struck her as strange, although they were distinct – a squarish face with triangular ears similar to a wolf's, with frost-white hair and a matching patch on his chin. She also remembered his skin being alabaster-hued with light pink tones, and his eyes were radiant turquoise. He had never hidden any of his facial features; she recalled rather liking the brief time she was in his company, but not because of his looks. She gave Gabriel a suspicious look. "Just how do you know so much about the elves?"

"I've told you, I've been wandering for a long time now. You pick up a lot of information on the road," he replied. "Mostly hearsay, but you'd be surprised how much of it turns out to be true."

"We gonna follow her, or what?" Chiriku said. "I know we're freezing our butts off, but I'm getting worse shivers from that woman."

Desert Rain glanced at each of her companions. *If the Elfë Taigas wanted to hurt us, they could have done so already, right? I mean, they can reach into our minds whenever they want. They must trust us if they're guiding us in*, she thought.

"This is why we're here," she finally replied. "We need to go in."

Warily, the four entered through the opening, leaving the light of the outside world behind.

The narrow hallway inside the glacier cast blue shadows along the frosted walls, and their snow elf escort waited patiently a few yards ahead of them. Without a word, the elf turned and started down the hallway, as the four guests had to walk single-file down the silent corridor, with Gabriel in front, and Desert Rain, Chiriku, and Mac behind him. It seemed no matter how quickly they tried to catch up to their host, she always remained the same distance ahead of them, although it did not appear that she adjusted her pace at all.

The deeper they went in, the more the ice around them took on a reflective quality, and Desert Rain realized she could see all their reflections in the walls. It created a multiplying effect, with both walls reflecting each other, so their reflections repeated over and over to look like a long line of doppelgangers were walking beside them.

How very odd, she thought. *Ice doesn't normally reflect like this, does it? I wonder why —*

She suddenly bumped straight into a wall, or mirror, in front of her. She silently berated herself for not paying attention to where she was going, but then panic grasped her when she realized she should not have bumped into a wall; she should have bumped into Gabriel. She glanced around at the figures around her, but they were all her own reflection, as if she were surrounded by herself. Her guide, and her companions, were gone.

"Gabriel? Chi? Mac?" Desert Rain's voice echoed through the empty hallways, and it reverberated in such a way it sounded like a chorus of her calling back. She tried to backtrack — perhaps she had missed a turn while she was distracted by the reflections? — but it became clear, quickly, that the hallways around her were a maze, and wherever she had come from was no longer apparent.

It also became clear that this had not been an accident, or a misstep on her part. Chiriku and Mac had been right behind her; they would not have strayed off a different direction without her and Gabriel. Something had happened during the brief period of them they had been following the guide, something that had been intentionally put into play. She looked around again, and somewhere past the mirrored surfaces of the walls, she swore she was being watched.

"Why did you isolate me from my friends? Where did you send them?" she called out, trying to keep her composure.

Only her echoes answered.

"We don't mean you harm!" she shouted, hoping her hosts could hear her, or at least read her thoughts. "I don't know why you felt the need to separate us, but you know why we're here. I need to find the Lightscale, to stop Katawa. Do you have it? Does it exist?"

Again, nothing but hollow echoes replied to her request.

Desert Rain took several deep breaths, calming herself. She was in the snow elves' territory now, she would have to abide by whatever strange rules they had in place. "What do you want from me to prove to you I am trustworthy? Can you not read my mind and see for yourselves that I speak the truth?"

The truth is subjective.

It was not a voice that answered, not even a voice in her head, the way Bellaluna had sounded in her mind. It was...Desert Rain could not quite describe it. It was more a feeling than a thought. Something deep in her blood and bones. Softly, as if she thought lowering her voice may be more respectful, she said, "Not this truth. Not my truth."

You are dangerous.

Was that the elves' belief? Or was that her own? "Not to you," she whispered. "Kidran could tell you—"

You are broken.

She paused. She stopped speaking and simply thought. *This is true. But I want to repair what is broken.*

You are weak.

Perhaps. That's why I need your help, Desert Rain replied.

How can you face the Distortionist when you won't face yourself?

Desert Rain closed her eyes. *Do what you will, whatever you would have of me to prove myself.*

When she opened her eyes, she was no longer in the hallway. She was surrounded by forest, by darkness, and by dozens of pairs of malicious, glowing red eyes. From out of the darkness formed the scrawny, filthy goblin band that she knew too well, brandishing their rusty sickles and daggers at her. Their nasty giggling laughter sent shivers throughout her body.

"The Zi'Gax?" Desert Rain cast her gaze at the bandaged, wrinkly faces around her. She realized that Silverheart was in her hands, but it was so unbelievably heavy, she could not lift the blade out of the dirt at her feet. "Sir Luce? Sir Luce, I need you!"

The goblins laughed harder, closing in on her. A taller goblin, gray-green in color and more gruesome than the others, raised his pair of sickles at her. "I'm supposed to be afraid of a scullery maid, am I? You're out of your league."

Wait, she had heard that before. She remembered him, the leader of the Zi'Gax. And he was dead, along with most of his band.

A memory. This was just a memory. Was this the power of the Elfë Taigas that Thunderpaw warned her about? They could literally bring her memories to life? Why would they do this, as some sort of test? She struggled to lift the sword again, if this was even the real Silverheart.

"You're not real," she murmured in a low voice. "None of you are real."

This fact would not deter the goblins, as they crept in closer. For being only a memory, their horrible stench sure seemed real.

Desert Rain's panic melted into the molten magma of anger. She dropped the sword, letting it clunk at her feet. "I'm not going through this again!" she screamed. "You will not make me relive having to take lives to save my friends. You will not make me relive my fears! Pull out of me all you want, any bad memory I have, but I will not accept this!"

She raised her hand, and with a burst of brilliant blue light, sent the Blueshine ripping through the goblins. It was a second-long flash, the searing heat of the magic flowing through her arm, but it subsided quickly. However, when the light faded and she could see again, it was not the frozen faces of the Zi'Gax before her. It was…

No. No, not this memory. Anything but this.

Andeas, Lional, and Tandre. Her brothers. Lying in the brittle dead grass, they had not been obliterated by the Blueshine, but their bodies had been damaged by the wild magic. They looked like frost-bitten corpses, though they breathed, just barely. Their skin was pale, caked in bluish crystal, and their hair stiff as glass. They could scarcely open their eyes, but what little they could, they looked at her with petrified terror.

Desert Rain swallowed hard, closing her eyes against the vision. *I was trying to protect my family from the thieves. I didn't know what I was doing! It was the first time I used the Blueshine. I would not do this to the people I love!*

The strange feeling rattled her being again. *You*

have no control.

She kept her thoughts calm. *I am learning control. You must know that.*

How can we trust you with something as precious as the Lightscale, if you are so reckless?

Desert Rain's anger subsided, as hope bubbled to the surface of her mind. *So you do have it! It does exist!*

It exists. We do not have it.

The hope plummeted into oblivion as quickly as it had risen. *Then where is it? Please tell me!*

Suddenly, a gentle familiar voice resonated in her head. *Haven't you put my granddaughter through enough? It's not her you're mad at. You're doing this to punish me.*

Desert Rain snapped her head up, holding her breath. *Grandma Luna? Can you hear me now? What do you mean, punish you?*

The voiceless sensation rocked her being again, but this time, it emitted a dark, malicious air about it. *We do not hold grudges, Bellaluna of the Blueshine. However, we believe in judgement, which you are due. Does your heir know of your transgression?*

Desert Rain thought she sensed a deep sadness, not her own, but then the world around her dropping away into nothingness, the ground beneath her transforming into mirror, and she was suddenly sucked into the mirror beneath her like diving into water.

*   *   *

She could feel the tightening of the delicate strands of magic that were holding their land together, strands she herself was woven into, and the tension sliced through her with a deep, tearing pain. Still, she raced, her muscles straining under the cuts of both the decaying magic and the sharp pieces of ice and stone raining down around her. The Hold of the Equanume had been one of their grandest masterpieces of architecture, a combined effort of sorcery to create an organic menagerie that was their home and haven, incorporating a symbolic piece of each of its builders. The steady earth, the vivacious sea, the gentle flora, the arctic ices, the dancing fires, and the unending play of shadows and light were all in its walls, its parapets, its crystalline ceilings and sweeping halls. Every room had once breathed joy and warmth, pulsating with the music of life like the chambers of a young heart. Now it was crumbling away before her eyes.

   The rest of the Hij-Urawran had all fled. It was their history, their fate, to flee the hardships of their failings. They had hoped this land could finally be their home, this once wild and untamed realm so far away from the Otherlands. All their hard work, the relentless years of toil to master the foreign mystical energy of Luuva Gros, had counted for nothing. They knew what had been put into motion could not be undone now.

   But Bellaluna could not let go. She would not allow it all to die.

   She remembered how the Sages had come to this place — what had been left of them, who had survived the journey across the waters — in the hopes of building a better life, or at least finding a final peace before their souls would pass into the gentle blue of the Eternal Deep. She recalled all the days and nights, for what had seemed centuries, she and the others had gently combed through and woven their own precious energies into the vicious and feral life-force of Luuva Gros, until after all the lashing and stinging the wild magic had retaliated back against them, it had eventually calmed and accepted them as its new caregivers. Then came the new forests, and the cleansing rains, the lively winds, the great fires of the south and the snows in the north, all a beautiful tapestry on which the Hij-Urawran painted their dreams and visions upon the land. The greatest memory of all, however, was that they had finally found families again among the native beings of Luuva Gros. The creatures had all been so fragile, so lost, uncertain of their present or future. The Hij-Urawran had so much to teach them, to guide them, and the natives had come to love the Sages as much as they loved their new children. Even these creatures changed over time, as the strands of magic reshaped their world, as the essences of the Hij-Urawran began to entwine within them. The land, its flora and fauna, all blossomed into a grand new manifestation.

That was why Bellaluna could not let this world fall apart. She would not allow her children to succumb to darkness and emptiness. She would save them, and she knew what she needed to do it.

The Hold of the Equanume continued to wither away as she burst into the central chamber, where the Equanume, the thriving Machine of Ancient Magic, was kept safe at the hold's core. The sight that met her eyes shattered her heart. It was what the other Sages had told her, what she had refused to believe. It couldn't be true...but there it was.

The Equanume was broken, torn asunder like an elder oak splintered apart by a tempest's spears of lightning. There beside it was a writhing shimmering figure, billowing up in curls of smoke to fill the room with a splash of midnight. Yellow-topaz eyes turned to meet hers, not ones of malice or evil, but ones of dignity and wisdom, eyes that she had come to love so dearly. Yet where she had once seen patience, now she saw cold determination.

"What are you doing?" she demanded.

"I am taking the part of the Equanume that is mine and leaving," the figure replied calmly, too calmly amidst the chaos he had evoked.

Bellaluna allowed anger to enter her, to smother the sadness in her heart. "How dare you…after all we worked to create, after all the things we were going to share. You choose to destroy it all!"

He did not blink, nor flinch at her words. "It will not be destroyed. This land will heal and continue as it always did, before we ever tampered with it. I must turn my plans now to more important matters."

"More important? What about the life force of this land? What about the creatures of Luuva Gros? Do you not consider them important?"

The room around them convulsed, as the elements around them broke apart in violent quakes. The mysterious being unfurled his massive wings and enveloped Bellaluna and himself, wrapping them into a dark shroud that banished all the noise and perils of the room crashing down around them. The sudden silence and stillness was startling, and Bellaluna was too shaken to remember what was happening. Her protector picked up right where she had left off.

"On the contrary," he replied with a chilling coolness. "I value life, but you know my responsibility lies in the end of it. Death is not capable without life, nor is life valuable without death. Your creatures, the ones you love so dearly, must be able to pass to the Eternal

Deep so as not to be lost forever. Thus, I must prepare them for their future, as well as mine."

"Your future..." Bellaluna breathed to stable herself. "It was going to be *our* future."

"No, Bellaluna. You know as well as I do that our essences do not make life together possible. Nor would such a union be fruitful."

Bellaluna shook her head. "We don't know that. Our kind hasn't had offspring in many millennia, but—"

"You have your 'children,' Bellaluna. When you wish to pass on your legacy, you can without difficulty. Your gifts will allow you to seek out such an heir. I, on the other hand, must find mine through other means."

"What do you mean?"

"The nature of my gifts, my energy, is too much for your gentle creatures of Luuva, your lovers of light who fear the dark and loathe the unknown. You and the others have taught them too well in your ways. Thus, I must take my piece of the Equanume. I will manufacture my heir."

Bellaluna, bewildered, locked onto his unblinking eyes. "Manufacture, from what? You don't plan to...try and create some new species?"

"Unnecessary. There is a new breed of creature already forming. They have been molded from all their inner pain and suffering, their anguish reflected in their appearances by all the magical changes we have thrust upon this land. They are the ones who have turned from the disdainful light and all its rigid conditions for acceptance and love. They have overpowered the fear within themselves, the darkness that destroys the soft hearts of your creatures. They can be strong enough to accept my legacy."

"No...the Wretched! You can't!"

"Luna..." The name dripped like honey in his voice, and Bellaluna felt a gentle warm touch nuzzle her under her chin. It retracted as quickly as she had felt it. "Take what belongs to you. Leave this place. Think of your own future now and do not be concerned with the future of others. You know where they will go to in the end. If in the end, you come to me, you will have nothing to fear. But if you pass your legacy on...teach your heir well."

Then he was gone, as well and the Hold. There was no trace of it, as if the shadowy figure had kept her enclosed in his wings for hundreds of years and time had done away with what was left of their once grand home. That was how quickly magic could unravel, and how centuries of labor and pride could vanish in an instant. Bellaluna was alone, in a place where she could no longer feel the heartbeat of the earth, or the joy of the winds, or the bond of the creatures for which she so ached.

All that was left was a remaining piece of the Equanume that lay at her feet. Slowly she reached down to place her taloned hand upon it. Cold. Still. Lifeless. For now.

*Teach your heir well...*His words echoed in her mind. Her pangs of loneliness and despair were slowly mending, as she remembered who she was, what her legacy would be. Knowing that, this world would have the one thing, the one unbreakable gift that would keep it from falling to destruction.

*   *   *

Desert Rain gasped as she felt herself break free of

the memory. She did not know how it was possible that she had seen it, other than she and Luna were linked, and the elves could access both their memories. But that was of little concern, compared to what she had just witnessed.

The Equanume...why did that sound familiar? Of course! It was what Anthron of the Ahshi had told her about, that it was the combined halves of the Darkscale and the Lightscale. This memory was from when it had been broken in two by that night dragon, whoever he was. Desert Rain could not recall of any such dragon from her history texts...

I value life, but you know my responsibility lies in the end of it.

His words echoed in her mind. She froze, the realization flooding over her. The Death Walker. That had been Balthazin the Death Walker. Bellaluna and Balthzin had been...*Oh, Guerda-Shalyr, Luna! What did you do?*

A hand — a real, physical hand — yanked her from the darkness. The next thing she knew, Desert Rain was standing in a small room, sparsely furnished, with a marble and pearl fireplace against a wall housing a meager fire to illuminate the surroundings. A child's bed sat on the far side of the room, and various toys littered the floor. Standing before her was a girl, seemingly human except for the bizarrely large black eyes, and downy white feathers that covered her heart-shaped face northwards of her triangular nose. Even her hair was made of long white-and-gold feathers that trailed down past her shoulders. It was almost as if she were wearing a mask or headdress, but Desert Rain could tell the eyes and feathers were all truly part of her. Given her short height and frail frame, the child could not have been more than six years old.

The girl simply stared at Desert Rain for a minute. Eventually, a beaming smile blossomed on her face. "Hello, Mother," she said.

CHAPTER THIRTEEN
The Trial of the Cursed Wanderer; Not All Memories are Bad

Gabriel blinked away the haze, unsure of where he was, until he realized he was surrounded by a tribunal of pale, gaunt faces. They towered over him, several rows on each side of him standing in high ivory jury boxes, looking down at him like a condemnatory choir. In front of him, five figures stood on a wide judge's bench. He stood upon a round dais, caged in by a cold, iron banister that came up to his chest.

Everyone around him resembled the elf that had led his party inside: white head wraps obscuring the upper halves of their heads, with only sharp noses, blue lips and pointed chins visible. They all wore some combination of feathers and fur, white and cloud-gray, creating the atmosphere of an overcast sky. Even without seeing their eyes, Gabriel could feel their piercing gazes on him.

The only one who did not wear a headwrap stood in the middle of the judge's bench, a notably taller woman that any of the others beside her. Yet, her solid white eyes, her long, ice-mint hair, and her skin so light that bluish veins could be seen through it, made Gabriel believe he was looking at a marble statue. Then she spoke, a hollow, cold voice that echoed throughout the cavernous court.

"Banished one, cast out because of the darkness in your heart, you stand before us an abomination and insult to life. You bring death and pain in your wake.

Thus, you must be put to trial."

Gabriel's face reddened in indignation. "For what crime? Who in Luuva are you, anyway?"

The woman lifted her nose. "I am the High Lady of the Crystal Court. I administer justice and maintain order here."

"Justice and order, huh? You say these horrible things of me, yet you don't know me. You permitted me in to your...whatever you call this. Do you treat all your guests this way?"

"You shall show respect." The High Lady sat down, and steepled her hands before her. "All of your companions come to us malformed. But you, you are the most malformed of all. We do not stand for weakness. We do not coddle frailty. Where there is a crack in the ice, it is bound to shatter."

"It sounds like you already find me guilty of whatever you perceive as a crime. Why put me on trial at all, then? Why not lock me away, or do whatever it is you do with criminals?" Gabriel refused to be intimidated by these elves, refused to be treated like an animal in a cage.

The woman showed no hint of emotion. "Because your circumstance is...intriguing to us. How does one such as you, the way you were made, survive? You may have surmised by now, we know everything about you. Your mind is open to us. We know who you are, or perhaps more accurately, who you once were."

Gabriel's face blanched. He took a deep breath, trying to focus so he would not say anything brash or stupid. But then, what could he tell them that they wouldn't already know? "My lot in life was not my choice. It is also of no consequence. What was done was done. I was cast out. I have done what I can to undo the wickedness inherent in my soul, but only those in the Eternal Deep may judge me. You have no right or authority to condemn me."

Still, the High Lady made no facial reaction. "Do you not agree that you are the reason Swordmaster Skyhan is dead?"

That question stunned Gabriel, and he could tell by the tiniest upward twist in the elf lady's lip that she smugly enjoyed his shock. "N…no. He died in battle against Katawa. I wasn't even there—"

"And it was because of your absence that he fell."

Gabriel was quiet for a long moment, trying to understand the accusation. "Why would I… how would that have changed anything? If anything, I was Skyhan's weakness…"

"Perhaps your memory has become unreliable because of your resentment of Skyhan," the High Lady said. "Fortunately, we can remedy that. Let us review, shall we?"

Gabriel suddenly felt an incredible pain in his head, like a thousand needles stabbing into his brain, and then he was looking through eyes that were not his own.

"Helio…" A lovely woman, with starlight hair piled in a loose bun atop her head, and two clear quartz markings in the shapes of lotuses were on the outside of each eye. She wore the robes of a healer, and she was applying a soft, warm touch to Gabriel's face—or, that was, whoever's face that Gabriel was peering out from. A tingling magic flowed through her fingertips, but eventually she shook her head and dropped her hand. "It's no use. My powers have healed your injuries as best they can, but cannot remove them completely. Whatever caused these scars was imbued with dark magic and some sort of acidic chemical. Those Darkscale are getting craftier by the day. I'm sorry. There isn't any more I can do."

Gabriel felt a mixture of heartbreak and fury within his host. "This is my fault," a deep, male voice said.

"No, brother! You have earned countless scars in battle, defending what is good and just. This is simply another. It doesn't change who you are," said the woman...a mage...Dahlia. His sister. Divine Beasts, it had been so long, how had Gabriel almost forgotten her face?

"But Purelight is supposed to protect me from dark magic," came a bitter reply. "It should rejuvenate me. If Purelight, or even your magic, can't undo this...then it means one thing. The dragons' magic won't work on an evil soul. I am not good enough to be its bearer."

Dahlia gave him a gentle smile. "You know that's nonsense. Veritas would not have picked you if that were true."

"There is darkness in me, I sense it! All this training, all this suffering, what good is it if I am not pure of heart? How can I overcome evil if it infects my soul? There must be a way to purify it, there must!" The host's voice was consumed with animosity, but a shocked look from the mage softened the voice. "I don't mean to frighten you, Dahlia. I must ask...did your dragoness ever reveal anything to you about healing a soul? Healing from within?"

Dahlia knitted her eyebrows in concern. "Halua

Mata always said the ailments of the body and the mind are connected, but the soul…oh, Helio, your worries are unfounded. I understand these new injuries are still a shock, but this will pass. Perhaps Veritas can give you some guidance—"

"Veritas doesn't…" the voice paused, then sighed. "Thank you for your healing. I need some time to think."

What Helio would not tell his sister was that he had not heard Veritas Lucen's voice in a long time. He did not know if it was because something had happened to Veritas, or to himself, or just that the dragon's spirit refused to speak to him anymore. It exacerbated his fears of his impurity, that he was growing more corrupt, and that Purelight was failing him. It festered in his mind, and no amount of meditation, practice, or distraction could alleviate his fears.

Gabriel could still remember the moment that the thought, the one thought that changed everything, slipped into Helio Skyhan's mind: *Why can't I just rip this impurity out of me?*

A sensation like lightning crackled in his brain. *Yes, of course!* The magic wasn't called Purelight for nothing, and Silverheart was more than a weapon. It channeled righteousness. It embodied virtue. It dissolved darkness. And while it had not been an instant decision—there were sleepless nights, and hours of reading spellcaster tomes for guidance, and desperate days of mentally beseeching Veritas to answer his questions, only to be met with silence—Helio made the choice. It would either purify him, or destroy him, and if it did the latter, then it was proof that he was corrupted beyond salvation.

With a quick, strong thrust, Helio plunged the

blade of Silverheart through his abdomen, and he let forth a scream of torment as he channeled Purelight into himself, into his blood and bones, feeling its power burn through him like dragon's fire.

It was dark then; for how long, Gabriel could not remember. But the next time he opened his eyes, they were his own eyes. He felt his brittle, wan skin, and it was his own. He touched his face, feeling the charred scars there, even more pronounced than before. Beside him, lying in the same pool of blood as Gabriel, was the Swordmaster reborn and without injury, radiant in his silver beauty. All that was left of the scars on Skyhan's face was the faintest pearlesque outline, but otherwise he looked angelic. Perfect.

Gabriel knew in that moment that he himself was not perfect. He was everything that had made Skyhan weak, scared, and flawed. Now Skyhan would be none of those things. He had waited until Skyhan came to, expecting the now pure man to do the logical thing with his evil half: run Silverheart through him, obliterating him permanently. But the Knight, apparently, had other plans.

"I do not know the consequences of remaining divided like this," Skyhan had said. "After all, a sword broken in two is not as effective as a whole sword. But a fractured sword can be forged whole again, and there could still be hope for you. Perhaps, now that you are revealed and not intermingled with my soul, you could be cleansed. Go into the world. Help the defenseless, protect the weak. Live by the Knights' Code as I have, and perhaps your corruption will melt away. Once it has, return to me, and Purelight can reunite us, fully purified."

Gabriel had hesitated, looking down at his frail body. "But what if I can't be cleansed? What if I stay like this, no matter what I do?"

The Swordmaster had a hard look on his face. He reached into a leather bag hanging from his belt and withdrew the Mask of Truth. He slipped the mask on, once used to hide his scars, but now it would remain on his face as a symbol for all to see, forever shielding him and those he protected from the darkness. "Then never return. And if you do, I must do what I do with all creatures of evil."

And so, the years had passed, and the nameless half of Skyhan—he certainly could not bear the Skyhan name in his current state, but somewhere along the road, he heard the name "Gabriel" and found that he liked it, so he adopted it—ventured forth, doing what he could to be good and virtuous. It was hard at first since people were repelled by his scars and sallow appearance. Over time, though, he found it became easier, as he developed muscles from doing hard labor on farms in exchange for lodging and food; his frail skin hardened and tanned under the sun; and he found that covering his scars with a hat was enough to make him more approachable. Yet, deep down, he felt like nothing was changing at all—he felt the same as when he started, lost, confused, and alone.

Broken.

"A sword broken in two is not as effective as a whole sword," repeated a voice, but it was that of the High Lady instead of the Swordmaster. "Now do you see? Despite his ambition to be pure, the Swordmaster was not whole. How can half a warrior have hoped to best a creature of complete malevolence as the Distortionist? Therefore, your absence led the Swordmaster to failure."

Gabriel's mind was back in the courtroom. He breathed steadily and gave the High Lady a glare. "It was Skyhan's decision to fight him. His foolishness. Even if we were reunited, there is no saying if the battle would have ended differently. It might have ended sooner, for all I know."

"But then you and the Swordmaster would have suffered the same fate. Why is it fair he should die, and you should live?"

That, Gabriel thought, *is a good question. He should have lived. I should have died.*

Of course, the High Lady could hear his thoughts clearly. "Then you admit your guilt?"

Gabriel lowered his gaze. "What punishment, exactly, do you intend to deal me if I do?"

The High Lady raised her chin a little higher. "Nothing so dire as death. But perhaps a little experimentation would be called for…"

*   *   *

"Stop it! Leave me alone!" Chiriku attempted to fight back, but the human and Falcolin bullies were bigger than she was.

Some Quetzalin girls stood nearby, laughing and saying nasty things at Chiriku. "Half-breed! Freak! She can't be a Quetzalin at all. Probably some Lejenous scum that her mom took pity on."

Nine-year-old Chiriku swug at one of the human

boys, her fist colliding with his nose. It made her feel good to hear the *crack* that resulted from it, and the boy yelped and staggered back as blood trickled out one nostril. "I may be a half-breed, but that means I have strong human arms, not weak Quetzalin ones. Who else wants their beak busted?"

The Falcolin boy tried to restrain her, but they were not used to a Quetzalin knowing how to fight. The same went for her legs as her arms; she had good strong legs and she kicked the Falcolin boy right in the groin, causing him to yelp and fall to his knees. She knew her stepdad would punish her for fighting back. She could hear his voice in her mind: "This is how the world will treat you. Get used to it. Fighting pure-born children would be disgraceful of you. Don't try to be better than you are."

But she didn't care. Her stepdad was a jerk, and someday her real dad would come and take her far away from Syphurius. She wouldn't miss anything here, not even her mother, who never stood up against her stepdad for her. Her mother always just stood there silently with a sad look in her eyes, while he berated Chiriku. She would tuck her in at night and sing her a soft lullaby after her stepdad went to bed...well, maybe Chiriku would miss her a little.

Just as Chiriku was tackled by one of the boys, she heard something pop and the boys let out a disgusted groan. She looked up to see the Falcolin boy drenched in some foul-smelling liquid, as a yellow orb flew through the air and hit the ground right next to where the Quetzalin girls were standing. The orb burst open, spraying them with the same horrible liquid, and they shrieked. The children ran off, leaving Chiriku alone—

although she wasn't alone anymore.

"Hey there, that didn't-ttk look like a fair fight-ttk," came a strange voice. Chiriku looked over to see a teenage human boy, maybe thirteen or fourteen years old, with red hair and freckles. He carried a peddler's pack and wore a simple tunic and a waist wrap that covered the top part of his trousers. He tossed one of the blobby yellow orbs up and down in one hand. "Hope you don't-ttk mind I wanted to get-ttk in on the fun."

"I didn't need your help," Chiriku replied, although not meanly. "What is that stinky stuff?"

"Trust me, you don't-ttk want to know. You okay?"

"I'm fine." She turned to leave, but then she looked back at him. "Why did you help me?"

The boy shrugged. "Where I come from, there's always-ss big fish tryin' to eat-ttk the small fish. I figure, the small fish should look-kk out for each other."

"You talk funny."

"You walk-kk funny."

Chiriku's face flushed underneath her feathers. "I'll give you a broken snout too, if you don't watch it."

"I'm just-ttk messin' with you. The name's Mac-kk." He held out his hand to her for a shake.

Chiriku eyed his hand warily. "You a thief?"

Mac looked positively aghast. "Never, little lady! Mac is as honest a merchant-ttk as you can come by. Cut my heart-ttk out in a fit, drown a beetle in my spit-ttk." He smirked a flashy smile.

"Shame. For a second, I thought you might be interesting."

Mac let his hand drop to his side when he realized Chiriku wouldn't shake it. "You don't-ttk trust a lot-ttk of people, do you?"

"No, I just don't trust weird red-headed boys. But maybe I'd trust you better if you buy me some candied nuts." Chiriku gave him an innocent grin, resorting to her natural child cuteness.

"Ah ha, so that's it-ttk. Feel like-kk you owe me one for helpin' you, but I could use a bit of a snack-kk myself in this heat-ttk."

After Mac bought each of them a treat from a roadside cart, he and Chiriku found a grassy spot in a park to sit and eat. Chiriku figured Mac must have come from the Bayou judging by his dialect, which would mean he came a long way to Syphurius, but he wouldn't be the first bumpkin to come and try to make his fortune in the big city. That meant he was an outsider too. That made her feel a little better.

"So, what do you, you know, do?" Chiriku said. "You said you're a merchant, but do you just sell stink bombs or what?"

Mac finished off his bag of candied nuts with a satisfied *mmmmm*. "Nah, I'm an entrepreneur. I just-ttk sell stuff I pick-kk up along the way to fund my business ventures. And one day, I'm gonna be so rich, I'll...I'll buy this-ss whole city!"

Chiriku giggled. "The whole city, huh? Would that make you mayor, or a king, or what? And can I be your advisor? Because I could tell you all the names of jerks around here you could officially banish and make this city a better place."

Mac laughed, but gradually, his laughter faded as a bothered look shadowed his face. "Hey, Chiriku? I think...something's wrong."

"Huh? What's wrong?" It clicked with her after a

second. "Wait, I didn't tell you my name. Not...yet." A cold feeling wrapped around her, even though it was a glorious sunny day. "You didn't learn my name until you guided me to my grandfather's shop. That's when I told you."

Everything around them seemed odd. The sun suddenly took on a strange, orange-brown tint, like looking at the world through a tea stain. The sounds around them, from the bustling crowds to the music playing from minstrels on street corners, was warped and muffled. This was not right. And somehow, both Mac and Chiriku knew it.

"Mac, what's happening?" Chiriku looked down at herself. Why was she wearing a wool coat on such a hot day? Why was she so tall? She was...sixteen years old. Not nine. She looked over at Mac, who was no longer a teenager, but an adult, also in winter wear. He stared straight ahead, as if lost in thought.

Chiriku tried to make sense of it all. "Where's...oh, where's Dez? And Gabe? Holy harpies, I totally forgot about them for a second! Where are we? Mac?"

The look on Mac's face was etched with growing terror. Whatever he was staring at, Chiriku could not see it...until, far ahead of them, she saw a kind of dark smudge hanging in the air. It began to pulsate, and swirl, and took on the form of a circular violet cloud. It seemed so far away, Chiriku did not feel too concerned at first, until it started to grow. Not just grow, but pull in the space around it; pull in the sunlight, the color, even the sound.

From within the cloud, Chiriku thought she saw small lights, like fireflies. Dread bled into her body as she realized those lights were eyes—dozens of pairs of glowing, yellow and red eyes. A soft, menacing murmuring rumbled from the cloud, someone saying something from a distance, or the echo of a long-lost conversation. Chiriku could not make out the words, and yet she knew they were not words of the Mutual Language, or any of the languages of the Noble Races. It was alien, and it was poisonous to the ear.

"Chi…" Mac's voice was barely audible. "I think-kk I made…a very bad deal…"

There was no more time to try and make sense of this. Chiriku grabbed Mac by the arm and yanked him along as she sprinted in the opposite direction of the cloud. "They're messing with our minds! The elves, they don't just read minds. They're making us hallucinate!"

"Oh." Mac's normally jovial tone was deadpan as he ran alongside Chiriku. "That's-ss a funny thing for them to do…"

"Mac, snap out of it! Now that we're aware, maybe we can break this spell." Without breaking stride, she punched Mac in the cheek.

He stumbled to the side, but regained his footing quickly and kept running. "Ow! What-ttk was that for?"

"I thought maybe pain might wake you up from whatever this is. And if one of us wakes up, maybe we both will."

"You could've just-ttk pinched me! But-ttk if this is all in our minds-ss, how can I even feel pain?"

Chiriku shrugged. "Maybe this is more than a dream."

"Great-ttk. So those damned Darkscale could actually hurt-ttk us, then?"

Chiriku looked behind them, as the violet cloud

continued to expand, to devour everything around them. "How do you know that's Darkscale magic? This can't be a memory. This never happened in Syphurius! The Darkscale Court has never come this far out of the Inbetween. Why are we imagining this?"

Beads of sweat dotted Mac's forehead. "I always knew...they'd find me..."

"Forget it," Chiriku huffed, figuring the elves were clouding Mac's mind so badly, he was saying gibberish. How in Luuva were they supposed to break free of whatever magic the elves were using on them? Desert Rain had a level of immunity to it...if she were here...where was she? Where was anyone? Why did Chiriku always have to fight on her own—

Chiriku...

The voice was so faint, Chiriku nearly missed it with her panicked thoughts raging in her mind. While the city was shattering around her, buildings and trees floating away into nothingness, there was a cool, gentle breeze that enveloped her, lifting her above the disintegrating street as the cobblestones crumbled beneath her.

"Chiriku! This way!" A jovial voice, this time much clearer, called to her from ahead. Chiriku found that she could control which way she floated, and she air-swam towards the voice, pulling Mac along by the arm. Soon, she spotted where the voice was calling from: a large, floating bubble, and inside of it was—

"Woasim?" Chiriku knew none of this could be real, that the snow elves were messing with her mind, but the sight of Woasim gripped her heart with both hope and grief. "Sim, what are you doing here?"

"Hmm, good question. I'm pretty sure I died,

which is kind of strange, but not as scary as you'd think," he replied with no sense of sadness, just an observation. "But Mum thought you needed some help. Navigating this mind magic isn't exactly our specialty, but maybe we can steer you in the right direction."

Chiriku floated up to him. "How? I mean, you're not really here, are you? You're just a…memory."

"I suppose so. But memories can both trap you, and free you. Looks like Mac's having some trouble freeing himself from his bad thoughts, and you got pulled in with him since you share this particular memory." Woasim stroked his chin in thought. "Why don't you come inside and we can think this through, before that demon cloud eats us?"

Chiriku pressed her shoulder against the bubble and discovered she could pass into it easily. She pulled Mac inside the bubble with her, and watched as Syphurius continued to be consumed by the violent Darkscale cloud. "I don't get it. Mac is having some kind of nightmare. Mac? You still with us?"

Mac appeared not to hear her. He stared wide-eyed at the chaos outside the bubble. "I didn't mean for it to go this far…"

"See? He's lost it." Chiriku could not help herself; she let go of Mac and gave Woasim a tight hug. "I know you're not real, but I'm sorry you're gone, Sim. I wish you were really here."

Woasim held the hug a while, but then leaned back and looked her in the eye with a smile. "That's what makes memories so lovely, Chi. Anytime you miss me, just think of me and I'm right there with you. But let's see if we can't find a nicer place to chat, eh?" With his hands, he started to roll the bubble, slowly shifting them away from Mac's nightmare, out into the calm solitude of space.

*   *   *

Desert Rain wrung her fingers together as she stared into the deep, black eyes of the child before her. "Uh, hello. How did I get here? I was in the corridor —"

"I pulled you in here. You were trapped in the Mind Maze, but when the others started focusing on the memories of the Moon Dragoness, they released you for a second, so I was able to sneak you away from them. I'm sure they're wondering how you did that, but they won't find you in here. Do you want to play?" The owl child went over to her toys and selected a couple of stuffed animals. "I never have playmates. You can be Mrs. Pinkley!" She held up a toy, a stuffed snow fox in a pink dress.

Desert Rain tentatively accepted the toy. She puzzled over the child; her first assumption was that she was of Quetzalin blood, but her avian qualities were only from her nose and up. Everything else was human, maybe elven, judging by her slender limbs. The more she thought about it, Desert Rain couldn't remember if she had ever seen an owl-like Quetzalin before. "Are you here all by yourself?"

"This is my room. The others come to check on me sometimes, but I'm not strong enough to leave this room yet." The child started to set up a crystal tea set on the floor.

"Oh. Are you ill?"

"No. I'm a goddess."

Desert Rain paused. She perceived that this wasn't

make-believe or play; she believed the child. "I see."

"I'm Emily. Or it is for now, until they give me a proper goddess name. I just like the name Emily." She started to hum a little melody.

"Well, it's nice to meet you, Emily. I don't suppose you know what's become of my friends?"

Emily nodded. "The elves are keeping them in the Mind Maze for now. But they're probably looking for you. But I won't let them find you. This'll be our secret, Mother."

Desert Rain took a deep breath. "I'm afraid you're mistaken. I'm not your mother. I mean, I don't remember every little thing that happened to me for the past ninety-ish years, but I'm pretty sure I'd remember having a child."

Emily giggled. "I know. I don't think I have parents, not like that. But you're all our mother. And I knew you would come. All I could do is wait, but now you're here and we can free Father too. Do you like tea with or without milk?" She held up a small cream pitcher from her tea set.

"Um, no milk." Desert Rain found it strange that a goddess played with imaginary tea, as nothing was in any of the vessels—could she not summon actual tea and milk? Then again, she did say she was not strong enough yet, nor did Desert Rain know what kind of goddess she might be. "You mentioned a father. Who's he?"

"The nice man with the pretty eyes. He has a dragon inside of him, like you."

"That's Kidran! Do you know where they're keeping him? Is he okay?"

Emily thought about it while taking a sip of imaginary tea. "He's fine, but they're hiding him somewhere I can't see. I don't know how, since I can see everywhere with my Hollow Eye." She held up a bauble that hung from a golden chain around her neck, a palm-sized orb.

Desert Rain walked over and sat down next to her on the floor, placing the stuffed fox among the other animal toys. She observed the peacock-blue Hollow Eye as Emily held it up to her – from within the Eye, there was motion, like a swirling galaxy of blue and green glowing stars. "That's very pretty. Is it magic?"

Emily shrugged. "This is how I knew you were coming. And I know all about that scary Wretched that's been after you. But if you stay here with me, he'll never find you. He's a stinky mean-pants."

Desert Rain couldn't help but smirk at Emily's assessment of Katawa. "Well, I have something magical too. It may help us find Kidran." From her pocket, she withdrew the Darkscale compass. "This can detect Hijn magic. Hopefully the snow elves' magic won't interfere with it. Do you think it will work?"

Emily looked at the compass with wide, awe-filled eyes. "Ooooh, a Darkscale doodad. Spooky! Can I have it?"

Desert Rain bit her lip. It seemed like a bad idea to make a goddess upset. "Yes, if you help me find Kidran. You seem to know how to mask our thoughts from the elves, so I could really use your help to find my friends. I'll give you the compass afterwards if you help me."

Emily clapped her hands together in excitement, but then her joy promptly withered. "But I've never been outside this room, and they say I can't leave yet."

"What would happen to you if you leave too soon?"

Emily shrugged again. "I could poof out of existence. Or lose my immortality. Or they'll send me to bed without dinner."

Desert Rain smiled at her reassuringly. "If anything starts to happen to you once we step outside, we'll come right back in this room. Otherwise, I'll do everything I can to make sure nothing bad happens to you. But it's your choice, Emily. I won't make you do anything you're not ready to do."

The feathers on Emily's head fluffed up as she giggled. "Oh, I do want to go outside! I'm so tired of this room. And once we find Father, then we can be a happy family!"

Desert Rain's heart ached for this girl. Even being a goddess, and having who knew what kind of divine powers, all she wanted was a family like any other child. "Yes, you should have a family. But we have a lot to do. Let's find Kidran and my friends first."

The door to exit was on the far side of the room. Tall, narrow, and carved with spiraling imagery of a winter storm into its ivory surface, there was no doorknob, handle, or keyhole. It appeared to be no more than a decorative panel in the wall. Desert Rain and Emily walked over to it, and Desert Rain attempted to push, then slide the door to no avail. "Do you know how to open this?" she asked.

Emily made one slow blink of her enormous eyes, and in the amount of time it took her to do that, the door vanished, leaving an open exit.

Desert Rain was startled by the sudden disappearance of the door, but she chuckled when she regained her composure. "So that's what they mean by 'in the blink of an eye,'" she said.

Emily frowned at the opening in the wall. "You promise you're not going to let me disappear, right, Mother?"

Desert Rain held out her hand to Emily. "I won't make you go if you're scared, but I promise I'll keep you safe."

Emily accepted Desert Rain's hand, however cautiously, and together, they took a synchronized step outside of the room. They paused, as if waiting to see if Emily would pop like a bubble or simply vanish like the door, but she remained as she was, no hint of corporal disruption. The child made a light squeal of joy and waved her little arms in the air.

"I'm strong enough! I'm strong enough!" she sang to an invented tune. "I'm still here! I'm outside my rooooooom!"

Desert Rain wondered if the whole "can't leave my room" notion was something that the elves had convinced Emily was true, when it wasn't. It simply may have been a means of control. She figured they should still err on the side of caution, however, and keep tabs on how Emily was feeling. "Do you feel all right to keep going?"

"Oh, yes! Let's find Father. Can I hold the compass?"

"Sure." Desert Rain gently handed the compass to the goddess, who flipped it around in her hands to look it over. "But be careful with it. It's delicate. Just hold it flat on your palm, and try to follow the direction that the silver ball inside rolls towards. Is the ball showing you a way to go?"

Emily squinted as she studied the compass, holding it as flat as she could. "Little silver ball...little silver ball…yes! This way!" She grabbed Desert Rain by the sleeve and pulled her with surprising strength, and they took off down the dark, cold hallway.

CHAPTER FOURTEEN
The Snow Elves' Secret; Mac Rattles Some Brains

The crystalline labyrinth extended on for what felt like forever. Desert Rain could not imagine how anyone could find their way through this place, with or without telepathy. Yet Emily maneuvered through the maze with such confidence, it surprised Desert Rain that this was her first time outside of her bedchamber. Or maybe it was just the confidence of a child who did not mind whether they got lost or not – she was enjoying the exploration.

"Are you sure you're following the compass?" Desert Rain asked.

"Uh huh. But now that I'm out here, there are so many voices," Emily said, casting her gaze at the reflective walls.

Desert Rain perked up her ears, listening. She could not hear whatever voices Emily was referring to – they were enveloped in dead silence. "Voices? Where do you hear them coming from?"

"In my head, when they all talk to each other with their minds. Don't worry, I don't think they can hear us. But I hear the lady's voice…oooh, I don't like her very much. But don't tell her I said that."

"The lady?"

"The High Lady. She visits me sometimes. But she's creepy. And she has bad thoughts, sometimes."

"How so? She doesn't hurt you, does she?"

Emily shook her head. "No, but she says someday

I'm going to save everyone, and if I don't, it'll all be my fault. And I know she wants to hurt Father."

Desert Rain felt a chill in her veins. "Hurt Kidran? Why?"

"She got mad at him, real mad. For talking to someone, I think. Another elf from far away. A rainforest elf. She got mad that Father talked to him, so she locked him away."

Desert Rain wiped a hand across her unexpectedly hot forehead. It must have been when Anthron used his Flightspeak spell to reach out to Kidran, when she and her friends were staying in Juka Basin. She had no idea it put Kidran in such danger. "What does the High Lady plan to do with Kidran? Just keep him imprisoned forever?"

Emily stopped walking. She turned to look at Desert Rain, her eyes full of sorrow. "She wants him to...It's something only your mortals do, so I don't understand it. It's when you stop...being. Like that yellow Yopeis-Gichen that was with you before."

Desert Rain's stomach lurched. "Death? Are you saying the High Lady wants to execute Kidran?"

"But she won't until I'm ready to be a goddess. I guess she likes having someone with magic powers around if she needs it."

Desert Rain tried her best to quell the rising panic inside her. *Everything's going to be fine. We're going to rescue Kidran right now. Then we'll find Gabe, Mac, and Chi, and we'll get out of here. Even if the Lightscale really isn't here, at least we'll save Kidran and we'll figure out a new plan of action from here. As long as we can avoid that High Lady and the other elves, we'll be... Grandma Luna, if you have any advice you could give me right now, I'd really like to hear it!*

The corridor ended, and they came upon a wide gallery, the walls lined with what appeared to be ritualistic carvings and engravings in ice and stone. From within the glassy walls, bluish lights bled through to help brighten the room, and the way the lighting shimmered across the walls and floor created the illusion of being underwater. There was no one else around, so Desert Rain and Emily quietly entered the gallery.

Desert Rain marveled at the carvings on the wall, depicting grand scenes of what she imagined must be snow elven history. There was such detail, such artistic passion, such...familiarity. She stopped before one carving that extended from floor to ceiling, and it dawned on her.

"By the divine beasts, I've seen this carving before," she gasped.

The stone carving was of a crescent moon lined with silver and pearls, and beneath the moon was a line of figures in temple garb – priestesses and monks, or perhaps acolytes, their hands extended upwards as if in prayer or ritual. Flying over them, above the moon, was the serpentine, magnificent form of a winged dragoness, her underside lined in faded gold leafing. There were hints that other precious stones might have been part of this carving once — there were small, empty impressions in the surface — but it was unmistakable.

"I have this same carving at home," she said in a half-whisper. "This one is better preserved, but the same exact image is in my house's lower tunnels. How is that possible?"

Emily looked up at the carving. "Oooh, what a pretty picture of Mother!"

Desert Rain turned her head to Emily. She pointed

at the dragon in the carving. "Is that who you mean by Mother? Bellaluna of the Blueshine?" She knew without a doubt that was who the dragoness in the craving was. But why would the Elfë Taigas have the same carving? "Wait a minute…Emily, how much do you know about the snow elves? Would you know why one of their carvings would end up in a temple in the Golden Dragon Desert?"

Emily twisted her lips in thought. "Well, I know the elves didn't always live here. They used to travel around from place to place, and had temples all over Luuva Gros. That was before they started to change."

"Change? Change how?"

Emily paused. She had a worried look in her eye. "I don't think Father wants anyone to know."

Desert Rain knelt to be on eye-level with Emily and gently grasped her by her shoulders. "Emily, this is important. There's a connection here, to Bellaluna. The snow elves must have some history with her. I get the sense they're angry at her about something. When I was in the Mind Maze, when they pulled that memory about her… Maybe if I understand this connection, I can get a better picture of what happened. There can be some reconciliation. Is there anything you know that can help me understand what's going on?"

Emily was quiet at first, but then she nodded. "It was back during the Great Manifestation. Bellaluna told all the Elfë Taigas to come here, to the north, once they started changing. It was because some of the land's wild magic resisted being tamed by the Sages, and it affected some people. She promised she would find a way to help them, to undo the changes. But then she left and never came back. After a long time of being forgotten, the elves were found by the Frost Dragon, who became their new guardian, and then chose Father to be his Hijn when he... stopped being. There's a lot more, but it's all...what's the word the High Lady uses? Com-pli-cate-ered."

Desert Rain furrowed her brow. None of that made sense. Why would Bellaluna promise to help the snow elves with whatever it was, and then abandon them? Did it have to do with the Equanume Balance splitting? Either way, it explained why the elves seemed to both respect Luna and were furious with her at the same time. She used to be their guardian Sage.

"Thank you, Emily. Once we find Kidran, maybe we can think of a way to make things right by everyone." Desert Rain stood up and took Emily by the hand as they walked through the gallery. "Although...hmm, how strange. He really was wrong."

Emily tilted her head at her. "Who?"

Desert Rain shook her head. "Nothing, it's just...when Swordmaster Skyhan..." Her thoughts drifted, the memory of him still tugging at her heart. "When he saw this carving at my house, he completely misjudged it. Which was strange, for him. I have no idea where he got the idea—"

"That it was bad?"

Desert Rain stopped in her tracks. She gave Emily a long, puzzled stare. "How do you know he thought that?"

Emily bit her lip. She looked down at the floor. "Father wouldn't want me to tell..."

"Emily, I need to know the truth. No one will be mad at you. But... Skyhan thought the carving was of Secret Sacroth design. Do you know what the Secret Sacroth are?"

Emily would not look up at her.

"They're one of the three Courts of the Wretched. The Secret Sacroth are demons. Why would Skyhan believe that? Why would he get this carving confused with them?"

Emily dropped the compass and put her hands over her face, shaking her head violently. "Father doesn't want anyone to know! I can't tell! I can't tell!"

Desert Rain held Emily close, stroking her feathered hair. "Shh, it's okay. I'm sorry. I shouldn't have pushed you. I'm sure there's a reasonable, perfectly logical…"

Suddenly, King Ragnor's words echoed in her mind. *Dragons speed, Mother of the Wretched!*

Why did Emily insist on calling her — calling Bellaluna — Mother? When everything she knew, she had learned from the snow elves…the elves who had purposely cut themselves off from the outside world and no one had any idea what they truly…

Oh no. Oh, Guerda-Shayler, no.

Before she could even process this horrible truth, the silence of the gallery was disrupted by what sounded like a chorus of ghostly wailing from beyond the walls, all around them but somehow far away, a blood-freezing echo. Emily dropped the compass and covered her ears, letting out a painful, surprised cry. "That noise! It hurts! Is this death?" she screamed, tears rolling down her face.

Desert Rain held Emily close, trying to calm her. She strained to hear what was causing such pain, but she sensed it was not a physical sound. "By everything in the Eternal Deep, what now?"

* * *

"Have you tried pinching yourselves?" Woasim asked hopefully.

"Pinching? She punched me in the face-ss!" Mac said, having regained his senses now that they floated far away from his destructive nightmare, and they hung in the quiet, star-scattered night sky, high above the world. He sat cross-legged in the bubble, arms crossed. "And it smarted, by the by."

"Besides, I think all that would do is confirm if we were dreaming or not," Chiriku added. "If all this is elf magic, how are we supposed to break free of it? How do we know we can't seriously hurt ourselves in this illusion? Like, what happens if this bubble pops and we all fall thousands of miles to our deaths? Do our brains just go splat?"

Woasim chuckled. "I'm not going to let the bubble pop, silly."

"Well, *he* popped one of your sky-boat bubbles and set the whole thing on fire," the Quetzalin replied, jutting her thumb at Mac. "Who knows what else he can totally ruin?"

Mac grimaced, but he tucked his hands under his armpits, as if his slightest touch might cause another calamity.

Woasim tapped a finger to his lips. "Hmmm, totally ruin, eh? Maybe we could use a talent like that. Like I always say…er, said…even a foul wind can bring you a blessing, if you know which way it's blowing."

Chiriku and Mac exchanged a look. "How?" the bird girl asked.

Woasim grinned. "Mac, if you needed to break someone's concentration, how would you do it?"

The lizard man cocked an eyebrow, but then he smiled. "Ahh. I figure you mean, *really* break-kk someone's concentration. As in, a real brain-rattler. That reminds-ss me of the time I was cornered by this pack-kk of bobcat-ttk bandits deep in the Bayou, big hairy brutes that smelled like day-old rotting meat-ttk, and all I had on me was-ss a blade of grass-ss and a comb—"

"Is there a point to this, Mac?" Chiriku huffed.

Mac stood up and rummaged through his many pockets, until he found and withdrew a small, brass whistle. "I know she doesn't-tkk look like much, but boy, you can hear this baby for miles. I used to sell these to kids-ss at festivals-ss until their parents-ss told me they were drivin' them crazy."

"Driving them crazy, that's perfect!" Woasim rubbed his hands together. "And I'll create a current that'll send it in all directions. This whole 'in the mind' stuff is new to me, but Mum says there are currents in the brain as much as in the breath."

Chiriku crinkled the corner of her beak. "Are you serious? How is a whistle supposed to free us from—"

"Uh, Chi?" Mac gave her a wink. "You might-tkk want to cover your ears."

Woasim cupped his hands and blew into them, and a churning ball of wind formed, spinning like a small tornado on his fingers. He then carefully maneuvered it over to hover over Mac's head. "Okay, let 'er rip!"

Chiriku covered her ears, not expecting much, but her eyes shot open and her beak clenched hard as Mac brought his lips to the whistle, and a shrill *screeeeeee* like a million boiling tea pots shrieking, on top of a flock of distressed starlings trilling, and a chorus of banshees wailing, escaped from the unassuming little tube.

The whirling ball of air over Mac's head shot out in all directions as tendrils of small cyclones, carrying the ear-piercing sound with them, spreading it louder and louder until Chiriku thought the whole sky might crack. But instead of cracking, the sky around them grew foggy, then lighter, and she could already feel like she was being released from a deep sleep. She could even feel it now, like some unseen hand that had been clamped tight on her head, was now being lifted.

She quickly reached out and grabbed Woasim for one last hug. "Sim, thanks. We all miss you, real badly."

Woasim hugged her back, his touch already fading as she pulled away from the enchantment. "Chi, Mum has something to ask you... soon..."

Chiriku's arms were empty. She was curled up inside a cold room, although calling it a room was generous since there was barely any of it. It was hard to see, as there was no direct light, but after a few minutes of letting her eyes adjust to the darkness, she could make out she was in a hexagonal-shaped space. As she tried to rise, her head hit the ceiling before she could fully stand up. She was surrounded by ice on three sides, but one wall was a more opaque, differently textured substance. She scratched a fingernail on the odd wall, as some of the white, pliant material peeled off easily.

"Is that...wax?" She pushed against it, but even though there was some bend to the wall, she was sealed in by the wax. She sat back down on the floor and with all her strength, she kicked repeatedly at the wax wall. With each kick, a little more of the wall gave way, until she finally broke through, and pieces of wax thudded to the floor outside her cell.

"Guess these human legs are good for something

after all." She climbed out of her cell, standing up straight and dusting herself off. There was more light out here, in this wide cavernous space, but what she could see clearly now mystified her. All along the wall beside her cell, and along every wall in the cavern, were rows upon rows of hexagon cells sealed up with white wax. Looking around, she got the impression she was looking at a design similar to…honeycomb?

"Mac!" She darted her gaze back and forth along the row of cells, but nothing indicated who or what might be in each cell. She picked the one immediately to her right, tapping lightly on the wall. "Mac? You in here? Say something if you can hear me."

From the cell on the opposite side, to her left, came some muffled words. She walked over to it and could tell that was Mac's panicking voice through the wax. She remembered now, he hated tight spaces. "Just kick the wall out, Mac! It's wax. Kick towards the sound of my voice!"

There was a pause, followed by a few *thump, thump, thumps* against the wax, but the wall was hardly budging. Chiriku instinctively reached for the sheath on her back but found nothing there. Those darn elves swiped her warhammer! She scanned the room, looking for anything that might indicate where they took her weapon, but that would have to wait. Mac was sounding more and more rattled as he kicked the wax wall and was not making progress. Chiriku, flustered, stepped back several paces, readied her shoulder, and barreled straight into the wall, making a good, cracked dent. Having weakened the wax, a few more kicks from Mac freed him, as he spilled out with the broken wax pieces onto the floor.

"Thanks, Chi. Where are we?" Mac looked around, cocking an eyebrow. "These elves-ss have a strange sense of architecture, don't-ttk they?"

Suddenly, all around them, they heard the high-pitched echoes of pain and panic coming from somewhere deep in the caverns, beyond this cave.

"I think we made the elves mad," she whispered, nudging Mac.

Mac slowly stood up, shaking off the last bits of the magic stupor. "Oh, wow, that really was all in our heads-ss, wasn't-ttk it?"

"We better move fast while they're distracted. I need to find my hammer. It's got to be around here somewhere."

Mac tapped Chiriku on the shoulder. "Uh, Chi? What's that-ttk?"

Far across the cavern, there was an archway, and from it came a pulsating teal light. There was also a moaning sound of anguish, and what sounded like a quick series of rapid tinkling, like glass tapping glass. A slow shadow passed across the light, and then a high wail emanated, so high that it set Chiriku's feathers on end.

Mac scrunched up his face with a terrified, unintended smirk. "Let's-ss not-ttk go that way."

"I think we have to. I don't see another way out of here. You got anything on you that we can use to defend ourselves?"

Mac patted his trouser pockets — apparently, the elves had found no reason to strip him of his various trinkets, since nothing seemed dangerous; either that or they figured he was harmless after reading his mind — and found the same brass whistle he had used in his dreamscape. "Funny that-ttk! I didn't just-ttk make-kk up that I had this thing. Bet it works-ss just as well on elves out here, as it did in here." He tapped the whistle to the side of his head.

"Great. Now shut it." She crept quietly across the floor, stealthily making her way over to the archway, with Mac following close behind her. They slid up to the doorway with their backs to the wall, and Chiriku, who was closer to the archway than Mac, peeked carefully around the corner to investigate the next room.

The blue-green light was coming from a massive crystal orb growing from a wall. The room had several crystal pillars throughout, all radiating a pulsing light, but the orb overpowered everything else. There were six pedestals, each with a marble orb on top, positioned in a half-circle around the glowing orb. The room appeared empty at first, but then Chiriku realized someone was in there — in the orb. Floating inside in what looked like a viscous liquid, was an unconscious...

"Gabe!" Chiriku forgot stealth and shot into the room, running for the orb. "Mac, help me find my hammer. We can use it to smash the—"

She was cut off as something from behind one of the pillars snagged her ankle, causing her to fall forward onto her stomach. Snapping her head around to look, she gasped as a gnarled, white hand grasped at her trouser leg. Mac made a beeline for her and stomped on the assailing hand which instantly released her. He leaned over to help Chiriku stand up, but then he caught full sight of what was causing the Quetzalin to stare, paralyzed in place.

It was an elf. Sort of. Some features were there — pointed ears, angular face, delicate pale skin and lips—

but the eyes…huge, protruding, glittering like they were made of thousands of tiny jewels. The head was bald, but a bizarre soft fuzz covered its body from the chest down to the hideous, bulbous, furry abdomen on the back end. And that tinkling noise? It came from two sets of thin, crystalline wings, shaped like an insect's, jutting out from its shoulder blades. Under its long, gaunt arms was another set of matching arms — four spindly arms in all.

The snow elf — that was not an elf — hissed at them with a mouth full of black, pointy teeth.

There was not much else for Mac and Chiriku to do in that situation other than the obvious — scream.

CHAPTER FIFTEEN
Uncovering Kidran

Desert Rain noticed, after a few minutes, that the tension in Emily's body subsided, and her crying dwindled to sniffling. "Emily? Is the pain gone? Are you all right?"

Emily continued to hold Desert Rain in a hug and nodded. "I think so. The sound stopped."

"What sound was it? Was it one you could only hear in your mind?"

Emily nodded again. "Uh huh. It was really loud. And now I can't hear any voices."

Desert Rain wondered what it all meant. Clearly, whatever Emily had "heard," the snow elves — whatever they were now — must have heard it too and it quieted them. Maybe that sound even prevented their mind magic from working. "Maybe it was something Kidran did," she suggested.

"I don't think so," Emily replied. "But it's so quiet now, I can't hear... there's something else. We should go this way."

Desert Rain retrieved the compass from the floor. "Don't you want to check the compass — "

Emily was already walking, as if compelled by a will not her own, towards an exit of the gallery. It seemed as logical as anything to trust a goddess's intuition, so Desert Rain followed her.

Down more frozen corridors, past more quiet rooms, Desert Rain was growing increasingly unnerved by how empty this bastion seemed to be. Shouldn't they have run into someone by now? There was more than enough indication of inhabitants — they came across what looked like a dining hall, grand with all its ice sculptures, ivory furniture and fur-and-wool tapestries, but it looked like it had been untouched for ages. Another room revealed what might have been a communal bathing spot of some sort, with marble tubs, soft mats, and piping that looked like it might have pumped in warm water from somewhere, but it too was barren, a petrified picture in time.

Eventually, the corridor ended, and the sight before them filled Desert Rain with serene awe. A city plaza stretched out through the cavern, with ice-carved gardens of crystal lotuses and flowered trees, marble and howlite-cobbled walkways, and an ornate fountain of milky quartz designed with a great dragon head atop, which would have spat spring water if the fountain was functioning. It was every bit as beautiful as the plazas in Syphurius, as it shimmered in the strange aquamarine light that glowed all around through the ice.

"Do you know where we are now?" Desert Rain asked.

"I think this used to be an important place," Emily replied. "Like, the heart of a city. But no one comes here anymore. Except that."

She pointed up to the top of the fountain, where Desert Rain realized a white bird, a snow bunting, was sitting. It was so still and blended so well with the fountain, Desert Rain had assumed it was part of the architecture. But it blinked its blue eyes and tilted its head curiously at them.

Desert Rain slowly approached the fountain,

staring at the bird. She realized its eyes weren't blue; they were a unique shade of turquoise, just like...

"It's one of Kidran's snowbirds!" she realized. She recalled he had brought some with him at the last Hijn Council meeting; all his birds possessed his eye color, because he could see and hear things through them, like his own stash of spies. He must have managed to sneak this bird past the elves, to be his eyes and ears while he was imprisoned. She looked down at the compass in her hands; the silver ball inside was hovering right in the direction of the bird. "That's what the compass was picking up on. The bird is imbued with Kidran's magic. Maybe he knew someone would come help him, and this bird is meant to lead us to him."

Emily cooed lightly to the bird, which flittered down and rested on her outstretched hand. "Of course that's why he's here. And now he can take us to find Father." She cooed again, and the bird took flight, heading towards a facade carved in the wall that looked like the front of a town hall or a guild house, with fluted columns and arched window lattices designed in snowflake patterns. The bird flew through the open doorway into the shadow-soaked structure, and the Hijn and goddess cautiously followed it inside.

"Do you have any idea why the elves..." Desert Rain paused, unsure how to even refer to them anymore. "Why *they* don't live in this part of the city anymore?" She was using the conversation to steady her nerves as they walked through the un-lit guild house. The only light to guide their way came from Kidran's snowbird, who gave off an aura of shining white as it flitted from room to room.

"They moved lower into the glacier. To hide."

Emily's voice was nonchalant.

Desert Rain hoped that was a good sign; if one of the elves were nearby, surely Emily would sense that and let her know. "Because of…what they've become?"

"Uh huh."

"Will they hurt us, if they find us looking for Kidran?"

"Not me. And I won't let them hurt you, Mother. Or Father."

Desert Rain was seriously beginning to wonder what she was going to do with this child. What would this goddess do once they got out of here, *if* they could get out of here? Was Emily expecting herself, Desert Rain, and Kidran to be a family after all this? How do you even care for a goddess? Would any of them, or Luuva Gros itself, even still exist if they couldn't stop Katawa and his Distorted from defiling everything?

"You really worry too much," Emily said dryly.

Desert Rain frowned. "Please don't read my mind without my permission."

"If you don't want me hearing your thoughts, don't think so loudly."

The Hijn wondered how she was supposed to think quieter, but then had another thought. "If Kidran is in here, why can't you read his mind? How are the elves containing him so he can't use his magic?"

"With that."

The snowbird had led them to a high room far in the back of the guild house, inside of which was a pyramid that looked to be made from pure silver, that reached from floor to ceiling and was almost as wide as the room itself. The bird alighted atop the pyramid, looking down at them expectantly. The bird's aura reflected off the silver surface, giving it a white sheen.

Desert Rain approached the silver pyramid cautiously. She noticed an emblem engraved on the side of the pyramid facing her; five open eyes placed along a ring, and in the middle of the ring were three connecting spirals. The symbol of the Secret Sacroth. She had seen it in one of her books at home.

"Well, you going to open it?" Emily asked.

Desert Rain looked back at her. "Open it? I don't even know what 'it' is."

"Silver is a metal that blocks psychic powers," Emily explained. "They use cells like this as holding rooms for traitors and criminals. Although they really tried to hide this one. I really hope someone's been coming to bring Father food and stuff. I don't know since I can't hear his thoughts yet. The bird's not being very clear on that."

"Wait, Kidran's inside this thing? How does it open? I don't see a door." Desert Rain knocked on the side. "Couldn't you make the pyramid disappear, like you did with the door to your room?"

Emily concentrated on the pyramid, blinking a few times, and then shook her head. "Guess my powers don't work on silver yet. But you could open it."

"How? There's no…" Desert Rain understood what Emily was saying. "Oh. You know what my magic can do. Then you also know there's a 50-50 chance, or more chance than that, my powers could also affect Kidran by accident. My control of my magic isn't… great."

Emily shrugged. "I thought you wanted to get Father out. I can't do it, so you have to."

Desert Rain took a deep breath and exhaled

slowly. Maybe since Kidran was inside the pyramid, he would be safe from the Blueshine. All she needed to do was affect the outside. She carefully placed her hands on the pyramid, closing her eyes. *Just concentrate. Don't think hard about it. You can do this. Just like with Woasim's chains.* Instantly, hot tears swelled under her eyelids. *Oh, Woasim... I messed up. I messed up so badly... you're dead because of me...*

Ooooh, Dez! How beautiful! I never knew you could do that! You're amazing!

Something about remembering Woasim's words renewed her resolve. Focus on that. Focus on that moment. Remember how you felt when you were doing it right.

I like Desert Rain. I wish you would, too. Because Desert Rain is the best.

Was Emily pulling these memories up in her mind? Desert Rain wasn't sure; the memories seemed so strong now. And it made her feel confident. Stronger. Powerful. She didn't even feel a chill in her arms and fingers — it felt like a cool, flowing river, like a gentle spring shower healing a drought, like...

"Desert Rain?"

She opened her eyes to see someone else's — bright turquoise — staring at her from the other side of the glass wall in front of her. Then there was an abrupt *smash* as the glass broke. There was no more silver pyramid; she had transformed the entire cell into glass, and realized that Emily had come over beside her and flicked the glass, causing it to shatter. Kidran covered his head from the raining glass, but strangely, the glass did not break into sharp shards — when the pyramid broke, it turned into bluish sand. While a good deal of it dumped onto him, it was no more dangerous than someone having poured a bucket of shore sand onto his head.

Emily looked up at Desert Rain with a funny grin. "That was fun!"

Desert Rain smirked. "Did you do that? Turn the glass into sand?"

Emily shook her head. "Nope. Glass is made of sand. When you accept the magic more willingly, it simplifies."

"I don't understand. How could I have done this, when I haven't even spoken dragon-tongue…" It dawned on Desert Rain, as she said that, that it was not the first time she had managed Blueshine without speaking the incantation. When she had used it on Katawa, she hadn't said a word. But all Hijn had to use dragon-tongue or specific gestures to summon Hijn magic. How could she…?

Kidran brushed the sand from his hair and clothes, a faded brown tunic and trousers. His feet were bare, and the usual cloak of furs he wore to keep himself warm had been stripped from him. He looked gaunt and ashen, the light hue of pink in his alabaster skin faded to gray. But his eyes were still bright, still hopeful. "Desert Rain? Thank the Divine Beasts, the Council sent you! And…you…" He looked down at Emily with amazement. "You left your room."

"Hello, Father." Emily went to him and gave him a hug around the waist. "I knew Mother would come to help me rescue you."

"Kidran, are you all right?" Desert Rain tried to inspect him as Kidran's bird landed on his shoulder, radiating some light over him. "How long have you been in there? Have you even been fed or given water? Did they hurt you at all?"

Kidran smiled warmly. "I'm fine. These silver cells suspend one in time, so to speak. One can go for months, even years, without food or water while inside one. Although now that I'm out, it's all catching up to me." His stomach gurgled in confirmation.

Emily blinked a few times, and a plush fur coat and thick boots formed on him, and a hot cup of cocoa appeared in his now gloved hand. He jumped in surprise at the sudden fabrications on his person, but then grinned at Emily. "Thank you. But how did you two get here? Are the other Hijn here as well? The last thing I heard from the outside world was from Anthron..."

"Yes, and that was weeks ago, maybe over a month at this point." Desert Rain was horrified to think of how long Kidran had been prisoner, essentially in a state of living death. "But now that we found you, I need to find my friends. They're lost in here somewhere. Do you have any idea where the Secr..." She caught herself, not knowing how to broach the awful truth with Kidran. He must know; but Emily said he didn't want anyone else to know. Would he be angry?

Kidran's eyes shot wide open. His shock slowly decayed into sadness. "You know."

"*I* didn't tell her," Emily insisted. "She figured it out."

Kidran sighed, running his fingers through his pale hair. He was pensive, closing his eyes momentarily before opening them again. "I suppose it was inevitable. I'm not sure how the rest of the Council will react to this. Are any of them here? Do they know?"

"There is a lot to catch you up on," Desert Rain said. "But no, it's only me and my three friends. And I will not reveal this to anyone until you are ready. But I must ask...are you... too?"

Kidran tightened his lips. "I...I'm not entirely sure, to be honest. I hope my Hijn magic has kept the corruption at bay, but the elves' transformation began deep down, underneath. It may not have surfaced in me yet. I cannot say."

Desert Rain went to Kidran and placed a hand on his shoulder. "Forgive me. It wasn't my place to ask, and no matter what the answer, you're my friend. It changes nothing. But I must find the others. Where do the Secret Sacroth dwell now, if not in the city?"

Kidran's face grew grim. "Desert Rain, this place is not what it once was. And where you want to go is dangerous. I will guide you there, but neither my magic, nor maybe even yours, may be able to protect us."

"What about me? I'll protect you!" Emily said with a grin.

Desert Rain grinned. "We do have an advantage, having a goddess on our side."

Kidran smirked. "Valid point. She is still so young though, and she has never been outside her room. And the High Lady is..." He swallowed hard and took a sip of cocoa to steady himself. "Okay. I'll take you. To the Crystal Court."

*   *   *

Gabriel slowly opened his eyes. He felt the harsh chill in his skin and bones, and when he tried to move his arms, there was resistance. He realized there was tubing in his nostrils and mouth, permitting him to breathe while being submerged in this strange viscous liquid, which clouded his sight with a hazy blue. He was not sure how he got there; one moment he was in the Crystal Court, and suddenly there had been an ear-shattering shriek that had thrown the entire court into convulsing screams and agony. Then, in an instant, he was here in this ooze, almost as if the shriek had woken him from a dream. Or was *this* a dream?

All Gabriel could figure was he needed to get out of whatever this was, immediately. He tried to move again, and while it was slow going, he found he could push himself upwards. After several struggling pushes, he managed to bring his head above the gel, and he spat out the tube in his mouth. Now he could hear the voices clearer, although he was still inside a glassy crystal closure of some kind.

"You stay away, now," resounded a familiar Bayou-accented voice, "or I'll blow this-ss here whistle again, I will!"

A pained shriek answered the threat, unworldly and inhuman. Gabriel freed his hand from the goop so he could yank the tubing from his nose, as he spat out some traces of blue goo from his mouth. "Mac, that you?" he called.

"Gabe!" Chiriku's call gave Gabriel relief. "Hang on, I'll get you out. Where'd you put my hammer, bug face?"

There was a warped, fuzzy sensation in Gabriel's head — the words *No, you cannot free him!* flashed across his mind — but it was faint, and it dissipated as quickly as it had formed. Mac and Chiriku were out there with someone, one of the snow elves, but it must be too weak to use its magic to full effect. Gabriel looked about his prison for a way out, a hatch or a door. How had he gotten inside here in the first place?

He did not contemplate the question too long, however, before he heard a loud smash in front of him. The crystal prison shattered open, and Gabriel spilled out along with the blue gel. A marble ball about the size of a cantaloupe rolled on the floor beside him, as it tracked a line of goo. Gathering his wits, he looked up to see Chiriku standing next to a marble pedestal, one of six that each had marble orbs atop them—except for the one she stood at, for she had used its orb to smash open the prison.

"Are you all right? What did these freaks do to you?" Chiriku helped him up, and Gabriel could see Mac was trying to keep a strange, insect-like monster at bay, wagging a copper whistler at it. The creature shirked away from the whistle, covering its ears with its frail hands.

"What in Luuva..." Gabriel could barely comprehend the creature writhing on the ground, with its humanoid face but huge compound eyes. But then he recalled the Crystal Court, the sharp chins and pale skin of the otherwise masked faces, and the familiarity hit him. "Wh...what happened here?"

"This nasty took-kk us prisoner, but-ttk we showed 'em!" Mac said. "They don't-ttk like loud noises. Wait-ttk 'til the snow elves find out what-ttk be living in here, they'll want-ttk to hire some pest-ttk control!"

"No, Mac." Gabriel stared long and hard at the bug-like beast. "I believe...that *is* a snow elf."

"Are you crazy? That thing?" Chiriku frowned, narrowing her eyes. "There's no way. We saw a snow elf, and she looked nothing like that!"

"It's the mind magic. They made us see what they wanted us to see." Gabriel wrung the blue gunk from his clothes, and he sniffed at it. "What is this, alchemical slime?"

Soul nectar, a faint voice echoed in his mind again. Given how all three of them turned to look at the elven insect, Mac and Chiriku must have heard the voice too. The snow elf, his wings shivering with an icy tinkling, was still prone on the ground, but slowly he was getting his wits back. *It allows us to understand certain properties of one's soul. Namely, how you were able to split yours in half.*

"What's he talking...er, *thinking* about?" Chiriku asked. "What does he mean, split your soul in half?"

The elf stared intently with his many, many eyes at Gabriel. *If the Swordmaster was able to purge you from his soul and body, then perhaps the process could be replicated. We can purge the wickedness from our beings. The High Lady will not let you leave until you divulge this information.*

Gabriel narrowed his eyes. "Skyhan did that, not me. I never asked for it. And without Silverheart and Purelight, it can't be done again."

The elf grinned its horrible black teeth. *Ah, but the great demon-slaying sword is here, within the Hive. And perhaps we lack Purelight, but there is a celestial dragon's power here. If we combine your memories with what she can provide, perhaps we can claim salvation.*

It dawned on Gabriel who was missing, as he looked back and forth between Chiriku and Mac. "Where's Desert Rain? She's not with you?"

Chiriku, concern etched into her face, shook her head. "Mac and I woke up in those strange cells, but I don't think Dez was in any of them. I don't know where she is."

Gabriel advanced on the elf, his face twisting into an enraged grimace. "Where did you take her? What have you done to her?"

"Tell us where Gila is-ss, or I'll blow again!" Mac threatened. "The whistle, I mean."

The elf shrunk away, instinctively covering his ears with his hands. *The Moon Dragoness is fine. She escaped our grasp, but even now she makes her way to the Crystal Court and the High Lady. There she will face true judgement, and we will take her penance that we are due.*

"Take us there!" Gabriel demanded. "To the Court, the real one. No illusions."

Chiriku poked Gabriel in the shoulder. "Gabe, we can't trust these guys. Any second, they could start using their magic on us again, and we wouldn't even know it."

Mac took Chiriku by the hand. "We just-ttk need to make-kk sure we stick together like moss on a log, Chi. And if you think-kk they start-ttk messin' with us, you let-ttk me know and I'll be the whistle-blower, okay?"

The elf frowned, but slowly steadied himself on his fragile arms and legs. *It is just as well. It is as the High Lady orders. Follow me.*

*   *   *

The true Crystal Court was nothing like the illusion Gabriel had been presented with during his interrogation. He, Chiriku, and Mac stood at the edge of a round hole deep within a lower cavern, where not even the eerie blue lights radiating in the glacier walls could reach. The hole was fifty feet in diameter, and from within it came a clattering of hundreds of tinkling glass wings. A strange, eerie white glow came from below to illuminate what was inside, and as the three of them braved to look, they saw tiers of honeycomb—or ice-comb, in this case—extending down, down, down, farther than they could see to the bottom.

And hundreds — thousands — of Secret Sacroth swarmed the hive.

"Oh, Divine Beasts save us-ss," Mac gasped, as his scales paled.

"Look!" Chiriku said in a tense but hushed tone, not wanting to disturb the hive. She pointed to the other side of the hole, where three figures were standing.

Gabriel did not recognize two of them — a little girl and a spectral-looking man — but the sight of the third filled him with relief. "Dez!"

Desert Rain perked up her ears, spotting her friends on the other side. She instantly brightened, waving to them. "Gabe! Chi, Mac! Are you well?"

Kidran immediately grabbed her waving hand and lowered it. "Reunions can come later," he said with quiet warning. "We must tread lightly now that we are in her presence."

Emily clung tightly to Desert Rain's trouser leg. "It's the bad lady," she said softly.

As if hearing Emily's words — which there was no doubt she did — up from the bowels of the hive arose a grand, glittering, gruesome beast. Its green-glass wings were nearly as long as the hole was wide, attached to a bulky writhing thorax and abdomen that were striped in pearl and storm-gray. The magnesium-white glow emitted from its tail end like a glow worm, shining a terribly cold radiance about the cavern. At the top of this monstrous form was a head bursting with silken spider-thread hair trailing down the length of the body, two long hooked antennae, and compound eyes like pieces of mirror, reflecting all she saw. A set of sharp, jagged mandibles grew from the thin-lipped mouth like a set of curved fangs. Six arms, each ending in a clawed skeletal hand, fanned out from her body.

Bad is an unfair assessment, echoed a warped voice in all their minds. *Even a goddess must learn respect, for without your believers, you are quite literally nothing.*

Mac nearly swallowed his tongue, his eyes bulging out of their sockets. Chiriku stared in disbelief, unable to think of a single snarky thing to say. Gabriel did all he could to calm his racing heart, breathing slowly. He glanced back at Desert Rain across the way — he had expected more shock, fear, or disgust on her face, but she appeared tranquil, if not a little anxious. Had she already known what the snow elves had become? Was the man standing next to her...wait, some vague memory was coming back to him, from his old life, from Helio's life...*Kidran*...

Kidran turned his gaze away from the High Lady to look over at Gabriel. He stared intensely at the human, as if searching for something. After a moment, a quick slip of a thought entered Gabriel's mind: *We'll talk later.*

"High Lady of the Elfë Taigas," Desert Rain spoke, her voice remaining calm but her ears shivering. "May we speak on friendly terms? As allies?"

The High Lady turned her eyes to Desert Rain, although her expression was pure ice, a mask of indifference. *You know our horrible truth now. You know what we have become. And yet, you extend friendship? To the Secret Sacroth, of the same ilk of Wretched that your people so deeply despise? This is not genuine. You do so out of fear.*

Desert Rain shook her head. "No, your grace. I extend it as someone who wishes to understand your pain. I know what it's like to hide away in a wasteland because of how the world changes you, because of fear of what harm we might be capable of—"

You cannot comprehend the pain we have endured. You may think you do, because of how your Hijn magic has transformed you, but you have never been reviled and persecuted as we have. If Bellaluna had used her powers when the Great Manifestation first began, she could have spared us this fate.

"I...I don't believe Luna's powers could have..." Desert Rain paused, taking a breath. "If there was a possibility that Luna could have prevented this, I am positive she would have. But whatever may have happened back then, I want to help you now. All we ask is for your alliance in return. All Luuva Gros is in great peril—"

Your quest is futile. The High Lady hovered closer to Desert Rain, her eyes reflecting hundreds of the Hijn woman's face in their mirrored surface. *Even if you were to discover the Lightscale, your brokenness would never allow you to awaken its abilities. We prayed such a device would be our salvation, but without a celestial Sage to operate it, it was useless to us. And then, it was stolen.* At this, the High Lady turned her sour gaze to Kidran. *His dragon smuggled it away, bestowing it to another. Ever since, the Lightscale has been lost to time.*

Desert Rain turned to Kidran, whose face was unreadable. "Kidran, why would the Frost Dragon do that?"

Kidran's brows furrowed. "Wintermane did not tell me his reasons before I acquired his spirit. But the Equanume was a machine of immense power. Since the Darkscale possessed one half of the Balance, having the other half owned by another clan of Wretched would be disastrous. I can only surmise he didn't want to risk the Courts of the Wretched gaining full control of such a machine."

Do you see? So quickly were we condemned because of what we had become, at no fault of our own! And now this traitor risks exposing our secret to the outside world, conversing with our forest brethren, luring you here. He can no longer be trusted.

Kidran raised his chin in defiance. "I kept our secret secured all this time, but where has it gotten us? I want to bring our people the help they need. But every time I wanted to address our circumstance to the Hijn Council, you—"

We only allowed you to hold place in that council to keep up appearances. So you could uphold the illusion that the Elfë Tiagas were untainted and strong. If you revealed us, they and the Knighthood would have come to destroy us.

"You don't know that!" Kidran's face reddened, but he restrained himself. "You have become so steeped in your illusions, you have lost your grasp on reality."

I say what is reality. Besides, we no longer require a Hijn for our protection, now that we have constructed our own divine source. The High Lady's eyes shifted to Emily. *This one will be far more powerful than any Hijn, once she comes to fruition. Allowing her out of her room before she is fully developed endangers us all. She will be returned to her quarters until I deem her ready. And you and your companions shall be put to use, serving the Crystal Court, for the rest of your pathetic lives.*

"No! I'm not going back to my room!" Emily shouted, indignant. "You said I would poof away if I left my room. You lied!"

Desert Rain placed a comforting arm around

Emily to quiet her. She again spoke to the High Lady. "I understand your anger, but you can't punish others for what was done to you. If you do not desire to help us, then let us leave. We won't divulge your secret. We will do everything we can to find a way to reverse your transformation. If we find the Lightscale, maybe we can figure out how to make it work to help your people."

The High Lady clacked her black mandibles, a threat. *If you truly wish to help us, then you will have your divided companion reveal to us how he split himself, dispelling his baser half from his noble half. If we can replicate the process, then we can dispel this wickedness from our bodies and souls as well.*

"My divided...what are you talking about?"

Instantly, a vision entered her mind. It was hazy, like recalling a dream. Was that Mage Skyhan talking to her? But she was speaking to someone else...who was Helio? Desert Rain realized it wasn't a dream, but a memory—not a memory of her own, but someone else's. Did Mage Skyhan just say "brother"?

She suddenly heard Gabriel let out a terrified yell. "Stop, STOP! Don't show this to them! Leave it be!!"

But the memory continued. Desert Rain felt her heart rip as she heard a familiar voice, that of a man she had once idolized, a man she had watched die. *"There is darkness in me, I sense it! All this training, all this suffering, what good is it if I am not pure of heart? How can I overcome evil if it infects my soul? There must be a way to purify it, there must!"*

Desert Rain was still aware of her surroundings, and as she looked between Kidran, and across the way to Chiriku and Mac, she could see their facial expressions change from confused, to stunned, to horrified. And she, too, was horrified as the memory shifted to another moment, as the Swordmaster plunged Silverheart through his body. She could even feel the residual pain, the echo of the blade and magic searing through skin and muscle. *Guerda-Shalyr! Why??*

The aftermath of Skyhan's actions made it clear. Two Skyhans…it was impossible…

She looked over at Gabriel. He buried his face in his hands, his whole body shaking. He had to relive that memory again, and everyone in the cavern had witnessed it as well.

Now you understand, the High Lady's voice resonated as the memory faded away. *You possess the sword. You possess the spirit of a celestial dragon. Now that you have seen how it was done, you can perform the ritual again for us.*

Desert Rain's hand went to the pouch at her side. She had wondered why the elves had not removed Silverheart from her possession, but now it was clear — Wretched could not hold the sword, and they wanted her to use it. Her hand tightened into a fist, and she shot the High Lady a furious glare. "How *dare* you. He wasn't ready to share that. How dare you force him to experience that again, and then expose it to us? For someone who's so damned terrified of her own secrets being revealed, you have no problem divulging other people's!"

Watch how you speak. You are not in power here.

"Really? You want me to use my powers and Silverheart to free you from your fate. But that's the funny thing about fate. It's hard to know whether it's truly preordained, or just random, or if maybe someone deserves it. Even if I could split you, remove your supposed wickedness from your body and soul, there is no removing it from your heart. You are cruel, your grace. Your evil can only be purged by you, and I don't know if you are capable."

Finally, the High Lady's face twisted into a reaction—full, unbridled, raw rage. *I can shatter your minds into a million pieces! Only by my kindness do I even permit you to think! You will free us from our twisted bodies, even if I must break your mind to do so!*

Desert Rain expected to lose her consciousness, her sanity, her mind at any second, and yet, she did not. After a beat, the High Lady's eyes widened even larger than they already were, and her scowl changed to a frown of shock.

"You won't hurt Mother," Emily said, her voice unusually low.

Looking down at the small goddess, Desert Rain suddenly noticed Emily's big eyes were no longer black, but glowing a strange green, like an animal's eyes reflecting in the dark.

The High Lady reined in her shocked expression, returning to her placid porcelain façade. *Sweet child, you do not understand. I do what is best for the Crystal Court. And this one is not your Mother. I can prove it to you. You are a goddess, thus you are above mortal beings. You do not succumb to age, disease, or wound. If this one were your mother, neither would she.*

The movement was so fast, Desert Rain could not comprehend it. Suddenly, one of the High Lady's long, spidery arms lashed out at her, and a sharp pain slashed Desert Rain across her cheek. It was both a burning and freezing sensation, and when she touched the cut, blood came away on her fingertips.

The High Lady gave her a smug smirk. *See? This one is mortal. Even with her Hijn powers, one day she will die. Do not grow attached to trivial things, as you will outlast them all.*

Emily looked up at Desert Rain's cut face, wide-eyed and her mouth open in a silent gasp. At first, Desert Rain thought her surprised look was from realizing that her "Mother" was, indeed, mortal, and therefore not what she thought. But then Emily's eyes glowed a deep red, and her mouth set into a gritty grimace. The feathers on her head stood on end, and her skin faded to gray and became riddled with veins of black, like streaks of ink pouring across her arms and legs.

The High Lady froze in mid-air, even her wings coming to a dead stop, but still she hung in the air. The cavern became so quiet, Desert Rain could hear her own breathing. She also heard a quick inhale from Kidran, and when she turned to him, his eyes screamed panic. He could not have looked more terrified if he was witnessing his own incoming death.

"You...hurt...MOTHER!" Emily's voice was no longer that of the kind child Desert Rain knew. This new voice was a bottomless well of horrors, a reverberating abyss of nightmares. There was no chance to extend comfort, no chance to try and calm the goddess, and the entire cavern — the entire glacier — exploded into millions upon millions of shards.

The next thing Desert Rain knew, they were all falling into nothingness.

She thought she heard screaming, but maybe it was all in her mind, as the hive of Secret Sacroth plummeted down into unending darkness. The High Lady was frozen, literally, as she fell away, and there was a sickening series of snaps as Desert Rain watched her break into pieces like a china doll thrown against a wall.

She saw Gabriel, Chiriku, and Mac all tumble from their ledge, and Kidran was falling beside her. Ice rained around them, filling the air with sparkling splinters, and Desert Rain would have found it lovely if they were dropping to their deaths.

A hand gripped her sleeve, and Desert Rain was gone.

CHAPTER SIXTEEN
Grandpa's Petting Zoo

It was warm—too warm. Desert Rain opened her eyes but blinked as harsh sun hit them. As her eyes adjusted, she recognized where she was.

Sand stretched out before her, miles of dunes and golden landscape. She was in the desert. She was home.

Is this part of dying? My life must be flashing before my eyes, she thought. But it all felt too real—the hot wind in her face, the earthy smells, and the faint sounds of a dune screecher somewhere over the dunes. She was also no longer in her winter apparel; she was in her plain tunic and trousers, and her pouch containing Silverheart still hung from her belt. Her feet were bare, and she felt the sun-heated sand slip between her prehensile toes. When she looked around, she spotted Emily standing next to her, looking up with her black, shiny eyes.

"Emily? Wha...how are we..." As Desert Rain's brain reconnected the dots, dread consumed her. "What did you do?"

Emily shrugged. "I wanted us to go home. So, I used the Hollow Eye to send us home." She glanced around at the desert around her. "This is so different from the Taigalands. It's so warm and pretty! I love it!"

Desert Rain fell to her knees, grabbing Emily by the shoulders. "Emily, we have to back, right now!"

Emily frowned in disappointment. "Why?"

"Everyone is going to die! There must be something we can do. We need to save everyone!"

Emily tightened her lips. "I don't want to go back there, Mother. There's nothing there anymore."

"What do you mean, there's nothing..." Desert Rain suddenly realized something. She touched her face where the High Lady had slashed her but felt nothing but a light, almost healed scratch. "How did...did you heal me when you sent us here?'

Emily shook her head. "No. It just healed on its own. When I brought us here, we jumped ahead in time too."

Desert Rain's ears drooped. "You can jump in time? How far ahead in time?"

"I think two, three...weeks? I'm not great with time yet."

Desert Rain's arms fell limp to her sides. "They're gone. They're all gone..." She gave Emily a desperate look. "If you can jump ahead in time, can you go back in time? Back to when, no, before the glacier fell apart? We can stop what happened, can't we? Please, please try!"

Emily thought about it for a painfully long time. "I don't think time works like that. Besides, if you could go back in time, you can't change what is written into past events anyway. It gets all messy when you try to do that. Like, collapse time itself messy."

Desert Rain felt the world fall away from her. Nothing seemed real anymore. Part of her hoped this was some awful illusion with which the Secret Sacroth was poisoning her mind, but with Emily here, she knew that could not be the case. She couldn't accept it. Mac, Chiriku...Gabriel...gone? And it was all her fault. She should have taken this journey alone. She should have refused to let them come along. There was a reason why she was always alone, and this was it. She was cursed.

She ruined everyone she met. No friends, no Lightscale, no way to stop Katawa. It was over.

Desert Rain plopped down on the sand, pulling her knees up towards her chest. She wrapped her arms around her legs and buried her face in her knees.

Emily sat down on the sand next to her. "I'm sorry. I didn't mean to make everyone go away. I got so mad that the Bad Lady hurt you. Please don't be mad at me." Her last sentence came out as a squeak, her rising tears audible in her tone.

Desert Rain felt terrible for Emily — poor child, barely able to control her emotions, let alone her goddess powers — but she could not respond. She half wanted to ask Emily if she could just poof her out of existence, but she knew Emily wouldn't do that even if she begged.

"I promise I won't ever do that again," Emily said quietly. "I'll be good from now on."

Desert Rain weakly raised her head. "It's not your fault. It's mine."

"You didn't do anything —"

"Emily, I'm sorry, but I want to be alone for a while."

Emily was quiet. Desert Rain thought maybe she had left, until the girl asked, "Where's your house?"

Desert Rain limply gestured towards a large hill of sand, and then flopped over onto her side and curled into a ball.

It was abruptly not hot and sunny anymore, as Desert Rain realized she was now curled up on her bed, in her bedroom, in her burrow. The sudden shift should have jarred her, but nothing seemed to affect her now. Emily stood at the foot of her bed, holding her Hollow Eye pendant in her hand. "You sleep. I'll be back." She then left the room, leaving Desert Rain alone.

Desert Rain had no idea where Emily was going to go, but it did not matter. The familiar smells of her house soothed her, but not much. Her bed was dusty from how long it had been since she left, but it was still soft and inviting. Maybe she could sleep forever and never wake up. The world would be a better place without her. She pulled one of her cushions to her chest, hugging it tightly, and now came the tears. She wept for all she had lost, for who and what she had loved, for all the things that were gone forever. The exhaustion and the crushing weight of her quest hung heavily on her body, and as she ran dry of tears, she succumbed to sleep.

*　　*　　*

"Mother, come see Grandpa with me! He's got a petting zoo!"

Desert Rain awoke in a daze, her body slow to react to the child shaking her. How long had she been asleep? Her stomach rumbled — skipping ahead three weeks in time was bound to make one hungry, she supposed. She finally realized she was also parched, as her throat felt sore and dry. As if in response to her thoughts, a plate of ginger cookies and a flask popped into existence next to her on the bed. Emily took one of the cookies and munched on it and nudged the plate closer to Desert Rain.

"Bad Lady never wanted me to have cookies," Emily said. "Said sugar rots the mind. But they're soooooo yummy."

Desert Rain couldn't argue with that. She managed to eat a couple of cookies, and when she drank from the flask, found it to be full of brown liquid…oh, chocolate milk. It was astoundingly sweet compared to the cactus milk she was used to, but it was cool and refreshing. "Thank you," she said hoarsely.

"Now come on, let's go visit Grandpa! He said I can pet the animals!"

Desert Rain propped herself up, and every muscle in her body protested her movement with aches and stabbing pains. She blinked groggily at Emily. "What are you talking about?"

"Grandpa. He's down by the little lake with all the pretty flower bushes. He wants us to visit him."

Lake? She must mean the oasis. It was a quaint reprieve from the desert barrenness that Desert Rain had spent years cultivating, but the last time she had been there, it had been with Katawa. She visibly cringed at the memory—how happy she had been back then, how foolish. She did not want to go there anymore; her lush sanctuary had been tarnished forever. But Emily was not taking no for an answer. She started jumping up and down on the bed, chanting, "Let's go! Let's go! Let's go!"

Desert Rain eventually lumbered out of bed, taking a deep breath and she got to her feet. Couldn't Emily just whisk her over to the oasis in the blink of an eye, without all this childishness? But when Emily took her by the hand and led her along, up the steps out of her burrow, out into the sun and across the sand, the goddess was humming a little tune as she skipped, and even ran about in circles, making designs in the sand with her footprints. Desert Rain realized how much Emily wanted to just…be a child. To play, and take walks, and eat cookies and drink chocolate milk. Sure, she could probably bend the entire world to her will, make Desert Rain and everyone do whatever she wanted, but she didn't care about that. She wanted a normal life, full of family and love. Desert Rain was grateful for that; with the High Lady having influenced her, Emily could have turned out completely different.

As they crested the dune overlooking the oasis, Desert Rain was startled by what she saw below. Yes, her oasis was still intact and in bloom, but it was also overrun by a whole farm's worth of animals. Pens had been set up for desert sheep with curling horns, and furry plump peccaries with brown snouts, and cute black pygmy goats, but none of them cared for their pens as they wandered about the oasis, munching on foliage. There was a tent of modest size, built of various animal hides and bones, decorated with beads and shells.

This was the camp of a nomad, most likely, but what sense did it make to bring your animals into the desert? Where in Luuva could this nomad and his herds be heading? Desert Rain sighed, hoping the animals would not eat all her vegetation—but then again, all of Luuva Gros would be a distorted dystopian wasteland soon, so what did it matter? In fact, it made sense now why these herds were here; it was probably the last place in Luuva Gros that was comparatively safe, given that Katawa's legions of Distorted were probably overrunning the rest of the land by now.

Emily squealed in delight as she skipped among the animals, petting them on their furry heads. Desert Rain dragged her feet towards the oasis' pool, allowing her feet to soak in the water. She noticed a goat drinking from the water, white in color, standing out amidst the other pygmy goats. When the white goat looked up at her, it started, as if surprised by her. It went stiff-legged and toppled over onto its side.

Desert Rain would have found this display amusing, but a strange sense of recognition crossed her thoughts. This little white goat...it reminded her of...its eyes, its muzzle, its odd little tuffs of fur around its face... "Gothart?"

The goat regained his consciousness and scampered away, ducking behind a bush and peeking out warily at her.

She gave the goat a narrow look. "Gothart Grandwitt, of the infamous house of Grandwitts, I presume? What are you doing, taking on a cute, sweet shape to trick someone? You're not fooling me. You ditched us when we needed you! Come on, turn back to normal. No hiding!"

"I'm afraid that is normal, for him." A deep, soothing voice came from the nearby tent, and out stepped another familiar face, one that took Desert Rain off guard.

"Grandpa!" Emily giggled, running to him and hugging him at the waist. "Mother's here now. I forgot to bring Father, but I don't think he'd like the desert very much. Can we have a tea party? I've always wanted one of those!"

The old man, dressed in antelope hide trimmed with rabbit fur, patted the goddess gently on the head. "Of course. But Desert Rain and I need to talk first. Why don't you go chase Gothart around the pool? He could use some exercise."

Emily went and chased after the white goat, who seemed put-out that he was being played with, but he trotted off as the goddess followed him. The shaman, with his braided greenwood staff in hand, approached

Desert Rain, who at first did not know what to say. She remembered him well; he was the one who had convinced her to pursue Katawa after he had betrayed her. He had given her the bracelet that had protected her fractured soul. She instinctively pulled at her sleeve, hoping he wouldn't ask to see it.

The shaman chuckled. "Don't concern yourself with that bracelet. I knew the moment you felt someone needed its power more than yourself, you would give it away. Besides, I sense you don't need it anymore."

"I don't? But you said a soul unravels when it's broken. Am I going to go feral without it?"

The shaman gestured for her to follow him, and he led her inside the tent. Inside was sparsely furnished: a pair of chairs, a thin sleeping mat, and a stone-lined fire pit. They both sat down. "You have undergone quite a journey, haven't you?"

Desert Rain tried to steady herself, but the sadness overwhelmed her and she burst into a renewed cascade of tears. "I killed all of them! I couldn't save them, they're all dead! And now Katawa is going to distort everyone and everything, I couldn't find the Lightscale, there's nothing left! If you're here to punish me for failing, get it over with."

The shaman looked at Desert Rain with genuine sympathy. He waited while she cried, giving her time to grieve. "No one said the journey would be easy. Life is full of gains and losses. But, like an oasis in the desert, there is always hope, no?"

"No, there isn't! What possible hope is there? I...I can't do this alone."

"Let me show you something." The shaman broke off a piece of his staff, handing it to Desert Rain. "When a plant is cut, it may lose its beautiful blossoms for a while. It is left a stump, a barely visible remnant of its former self. But, with time and perseverance..."

Slowly, his staff regrew its missing piece, and the braided wood intertwined again. The piece of staff in Desert Rain's hand also grew, sprouting its own little branches and leaves until it was a tiny tree in her palm.

"As long as there is something to grow from, and if they are given light and rain, plants can grow again and thrive. Anything that lives can regrow from even the darkest times, growing even through the stones of hardship and turmoil. So it is with love, hope, and souls."

Desert Rain looked up at him. "Souls? Souls can regrow?"

"Oh, yes. It's their nature to grow, even when broken. Especially when broken. And yours has grown back rather nicely, I should say." He smiled warmly.

"But...Katawa said—"

"Katawa is a devil, and you know it. He thrives on the belief that people are inherently wicked, so he believes he reveals people for what they are. Bringing their inner twistedness to the outside, ha! Now *there* is someone whose soul is broken and refuses its nature to grow." The shaman leaned close. "That is the key. No one can heal their soul other than themselves. It has even been reflected in your magic, has it not? Once you accept yourself, the magic accepts you, too. Magic from a broken soul is distorted. Yours is healing. It was smart of you to pass the bracelet to your friend, for he needs time to regrow as well."

Desert Rain was washed in relief from the shaman's words. "So...I won't go feral?"

"Not unless you want to. Although I don't advise it. Might be fun at first, but causes lots of problems down the line." The elder man rose from his seat. "Now, I need a little help rounding up my herds. Would you mind lending a hand? These old legs aren't as fast as they used to be."

While Desert Rain found some comfort in knowing her soul was not only intact, but healing, the reality of the situation kept her mired in despair. "You do know there's an insane Distortionist destroying our world, right? Doesn't that make everything else seem a little...pointless?"

"The world will always have its great evils. That doesn't mean the little things don't still need tending to. While the stars still shine, the wind still blows, and the snow still falls, we need to be the stewards of the creatures of nature."

Desert Rain rose from her chair, as a thought came to her. "The snow still falls...Kidran! Kidran was there, maybe his magic was able to stop the cave-in. Maybe they're still alive! Do you know?"

The shaman pulled back the tent-flap to the entrance. "Despite my wisdom, I cannot see all. But sometimes, it's hope alone that urges us on. That makes it quite a powerful force, doesn't it?"

Outside, the two of them gradually rounded up the sheep, goats, and boars, although it proved to be more challenging for Desert Rain than the shaman. As quick as she was, some of the animals were more inspired to eat the bushes than return to their pens. Only when she finally tore off a few of the more delectable branches from the oasis shrubs and used them to guide the animals into their pens did the task get done.

"By the way," she said, eying Gothart as Emily carried him around in her arms like a pet, "what happened to him?"

"I apologize for the grief he caused you," the shaman said, wiping his brow. "Some time ago, he got into my collection of talismans and ate one. It was imbued with magic, and it gave him temporary abilities. He's always been a rascal, but he became a little drunk with power, should we say? I pursued him when he ran away, but he was always too fast for me. Not until the talisman's magic wore off was I able to collect him."

"So, he's always been one of yours?"

"Naturally. We'll have to think of some way he can make it up to you."

"Don't. I'd rather have nothing to do with him again." She shot Gothart a dirty look, and the goat stuck out his lower lip at her. She looked back at the shaman. "May I ask, what are you, exactly? You clearly have ancient magic, so you're not one of the Syphurian spellcasters, nor an alchemist. Yet, I can't quite pin down what your magic is—elemental, ethereal, dark, light? If you don't mind me asking."

"Grandpa, when are we having our tea party?" Emily asked, her eyes hopeful.

"Why don't you get the tea party set up, and we'll join you?" the shaman advised. Emily giggled, with Gothart still swinging from her arms and she scurried off to find the right spot to host her party. The shaman grinned at Desert Rain. "Do you know why she calls me Grandpa?"

"Because she likes giving people familial names?"

"Yes, there's that. But you are Mother. Therefore, it follows that I am Grandpa."

Desert Rain chuckled. "Well, she really means Bellaluna is Mother, as in she was the matriarch to the…" She paused, finally processing what the shaman meant. She stared wide-eyed at him. "You're Bellaluna's father."

The shaman chuckled, and then his features shifted. He remained the same height, same stature, but his face morphed into a more pronounced muzzle, with a series of short copper horns along the sides of his face and head, and bright golden scales coating his skin. His eyes, however, remained kind and wise. He was rather handsome and dignified, as far as dragons went.

Desert Rain could only reply in a whisper, "Dear Guerda-Shalyr…"

"Yes?"

"Hmm?"

"You said my name."

Desert Rain blinked in surprise. "D…did I? I just always say that. It's something I picked up a long time ago."

The Sage smirked. "And where did you pick it up from?"

Desert Rain thought about it. She had always assumed she heard it from the people in Ulomin, and she had been saying it for decades without much thought. Now that she thought about it, she could not recall any specific person having said it to her at any point. Where had she originally heard it from?

"I told you, Desert Rain, that I have always been here. And part of you was always listening. You just didn't know what you were listening to. You heard my name in the wind, in the sands. After all, this is my home. The Gold Dragon Desert." Guerda-Shalyr cocked his head at her. "Interesting, as well, that you adopted my hues. Perhaps there is some sun magic in you, as well as moon."

It was true; while Bellaluna had had a gold-tinted chest and underside, her scale color had been moonlight-blue. Desert Rain had always wondered why that had not been her skin color when she changed. But sun? Guerda-Shaylr was the Sage of the Sun? She figured it made sense that he hid in the desert, then. She scratched herself behind her ear. "I don't understand. I thought Bellaluna died of old age. But you're her father. How—"

"It's a bit different for a Salamandrian Sage. You see, we could live on, and on, and on, but there comes a time when we know we must travel on from our mortal coil. And the only way we can do this is to select an heir, a Hijn. I just...never did." At this, his grin melted into a sad frown. "That's my own fault, I suppose. Anyone I thought had potential, I found too selfish, or too weak-willed, or this or that or the other. I was too determined to find the perfect heir. The fact is, to live forever but not pass on your centuries of knowledge and wisdom—that is truly the selfish act. Not to mention, the bond between a Sage and their Hijn is the greatest joy for a dragon." He sighed, sitting down on a stone, grasping his staff in both hands as if it was all he had left.

Desert Rain put her hand on his shoulder. "It's not too late, you know. If there is still a Luuva Gros after all this, we always need another Hijn."

Guerda-Shalyr patted her hand with his own. "I know. Which means, someone still needs to do something about saving it."

Desert Rain's shoulders slumped. "Guerda, I've tried. You know I've tried. But I've faced Katawa again and again, and I freeze up every time. And now I have no one. It's just me. And I have no Lightscale. The one thing I had placed all my hope in, I have no clue where it is, if it even still exists. What am I supposed to—"

"Tea's ready!" Emily bounced over, pointing to a table over by the pool. A purple porcelain tea set sat upon the table, along with cupcakes, cookies, and lots of flowers adorning everything. Gothart, still hanging from Emily's arms, munched on a clump of lavender.

"Ah, yes. How about some tea before we stress about saving the world?" Guerda advised.

Desert Rain's initial impulse was to argue something along the lines of, "How can we have tea at a time like this?", but it dawned on her that without a plan, there was no point rushing off. Besides, if Luuva Gros was falling into ruin, maybe one last nice day was all she could afford. It felt a little selfish, but what else could she do until she figured out her next step?

As they sat down at the table, and Emily poured them each a sweet-smelling herbal tea, Guerda-Shalyr snacked on a cupcake. "You're not alone, you know. How's old Sir Luce doing these days?"

Desert Rain sat up straighter at the question. "Oh. Sir Luce! Right! He's…in the sword."

Guerda-Shalyr chuckled. "Yes. He's been training you well?"

"Yes, although everything's been chaotic lately. I should probably check in with him."

"You should heed his advice. He's a very wise warrior. But I know, you miss your flesh-and-blood companions. I know there's one who has missed you a great deal." He placed his fingers on each side of his mouth and let out a long whistle.

A soft yipping sound came from the other side of

the oasis. After a few seconds, Desert Rain saw a small shape running towards them across the sands — it ran strangely, as if its four legs didn't quite match in length. It was a mix of purple-bruise and orange hues, but once she saw his little face, there was no mistaking who it was. Desert Rain jumped up from her seat and ran to her long-lost friend. "Jubis!"

The sand fox was still in his half-distorted state, but he no longer appeared to be in pain. He yipped in joy, although the Distortion in his face and throat made his yips sound different. His eyes were still the same sweet, loving eyes she always knew. She picked him up and held him to her chest, as he licked her face. "I thought you were going to die. I'm so relieved!"

"I cannot undo the infliction done to him," Guerda-Shalyr said as Desert Rain sat back down at the table with Jubis in her lap. "But he is a resilient creature. I know he was determined to wait for you."

Desert Rain's heart still ached at Jubis's unfortunate condition. She glanced over at Emily. "Emily, do you think you can change him back? You can change just about anything, can't you?"

Emily nodded. She stared intently at Jubis. At first, it looked like something was indeed happening. Jubis's twisted jaw and muzzle began to morph back into proper place, his warped leathery skin began to grow back tufts of brown-orange fur. It got as far as his face returning to almost normal, but then Emily winced and rubbed her eyes. "This is weird," she said.

"What's weird? Are you okay?" Desert Rain knitted her eyebrows in concern.

"I think so. But something about that bad magic is really strong. It makes my head hurt." When she stopped rubbing her eyes, Desert Rain gasped to see spots that looked like small bruises around her eye sockets.

"Emily, stop! I think when you tried to remove the Distortion, you started to absorb some of it by accident." Desert Rain had not even thought that a possibility. Distortion could even affect a goddess? The extent of Katawa's abilities was truly terrifying.

Emily touched lightly around her eyes and gaped her mouth in horror. "It's because that scary man has death in him!" she cried, and she ran to Desert Rain, hugging her and sobbing.

Katawa had the Death Walker's spirit inside of him—that power fed into the Distortion. Balthazin must have been a very powerful Sage that his magic could affect divine beings. Of course, Emily was still a young goddess who had not come into full power yet, and Desert Rain still was not sure exactly how the Secret Sacroth had made her. All Desert Rain knew was, she couldn't put Emily at risk, and not put anyone else at risk of Emily's powers until they understood them better.

Desert Rain gently smoothed Emily's head feathers. "Shh, shh, it's okay. You're going to be okay. Those spots will go away, you only absorbed a little bit. I had Distortion put into me, and it went away because it didn't have a chance to take hold. But it's best that you don't do that again. Thank you for trying."

As Emily calmed down, Desert Rain wiped away her tears and checked her face. She could already see the Distortion bruises receding, thank goodness. Even with a little of the Distortion having been removed, Jubis looked so much better, only one of his front legs and paws remaining twisted and the skin on one side of his body still bald and leathery. It was a blessing to see his normal face again, even if one corner of his mouth was still contorted.

"There is another friend who misses you as well," Guerda-Shalyr said, taking a sip of tea. "She was on her way from the rainforest to find you."

"She? Rainforest—Clova?" Desert Rain remembered what Woasim had told her, about Clova Flor gathering elves and elk. "Wait, she left Juka Basin to find me? How do you know that, if you 'can't see everything' as you put it?" She tightened her lips. "I mean, with all respect, Guerda-Shalyr."

He smiled, showing no offense to Desert Rain's brusqueness. "The sun's skyward eye sees much, but it doesn't see everything, correct? And unfortunately, she has passed into darkness, so I don't know where she currently lies. She needs a light in the darkness, so I believe it best you go to her."

Desert Rain's ears flattened against her head. "Darkness? When did that happen? Where is she?" She turned to Emily. "Can you use your Hollow Eye to find her? I think she'll be with a band of rainforest elves, if what Woasim said was true. She would have traveled from Juka Basin."

Emily took her Hollow Eye in hand and finagled with it for a minute. After much rolling around in her hands, the pendant glowed a dim, purplish glow. Her eyes went wide. "Ooooh, she's in the bad place, Mother. The really, *really* bad place. It's hard to find anything there. I can't see much."

The really, *really* bad place. There was one really, *really* bad place in Luuva Gros. "She's in the Inbetween? What in Luuva is she doing there?" Desert Rain realized that was a silly question; Clova was most likely on her way to the Taigalands, where Desert Rain had told her she was going. If the Ahshi elves had gotten word that the ocean was too dangerous to cross because of Merros, then to go north they had to pass through the Inbetween. Now that so much time had passed, who knew where Clova was and what had happened to her.

"Best you go find out," Guerda-Shalyr replied. "Don't you think?"

Desert Rain felt her heart creeping up her throat. She had never been in the Inbetween before. No one who had an ounce of sense went there. But she could not let Clova wander around lost in there. Not to mention, Katawa had to be somewhere in there, if he was still bent on destroying the Darkscale Court. She had no doubt he was still alive after his confrontation with King Ragnor and his men. She knew him too well, knew what he was capable of even when weakened. What if Katawa hunted down Clova and the elves? He still had all the other Hijn under his control; he would either capture her too, or find Clova's abilities of little use to him, so he might...

Her face hardened with determination. She gave Jubis a tight hug. "I'm sorry, Jube. I know I just got home, but I still have work to do." She gently set him down on the ground, and even though Jubis whined, he seemed to understand. "How do I find her? It'll take me about a week to reach the border of the Inbetween from here, and she could be anywhere by then."

"Oh, I can take you!" Emily held up the Hollow Eye excitedly.

Desert Rain smiled kindly at her and reached out to brush her feather-hair. "Emily, you have been so kind and good to me. I forever thank you. But we don't quite understand your powers, and you have trouble controlling them. And Katawa's Distortion can hurt you. You'd be safest here, with Grandpa for now. Will you please stay at my home, where it's safe? That would make Mother feel much better."

Emily pouted, lip jutted out, but she nodded. "Okay, Mother. Don't let the scary man hurt you."

Desert Rain kissed her on the forehead. She looked at Guerda-Shalyr. "Would you watch over her while I'm gone?"

The old dragon bowed his head. "I would be honored."

Emily removed the Hollow Eye from around her neck and held it out to Desert Rain. "The Hollow Eye can take you there."

The Hijn was flabbergasted. "Emily, are you sure? Don't you need this?"

"I'll be here with Grandpa. You need it to find your friend. It's easy, just think about where you need to be, and the Hollow Eye takes you there." Emily placed the pendant in Desert Rain's hand and folded her fingers over it.

"Thank you, sweetheart." Desert Rain pulled Emily into a hug.

Guerda-Shalyr stood up. "The Inbetween is shrouded in mystery and danger. The least I can do is send you with an escort. Let's see…ah, yes." He eyed Gothart, who was munching on the other flowers around the tea table. "Gothart, you have some making up to do for your trickery, don't you?"

Desert Rain held up her hands in refusal. "No, no, no. I've had enough of him. Anyway, he's a normal goat again. He'd be an easy snack for any of the beasts in the Inbetween."

Gothart clearly understood what she was saying, for his mouth fell open, the mouthful of blossoms tumbling out.

Guerda-Shalyr laughed. "Excellent point. We'll have to make him less appetizing, then. And a bit more useful." He patted the various talismans hanging around his neck, sorting through them until he located one, a clay figure the size of a thumb.

Gothart jumped up to run away, but suddenly, the clay talisman was around his neck in a flash of golden light. Another flash of sunlight, and he was six feet tall on his hind legs with a humanoid physique. He was not so splendid as he was before, when he had been dressed in fine white-and-gold coat, breeches, and gloves. Now he wore plain green tunic and trousers. Even his horns were not the long, spiraling marvels they had been; they were two little stubs atop his head.

"Whaaaa...." His word came out like a stunted bleat, and he cleared his throat and he attempted to formulate his words around his natural goat sounds. "Whaaaaat is going on here?"

Desert Rain wrinkled her nose at him. Unless Guerda-Shalyr's talisman had completely rewritten Gothart's personality, which she doubted given the smug look on his face, he was no more trustworthy now as he was before. However, facing the Inbetween with someone at her side was better than being alone.

"Let me pack you a lunch," Emily said. She focused her eyes on Gothart, and a large, heavy pack blinked into existence on his back. He almost toppled over from the sudden weight, and he stumbled about for a few seconds to regain his balance.

"This is lunch?" he gasped. "I hate to know what

your idea of supper is!"

Desert Rain grinned. After lugging Gothart around in her belt pouch, it seemed fitting he do some of the heavy lifting. She went over to Guerda-Shalyr and hugged him. "Thank you, Grandpa. For the hope."

"Keep it close to your heart. You'll need it." He smiled.

Gothart grimaced as Desert Rain came to stand beside him. "Now, hold on a minute. Can we talk this over? I didn't even get a say in this! Did anyone ask if I would prefer to just stay behind and eat flowers? Does anyone care an iota about what I—"

He did not get to finish his irate rambling before Desert Rain held the Hollow Eye in hand, thought as hard as she could, *Take me to Clova Flor*, and grabbed onto Gothart's arm. The two of them vanished.

CHAPTER SEVENTEEN
(Un)Welcome to the Inbetween

" — think?" Gothart realized he was not where he had been a second go.

The Inbetween. The place of exile, where the Knights of Luuva drove the Courts of the Wretched long ago to keep them always surrounded by the Noblelands. It was poisoned by the Darkscales' alchemy and the wastes of the Bloodburns' machines, rendering the belt land in the middle of Luuva Gros a sick and nightmarish wilderness. The air was stifling, smothering, thick with stale and acidic smells. What met Desert Rain's eyes was, at first, too difficult to comprehend. Anything familiar — trees, grass, stone, sea, sand, red clay or plain brown earth — was absent from this place. The only thing she could immediately recognize were the clouds above them, but even they were unlike any clouds she had seen before. They were saturated with shades of grisly green and corpse black, as veins of jade lightning danced through them like thread-wraiths chasing one another. They provided brief flashes of illumination, which was the one source of light as the clouds refused the sunrays' admittance.

Around them on the ground, the world was abstract. Spires of rough fluorite that bent at odd angles, perhaps this land's confused attempt at trees, reached up into the clouds and clung to the ground with elevated tentacle roots, or claws, or whatever they might be. The ground itself seemed like a tight stretch of speckled reptile skin, spongy and crusty at the same time – under Desert Rain's bare feet, it felt weirdly warm, and she swore it even had a heartbeat. What might have been tumbleweeds were jumbles of jagged glass pieces, rolling along with an unexpected weightlessness, but Desert Rain was certain it would be painful to have one roll into her. Umbrella-like fauna, or possibly flora, with purplish tendrils hanging down floated above them like airborne jellyfish. Again, all this could only be seen when the green lightning occasionally streaked down from the toxic heavens and struck the top of a random spire – in the lapses of darkness, it was a realm of silhouettes and shadows.

"Lovely. And here I was hoping I'd never have to see this place again," Gothart said with a grimace.

Desert Rain steadied the shivering of her ears as another vein of lightning skittered down to electrify a spire. "That's right, you've been here before, when the Darkscale hired you to steal Katawa's memories. How did you get mixed up with them, anyway?"

"Unfortunate circumstances, let's leave it at that."

"I never could have imagined what this land would be like…" Desert Rain glanced around for anything that indicated where they should go but found nothing. "Do you know where we are? Does anything look familiar to you?"

Gothart scratched his bearded chin. "Oh, yes! Of course, just drop me anywhere in this valley of pure horrors, and I'll know exactly where we are. Oh ho, this green rock! Hello, green rock, I remember you fondly. And this…whatever this is…" He pointed at one of the floating jellyfish flora. "Heigh ho! I named it Wally Wickerby. Good to see you again, Wally!"

Desert Rain frowned. "You could've just said no."

"You could not ask dumb questions."

Desert Rain sighed. "I asked the Hollow Eye to bring us to Clova, but I don't see her. Maybe it brought us to where it last spotted her. She must have recently been here."

"Well, if it's all the same to you…" The goat man gracefully slid the pack off his back and dropped it at Desert Rain's feet. "It's been a delightful reunion, but I have better things to do, now that I have my proper extremities back. I bid you a fond farewell." He turned around in the opposite direction and made a mighty leap—only to fall flat on his face. After a moment of regaining his composure, and chuckling in embarrassment, he stood up and tried again to bound away, but only succeeded in landing hard on his rear. A small "uh oh" escaped his lips.

Desert Rain was in no mood to humor whatever Gothart was trying to do. "Goodbye, Gothart." She picked up the pack, hoisted it over one shoulder, and started off away from the goat. She had gotten a few yards' distance when Gothart was suddenly at her side again, a big adoring smile on his face.

"Dezzy! Sweet Dezzy, beautiful Dezzy, wise and intelligent Dezzy," Gothart crooned. He went straight for the pack, removing it from her shoulder. "Oh dear, let me take that heavy pack from you. I would be heartbroken should you strain your back under such burden, my dearest and best friend."

Desert Rain rolled her eyes. Even he must know how thick he was laying it on. "What's the problem?"

Gothart hefted the pack onto his back with a grunt. "Problem? Ah, well, the problem is, it would seem that I don't have any of my previous talents. A nasty trick by the old dragon, I'm sure. Therefore, it would behoove us both to travel in tandem, don't you think? I scratch your back, you scratch mine?"

Desert Rain smirked. "What you're saying is, you're not really that useful to me. Why should I?"

Gothart looked taken back and gave her a puppy-dog look. "You wouldn't leave your good pal Gothart all the way out here, would you? Besides, goats are the best traveling cohorts. Sure-footed, strong, dependab… reliab… loya…" He couldn't seem to come up with the last word—not a truthful one, at least—so Desert Rain decided to spare him the stress.

"All right, you can help me keep an eye out for any beasts. But no tricks!" She wagged a finger at him.

"Who, me?" Gothart batted his eyes innocently at her. He then frowned. "Trust me, this isn't my idea of a good time either."

The Inbetween was at least, despite its unsettling appearance, quiet and serene. Perhaps a bit too quiet, as there were no sounds of wild animals, no birdsong, not even a rustling of wind, although there were no natural trees or leaves for wind to rustle. Desert Rain and Gothart trudged along, selecting a direction on a whim as every direction looked identical and the Darkscale compass was not any help. After all, it only indicated the presence of Hijn magic, not geographical direction. Or, could it?—as Desert Rain took it out of her pocket and inspected it, the little silver ball inside seemed to be shivering slightly towards the west side of the device. Could it be detecting Clova? Or, as another thought caused her stomach to lurch, was it detecting Katawa or any of the other Hijn he had abducted…

"Here's a thought," Gothart abruptly chimed in, "Why don't you use that magical Eye whats-its to take us somewhere nice? Someplace with sun, maybe an inn on a beach, and delicious food and drink, and we'll just have a lovely holiday? Sounds better than all this stomping around and chasing after a mad man who could literally turn us inside out, don't you think?"

Desert Rain felt like her whole body was dead weight, and it weighed on her even more so thinking of the possible escape Gothart was suggesting. She tucked the compass in her pocket and took the Hollow Eye in hand. She looked at it from a few angles, trying to understand exactly how this device worked. It could take her anywhere, see anything in Luuva Gros…a whisper of hope crossed her mind. What if her friends were still alive? The Hollow Eye would be able to find them, yes? She focused her eyes on the small trinket, concentrating. *Gabriel…Mac…Chiriku…Kidran…where are they? If they live, show me!*

Swirls of purple and green smoke filled the Eye and settled there, a rotten fog muddling the surface. Desert Rain's heart sank, both puzzled and disappointed by the Eye's reaction. What did that mean? Was the Malaise Cloud blocking the Hollow Eye's ability to see? Was the Inbetween itself affecting its magic? Or did that mean there was nothing to be found?

"Don't tell me that you broke it already!" Gothart bleated, noting the Hollow Eye's cloudiness.

Desert Rain turned her weary gaze to him. "Gothart, I'm doing my best here. As for your sunny paradise, none of that stuff will even exist if Katawa continues distorting everything. Maybe not even sun…" She looked up at the Malaise Cloud above, wondering how far it could spread if not contained to the Inbetween.

"But I don't want to be stuck here!" Gothart whined.

Desert Rain groaned irritably. "Do you ever think about anything else other than what *you* want?"

Gothart balked in mock disgust. "Of course I do! I think about what I *need*. Such as, a warm bath and lemongrass. Do you know how long it's been since I've had either?"

The Hijn grimaced, her green eye flaring a hot fire. Her voice lowered, sharp as a knife's edge. "You know what? Leave. Turn around and keep walking until you're out of the Inbetween. Go find your damn inn on the beach or whatever you want. I'm going to find Clova. I'm going to find the Hijn Council, and Katawa, even if it kills me. If all you're going to do is annoy the Eternal Deep out of me, then for once, do what's best for someone else, for *me*, and get out of my way."

Gothart's eyes went wide. He opened his mouth to retort, but then he shut it. He looked around, seeing nothing but the harsh, toxic land around them. "You'd just leave me out here?" He bit his lip. "All alone —"

The Hijn's voice exploded in raw, exhausted rage. "I've been alone my whole life! I'm going to be alone until I die! I lost my friends, my family disowned me, and anyone I ever loved is gone. We all end up alone. Get used to it!"

The goat cringed at Desert Rain's words. He suddenly seemed less proud than he had, his gaze turned down. "And here I thought you were this eternal ray of faith," he muttered. "Maybe that's why I liked following you around. There's so little of that left in the world, even before all this Distortion took over."

Desert Rain raised an eyebrow at him. "You *like* following me around?"

Gothart scratched the nape of his neck. "In case you hadn't noticed, I don't have a lot of friends. And you weirdly trusted me, for a while. Sad to say, you're kind of the closest thing I've had to a friend. Not that I suppose that means much to you."

Desert Rain placed her hands on her hips. "Is this another trick?"

Gothart shook his head. "Dez, I have no powers. And I'm aware I'm not that clever without them. I'm just a goat, and I'm...I'm scared."

The Hijn paused, observing what appeared to be genuine fear in Gothart's eyes. She figured he would not attempt to fake fear; why tarnish his otherwise confident, perfect image? She sighed, her eyes softening. "Me too, Gothart. But if you want to stop being afraid, then we must stop the danger. We must stop Katawa if we ever want to feel safe again. I don't know if I can even use the Hollow Eye in this place, to transport you somewhere else. So, I think we're in this until the end. Can you do that with me?"

The goat tapped a hoofed foot rapidly as his mind raced. Eventually, he swallowed hard and gave Desert Rain a small nod. "Just don't ask me to do anything *too* heroic. That's not really my style."

Desert Rain gave him a tired smile and prepared to turn around to keep walking when suddenly, Gothart grabbed her arm. He sprinted, with a sudden speed despite the pack on his back, and yanked her over to one of the rock spires and ducked behind it.

"What in Luuva—" Desert Rain started, but the goat slapped a hand over her mouth.

The fear in his eyes was bubbling over as Gothart mouthed the word, "*Monster.*"

Desert Rain's ears folded back against her head. As slowly and quietly as possible, they snuck a glance around the edge of the spire. In the not-too-far distance, there was a hulking silhouette against the dark landscape. A flash of lightning revealed a momentary glance of the shape: it was covered in muddy fur, stood on four oddly bent but muscular legs, and had a long, wide muzzle full of crooked, sharp teeth that jutted out of its mouth. It seemed to be sniffing around, as if hunting.

Desert Rain furrowed her brow in thought. That monster was huge, and there was little in this terrain that would serve as good cover. She was not familiar with creatures in the Inbetween, but something about the creature's uneven walk struck her as strange. It seemed to be having trouble, its sniffing strained, its breathing labored. It swung its head from side to side erratically, as if it had issues seeing. When it turned its face in her direction, she realized what was wrong — its face, in fact its whole body, was a mass of twisted knots and pulled skin, and its eyes and nose were so molded out of sorts that it could barely see or smell. It was mostly all mouth and teeth, but little good that did it when it could not find food.

It's a Distorted, she thought. *But why is it all by itself? Katawa normally keeps his Distorted all together.*

"What do we do?" Gothart rasped, his grip on the straps of his pack tight.

"It looks like one of Katawa's creatures, but it must have gotten separated from the others," Desert Rain whispered. "It looks like its senses are muddled by the

Distortion, but maybe we could...Gothart, I need you to do something for me."

The goat man's eyes were wide. "Curl into a ball and weep in terror? I can do that."

"No. I need you to lure that Distorted over here."

Gothart's jaw dropped open. "Are you insane? Why would I do that?"

"I have a plan, but I'll need to take it by surprise. I need you to lure it closer."

The goat crossed his arms and glowered at her. "How about *you* lure it closer, and I...what is it you want to do?"

"That Distorted may know where Katawa and the Hijn Council is. If we can get it under control, it could lead us to them."

"You expect that big, dumb animal to just do what we say?"

Desert Rain grimaced. "If you have better ideas, I'd love to hear them. And the Distorted aren't big dumb animals. They were people once. I haven't had a chance to try...if Emily was able to reduce the Distortion in Jubis, maybe there's a way we can do that too. Maybe Silverheart..." She placed a hand on the pouch at her belt. "Purelight has purifying powers. Perhaps Silverheart could — "

"Oh, so *you're* the Swordmaster now?" Gothart gave her a condescending smirk. "Because as I understood it, only the Swordmaster could use Purelight."

"I know. But Sir Luce...if Sir Luce is in the sword, then perhaps he could channel Purelight for us. Hijn magic comes from the Sages' souls, and since his soul is in here, maybe the magic still works. Purelight could tame that Distorted for sure."

Gothart snuck another look around the pillar. "You better pray your plan works, because that thing is not leaving."

Before Gothart could do anything, Desert Rain grabbed at his chest and yanked on the talisman. The strap of the talisman snapped, and the tall Trickster was replaced by a small, white pygmy goat. The goat looked around, realizing its height had drastically changed, and then it looked up at Desert Rain with sour disdain. She motioned for him to go with a reassuring smile. The goat stamped its little hooves in protest and gave her leg a headbutt, but he realized he would not get the talisman back until he did what Desert Rain wanted. With a light grunt of frustration, he cautiously tiptoed around the pillar and then started to prance warily out into the open.

Desert Rain placed the talisman on the ground and withdrew Silverheart from its pouch. She took a deep, calming breath. "Sir Luce, we need to try something. I could really use some Purelight. Would you please take control to channel it? I know I'm not Skyhan. I know I'm not worthy of Purelight, but if you could just this once—"

"And who says you're not worthy of it?"

Desert Rain realized she was in the arena again. Or, a slightly altered version of it. The rocks that had littered the sand of the arena were cleared, and the statues were draped in moss and vines, morning glories sprouting from them. It looked like much time had passed here—or had time gone in reverse? Sir Luce stood in the middle of the arena, pulling along a wooden rake of sorts, creating lines in the sand. He was dressed in robes, barefoot, and wore a different mask on his face—

not a war mask, but a simple wooden one without ornamentation, possibly made of bamboo.

"Wait, you can do this to me when I'm awake?" Desert Rain asked.

"When your mind is calmed and focused," Sir Luce said. "Sleep tends to make the connection easier. But you ask for Purelight, while you are still mastering your own magic? No Hijn has wielded two dragon souls before. The consequences could be overwhelming, perhaps even fatal."

Desert Rain thought on this. She could barely keep Blueshine under her control; how could she assume she could control Purelight? Even the Swordmaster had gone too far with it when... She couldn't think about that right now. "I'm not asking to inherit Purelight. Just for you to channel it through Silverheart. To see if it might work on weakening Katawa's hold on that Distorted, so we can communicate with it. Relieve it of some of its pain. Is that possible?"

"Magic wielded without a proper vessel can be chaotic. Untamed. When the Salamandrian Sages first came to Luuva Gros, that's exactly how the magic in the land was. We tamed it to create order, to create balance."

"That was all during the Great Manifestation, I know."

Sir Luce stopped raking, looking Desert Rain in the eye. "When our bodies were no longer able to do that, we needed new vessels to maintain the balance. If you do not command the magic, it will do what it wants, and magic by nature is unbridled and without thought. Control is key. You must control it."

Desert Rain rubbed her chin in thought. "Oh. Then how about for a few minutes? You know, I'll just sort of borrow it?"

Sire Luce sighed, shaking his head. "Always looking for loopholes, these young ones. You have your own light, Desert Rain. You don't need to borrow another's."

"But the Blueshine doesn't—"

"I'm not talking about the Blueshine. That is Bellaluna's light. I'm talking about yours."

Desert Rain blinked, her confusion unmasked. "What do you mean, mine? I don't have any magic apart from Luna's."

Sir Luce's eyes shifted, and Desert Rain could tell he was smiling from behind his mask. "Silverheart has a deeper secret than you know. You see, Purelight in itself is nothing. A heart of darkness who would command Purelight will receive only more darkness. Purelight is simply...a glass of sorts. As is the sword. It magnifies. It intensifies. Silverheart will respond to *your* light, Desert Rain. Why don't you give it a try?"

The sharp, panicked bleat of a goat brought Desert Rain back to the Inbetween. Looking around the pillar, she saw the pygmy goat bolting towards her, bleating enough for a whole herd of goats, being pursued by the burly Distorted—whose hearing proved to be good enough, as it made a straight beeline for Gothart's high-pitched shrieks.

Now is a really bad time to suggest I try something new with this sword! She thought. If she had to, she could maybe fight or scare off this Distorted, but she had to do something. The sword magnifies your own light...*what's my own light?*

She stepped out from behind the pillar, Silverheart at the ready, as Gothart reached her and scurried behind her legs. The Distorted kept barreling towards them, its massive maw gaped wide, a mucus-slathered tongue lolling out from it.

Desert Rain did not want to hurt this thing. It was not the Distorted's fault it was this way. It was probably some poor soul that just had the misfortune of crossing ways with Katawa. It probably felt so much pain, so much fear… She had to help it, to save it somehow…

The Distorted stopped dead in its tracks, scrambling to a halt, as Silverheart abruptly was ablaze with a blinding white. Even though the beast could not see well — Desert Rain could now observe, up close, how twisted and mangled its face really was — it could sense the light. It shrunk from it yet did not run away. It hunkered down, shivering, while gnashing its teeth.

Gothart recovered his talisman from the ground and held it in his mouth. He popped back to his tall, two-legged self, and retied the strap of the talisman around his neck. "Next time, warn a goat when you plan to do that. But I see you got the sword to comply. Lovely trick. Not such a tough monster now, are you?" He blew a raspberry at the Distorted, who was petrified.

Desert Rain looked Silverheart up and down. Was this her light? Or had Sir Luce simply been playing with her and was channeling the magic himself? As she looked down, she noticed the Hollow Eye around her neck…it was slowly floating up, floating towards Silverheart. Why was it doing that? The Eye hovered out as far as it could go on its chain, drawn to the sword's glowing blade. Were enchanted objects attracted to each other, through some magnetic force? She would have to sort that out later. She tucked the Hollow Eye under her tunic collar and returned her focus to the Distorted.

"Now look, we don't want to hurt you. I don't know if you can understand me, but—"

"STOP! DO NOT HURT! STOP!"

Desert Rain snapped her gaze to something approaching from behind the Distorted. Another Distorted, this one long and lean, ran towards her on spindly legs. Just like the first Distorted, its face was also twisted to such an extent, it seemed impossible it could see or smell, but this new Distorted had a...rider? Yes, there was a small someone on its back, guiding it by holding onto tufts of fur on its back. The small rider was not a Distorted, and as they approached, Desert Rain recognized the white fur, the muzzle, the black eyes, and the yelping voice.

"G...Gank?" She could barely believe it. What was one of the Vermin Brothers doing all the way out here? And riding a Distorted? The last she had seen of the Vermin Brothers was when their ship had been destroyed back on the sea and they all had been separated.

Gothart wrinkled his nose. "Is that one of those pungent Lejenous boys from the Bayou? They weren't kidding when they say 'it's a small Luuva after all.'"

Desert Rain was certain she had never heard that expression before, but she dismissed it as she lowered Silverheart. "What are you doing here? What happened to you?"

Gank yanked his Distorted's fur to make it halt and slid down from the creature's back. He ran over to the cowering Distorted and threw his body over it, to protect it. "No hurt, no hurt! Please, we just want to get away..." He looked up at Desert Rain, finally getting a good look at her. He gasped. "Dragon lady? Oh, dragon lady! Yes, yes! Nice dragon lady won't hurt us." He spoke to the two Distorted. "Dragon lady help us now! You see...oh, no, you can't see. But she's here!" He turned back to her, his hands clamped together in pleading. "Please, hide us from him! Can't go back there! Horrible, horrible!"

"Gank, calm down. Breathe." Desert Rain slid Silverheart back into its pouch and knelt to be closer to his level, placing a hand on his shoulder. "Now how did you get here? And why are you with these..." The answer to her second question became all too apparent as she looked at the two Distorted. She could see it now, what small traces were left of who they used to be. Patches of brown and black fur, the muzzles...*oh Divine Beasts!* "Are these...oh, no. Goude, Gimch. I'm so sorry."

"Bad man hurt them." Gank went back over to the Distorted Goude and put his arms around him. "Thought he would do same to me, but he made me his servant. Small things, bring him food, wait on him. He said he liked to see me cower, liked the fear in my eyes. But brothers...he said they were strong, would make good soldiers. But now monster army is so big, bad man didn't pay attention to us. I got us away, ran away! But we don't know where to go. This place...this horrible place, so big!"

Desert Rain gulped, wondering how big Katawa's army of Distorted was now that he did not notice the Vermins sneaking off. But she would deal with that when the time came. Right now, she had to help these poor boys. "Gank, we'll get your brothers help. We'll undo this, somehow. But you need to tell me where you ran away from. You need to show me where Katawa is."

"NO, CAN'T GO BACK THERE!" Gank sobbed

into Goude's fur. "WON'T LOSE BROTHERS AGAIN!"

"Of course not," she said kindly. "I just need you to show me most of the way. Then we can use the Hollow Eye to take you home. It's a magical item that can take you there instantly."

"I thought you broke it," Gothart mumbled.

Desert Rain gave him a look. "It's not broken, I don't think. We're...just not in a good spot. We'll find one. And when I find Katawa, I'll leave the Hollow Eye with you, so you and the Vermins can leave this place. Take them home, and then you can use the Eye to go wherever you want. Okay?"

Gothart had a befuddled look on his face. Desert Rain thought he'd jump at the idea to get out of the Inbetween, but instead he asked, "But then, how are *you* supposed to get back?"

Desert Rain was mystified at the sudden concern, although she tried not to show it. "Let's be honest with ourselves. I don't think I'm going to come back, Gothart. I don't even know if I can stop Katawa, let alone come out of this alive. But I have to try."

Gank's eyes went wide as he looked at Desert Rain. "Dragon lady shouldn't fight bad man. I like dragon lady. Come with us. We'll hide good in the swamp!"

Desert Rain smiled, patting Gank on the shoulder. "It'll be okay, Gank. We cannot afford to be afraid. We need to be brave, for your brothers, for everyone. Can you please show me where Katawa is? Just as far as you can go, and I'll go the rest of the way."

Gank sniffled, rubbing his nose. "Okay, will be brave. We can show you. Goude, carry dragon lady and goat, okay?"

Goude slowly rose, sensing the threat of the sword was no longer present. He also apparently understood, as he lumbered over to Desert Rain and lowered himself enough so she could mount his back.

"That's all right, I'll follow on foot," Gothart said, handing Desert Rain the pack. "I'd rather do that then ride on what is undoubtedly a bustling metropolis for fleas and ticks."

Gank mounted Gimch and gave Gothart a sour look. "I wish. Fleas and ticks are yummy. Haven't eaten in days."

"Let's find some cover first to set up camp, and then we can tend to that," Desert Rain suggested, wincing as another lightning bolt crackled against a spire.

"COVER, YES! We know where cover is. Follow us!" Gank tugged on Gimch's fur and they broke into a run towards the west. Goude followed, lumbering along at a fast pace to stay at pace with his brothers. Desert Rain looked behind to see Gothart was managing to keep up, but he clearly had not anticipated how fast the Vermins would be, and he was sprinting at full speed.

Clova, wherever you are, I hope we can find you too, thought Desert Rain. *We need all the help we can get right now.*

CHAPTER EIGHTEEN
Scramble in the Bramble

Gank and his brothers led Desert Rain and Gothart to what could, indeed, be considered cover, but it was not the kind of cover the Hijn and goat hoped for. What had initially looked like a modest field of brambles in the distance — the first sign of vegetation that Desert Rain had yet to see in the Inbetween — grew more and more into an unruly tangle of woody vines and thorns that stretched for miles as they approached it. The Bramble, coiling as large and long as dragon tails, grew in a tightly woven mass well over fifty-feet tall, a variable palace of prickles. Berries the size of beehives dangled from the vines, glistening burgundy red and dripping with an intoxicating juice.

"Don't eat the berries," Gank advised, pulling back his lips into a disgusted snarl. "Smell like death and they burn skin."

Gothart frowned, glaring at the berries. "And they look so delicious, too. What else can disappoint me today?"

They squeezed their way through the knots of brambles, wincing as thorns inevitably bit at their skin, hair, and fur. After a few minutes, they found an opening in the vines that served as an enclosed space for them to rest. They sat down, the ground warm and pulsating beneath them.

"We should be well hidden for now," Desert Rain said. "But I know you're all hungry. Emily said she packed...er, poofed up some lunch for us." She placed the pack in her lap and opened it. She reached in and pulled out—

"COOKIES!" Gank wasted no time plunging his hands into the pack and pulling out a handful of what smelled to be cinnamon cookies. He fed cookies to each of his Distorted brothers before he shoved the pastries into his own muzzle, scattering crumbs everywhere.

Desert Rain sorted through the pack, finding a large leather canteen. She opened it and sniffed. "Of course. Chocolate milk. She gave us cookies and chocolate milk."

"That's why you don't let a child pack your provisions," Gothart snorted. "But I'll take what I can get." He took a cookie from Desert Rain and nibbled at it, grousing.

Desert Rain passed the canteen around so everyone could have a drink. "All right. We'll rest for a bit, then I'll scout around to see if I can find any...well, anything. I don't suppose you saw anything while running away from Katawa, Gank? Anyone? Maybe, any signs of elves?"

Gank crammed another cookie in his mouth and shook his head. "No elf. Just rocks, and this bush. And dirt. And tracks."

"Tracks? What kind of tracks?"

Gank shrugged. "The foot kind? Not monster foot, though. Kind with..." He wrinkled his forehead and tried to draw the shape in the air with his finger. "Long, flat, not deep. Smelled like apples."

"Apples?" Desert Rain's face lit up. "Apple leather! You smelled boot soles made of apple leather. And there's only one race in Luuva Gros that knows how to make apple leather. Will you show me—"

A long, viscous slime of crimson juice dripped down right in front of Desert Rain's face. She scooted back from it, heeding Gank's previous warning that the berries' juice could burn her skin. Looking up, she spotted a berry hanging directly overhead—and it was twitching.

Gothart stared at the berry, his lip curled in revulsion. "Is that normal for Inbetween fruit?"

One of the drupelets of the berry suddenly burst, a spray of juice—or was it juice at all?—spurting out as something punctured the fruit from the inside out. A tiny claw, a hand, and then a head, squeezed its way out. Then another drupelet popped, and another, and another, all revealing tiny creatures. The creatures, no larger than a human hand, were deep plum in hue, with beady black eyes and wide mouths with pointy red teeth. With roundish bodies, long saltatorial hind legs for leaping, and magenta grasshopper wings, they fully emerged from the fruit and looked down at the intruders below.

Desert Rain blanched. "Those aren't berries… those are egg clusters!"

Gothart grimaced. "Bramble imps. Just what I was lacking in this otherwise seamless situation."

Gank didn't feel like adding his own quip—he immediately screamed and took off, squeezing his way through the thorny vines and not caring if barbs scratched his skin. His brothers, oblivious to any pain other than the Distortion, broke into a lumbering run and cracked, snapped, and trampled the brambles, making a path for Desert Rain and Gothart to follow in quick pursuit.

The buzzing of wings crescendoed to a deafening degree as they were followed by the swarm of imps, who were hungry for any source of food in the Bramble. Despite Goude and Gimche clearing the way, the group was inhibited by their surroundings, and Desert Rain could feel imps crawl into her hair. She batted them away, pulling them out of her long tresses as the little vermin tried to bite her.

"You know, *magic* would be helpful in this situation!" Gothart yelled, as he yanked an imp off his neck and threw it aside.

Desert Rain ventured to look behind her. *Divine Beasts, there are so many of them!* She didn't think one blast of Blueshine could get them all, but some would be better than none.

"Get behind me!" She allowed Gothart to run past her, and she extended one hand upwards as the closest cluster of imps appeared overhead. She was preparing to speak her dragon incantation, but suddenly a burst of blue exploded from her fingertips — the magic was ready without command. The burst billowed above her, into the brambles, coating everything it touched. She watched as twenty imps were dusted in Blueshine, frozen into glass statues along the equally glazed branches, before poofing into a spray of sand that sprinkled onto the ground in shimmering dust.

This, however, did not deter the several hundred more imps closing in on her.

Another blast of Blueshine, and another, and another. The air became thick with bluish glittering sand, to the point that Desert Rain had to cough and wipe sand from her eyes. She had cleared all the brambles around her, along with several dozens of imps, but all this had done was eliminate her cover. She was now in the open, surrounded by sand and hundreds of imps continuing to close the gap as they flitted towards her.

At least the others got away, I hope, she thought. She breathed heavily, as sweat rolled down her face and she felt her legs wobble. *Guerda-Shaylr, I forgot how much energy magic takes. I don't know how much more Blueshine I can keep flinging...*

She reached for Silverheart in its pouch, but even as she gripped the handle, it seemed to weigh a ton. She grimaced, using all her remaining strength to draw it out and hold it high. She managed one good swing and sliced an imp, which squealed and fell to the ground in two clean-cut halves. Now if only she could do that a few hundred more times...

Another bramble imp suddenly fell to the ground, but not by Silverheart's doing. Desert Rain looked down at the writhing creature to see a long, wooden shaft sticking out of its gut.

She looked up to see an impending rain of arrows coming down around her. Instinctively, she lunged away towards the nearest covering of bramble, falling on her stomach and covering her head with her hands. She listened to the hundreds of whooshes, shrieks, and soft thunks of little bodies hitting the ground mere feet away from her. When the sounds ceased, she risked raising her head to look. A field of arrows filled the open space where she had just been standing moments ago, each arrow claiming a bloody bramble imp that was now pinned to the dirt. The buzzing of wings had stopped entirely; there wasn't a single imp left. Every arrow had hit its mark.

A soft scuffle of boots came up beside her head.

Desert Rain looked up at the boots' owner, someone tall, dressed in green-tinted and brown leather armor and carrying a longbow. From under his leather helmet, two pointed ears stuck out, and his face had swirls of green moss on his cheeks.

"While I'm sure you had everything in hand, Madam Hijn," the Ahshi elf said, "I hope you don't mind that we lent a hand."

He extended his hand to Desert Rain, and she accepted it as the elf helped her stand. She steadied herself, exhaling a long sigh. "Thank you. I'm so relieved I found you. I'm looking for Clova Flor."

"We will take you to her, you and these Distorted we captured. We were scouting the area when we saw them rooting around the Spire Stones, and we hoped they'd lead us to their master. You are no longer their prisoner."

From out of the Bramble, more armored Ahshi elves appeared as if they had materialized from another plane of existence. They came through the remaining Bramble without hindrance, snaking their way around the thorny vines as if they had lived here their whole lives. Among them, Gothart, Gank, Gimch and Goude were bound by ropes tied around their necks, as the elf soldiers held them captive.

"Found boots that smell like apples!" Gank called out to her, as if this was helpful.

Desert Rain retrieved Silverheart from where it fell to the ground and returned it to her pouch. "These are my companions. I wasn't their prisoner. They escaped from Katawa! We were trying to find you all."

"I told them all that!" Gothart said with a huff. "But apparently a goat's word isn't worth a farthing around here."

The elf soldier bowed his head. "Our apologies. But those two are possessed by the same dark poison that is ravaging all Luuva Gros." He pointed to Goude and Gimche. "We thought they were in the Distortionist's thrall."

"They're on our side, I promise."

The elf nodded, but his expression showed that he was not convinced. "General Flor will sort this out. She instructed us to keep an eye out for you, Madam Rain. She wasn't sure if we would find you, but it will lift her spirits to see you."

Desert Rain thought she had misheard at first— *General*? Clova had always been a guiding hand for her people, but not a soldier. "Is she well?"

"As well as one can be in these troubling times. Come, we will bring you to our camp."

They traversed deeper into the Bramble, and the vines seemed to get thicker and thornier, but the Ahshi navigated it with ease while Desert Rain and her companions continued to stumble through the brush. After what must have been a few miles, the Bramble began to thin, and Desert Rain could see light up ahead— a light that was already beginning to fill her with a sense of warmth and safety.

The brambles slowly moved apart as if of their own volition, with a few creaks as the woody vines peeled away. But Desert Rain already knew this was not of the Brambles' doing—only the Forest Hijn could bend the will of plants—and as the vines pulled back, she could see the enclosed camp hidden inside the Bramble. It was massive, hundreds of tents stationed as elves and riding elk populated the place. Supplies, bows, arrows, and packs were kept in precise inventory, and small campfires illuminated the encampment.

A welcoming party stood at the entrance to the camp, expecting the scouts' return. Among them was a Knight, resplendent in a suit of full armor, painted with emerald green and gold, with the insignia of Earthbelly over her heart.

Desert Rain was not aware that the Ahshi Elves had a member of the Knighthood of Luuva among them, until she recognized the face and was completely astonished. "Clova?"

Clova Flor's eyes bulged as if she had witnessed the dead rise. "Dez? Oh, praise Earthbelly!" She broke formation and ran straight to Desert Rain, wrapping her in a tight embrace. "I thought you might be lost to us. But I never stopped hoping you were alive."

"Clova, you have no idea what a weight this lifts from my heart," Desert Rain sniffled, fighting back tears. "But how is this possible? How did you get here?"

"There will be time for that. You must be starving. Come, you and your...friends..." She scrutinized the two Distorted, the small rat-like boy, and the scruffy goat man. She frowned at first, but then smiled at Desert Rain again. "You always did befriend those whom others turn a blind eye to. But we are all united against a common enemy here. Your party is welcome in my camp."

"Well, it's about time!" Gothart lifted off the noose from around his neck and tossed it at the elf holding the other end of the rope. "Some lemongrass tea would be refreshing. And I must have eight hours of uninterrupted sleep, so I will require a tent of my own and plenty of soft cushions. Oh, and clean garments. Surely one of you has some fresh tunics to spare, preferably silk."

Clova Flor's eyes narrowed as she walked straight up to Gothart, her face an inch from his nose. Her voice deepened, and her tone shifted to stern seriousness. "You will eat what is offered and you will sleep where we put you. Everyone must make sacrifices here, and we will not offer special courtesy even if you are Desert Rain's attendant. Do you understand?"

Desert Rain was caught off guard — she was not used to hearing Clova be quite so forceful — but it did make her grin.

Gothart bit his lower lip into a goofy smile. "Y-y-yes, ma'm. I mean, sir. I mean, whatever you want to be, please don't hurt me."

*　　*　　*

Clova's quarters were modest but comfortable, a simple woven-cloth tent on the outside but a makeshift greenhouse on the inside. Her plants here were not like the ones she grew in Juka Basin, however; these were flowerless, but the patterns on the leaves echoed the skins of leopards and tigers. Desert Rain gently touched the flat broad leaves that in the dim light of the overhanging lanterns seemed to glow an eerie blue.

"I've been experimenting with the soil in the Inbetween," Clova explained, as she noted Desert Rain's curiosity. "Most of the seeds from the Noblelands I brought with me did not take to it, and there's so little sunlight here they had nothing to feed on. But the native plantlife is malleable, susceptible to my magic's guidance. That gives us an advantage. If I can use my earth magic here, then we control the terrain over our enemies. I've found that influencing the plants has even encouraged them to provide new nutrients into the soil here through their roots. That means the Inbetween, over time, could be terraformed into a more thriving place. Isn't that amazing?"

Desert Rain gave her a tired smile. "It's good, Clova."

The Forest Hijn's mood shifted to concern. "Of course, here I am prattling when you must be exhausted. We have plenty of food and drink for you, and then you can rest here."

Gothart glanced around the tent, while the Vermin brothers sat in a corner gnawing on the dried fruit jerky that the elves had provided to them. The goat sniffed warily at the plants. "Ugh, everything smells like rotten cabbage. I never thought I'd appreciate plain old grass."

Clova went to an upright barrel upon which a wooden tea set was sitting. She poured a cup of steaming liquid and held it out to Gothart. Her face was stoic, but there was an edge to her tone. "Tea, then? You best keep yourself healthy, as I cannot tolerate delicate constitutions in my camp."

Gothart carefully took the cup from her, as one might take a piece of meat from a lioness's mouth. "Thank you, general. Your graciousness is only matched by your wisdom and beauty."

"I don't appreciate pandering insincerity." She turned away from him, eying the Vermins in the corner. Gank looked at her with nervous eyes and flashed a too-big smile at her. The two Distorted huddled close to each other, mindlessly chewing the food with some difficulty as their teeth did not align properly anymore. Clova gave them a long, hard glare. "Do they speak, little one?"

Gank's smile dropped at the question. "Um, they

haven't really, since the bad man changed them. They try, but I think it hurts them."

"I'm sorry for their pain, and yours as well. If there is anything we can provide that might alleviate their suffering, let us know." Clova walked back over to Desert Rain. "I need to discuss a matter with you, in private."

She led Desert Rain outside the tent, leading her away to another tent. A few elven soldiers inside bowed as Clova entered, and with a wave of her hand, they took their leave so the general and Desert Rain could have seclusion.

Clova leaned in close. "Dez, if I may…those two Distorted. I realize you are trying to protect them, but can they be trusted? How do you know they truly escaped? Isn't it possible their master sent them out on a mission? Even the small Lejenous with them could be a servant to the Twisted One."

"No, they wouldn't…" Desert Rain paused. She inhaled a shaky breath as she recalled how Katawa had taken control of Merros's mind when he was infected with Distortion. Could Katawa do the same with the two Vermins? What if he let them run away on purpose? To be his eyes and ears, to warn him if enemies were nearby?

If she told her suspicions to the elves, they would kill Goude and Gimche right now. No, she had to figure this out. After all, Katawa loved to show off so much, he wouldn't keep it hidden if he were puppeteering the two brothers. Besides, they did not make for very good "eyes", as their Distortion had twisted their eyelids nearly shut.

"I don't believe that," Desert Rain said firmly.

"They're scared, Clova. They're just boys, and they need our help. We can't let suspicion make us cruel."

Clova inhaled deeply, and slowly exhaled. "I know you mean well. And I don't intend to come across as cruel. But I cannot afford to be naïve. I will be vigilant and do what must be done. As you should, too. Now, please get some rest. I'll need your help at the next briefing."

"Of course, whatever I can do." Desert Rain was not sure if she was familiar with this side of Clova — where was the lighthearted free spirit she had known for decades? Had Katawa robbed her of that, too? Not that Desert Rain could blame her. Clova had to be a leader now, and that meant making tough decisions. But Desert Rain silently mourned the loss of what her friend had been before, and could only hope maybe Clova could rediscover her old self once all this passed.

*   *   *

The group of elven captains gathered with Clova around a rough table, upon which a length of reed paper was spread. The paper displayed a crude map drawn in black wax, one that the elves had tried their best to document what areas of the Inbetween that they had traversed. Large portions of the map were still blank.

Desert Rain stood quietly at Clova's side as she spoke to her soldiers. The general pointed to various spots on the map. "From what the scouts have observed, these areas have the largest groupings of Distorted, but the trajectory of the Distortionist's forces seem erratic. We're not sure if they are aware of our presence and are trying to throw us off their trail, or if they have no clear destination. As they continue to spread out their units further west and south, it would seem they are searching for something." She turned to the desert Hijn. "Desert Rain, if anyone might know the mental machinations of this enemy, it would be you. Is the Distortionist searching for something?"

Desert Rain held her breath, and she felt her face grow hot. "Well, I...I think once he's gathered enough army, he wants to locate the gates to L'Teth Zurên."

The elves murmured among each other in confused hums. Clova held her gaze on Desert Rain. "We are unfamiliar with this location. What is it?"

"It's the hidden bastion of the Darkscale clan. Goth—" She was about to say Gothart would know more, since he had been there already. But then she'd have to mention that Gothart had been employed by the Darkscale in the past, and as much as the goat had caused her so many problems, she did not need him to be held captive as a possible Darkscale spy. "Gods of Luuva only know where the entrance is, though. Apparently, the Darkscale use their abilities to shift the location of the gates throughout the Inbetween. Katawa doesn't possess any devices or magical implements that would allow him to find the gates, as far as I know. He's probably hunting blindly."

"That would explain why he's distributing his forces. And our scouts have been unable to discover where he might be keeping the Hijn Council. If they're not currently with him, then he's keeping them in reserve until he finds the Darkscale clan. Until then, they should be safe, or at least alive." Clova tightened her lips as she thought. "That means now is the time to strike. Our army against the combined powers of the Council wouldn't stand a chance. But if Katawa has them imprisoned somewhere, then it's just him and these Distorted. If we attack the Distorted head on, and attack him from a distance, we can reduce his numbers and maybe weaken him before he can reach his destination."

Desert Rain's heart skipped a beat. "Clova...I mean, General, the Distorted are innocent people that Katawa has twisted to his will. They need our help. We can't just treat them like war fodder—"

"I understand your concern," Clova interjected. "But you said it yourself. These Distorted are in pain. They're suffering, and no longer who they used to be. As far as we know, there is no undoing the Distortionist's damage. They will destroy us at his command. I'm sorry, Desert Rain. This is war. We do what we must to save what's left." She picked her helmet up from the table and placed it on her head. "We need to gather our troops immediately. Desert Rain, you may stay here and look after the camp—"

"No!" The word came out much more forcefully than she expected, and she could sense all the elves grow tense. She softened her tone. "If you're going after Katawa, I need to be there. I don't have the weapon I was hoping for, but I do have resources that can help."

"What resources?" asked one of the captains.

Desert Rain paused, but then she stepped back from the table, drew out Silverheart from her pouch and held it up.

A smile graced Clova's lips. "Silverheart, of course! And you wield it so well. But, Dez, do you feel prepared to battle? You've been through so much—"

"I also have this." She held up the Hollow Eye hanging around her neck. "I'm not fully certain of its powers, but it allows the wearer and anyone at close range to shift location. It seems a bit more limited here in the Inbetween, but it can get us out of a tight situation quickly."

The Hollow Eye suddenly began to glow a subtle cerulean blue, and it floated into the air, hovering in front of Desert Rain's face. Silverheart glowed as well, a shimmering blue-white aura. The elves stepped back, unsure of what power was coming to life in front of them. Desert Rain looked back and forth between the Hollow Eye and Silverheart—why were they responding to each other? This was just like back at the Spire Stones, but it was no clearer what was causing the reaction now than before.

"Dez?" Clova ventured a closer look at the Hollow Eye. She gently touched it, finding it caused no harm. "Where did you get that?"

"I...there was a little girl, with the snow elves." Desert Rain decided now was not a good time to discuss that the Elfë Taigas were in truth the Secret Sacroth, or if that even mattered now, if any were left. "She had this, and she gave it to me."

"With the snow elves..." A strange expression crossed Clova's face, and she looked at the Hollow Eye like it might burst into an inferno any second. "This is what you found in the Taigalands? This is what the Elfë Taigas gave you?"

"I don't think they intended for me to—"

"Thank you, Desert Rain. This is most helpful. Everyone is dismissed. Move quickly." Clova went straight to the flap of the tent, throwing it open as she ushered all the elves out.

Desert Rain was left alone with Clova. "Clova?

Did I—"

Clova returned to her, urgency in her voice. "Dez, the snow elves possess incredibly powerful magic. Even with something this small..." She began to pace, rubbing her hands together. "It must be of great importance. But tell me, what of your quest? Did the snow elves say anything of the Lightscale?"

"All they said was, that it exists, but they didn't have it anymore. The Frost Dragon sent it away with someone a long time ago."

Clova's hopeful intensity dropped. "Did they say who? Can it be recovered?"

Desert Rain shook her head. "I don't know."

"But they gave you this instead. Surely, it must be the key..." Clova came back over to the hovering Eye. "If this can shift the location of the wearer, then surely it can bring you to the Lightscale! That must be why they gave it to you!"

Desert Rain couldn't believe the idea had not crossed her mind. She had been so eager to find Clova, that she hadn't thought to ask if the Hollow Eye could take her to wherever the Lightscale might be. "Of course! If the Hollow Eye can see it, it can bring us to it. Its power seems a bit off due to the Malaise Cloud, but we could give it a try."

Clova took Desert Rain's hand. "Will it take us both?"

"It should. It's allowed me to bring a passenger before." Desert Rain took the Hollow Eye in hand, holding it close to her heart. "Take us to the Lightscale, wherever it is. Please."

Nothing happened.

Desert Rain swallowed hard. She closed her eyes.

Please, if you sense the Lightscale anywhere, take Clova and me to it. Even if you remember the last place you saw it, take us there!

She opened her eyes. Still, nothing.

Desert Rain sighed with a shrug. "I don't think it can see beyond the Inbetween..." But when she looked down at the Eye, it was not cloudy like before. Instead, she saw something she hadn't ever seen in the Hollow Eye before — it was a solid, pale blue with an iridescent sheen. A moonstone. And it had a growth on the bottom — a short, thin, silver shaft with a crescent-shaped bit on the end.

"I don't understand." Desert Rain gave Clova an unsure look. "It hasn't done this before."

"I think...it really *is* a key," Clova whispered.

Desert Rain let slip a groan of exasperation. "A key to what? We don't have anything that this could go to—"

That's when she turned her gaze to Silverheart. For the first time, she noticed the small hole in the top of the pommel. She would have sworn it wasn't there before, that she had handled this sword enough to have noticed it long before now. But there it was. A keyhole.

Desert Rain locked her gaze with Clova's. Her eyes asked the question. *Should we do it?*

Clova's eyes spoke uncertainty. But she nodded.

Cautiously, Desert Rain slipped the moonstone key into the keyhole and gave it a gentle turn until she heard a soft click.

The world when completely white for a few seconds as light exploded in the tent. Desert Rain was positive that she was blinded, but it took a moment or two for her eyes to adjust. When she could see again, the room was still awash in light, but the spectrum shifted across every color—pinks, blues, greens, golds, silvers, purples, all of them. Her hands were empty, and Silverheart now floated in the air before her. But it was no longer Silverheart.

The blade was much, much longer; it was now longer than Desert Rain was tall. It was also no longer a flat sharp metal, but a twisting staff of silver-scaled dragon tails all the way down from the top of the tent to the floor. The cross-guard was longer across, stretching out like two extended eagle wings of golden feathers. On each end of the cross guard were swirling balls of brilliance, miniature galaxies of gleaming stars, planets, moons, and comets contained. Atop was the Hollow Eye, although now it was a beacon of starlight, inside of which constellations danced and played. It was pure radiance, pure glory, and Desert Rain felt the essences of warmth, courage, and love envelope her in its presence.

Clova was too stunned to speak at first, but she eventually found the words. "It's...the Lightscale!"

CHAPTER NINETEEN
Railroaded

The elven troops marched across the plains of the Inbetween, most on foot but many on elkback, as they departed the Bramble a few hours later. Desert Rain sat behind Clova on her elk, still bewildered by the secret they had discovered. Bewildered, and fuming—she felt there were at least half a dozen people she had met recently who could have told her about the Lightscale, that Silverheart and the Hollow Eye were its two significant pieces. Guerda-Shalyr, Emily, the High Lady, probably even the winter gryphons who had such a deep connection to the Secret Sacroth—there was no way none of them knew the truth. Was it that everyone in Luuva Gros just loved messing with her?

Clova, meanwhile, had a renewed sense of confidence at the discovery—perhaps overconfidence, in Desert Rain's opinion—so much so that the general wasted no time rallying her troops and heading out to face their adversaries. Never mind that Desert Rain still did not know what to do with the Lightscale—at least, not beyond putting it together and taking it apart again for easy carrying. Silverheart was tucked safely in her pouch again, and the Hollow Eye hung around her neck. But Clova had simply said, "The Lightscale possesses a power beyond any of our understanding, but it has a life of its own. It will guide us in what to do."

Guide, huh? Desert Rain frowned—she thought about another who, without a doubt, must have known

Silverheart was a part of the Lightscale. Sir Luce! How could he not tell her? Why must he always be so cryptic? In fact, she had half a mind to tell him off right—

"You're upset with me."

Desert Rain was learning quickly not to be surprised by Sir Luce pulling her into his mental arena, even when she was awake. Except now the arena was full of blue sand, sparkling like grain-sized sapphires around her. One might have confused it for water, if she had not been standing on it. Yet it felt cool and smooth, not grainy, between her toes. The arena was surrounded by space, ribbons of heavenly light streaming around them in greens, blues, and pinks.

Sir Luce was no longer his knightly form; he had returned to his Sagely appearance, a long, winding silver dragon. He sat patiently on one side of the arena, flicking the end of his scaly tail.

"Of course I'm upset!" She placed her hands on her hips. "You must've known you've been inhabiting part of the Lightscale all this time. Why didn't you tell me?"

The knight-dragon regarded her evenly. "The desire to tell you ran through my mind many times. At first, I thought it was needless to tell you unless you found the missing piece to awaken Silverheart's true form. What good is a bow without an arrow, or one piece of flint to start a fire?"

"That's not a good enough answer, Sir Luce. If I had known—"

"You're right. It's not good enough." He let out a long, rumbling sigh. His voice shifted to sadness. "While that was part of it, there was a more troubling issue. You know now of Skyhan's secret. His rendering of himself.

The truth is, his act rendered me as well, although he did not know it."

Desert Rain's anger subsided. "It did? Does that mean there are two halves of you as well?"

"Not quite like that." Sir Luce slowly laid on his side, extending out his long neck so his chin rested on the ground. "I realized, if Skyhan believed that was the only way to be pure, I had not been a good guardian or teacher. It broke my heart. And because of that, I feared...I *fear*, that being within Silverheart makes it weakened as well. And I worried that it would make the Lightscale unable to be activated. Even now, I still fear it may not work at its full abilities. Yet, if I am to leave Silverheart, where would I go? A Sage needs a vessel. Otherwise..." He fell silent, unable to finish.

Desert Rain walked over and sat on the sand beside Sir Luce's head. "I wish you had talked to Gabriel about this. He was part of Skyhan once. He was part of you."

Sir Luce closed his eyes. "So much betrayal. So much pain. He thought I abandoned him. He was better off without me."

It hurt Desert Rain to know Sir Luce felt this way. She had never thought a Sage could feel so...human. "I realize now what you and Skyhan had in common. You both wanted to be so perfect. So unfailing in your virtue. But that's not how people are. We mess up sometimes. But we still have a chance. We can still make things right. You can't be so scared of failing that you don't face the truth. I need your help now. Can you teach me how to use this Lightscale against Katawa? To undo the Distortion?"

Sir Luce turned his head to look at her. "You seem

to misunderstand. The Lightscale cannot undo the Distortion. It is a component of balance, not a cure-all."

Desert Rain would have, normally, tried to keep the surmounting anger boiling inside of her under control, but in this mental realm, her scream reverberated across the mind-scape as if it could shatter the sky. "What do you mean, the Lighscale can't undo the Distortion? What in Luuva have we been doing all this for if it won't fix everything?! Why did I lose ALL my friends, my home, my faith, for nothing??"

Sir Luce growled deeply at the back of his throat, but his eyes remained patient. "I didn't say the Lightscale couldn't help. You simply don't understand its properties. Nor do you seem to understand what can truly undo this Distortion. Now, are you going to listen, or keep screaming?"

Desert Rain took several deep breaths until the knot of fury in her stomach loosened, although it lingered there. "Fine. Yes, I'm listening. Just don't withhold information from me anymore, promise?"

"Very well, I promise." Sir Luce lifted his head and rolled back into the sitting position. "For starters, those that can awaken the Lightscale have a unique bond with it. It is more than just its default shape."

As he spoke, a smaller version of the Lightscale materialized before Desert Rain's face. It was now roughly the same length as Silverheart, about forty inches long. It radiated with the same celestial glory but was easier to comprehend at this more manageable size.

"What do you mean?" she asked.

"Take hold of it," Sir Luce instructed.

Desert Rain reached out and took hold of it by the top end, where Silverheart's hilt would normally be. She gasped as it flashed a white blaze for a second, and then she realized she was holding a sword — but not Silverheart. This one was golden, with extended wings for the cross-guard, a ruby dragon's head for a pommel, and the reddish blade alight with astral fire. She was afraid she would be burned by this sword, but it remained cool in her hands.

"Ah, Burning Talon. He was always short tempered, but righteously ferocious." Sir Luce sounded wistful.

Desert Rain looked over the sword curiously. "Burning Talon? You mean, part of him is in the Lightscale? But I thought his soul was in Fierno Ginso."

"When we Hij-Urawran crafted the Equanume, each of us instilled it with a drop of our magic. And each of those magics can alter the Lightscale to whatever tool you need. It's no wonder that you summoned Burning Talon's magic first — your anger still runs hot. Try thinking… Waterweaver. The flow of water, moving around your obstacles."

Desert Rain closed her eyes, concentrating. She thought about her oasis, the traces of flowing water she could find in the desert…flowing, cool, life-giving… When she opened her eyes, she discovered she now held a glistening trident, the handle made of aquamarine and the three prongs on top glowing with blue rune markings. She tried again…Earthbelly, solid, firm, grounded…and the trident flashed into a bronze warhammer, with a Tiger's-eye-décor head twice as big as her own, with toothy spikes on both of its faces.

"That's incredible!" Her astonishment faltered. "But I'm not sure what to do with a shapeshifting weapon. We've only covered sword fighting."

"And what do you think I'm for? Moral support?"
Sir Luce gave her a big smile.

*   *   *

"Dez? Are you all right?"

Desert Rain snapped to attention at Clova's voice.
Returning to the real world from her mind-arena was
always jarring, especially after training for what felt like
two weeks. And again, her body felt all those weeks of
training, although she had been sitting behind Clova on
her elk the entire time.

"Hmm? Oh, I'm…I was just thinking." Desert
Rain blinked a few times, reacclimating to her
surroundings.

Clova looked over her shoulder at her, brow
knitted in concern. "You've been very quiet for the past
few hours. I thought maybe you fell asleep, and you
sounded a little distressed at one point. Like you were
having a bad dream."

"No, just a really, um, active dream. I'm fine."

Clova turned a little farther around to get a better
look at Desert Rain. "When did you bruise yourself?"

Desert Rain touched a spot on her cheek, wincing
at its tenderness. She probably had a fresh batch of
bruises all over—Sir Luce had not taken it easy on her,
and just like before, what happened in the mind-arena
left its evidence on her physical body. "It's a little
strange, but…I've been weapons training. The bruise is
from that."

"When did you have a chance to train? I know you
didn't have that bruise this morning."

Desert Rain grinned awkwardly. "You're going to

find this a little...odd..."

She went on to tell Clova about it all—Sir Luce, the shapeshifting Lightscale, the sleep training and sometimes awake training, how time passed faster in her mind than in the real world. The elf listened patiently, keeping her eyes ahead as Desert Rain talked. When she finished, the two were silent for a minute before Clova said, "Gracious, Dez, you'll need to write a book about all this when we go home." She looked at Desert Rain over her shoulder again, smiling. "Sir Skyhan would be very proud of you. Tell Sage Veritas I say hello next time you train."

Desert Rain smiled back. "I will." Her eyes drifted to the stark, sparse landscape. "Although 'going home' seems like such a long way off right now."

Clova murmured softly. "Thinking about all the beautiful things to go home to is what keeps me going. And maybe we could spend some time together, in my gardens, to help grow things. You would like that, wouldn't you, Dez?"

Desert Rain let out a soft chuckle. "I'm a desert dweller, Clova. I don't grow a whole lot of anything out there."

"I know, it must be so empty and lonely. Which is why you should get out of that desert and come live with me."

There was a strange, long pause as both women seemed to process what was just said. It was Desert Rain who broke the silence. "You mean to visit, right?"

"Yes, to visit. Of course." Clova paused, and then her next words tumbled out like pebbles from a pail. "Or not. You could, you know, stay. Longer than a visit. Maybe, all the time. With me. I don't mind. I'd like it, actually. Very much. If you would stay. But only if you want to. Of course."

Desert Rain opened her mouth to reply, but nothing came out. She blinked a few times, as if the blinking would help make sense of it all. "Are you asking me to move in with you? Why?"

The elven general was quiet again, and she shifted awkwardly in her saddle. "Because…we're friends. And we go decades without seeing each other, so…we have lots of time to make up for. Don't you think?" But there was a tinge of croakiness to her voice—her words were frogs trapped in quicksand and could not quite hop themselves to freedom.

"Clova, is there something else?"

Gradually, Clova's shoulders relaxed, and her grip on her elk's reins loosened a little. "I know you don't feel about me the way I feel about you, Dez. I figured maybe that's why you avoided me for so long—maybe you sensed how I felt and it scared you. And I don't want to do that. I know you were in love with Skyhan, and I was happy for you, I really was. I mean, how could someone like me remotely compare to that, anyway? So, I decided I was going to let my feelings go, if that meant I could keep you in my life as a friend. But…feelings are a lot like clover. You can pull them out by the roots again and again, and yet the next year, so much more grows back. But that's all right. It's a good kind of pain. Better than feeling…nothing. And I'd rather have you around than nothing."

Desert Rain felt her heart thumping—she wasn't sure why, as she was confused by Clova's admission more than anything. Maybe she *was* scared, but not of Clova's feelings. What could they possibly do from here?

Desert Rain looked down at her hand, at the finger where Clova had given her a jade and silver ring when they parted in Juka Basin. She had simply thought it a gesture of friendship — how could she not have realized? She knew she couldn't reciprocate Clova's feelings, not in the way she would want. Would they have to part ways after this war, for Clova's own sanity? Or could they stay friends, even if it ate away at Clova's heart every day?

"I…don't know what to say," were the only words Desert Rain could find.

"You don't have to say anything. I know that must've been a shock. But I had to say it. You can forget it now. We don't ever have to talk about it." Clova sat up straighter, her eyes forwards, her grip on her reins tight again.

Desert Rain knew she couldn't leave it at that. Forget about it? Clova laid her soul bare, and Desert Rain had rewarded her courage with *nothing*? No, Clova deserved better than that. She took a few minutes to contemplate a response. "I…I'm sorry, Clova. I do love you, like a sister. But it can't be more than that. To be honest, I don't think I could love anyone more than that ever again. Losing Skyhan, even losing the love I believed I had for Katawa, even though it was all a lie…my heart's about dried up. So, you have as much of my love as I can give, without me fearing I'll lose part of myself. I hope that can be enough."

Clova continued to look ahead for a few seconds, but then slowly looked over her shoulder at Desert Rain. She smiled, her eyes brimming with tears. "That is a gift I will happily accept, Desert Rain. It is more than I could hope for."

*   *   *

The flat landscape morphed into terrain of glassy obsidian—it was like walking upon a vast lake of shadow, with sharp-edged waves frozen in time that made traversing it precarious. Jagged mounds of garnet and onyx dotted with spiky shrubbery that resembled sea urchins rose from the black rock, and as the troops progressed through this land, the mounds gradually grew into hills, and beyond them loomed a mountain range that reminded Desert Rain of obelisks, thousands of sharp fingers flexed towards the clouds above.

Far ahead of them, up the pass through the hills, a figure came bounding towards them. It was an elven scout on elkback, a young lad wrapped in a brown tunic, and he made his way straight to Clova. The general held up a hand to halt the troops, and the procession slowed to a standstill.

"General, ahead, through the pass," the scout reported breathlessly, "...a valley...it's full of them! Hundreds of those monsters!"

Clova nodded. "Thank you, young one. Was the Distortionist with them?"

"I couldn't see," the scout replied. "I couldn't even make one beast out from the other. It's like a sea of bodies over there. He could be hiding among them, but there appeared to be no order or direction to the beasts' assembly."

With a gesture, Clova dismissed the scout. She looked over her shoulder at Desert Rain. "This could be a good opportunity to test the Lightscale. We can see exactly what the extent of its abilities are and its range."

"But we're not even certain what it will do,"

Desert Rain countered. "Even with what training Sir Luce gave me, I only know the beginnings of its magic, and that was in one-on-one combat. I have no clue how it would work on an army that's as big as what your scout just described."

"We must test it. And if it isn't as effective as we'd hope, then we'll have to sort the Distorted out in battle. I wish to avoid bloodshed as much as you, Dez, but we must do what we must. Hopefully, your Lightscale may be the more peaceful alternative."

Desert Rain furrowed her brow. What did Clova hope the Lightscale would do? Just make all the Distorted poof into thin air? Any chance that the Lightscale could undo the Distortion was unthinkable, according to Sir Luce — or, at least, not in the way Desert Rain had thought. *You don't understand what can truly undo this Distortion,* he had said. And, as usual, he hadn't offered any clear answer as to what that could be.

Clova was right. They had to find out what the Lightscale could do, and this was as good a chance as any, while they had the element of surprise. She reached into her pouch and drew out Silverheart. "What's the order, General?"

Clova smirked. "You're not my subordinate, Dez. No formal titles, okay?" She took a deep breath. "A small party will make it easier to sneak up on them and get a good look at what we're dealing with. I'll bring soldiers who are fleetest of foot in case we're spotted, and they need to retreat." She looked past Desert Rain towards her army. "I need the young Lejenous who was with the two Distorted in our custody. Someone bring him to me."

Desert Rain cleared her throat. "Could we not use that term? Gank is a normal boy, not a 'lesser one.'"

Clova tightened her lips. "I see. My apologies."

In a matter of minutes, Gank was dragged over by two soldiers and deposited in front of Clova. The general dismounted her elk and looked down at the shivering Vermin boy. "You were imprisoned among these creatures. What can you tell us about these Distorted? Do they have any special abilities? Attack patterns? Anything that would be helpful to us?"

Gank nervously shrugged. "They don't seem to think, much. They do what the bad man says. When he's not around, they get twitchy. Like they don't know what to do."

"He has no second in command? No one who dictates his orders when he's not around?" Clova asked.

"The wizard with the red eyes sometimes did, or the blue lady with the long hair. But I haven't seen them lately," Gank replied softly.

Desert Rain's face flushed with worry. Gank was describing Merros and V'Tanna. If Gank hadn't seen them recently, what had Katawa done with them and the rest of the Hijn Council?

Clova narrowed her eyes. "I see. So, if the Distortionist isn't here, they should be easy to overtake. If he *is* down there, we could be in for a vicious battle."

"You're not going to make me go back there, are you?" Gank whimpered. His eyes went wide with panic. "Can't go back! Brothers must stay away!"

Clova shook her head. "You and your brothers stay with the troops. Under close supervision." She turned to Desert Rain. "You, I, and a dozen of my best guards will go. We'll have to go on foot. The elks' hoof-steps are too loud on this terrain."

Desert Rain slid down from the elk's back. She

steeled her resolve. "Okay, let's go."

The scout had not exaggerated about the size of the Distorted congregation—if anything, he had not been descriptive enough. "Hundreds" were more like thousands, but it was difficult to tell with how tightly clustered together they all were. They almost seemed to move like one massive organism, crawling over, under, and among each other, leaving no room to breathe. Desert Rain wondered if this behavior was to keep any Distorted from wandering off in Katawa's absence, the way the Vermins had.

The reconnaissance party found a craggy path up to an outcropping of rocks above the valley to hide behind, giving them all a good vantage point. It was a steep decline from there down to the valley, steep enough that they hoped that if they were spotted, the Distorted would not be able to climb the descent to reach them. It also meant if anyone lost their footing, they would tumble down straight into the enemy's clutches.

"We have the high ground," Clova whispered. "Dez, is the Lightscale capable of a long-range attack?"

Desert Rain scanned the swarm of Distorted below, taking in the sheer multitude. "I'm not sure what good a long-range attack could do against so many. I mean, even if I could turn the Lightscale into a cannon, or a trebuchet, which I've never done before—"

"And that's not exactly the type of weapon we have space for, from this spot," Clova agreed. "I was hoping we could summon offensive magic. Fire, ice, lightning. Cast it as a wide net over them instead of individual attacks."

"A wide net..." Desert Rain pondered for a moment. "Clova, that could work! But not over them—

under them. You said you've managed to get the Inbetween flora to respond to your magic, right?"

"Yes, but the ground here is molten glass, and from what I can tell, it's several meters thick. The soil underneath might be fertile, but I can't get to it if there's no way to break through this rock."

"That might not be a problem, if my plan works the way I think it will. But I'll need your help." She drew out Silverheart and took the Hollow Eye in hand. She paused. "Clova, once I summon the Lightscale, you know how bright it'll be. We'll give away our position, so we'll have to act quickly. Are you ready for me to do this?"

Clova turned to three of the elven guards, nodding once to them, and they gestured an Ahshi signal of respect before silently retreating towards the pass. She then focused on Desert Rain. "What do you need me to do?"

Desert Rain grasped the sword's hilt tighter. "Just…try to keep me from botching this." She closed her eyes and concentrated — which weapon was it that she wanted? She needed one that could break up the molten glass under the Distorted army's feet. She considered Earthbelly's hammer to cause a fissure beneath the Distorted, but that could cause the hill she was standing on to crumble under her. Maybe Stormhowler's Bow? That could summon a torrent of lightning-crafted arrows with one release of the string, but Desert Rain had a better idea of how to use it.

"Clova, when I ask, I need you to channel your magic into the Lightscale," she said. "Do you think you can do that?"

The general pursed her lips in thought. "I've never

tried imbuing a weapon with my magic before, but it can't be too different than channeling my magic into seeds. Theoretically."

One more deep breath, and Desert Rain willed for the Lightscale to take the form she visualized in her mind—thanks to her training, she now had a good visual for all the Sages' specific weapons. A burst of light emanated from her hands, and she knew the Distorted would see it, that was for certain. She opened her eyes, and in her grasp was a grand bow, carved from yew and decorated with pearls and jasper along its limbs. This had come to be one of her favorite weapons to train with, as she had been raised by her family to know how to use a bow for hunting.

She could hear the commotion of the Distorted below drop to silence. Desert Rain felt her veins turn cold as all the twisted, mangled faces looked her way, even as the brightness of the Lightscale diminished as Stormhowler's Bow settled into its form. Then the silence broke into a cacophony of screeches and howls, the deafening rage of the Distorted realizing they were being watched.

Desert Rain, maintaining her composure as she drew back the bowstring, focused on pulling out Stormhowler's drop of magic, and it formed a straight beam of lightning at her fingertips. Once the string was taut, she shouted over the din of the monsters below. "Now, Clova! Channel your magic into the arrow!"

Clova hesitated—she had no idea what touching the lightning arrow would do, but she saw Desert Rain was not hurt by it—and then laid her fingers on where the fletching of the arrow would normally be. Desert Rain could feel the surge of magic, as the lightning's bright white radiated with a greenish shade. When she felt that the combined magic of Stormhowler and Earthbelly was at capacity for the bow to handle, she released the bowstring, sending the green lightning arcing through the air towards the center of the Distorted mass.

From the crater, green life erupted. Dormant seeds, buried in sleep under the layers of glass, responded to Clova's magic transported through the lightning. Almost frenzied by their desire to grow outside of their prison, gnarled vines and brambles poured out of the crater as freely and wildly as a geyser. The Distorted, driven by their blind rage to catch their enemies, did not comprehend how they were suddenly ensnared by thorned coils that wound their tendrils around legs, arms, and bodies. Any Distorted that tried to bite or claw their way to freedom found themselves immobilized, dragged down onto their backs and bellies by the crushing creepers.

The lightning struck the ground with a concussive blast, sending Distorted nearby flying away from the impact. Molten glass exploded everywhere, raining down shards, and where the lightning had struck was now a crater several yards deep, exposing earth beneath. The Distorted bellowed again, turning their attention back to Desert Rain and Clova. The whole herd heaved its way towards their position, clawing their way up the steep hillside.

Desert Rain and Clova fended off the advancing Distorted, launching a few quick lightning bolts at the feet of their attackers to send them tumbling back down the cliffside. They did not have to do this for long before their bramble brigade had caught up to the outermost rim of Distorted. The two Hijn surveyed the valley, observing how all the Distorted were now restrained — or, for a handful that managed to elude the net of creepers, they escaped out the other side of the valley, retreating in a panicked haste.

"That was fabulous, Dez!" Clova said, catching her breath as she scanned their captives. "This should hold them long enough for my troops to come through and deal with them."

Desert Rain shot her a bewildered look. "Deal with them? We just did! We don't have to hurt them now."

Clova's smile wavered into a grimace. "Dez, we can't leave them like this. It's crueler to leave them this way to starve than to…understand, it gives me no pleasure, but this is war."

"No! Just…give me a second. There must be something I…*we* can do. If I could just show you the Distortion can be lifted…" Desert Rain's brain crackled with a storm of thoughts, and then she clutched her fists around her bow. "Wait! Mage Skyhan's dragon… Halua Mata! Her healing magic is in the Lightscale, maybe magic that Mage Skyhan herself hasn't tapped into yet."

Clova furrowed her eyebrows in concern. "I know you want to spare these creatures, but we can't get too ambitious with something we don't fully understand right now. You're not versed in healing magic, and if it's magic that even Mage Skyhan hasn't attempted —"

"Just let me try! Like you said, the Distorted are secured. You can afford one minute for me to try."

The Forest Hijn's face hardened, and Desert Rain thought she would retort. But the general sighed instead. "One try."

Desert Rain closed her eyes, visualizing…what had been Halua Mata's weapon? It was not one she and Sir Luce had used much in training, since in her mind-arena, Desert Rain wasn't injured beyond bruises and therefore had not needed magic to heal. A healer typically used…a staff! That was it! In another flash of light, Stormhowler's Bow morphed into Halua Mata's Staff: a tall, braided length of ash wood, atop of which sprung clusters of healing herbs such as sweetgrass, goldenrod, and sage. It was plain and simple compared to the other Lightscale weapons, but it had no need to be showy.

She figured using the staff could not be terribly different from how she activated the other weapons in the Lightscale. It took focus, will, and confidence. She had also seen Made Skyhan speak healing spells before; there seemed to be no specific order to the words in her incantations, as long as they were in Dragontongue. Desert Rain held up the staff, chewing on a few words in Dragontongue that felt appropriate…

Drive out the disease…

Mend what has been inflicted…

Heal until the body and mind is restored!

From the top of the staff, a spray of sparkling mist wafted on the wind, slowly spreading out over the valley in a cloud of sweet-smelling vapor. Desert Rain could feel this magic was gentle, compassionate, and comforting.

Clova sniffed at the air. "Lavender and lemon balm. Those relieve physical and mental pain, which is what you essentially asked for, although—"

The Distorted stopped struggling in their vine restraints as the scents from the healing magic descended on them. They smelled the strange magic settling on them, seeping into their noses and snouts. One of the Distorted shriek a long, shrill cry, and this was followed by the others in a cacophony of horrid squeals and screams. They thrashed about more wildly than before, biting and clawing at the vines with a greater sense of urgency.

Desert Rain looked about in panic as the Distorted turned more feral by the second. "Why are they acting that way? The healing magic should make them feel better, and they're acting like they're in more pain!"

Clova grabbed the staff from Desert Rain, throwing it back behind them to stop the spraying mist. "We don't know what Distortion is other than evil magic, Dez! Some magic is immune to other magic, even designed to undo another magic's effects. We need to get my army here before they break through those vines!"

Already, they could hear the snapping and cracking of vines below, and the Distorted were already untangling themselves from their floral prison. Dozens started climbing up the cliffside towards them again, gnarled faces and maws snapping in fury. Desert Rain ran and picked up the staff, hoping maybe a more specific spell might correct her mistake, but Clova forcefully grabbed her arm and began dragging her down the path back to the pass. The general reached into one of her pouches, withdrawing a curved elk horn. She blew into it, and a resounding burst of sound filled the air. Desert Rain knew the elven army would be there in minutes at Clova's call, but the Distorted were scrambling up, up, up the cliff with veracious speed, clawing up and over one another with the tenacity of rats to rotten meat. Desert Rain thought she and Clova might be able to outrun them, but the two women jerked to a dead stop as they saw Distorted charging at them up the mountain path, blocking their escape. Clova was already drawing out her bow, and Desert Rain knew she had to summon another weapon, forcing herself to focus on calling Silverheart—

Another loud, high howl filled the air. But it did not come from Clova's horn—it came from the other side of the valley.

An abrupt cold wind ripped through the hills, and Desert Rain and Clova noticed tiny, white fluff begin to fall around them. They turned back to look to see gray clouds floating above, separate formations from the Maliase Cloud, and a gentle snowfall trickled down across the valley and mountains.

"You didn't do that, did you?" Clova asked.

Desert Rain looked at the staff in her hand, as if it might answer the question. "I don't think so."

The roars and shrieks of the Distorted, which had been deafening, gradually faded into a discomforting quiet. The two Hijn watched as the Distorted who had been charging their way slowed, their legs and arms dragging with sudden heaviness, until they collapsed in a heap and remained still. Looking down the cliff, the women saw the Distorted sliding back down the precipice, their movements growing sluggish. The pandemonium in the valley settled into calm, and it was still except for another bellow from across the valley that sounded much closer now.

Desert Rain perked up her ears, and suddenly recognized that sound. "That's a train whistle," she gasped.

From a mountain pass, a familiar train rumbled

along on iron treads, its teethy front catcher pushing a mass of Distorted in front of it to make way. The Grand Imperial Battle Train chugged along through the valley until coming to a grinding halt in the middle, letting out a blast of smoke from one of its stacks.

"Is that a Bloodburn battle train?" Clova asked, her eyes wide in bewilderment.

"Not just any Bloodburn battle train," Desert Rain replied. She felt a strange combination of both relief and trepidation in her chest. "That's King Ragnor's train! He must be here to help us fight the Distorted!"

Clova's jaw opened an inch, but no words came out as she stared searchingly at her friend.

"Very long story, but King Ragnor respects the Moon Dragoness, so the Bloodburn are our allies. And this—" She gestured towards the snow, "must be a secret weapon they have to...put the Distorted to sleep?"

That was about the gist of it, for the Distorted had slowed to near paralysis except for heavy breathing, and they littered the ground in what appeared to be deep slumber.

"But why does it put *them* to sleep and not *us*?" Clova wondered. "Bloodburn don't possess magic that can target specific enemies. Not to mention Bloodburn never pass up the chance for bloodshed over a peaceful solution."

From the window of the train's engine, a head poked out and looked around. Desert Rain's heart nearly exploded as even from that distance, she could make out the red hair and recognized the voice that shouted, "That'ttk did the trick all right-ttk! That's-ss some mighty magic-kk you got-ttk, Frosty!"

"Mac! MA-A-A-A-C!" Desert Rain called, waving

her staff in the air like a flag.

It took the lizard man a few moments of glancing around in all directions, but eventually his eyes fell on Desert Rain up the cliffside. He nearly fell out the window, letting out a whoop and holler. "GILA GUL! Ha ha! Paint-ttk me green and call me a toad! Everyone, it's Dez!"

Desert Rain couldn't contain her joy; she dashed down the mountain path, down the cliffside, stumbling and tumbling the whole way. She zipped around the sleeping Distorted, jumping and crawling over them as she needed, until she was within spitting distance of the train. Her heart swelled more as she saw people disembark: Kidran, looking much healthier and pinker in hue than when she had last seen him; Mac, dirty from his travels but smiling from ear to ear; and…someone new. Desert Rain had never seen this yellow-feathered woman before. But the Quetzalin looked her in the eye, and Desert Rain realized…

"Chi? Is that you?" Desert Rain ran over and embraced her. "Thank the Divine Beasts you all are alive! And you're so…yellow!"

Chiriku smirked. "Just don't say I look like a chicken, okay? It wasn't funny the first time a jerk said it."

"One time!" Mac retorted. "I said it-ttk only the one time!"

Desert Rain suppressed a laugh and couldn't help but smile. Her smile broadened when one more person came out from the train. Gabriel, despite the dark circles under his eyes from exhaustion, brightened as his gaze fell on Desert Rain. "Dez…"

"Gabe!" Desert Rain ran to him and hugged him,

and much to her surprise, he embraced her back with surprising strength. She allowed the hug to linger before pulling back to smile at him. "What happened? How did you all survive the cave-in? And why do you look—"

"There's much to explain," Kidran said, as he glanced up at the falling snow. "And I'm sure you have much to tell us as well."

"So, the snow is your doing," Desert Rain said. "I should've known."

"It's the same hibernation spell the Elfë Tiagas placed on me, just a wider cast," he explained, looking around at the sleeping Distorted. "They'll be asleep for a while. I find this helps us to keep moving faster than having to battle all these beasts. Less messy as well."

"Yeah, Frosty's-ss been a real pal handlin' all these Nasties-ss along the way," Mac said, clapping Kidran on the back like he was an old friend.

Kidran coughed from the back smack, and grimaced. "I assume telling you to not call me 'Frosty' for the hundredth time will not dissuade you at this point, will it?"

CHAPTER TWENTY
A New Chiriku; Finding the Council

As they sat around the campfire that evening, in the new camp that the elven army set up several miles past the mountains where they left the Distorted to sleep, Desert Rain recounted the events she had endured since her separation from her friends—what had been mere days for her, thus her account was brief. Upon her revealing that she had the Lightscale in her possession, the others were stunned into silence, except for Mac because very little struck him silent.

"Curl my tail and call me a chameleon!" he said, an ecstatic smile on his face. "Don't-ttk that beat-ttk all. Who knew it was Silverheart-ttk the whole time? Now we're sure to stop that-ttk demon!"

Kidran stared at Desert Rain evenly. "Desert Rain, your gift to awaken and use the Lightscale speaks more than enough of your capabilities, but this is the most powerful object in Luuva Gros. We need to form a plan to ensure its, and your, safety."

"I agree," Clova replied. "As we three are the only remaining Hijn Council, it falls to Dez, Kidran and I to protect the Lightscale."

Mac shot a glance between them and Chiriku. "You mean, the four of you."

Chiriku swatted his arm. "Shut up, swamp breath!"

"What-ttk? They outta know!"

It looked as if Chiriku might raise her fist at Mac,

but Desert Rain held up her hand as a gesture for the bird girl to calm down. "We should know what? Chiriku, what happened to you?"

The Quetzalin clenched her beak shut, but after a few seconds, she let out a long exhale. "I was going to tell you later, maybe, but something happened back in the snow elves' place, right after you disappeared…"

*   *   *

She remembered falling in what felt like delayed time. Ice shards hovered before her eyes as everything else around her vanished, and she tumbled through a white void. Her whole body was numb, but she could still feel hot tears welling up in her eyes. All she heard was the voice inside her mind. *I'm about to die. This sucks.*

Then Chiriku was no longer falling. She was no longer numb or scared. She just…was. When she felt something hug her around the legs, she looked down to see a familiar face.

"It's all right, Chi," said Woasim, looking up at her with his wide eyes. "Mum wants to talk to you."

It did not fully process in Chiriku's mind what was going on — what had been happening moments ago felt like a distant memory. "Mum?"

"Uh huh. Walk with me."

Chiriku realized she was not in a white void after all, but walking through a field of golden grass swaying gently in a cool breeze. The sky was bathed in the evening palette of pink and purple, speckled with a smattering of stars. Woasim took her by the hand to guide her, but it was clear where they were heading — a large magnolia tree, the only tree in the endless field, stood fifty yards ahead of them. Sitting under the tree was, what Chiriku first thought she saw at that distance, a giant swan, nearly as tall as a horse but having the unmistakable curved neck and feathered body. As they approached, the Quetzalin could identify four wings upon its back, and it rested upon four folded legs, each ending in a raptor-like foot with ivory claws. Four white illicia, each with a small pearl-like bulb on the ends, sprouted from its face — two at the brow-ridges above its eyes, and two on each side of its equine nose. The eyes of the dragon, for indeed that's what it was, had the softest, calmest blue Chiriku had ever seen.

"Hello, Chiriku," the Sage said, and her breath smelled of wildflowers. "I asked Woasim to bring you here so I can ask you something."

As Chiriku and Woasim were within a few feet of the dragon, the bird girl found her mouth dry. She had never seen a Salamandrian Sage in person before — no one of her generation had, and she found herself deprived of words save one. "Mum?'"

The wing dragoness chuckled. "My name is Zephyrsong, but Mum is fine too. I have something very important to ask of you, Chiriku, but the choice is entirely up to you. We Sages need a vessel to bond with for our magic to survive in the world. Our spirits can linger for a short while without one, but without dear Woasim…" With sadness in her eyes, Zephyrsong extended a hand to Woasim and caressed his face. "…I will need a new vessel. I asked Woasim who he advises to be his successor. He said you are brave, loyal, and truthful, all aspects I seek in an heir. I would like it very much if you would be my Hijn, Chiriku. But the decision is yours, and yours alone."

Chiriku stared dumbfoundedly at the dragon for a long pause, before squeaking out, "Huh?"

Woasim giggled. "It's a bit overwhelming, isn't it?"

"I understand the weight I am asking to place on your shoulders," Zephyrsong said. "And you are still so young. Also a bit quick-tempered, so I have heard. But your heart is kind, even if you don't believe it yet. I would be honored if you would accept my offer."

Chiriku wasn't sure if she believed what she heard. "*You'd* be honored? You're a divine dragon, for the love of Luuva! I'm nobody. A halfling freak. Why would *you* be honored?"

Zephyrsong smiled. "A halfling, from two different worlds? Hmm, no, I wouldn't know what that's like." She fluffed up her neck feathers, and then yawned, revealing her mouth was full of sharp, reptilian teeth. "But being from two worlds simply means you are more. You are a symbol for love crossing boundaries, overcoming odds, defying those that would stain pure hearts with hate. You've experienced great cruelty, and yet you embrace love rather than deny it. That is courage, Chiriku. And that is the kind of person I would be honored to be a part of."

Chiriku found it hard to breathe; so much about Zephyrsong reminded her of someone she had not seen in such a long time, someone who had told her similar things once. This gorgeous swan-dragon was so like the graceful egret Quetzalin that Chiriku had once called Mother…

"I…my friends!" Chiriku suddenly realized she had no idea what was going on outside of this…this dream? Wherever she was, there was a catastrophe happening back in the real world. "My friends are falling to their deaths! If I accept your offer, can your magic save them?"

"Yes, the magic can save them. But it won't be mine. It will be yours."

"Fine, whoever's magic it is! Yes, yes, I accept!"

The dragon breathed a cool breath over Chiriku. "Calm yourself. Time is relative. Do not make promises in haste. But I admire that you wish to use the magic to protect your friends. You must promise to use my magic for good, for the benefit and safety of others. You will use it as a guiding hand for the lost, and to quell the storms of darkness. Will you do that, Chiriku?"

Chiriku took a few calming breaths and nodded. "I promise."

Woasim gave her another enthusiastic embrace. "You'll do so good, I know it!"

Chiriku knelt and gave him a proper hug. "Thanks, Sim. Will I see you again?"

The Yopeis chuckled. "Of course. I'm just a whisper away."

Chiriku suddenly felt a wave of warmth throughout her being, a thunderous howl in her ears, and then Woasim, Zephyrsong, and the field disappeared. Every feather felt like it was lightning-kissed, and her whole body radiated light. The brown of her feathers evaporated and beneath shined a new hue of sunlight yellow. The chill of reality hit her once again, and she felt herself falling again.

Chiriku slammed hard onto a cold, slick surface. It dazed her momentarily, and she struggled to retain consciousness as she looked around to realize an ice bridge had miraculously formed beneath her. She heard

the heavy thuds of other bodies landing around her —
Mac, Gabriel, and finally Kidran, who hit the bridge
headfirst. She winced at hearing the side of his head
crack against the ice, and his body went limp.

"Wha…" She pieced together quickly that Kidran
must have used his magic to form the ice bridge to catch
them, but did not allow time to plan how to land safely
upon it. She hoped his magic could persist with him
unconscious — she sure hoped he was only unconscious.
"Guys! Are you all right? Is Kidran…?"

Gabriel had fallen on his arm, and winced,
clenching his teeth in pain, but he managed to scoot over
to Kidran and felt his throat for a pulse. "He's still
breathing. But he hit his head hard. We'll have to drag
him out of here."

"Which way is out-ttk of here?" Mac snapped, his
eyes staring up at the chasm they had all fallen into.
Panic grew in his voice. "Where's Dez? She didn't-ttk fall
past us, did she?"

"I…I don't know. I didn't see her. But…" Chiriku
looked down, her heart leaping into her throat at the
looming darkness below. "I didn't see that little girl
falling either. Maybe they caught a ledge or something."

An abrupt cracking silenced them. Chiriku's heart
rapped inside her rib cage as she watched veins of white
crawl through the ice beneath her, extending out along
the bridge as the group's combined weight tested the
strength of the precarious structure.

Everyone cast panicked glances at each other.
Their eyes did the talking — Do they stay still? Move?
Where would they move to?

Chiriku heard a whisper in her ear. It was a word
she did not understand, in a tongue that both mystified

and unnerved her. The word touched her mind with a soothing coolness, and suddenly she understood it. It was like a buried memory from a past life, or a childhood dream long gone. She echoed the word, letting it escape from her throat like a melody yearning for freedom. And she knew, somehow, that it was Dragontongue.

As the ice bridge collapsed under them, a howl consumed the silence, and a hurricane wind erupted from the abyss below. It was terrifyingly freezing, and Chiriku thought she would be petrified on the spot, but instead she felt her body rise, rise, rise away from the darkness. She could barely see against the wind, but through the gap in her eyelids, she could make out the others rising around her, suspended in the air like ascending kites. The gale blustered around her, whipping her around in spirals, and she curled up tight into a ball to protect herself from its force.

Chiriku tried to scream, "Stop! That's enough!", but her voice stuck in her throat. Another word whispered to her…another unknown yet comforting word…and she squeaked it out, another melodic command. The wind instantly hushed, the cyclone ceasing its swirling. She felt herself land softly on solid ground—then she ventured to open her eyes.

Snow. Blue sky. Calm. That was all that remained—well, that and the massive chasm in the ground a few yards away. Around her, Mac, Gabriel, and Kidran lied in the show, scattered about like tossed toys but all in one piece. Mac slowly sat up, looking around, before settling his gaze on Chiriku.

"Chi…" His mouth hung open as he gawked at her. "You're…you're shining!"

Chiriku was not sure what weird joke he was

trying to make, but then she noticed her hands, her arms…her coat had been blown clean off in the cyclone, but she barely noticed the cold as she marveled at her radiant, golden feathers.

And beside her, placed unscathed in the snow as if it had been gently hand delivered, was her grandfather's warhammer.

*   *   *

Desert Rain was silent after Chiriku finished her story. Then, a huge smile bloomed on her face. "Oh, Chiriku…you're Hijn!"

Chiriku shrugged as she shifted her warhammer against her back. It was in a new makeshift sheath that was crafted from rope. "Not that I really understand what that all means. I mean, I get I have wind magic now, but I don't know how I did it, or if I could do it again."

"You'll figure it out-ttk," Mac said, and he popped a few dried berries into his mouth. "We wouldn't be here right-ttk now, if you hadn't-ttk saved our tails-ss."

"Speaking of being here, how did you get that train?" Clova asked. "That's a Bloodburn battle train, isn't it?"

"Finders keepers," Mac replied, as if that cleared up everything.

Gabriel spoke up. "After the cave-in, the Haven Enders found us. How they knew we needed their help, I don't know, although I have my suspicions." He gave Desert Rain a knowing glance. "They helped us travel through the Taigalands to the southern border, and from there, we traveled on foot for weeks to get to the next town. But on the way, we came across the train, abandoned but still functional and with fuel."

Desert Rain was pensive. "There was no trace of anyone? King Ragnor?"

Gabriel shook his head.

Desert Rain frowned. Had King Ragnor and the Bloodburn abandoned the train during their fight with Katawa, and moved the battle far enough away to not want to return for the train? Or had Katawa…

"It's always good to have more resources at our disposal, even if it is mechanical," said Clova. "It can at the very least help us transport supplies."

"Where are you heading?" Kidran inquired.

Clova brushed strands of her hair from her face. "We have been following the trail of Distorted, hoping it will lead us to wherever the Distortionist is hiding. If he is heading for the Darkscale hold, L'Teth Zurên, then finding its location will take nothing short of pure luck."

Desert Rain rubbed her chin in thought. "Maybe not. Chi, as the Wind Hijn, you can command the winds to move clouds, yes?"

Chiriku shrugged. "Maybe."

Desert Rain's mood shifted to excitement as she rattled out her thoughts. "Then you can part the Malaise Cloud! Something about it is keeping the Hollow Eye from seeing properly, so I haven't been able to teleport with it since I got here. But if you can move the clouds, then it could get a better view from above, and we could ask it to take us to L'Teth Zurên, wherever it currently stands."

"And…" Clova stood up as hope rekindled in her eyes. "You could ask it to take us to wherever the Hijn Council is being held captive! Once we rescue them, all of us united stand a chance against Katawa."

Desert Rain nodded, although not in complete agreement with Clova's sentiment. Katawa had managed to get the upper hand on the Council the first time. Then again, the others underestimated him and had not worked together. Also, they now had Kidran and Chiriku's magic too. Once the Council was rescued, that would deprive Katawa of his strongest weapon against the Darkscale Court; maybe they could stop him before he could bring any war to his clan.

Chiriku looked up at the putrid clouds above. "I think I can move some of that. Yeah, that should be a…breeze." She caught her own bad pun just as it left her mouth, and she flushed in embarrassment.

Mac stifled a laugh. "Wouldja look-kk at that-ttk? She gets-ss magic powers-ss, and a sense of puns too!"

Desert Rain lifted the Hollow Eye on its chain around her neck. "Okay, Chiriku parts the clouds, and the Hollow Eye can take me to the Council. I've been able to transport others with me before, so hopefully it can teleport everyone back here once I find them—"

"You're not going by yourself." Gabriel wasn't posing a question.

Desert Rain looked around the group, who all looked back at her with the same stern glare as Gabriel. "But, if Katawa's there with the others, then only I risk getting caught and the rest of you can—"

"Gila, you should know better by now," Mac said with a smile. "We're a team, whether you like-kk it or not-ttk."

"Right. You really think we're going to let you deal with that slimeball?" Chiriku said. "Besides, now I can knock him out *and* blow him away!"

Desert Rain smiled. Of course, how could she separate herself from her friends again? She looked at Clova and Kidran. "You both should stay here and prepare the army in case we can't bring back the Council. That hibernation spell can protect you all if another wave of Distorted comes your way."

Clova's lips pinched together as if she didn't like the idea, but she took a deep breath. "If you find them but it's too difficult to stage a rescue, please return immediately for reinforcements. But a small group may prove a better choice for stealth. How do we find you should you get lost or if things go awry?"

Desert Rain thought on this and then rummaged through her pockets and pulled out the Darkscale compass. "This is what we used to find Kidran. It detects ancient magic, although not the magic of the Hijn holding it. At least, so far it hasn't. Use this to track us should we take longer than a few hours." She handed it to Clova.

Mac crinkled his nose as he watched Desert Rain hand off the compass. "You know, I just-tkk realized... we might-tkk run into some those Darkscale nasties if that Katawa's already started a fight-tkk, don't-tkk you think-kk?"

"Let's pray he hasn't," Gabriel said, standing up and walking to stand beside Desert Rain. "And if we do, we stick together, right?"

Desert Rain smirked. For someone who was such a lone wolf before, Gabriel had certainly come around. She liked that. "Right. Ready, Chi?"

Chiriku stood up, stretching and cracking her knuckles. "All right, here goes." She looked up, raising her hands towards the dark, gloomy sky. "Okay, Mum, what's the word?"

She closed her eyes, listening. She focused quietly for several minutes, until a soft, barely audible word rolled from her tongue, and Desert Rain recognized the shape of the word.

A slow wind began to stir. Chiriku murmured more words, and the wind intensified. Everyone retreated a few paces as the wind concentrated around Chiriku, forming a tunnel around her. The tunnel extended up higher and higher, a whirling vortex that cut through the darkness above. The vortex moaned as it grew taller, a finger reaching up as if to point the way. The vacuum within the whirlwind slowly inhaled a cluster of clouds, pulling them down and dissipating them within the belly of the vortex. Finally, a strand of gossamer light broke through the gaseous ceiling, and the strand widened as the clouds parted, revealing the pale face of *Ia Ternaut* in the clear night sky.

"That's it! You did it, Chi!" Desert Rain could already feel her spirit strengthening as the moonlight poured down. "Okay, let's do this before the clouds shift."

As the moonlight bathed the earth below, revealing what had been cloaked by shadow, something caught Desert Rain's eye in the distance. It was a streak of crimson near a rock formation, and she might have missed it entirely if it wasn't for two spots of reflected yellow light staring at her. Then she made out the steel-blue hair, and the lavender-tinted skin.

She managed to overcome her terror enough to point and scream, "Katawa! He's here!"

Everyone instantly snapped their heads in the direction she pointed, but Katawa was gone.

"Where? Are you sure?" Kidran asked.

"Yes! He ducked behind those rocks, I swear it!" Desert Rain could not fathom how he'd found their location…unless, the Vermins…had Katawa been watching them all through the Goude and Gimch's eyes this whole time? No, she couldn't believe that. It could have been any of the other Distorted they had encountered that had been the culprit. It didn't matter, either way—she reached into her pouch for Silverheart.

Clova placed a hand on Desert Rain's arm to halt her. "If he's here, then you must go and rescue the Council now while we detain him."

"What? No! Clova, you have no idea how dangerous he is. He can't be killed—"

Kidran was already muttering Dragontongue under his breath, which began to cloud the air around his lips with frost. "I'll cast my hibernation spell over the whole area. It should render him unconscious like the others."

Gabriel locked eyes with Desert Rain. "We'll have to move fast, but this may be our best shot to save the Hijn while he isn't guarding them. Once we have everyone back, we can move full force on him."

Desert Rain nervously darted her eyes from one person to another—how could she leave Clova, Kidran, and the Ahshi with Katawa around? But Gabriel was right; this may be the best chance they had while they knew where Katawa was. If Kidran's magic could at least slow him down, then maybe the elves stood a chance until they returned.

"Okay," she relented. "We'll come back as soon as we can. Please, be careful. Keep your distance from him, if you can."

Chiriku placed a hand on Desert Rain's shoulder. and Mac placed his hand on her other. The lizard's grip was tight. "Let's-ss all hope that Eye of yours-ss can see straight-tkk."

Your words to dragons' ears, Desert Rain thought. She gently took Gabriel's hand, and he squeezed hers in return. Holding the Hollow Eye in her free hand, she closed her eyes and whispered, "Take us to the Hijn Council."

In a blink, the four of them vanished.

*   *   *

The grand mausoleum loomed before them. It was larger than any Desert Rain had seen before; it bordered on being a modest castle, and not the sunny storybook kind. The structure stood in a murky wasteland where nary a tree, rock, stream, or any other accessory of nature was to be seen. It was not just a land of death—it was a land of emptiness.

Mac cocked his head at the mausoleum, and then glanced at their surroundings—or lack thereof. "So, do we just-tkk charge in, or knock-kk, or..."

"We need to determine if any Distorted might be guarding the place," Gabriel said. "I don't like being exposed in the open like this."

"How about I huff and puff and blow their house down?" Chiriku said with a grin. "I think I heard that from a story once..."

Desert Rain stared at the entrance, which reminded her of her home's front door—a thick, round slab of stone blocked the way in. "Maybe I can disintegrate that stone door like I did with Kidran's prison. Now that the moon's full, my magic should be at full strength."

"Or you can disintegrate the whole building," Chi suggested. "Less fun for me, but I'd like to see that."

"Can we take cover while we chit-chat?" Gabriel hissed. "You don't know who might be lying in wait."

"Take cover where?" But Desert Rain didn't get an answer as Gabriel dragged her by the arm to the front wall of the mausoleum, pressing up against its cold surface. There were no windows or archways, just marble pillars. Mac and Chiriku followed them, each hiding behind one of the pillars.

"We haven't seen any guards on the outside, but that doesn't mean the inside's not swarming with them," Gabriel said. "Or this place could have traps —"

"Or, again, Dez can just dissolve the building which would also dissolve any traps, and then I blow away any Distorted inside," Chiriku said. "Seriously, we're way overthinking this."

Desert Rain took a deep breath. "You're right. We're wasting time. Let's go."

She slipped over to the slab blocking the entryway and placed her fingertips on the cold stone. She closed her eyes, reaching deep within to remember that feeling she had back when she freed Kidran. That feeling of empowerment, or confidence. *I can do this. My friends believe in me. I can do it.*

Gradually, she felt cool sand drifting around her fingers and heard the *sssshhh* of it falling to the ground. When she opened her eyes, there was a pile of bluish sand at her feet, and a gaping maw of the mausoleum before her, stretching into drafty darkness.

"Now that — was — cool," Chiriku said. "My turn

now? How about I send a raging cyclone through there to blast away any Distorted —"

"You could accidentally blast away the Hijn Council," Gabriel noted. "We need to investigate."

"Aww, darn," the Quetzalin groused, but she shoved her hands in her pockets and followed the group into the dark entryway.

The passageway within was dank and chilling to the bone. Desert Rain hoped the other Hijn had not frozen to death in here — maybe Fierno Ginso kept a bonfire going, wherever they were being held. As there were no windows or sources of light, she took Silverheart out from its pouch and attached the Hollow Eye at the pommel, thinking of an illuminated form it could take. Suddenly, it was Burning Talon's sword, the blade blazing with a golden-red fire.

Mac jumped back as the sword radiated its enchanted fire. "Woo! That's-ss a fancy torch."

Gabriel eyed the sword cautiously but said nothing.

At the end of the hallway, they came upon an open space, a circular parlor of sorts, with a stone staircase leading up to a second story landing that wrapped around the room. Dust and mold covered the floors and walls, and various arched doorways led to more darkness. Desert Rain could imagine spirits hosting macabre balls in a room like this. She spotted rusty sconces holding torches along the walls, and hoping they were dry enough, tapped her sword to one of them, which crackled into fiery life.

Gabriel took the lit torch from its sconce. "This place is even bigger than it looked outside. Since we haven't run into any guards yet, I think we should split into teams of two, one for this floor and one for the second."

"One Hijn per pair!" Chiriku said. "That way, both teams have magic mojo."

Desert Rain nodded. While she didn't like the thought of splitting up, they did need to cover ground quickly. "Okay, Mac can go with Chiriku and scout this floor, while Gabriel and I check out the second—"

"Actually, if you don't mind," Mac interjected, rubbing the back of his neck, "maybe Dez and I could check out the second floor and Chi and Gabe pair up down here."

Chiriku grimaced at him. "What, you don't trust I can protect you? Your loss, scale butt. Come on, Gabe." She headed off towards one of the adjoining hallways, while Gabriel glanced back at Desert Rain while he followed.

"We'll have Chiriku send a wind message to you should we find anything," he said, holding his torch high as he walked off.

Desert Rain and Mac ascended the stairs, the second story landing somehow managing to be colder than the first floor. There were rows of doorways that led to rooms with various tombs, both secured in the walls and in marble caskets on the floor, and Desert Rain wondered how many people could be buried here. She also remembered Mac's aversion to burials and death rituals—his terror of his former undertaker boss back in the Bayou was clear in her memory—so she hoped he was faring all right. When she looked at him, his tense facial expression indicated otherwise.

"Is there something you wanted to discuss with me, Mac?" Desert Rain said, hoping to distract him from his fear. "It felt like you wanted to pair up with me for a reason."

Mac blinked back to reality from whatever stray thoughts had been preoccupying him. "Oh…well, yes, there is-ss something. We might have to fight-ttk that Katawa creep if he makes it-ttk to the Darkscale place, right-ttk?"

"If we find the Council and we all can stop him before he gets there, then hopefully not. Why?"

"There's-ss…something I need to tell you." Mac took a long pause, breathing deeply several times, and he trembled from head to toe. "I hope you won't-tkk hate me for this-ss. For not-tkk telling you sooner."

Desert Rain stopped walking and fully turned to him. "I could never hate you, Mac. Please, trust me. What is it?"

Mac looked like he was on the verge of tears, but he swallowed them back. "I've been there before, Dez. To the Darkscale place."

It was Desert Rain's turn to take several deep breaths to steady herself — more out of fear for her friend and what he may have endured than herself. "You have? When?"

Mac leaned against a wall, as if to keep his legs from buckling under him. "I lied, Dez. I told you I was born with this ability, to look human. I wasn't-tkk. I was just-tkk a normal lizard, but when I was young, some bad Nasties came through the Bayou. They took a lot-ttk of young ones, like-kk me. We Bayou folk, what could we do in the face of them Nasties? And the Nobles-ss, they wouldn't-tkk help us Lejenous-ss, and the Nasties-ss know that-tkk. They brought-tkk the young ones to that place you keep talking about, L'Teth whatever. And they…experimented on us-ss, Dez. They call themselves 'alchemists-ss', and they did strange things with magic-kk and science. I think they were trying to figure out-tkk how to change us to look more like Nobles-ss. Maybe to use us as spies-ss, maybe to use the same process on themselves if it worked, who knows-ss. I was a lucky one, their experiment-tkk worked on me, mostly…so many of those kids-ss, it didn't-t work-kk. I saw so much…death…"

He choked on his words, his tears escaping his eyes and pouring down his face as he continued. "The Darkscale told me, they would use my services-ss one day, and I couldn't-tkk refuse. They left-tkk me alone for a while, and I used my human form to sell things to the Nobles, to make-kk good business. But then, the Nasties sent-ttk one of their messengers to find me. He said they needed me to go to the desert-tkk, to find out if anyone around there might-tkk know of a rogue Darkscale who was left-tkk out there for dead. They worried he might-tkk be alive, and someone powerful could be protecting him. And when I got-tkk out there, I heard rumors about a Charmer who lived outside of Ulomin, and I thought-tkk she would know something…" His voice cracked, his breathing labored. "I'm sorry, Dez! I should've told you everything, but-tkk if we go to that place, the Darkscale will recognize me. They'll say I'm their property. I couldn't-tkk have you find out that-ttk way. I'm not a traitor, I'm not-tkk! I don't-tkk want to turn you in to them. I don't-tkk, please believe me…"

Desert Rain needed time to process this, although she knew she didn't have time at that moment. "That Darkscale compass you gave me…it wasn't the one I lost, was it?"

Mac shook his head, staring at his feet. "They gave it-tkk to me because they thought-tkk it would help me find Katawa, or whoever was with him. It led me to you, that night-tkk at the Banishing Festival. Or it might-tkk have been Miss Clova, I'm not sure."

That also explained his initial interest in scoping out her home when they first met — he must have been looking for any trace of Katawa's presence there. Desert Rain could only go with her gut feeling to respond. Without a word, she went to Mac and gave him a hard, lingering embrace.

Mac's body jerked in surprise. He whispered, "You not-tkk...mad?"

Desert Rain stepped back, looking him square in the eye. "Of course not. I know you're my friend. You could've run away at any time to report back to the Darkscale about me, but you stayed by my side. You've fought alongside all of us. You have a good heart, Mac. I'm so sorry for all the pain you've been through. I'm glad you told me about it."

Mac smiled, wiping away the last few tears. "You're a better friend than I deserve."

"Nonsense. We can talk more about it later. For now, let's — "

A strange, strangled sound came from a doorway ahead. Desert Rain and Mac instantly hushed. They crept along the wall, halting as they came to the archway where the sound was coming from. Desert Rain gripped Burning Talon's sword in both hands, slowly turning to look into the room as she allowed the light to bathe whatever was in the space beyond.

Inside the room, the Hijn Council stood along two walls facing each other, three people on each wall. They were propped up inside what looked like molded marble, egg-shaped display cases, products of Katawa's twisted art. Their arms, legs and torsos were secured in place by malformed, thorny coils that melded with the marble prisons. Merros, V'Tanna, and Rukna were on one side of the room, and Fierno, Guargos, and Mage Skyhan were on the other—and the strangled noise was coming from Mage, who was struggling to speak against the black bile oozing from her lips and eye sockets. She was the only one who appeared to be conscious, as the others lied against their slabs motionlessly.

Desert Rain made a quick scan of the room, seeing no guards, and rushed over to inspect the conscious Hijn. She wanted so badly to rid Mage of the bile; there had to be some way to clear it. It was viscous but liquid, so she shifted her sword into Waterweaver's trident. With it, she touched the tip of one of the prongs to Mage's lips, softly speaking the Dragontongue word for *flow*.

Instantly, Mage Skyhan hacked up a huge stream of black liquid, which became more like ruddy water, and it splashed onto the floor. Enough of it escaped Mage's esophagus and lungs for her to finally, after Divine Beasts knew how long, to intake the deepest, cleanest breath.

"Ooooh, bless you, Desert Rain!" Mage wheezed and coughed, her voice raspy. "How did you find—"

"I'll explain later," Desert Rain interrupted her. "I can teleport all of us out of here with the Lightscale. Mac, you stay here while I find Gabe and—"

When she turned around, she met a pale, wide-eyed Mac, whose skin was crusting over with a bruised, purple-green tinge at his throat. He was petrified, as was Desert Rain, as she saw Katawa standing directly behind him, one of his clawed fingers raking Mac's neck.

"Look who's come to visit me," the Distortionist said, his wicked smile freezing Desert Rain's heart. "Oh, how I've missed you, Dezzy."

CHAPTER TWENTY-ONE
A Lethal Waltz; The Homecoming Party

Desert Rain held the prongs of the trident towards Katawa. Even if she couldn't stab him to death, she was more than ready to perforate him with more holes than a sieve. "How did you get here so fast? You were at the camp, I saw you!"

Katawa dug his claw into Mac's shoulder, causing the lizard man to suck air in between his teeth. "Yes, you did! Although you wouldn't have seen a blasted thing if that moonlight hadn't come out from behind the clouds."

Desert Rain's skin crawled as she realized the truth. "That was your ghost."

"Ghost, self-projection, call it what you will. I've been here, resting after taking care of those idiotic Bloodburn you and that decrepit king set upon me. But enough about me." He gave Mac a hard shove, knocking the poor man to the ground and advancing on Desert Rain. "I believe I heard you say you brought me a gift? The Lightscale. I knew I could count on you to find it! Oh, what wondrous things we will accomplish—"

Desert Rain was sick of his voice. She lunged at him, the trident snagging his jacket and ripping through it as he nimbly stepped to the side. Even Katawa probably didn't know what the Lightscale could do to him, even if it might not kill him. With a summoning thought, she transformed the trident into Stormhowler's Bow, readying to shoot three arrows of lightning aimed straight at Katawa's heart—of whatever was in his chest.

"Impressive." Katawa seemed genuinely amazed, but his awe was tainted with disdain. "But temper, my golden girl. We're in close quarters. It would be a shame if your little bolts brought this room down on your friends' heads."

The thought had already occurred to Desert Rain, so she was prepared to retort. "Then let's take this outside!"

Instantly, the bow slithered into the shape of Wintermane's Whip, a sleek length of frosted chain laced with silver barbs and ending in an icicle spike. She lashed it at Katawa, who raised an arm to block the attack — exactly how Sir Luce had taught her most enemies would. The chain caught and wrapped around his arm, digging its barbs into his skin, and Desert Rain yanked with all her strength. The Distortionist was pulled off his feet — judging by his shocked expression, he had not expected this feat of strength from her — and he flew past her and hit the wall behind her straight on in the face. Before he could regain composure, the whip became Earthbelly's hammer, which Desert Rain slammed into Katawa's back, sending him clean through the wall in an explosion of stone. Katawa was propelled as if ejected from a cannon, and plummeted from the landing, crashing into the parlor below with a satisfying crunch and hailing of rock on his battered body.

Desert Rain reveled in her feeling for a second — *Guerda-Shalyr, that felt great!* — before she rushed to Mac, who was still prone on the floor. "Mac! The Distortion…can you breathe? Is it spreading?"

Mac rolled over and reached up to the patch of Distortion on his neck. He had reverted to lizard form, his red scales tinged purple from where Katawa had touched him. He scratched at the skin around the spot, and in a methodical way as he had done a thousand times before, peeled away that patch of contaminated skin. Underneath was pink, unharmed skin, and he tossed the shed skin aside.

"Was-ss only skin-deep, Dez," Mac said groggily. "It was about-ttk time I shed anyway. Now go wallop that hog's warty bottom!"

Desert Rain was stunned. Did Mac just...shed Distortion? Granted, her body had rejected it too, but he had barely been fazed. Maybe Katawa and his powers were weakening. Maybe she stood a chance.

With renewed vigor, sprinted out of the room and looked down from the landing. Katawa had more than the wind knocked out of him, as he staggered to get back on his feet. Raising the hammer over her head, Desert Rain leapt from the landing, bringing her hammer down toward Katawa's head. The Distortionist sensed her attack, spinning out of the way with a split second to spare. When the hammer hit the floor where he had been standing, it shook the parlor with a thunderous earthquake, causing both opponents to struggle to maintain their footing. Desert Rain mentally called for a lighter weapon, AshenClaw's twin magma war axes, which blazed with volcanic fire. Before Katawa could comprehend the weapon's change, she swung one of the axes at him. The smell of searing flesh filled the air as she landed a gash across his chest—not deep, but the heat of the magma metal scorched like the hand of a sun god.

Katawa stared dumbfounded at his bleeding wound. "For the love of Luuva, Dezzy...you never cease to astound me."

"Don't mock me," Desert Rain hissed, and she

swung again, aiming for his neck. This time he dodged, and they were suddenly in a mad waltz as they traversed the room, her precise swings missing him by a hair. She was waiting for him to strike back—seriously, what was he waiting for?—and it dawned on her that he was analyzing her, taking sick enjoyment in watching her fight. Although, that nervous glint in his eye indicated it wasn't all fun for him...

A gust of wind rushed into the parlor. A hurricane fist of air slammed into Katawa, smashing him against a wall hard enough to force him an inch deep into the surface. Gabriel and Chiriku stood on the far side of the parlor, and the Quetzalin's feathers were ruffled in fury. "Save some of the fun for me!" she shouted, with a fervor that was both excitement and rage.

Katawa pushed himself out of the wall, snarling. "That squawking child is Hijn now? I kill one, and another pops up like a cockroach."

Chiriku didn't take kindly to the comparison. With a circle of both arms and Dragontongue words, she sent another funnel of wind at him, this time lifting him clean off the floor and up towards the ceiling in a whirling spiral. Desert Rain took the opportunity to transform her axes back into her silver-studded whip, which she lashed out and snagged Katawa around the leg with it before pulling him down and slamming him into the floor.

"Teamwork, I like it!" Chiriku said, and she continued commanding her funnel to lift the Distortionist again. Katawa was ready this time, however, and since the whip was still snagged on him, he kicked back his leg and jerked Desert Rain up into the cyclone with him. They grappled as they circled the room, Desert Rain trying to free her whip from him, but he grabbed her by the wrists, trying to keep control of her. She tried to push the length of whip between her hands against Katawa's throat, its barbs jabbing into his skin, but all he did was curl his lips into a condescending grin.

"Kill the wind, Chi!" Gabriel shouted over the churning wind.

Chiriku struggled to pull her arms out of the whirlwind she had created, to no avail. She tried to speak words of Dragontongue, but the wind seemed to have a mind of its own. "I...I can't calm it down! It won't listen to me!"

While Gabriel grappled with Chiriku's arms to try and lower them, Katawa and Desert Rain were oblivious to the cyclone they were swept up in—all they focused on were each other, their eyes locked in ferocious battle. They both hit the wall on the second-floor landing, with Katawa's back against it while Desert Rain pushed in on him, and the wind pinned them there. Smacking into the wall had caused him to release his grip on her wrists, and she resumed pressing the whip into his throat in a choke hold.

Katawa gritted his sharp teeth. "Aren't you getting tired of this silly dance, Dezzy? You're only prolonging the inevitable."

"Shut—up," she ordered, her green eye glowing pure hate.

He laughed. "Look at you! I knew if I was patient, you'd become everything I needed you to be. You'll have to show me how your lovely device works."

It was Desert Rain's turn to give Katawa a smug grin. "The Lightscale can only be commanded by a Hijn of a celestial Sage. It repels darkness and those who serve it. And I bet you figured as much, since you've done your best to avoid touching it."

"Smart girl," he replied. "You know, I've been meaning to return to you that little gift you gave me a while ago."

He reached under his tunic collar, pulling out a familiar token—the golden rose that he had used to steal the piece of Desert Rain's soul all those moons ago. He had been wearing it around his neck this whole time, although now it looked dry and withered. Seeing it brought back the horrid memory of that day, the day he had revealed his true colors and ruined her life, and it made Desert Rain seethe. She brought her face close to his in a menacing grimace. "I don't need that anymore, Katawa. I grew my soul back, and it's stronger now. You don't control me anymore."

Katawa returned her gaze, amused. "I admire your tenacity. Although, this rose still holds a piece of your soul, a piece of *your* Bellaluna's magic." He clapped his hands together, crushing the rose and rubbing his palms together until glittering gold dust covered them. "The question is, is your precious Lightscale going to be able to tell the difference?"

Desert Rain couldn't comprehend his meaning, not until he placed his hands on the whip—no electric shock, no defensive ward to resist him—and it brightened in response to his disguised touch.

"Take us to L'Teth Zurên," he said.

Desert Rain sensed the surge of magic, and didn't have time to scream "NO!" before the two of them were blinked away in a flash of light.

*　　*　　*

It was dark at first. Desert Rain squinted, waiting for her eyes to adjust to the dimness, but her eyelids burned. A wash of lethargy soaked into her muscles and bones, making it hard to even move. She lied on hard, gravelly ground, and she managed to sit up despite her aching body. The air around her was heavy, stifling, and she started to wonder if maybe she was drowning. But then there were sharp pains in her wrists and forearms, dozens of little teeth. She finally opened her eyes, and saw that Winterman's Whip was tied around her arms, its silver bards snagging her skin. At the other end of the whip was Katawa, sitting on what looked to be the stump of a salt pillar. He grinned as she focused on him.

"It's oppressive, isn't it?" he said, sniffing the air. "It's the ward they've set on this place. All those alchemic fumes. Only Darkscale can resist its toxicity. It weakens anyone else who comes within a stone's throw. Kind of like how I was weakened when you first used this contraption on me." He gave the whip a slight tug, which made Desert Rain wince as the tug tightened her binding. "But now I'm feeling a bit better, thanks to your protection on my hands. And I suppose one always feels better coming home."

A chill ran up Desert Rain's spine as she realized where they were, and she looked up to see sky-tearing steeples upon a grand bastion, shrouded in shadows beneath the Malaise Cloud above. The Cloud was somehow even thicker here, even more foreboding, like it was the belly of a night beast pressing down on the world.

Somehow, the Lightscale had found L'Teth Zurên.

Desert Rain looked back at Katawa, grimacing at his hands. "How did you know that would work?"

"What, this?" He held up one of his hands, the golden dust still shimmering on its palm. "Oh, I've had so many years to experiment with such things. We Darkscale are alchemists, and I grew up playing around with all sorts of things in my clan's laboratories. I always had an affinity for the magic stuff — I loved it when I'd see a fresh load of spellcasters carted in from the Noblelands, being prepared for…well, let's say the grinders never got dusty from lack of use. Their souls weren't as potent as yours, not by a longshot. But using coagulated essence as a salve is a fun trick, don't you think?"

Desert Rain closed her eyes, trying hard not to visualize what Katawa was describing. "So, you've always been this cruel."

Katawa clicked his tongue behind his teeth. "I'm just a product of my clan, Dezzy. The Court of the Darkscale trained me well. Dare I say, I have a few fond memories of my childhood in this place."

"I thought your clan tortured you."

"Oh, they did. I could only hide my deformity for so long. But before that, I was quite the alchemy prodigy. Now, if I had been in their position, I would have at least dissected me to learn the root of my Distortion, rather than throw me into the furnace like I had some contagious plague. But I always had better foresight than they did. Speaking of which, how about we go in and say hello? My family's going to love meeting you!"

He stood, yanking her to her feet. She bit her lip hard, holding back a yelp as the whip's barbs pulled at her skin. She looked incredulously at Katawa. "What? You're just going to walk in there, all by yourself? After you built that Distorted army, kidnapped the Hijn — "

"Don't worry, my army is coming," Katawa clarified with a smirk. "Now that I found this location, I've already summoned my Distorted to converge on this spot. And here I thought I'd have to have them tear the entire Inbetween apart to find this place. As for your Hijn friends, I think I'll keep them. They make such a nice collection. I'll display them in my court. But you changed the game, Dez. Now that you found the Lightscale, we hold the power we need. These Darkscale fools will crumble before it."

Desert Rain tried to get her fingers around the whip—maybe she could free herself the way she had freed Woasim from his shackles. But then, she might damage the Lightscale—or, more likely, her powers might feed it, not break it, and she couldn't allow Katawa to have more power. She glowered at him. "What do you still need me for? You have the Lightscale. Isn't that all you want?"

Katawa dragged her along toward the gates of L'Teth Zurên, a tall archway shaped like a setting sun, fitted with triangular obsidian stones set to look like rows of pointed teeth. "This soul salve is only a temporary solution. It's more like a glove, and it will eventually wear through. You're the one who activates the Lightscale's magic, and now you're strong enough to do exactly what I need you to do."

Desert Rain didn't even want to know what Katawa's intentions were for her. She tried to twist her way out of her binding, to no avail and more pain. "And you assume I'm going to go along with whatever you have planned? You've taken everything from me, what more can you do to force my compliance?"

"I don't have to force you. Because," he said,

pulling her close with the whip until she could feel his breath on her face. "It's our destiny, Dez. You have no idea how deeply this is carved into your very being."

Desert Rain stared daggers into his eyes. If only she could figure out how to get the Lightscale back under her control — how to use it to make this Wretched breathe his last breath — but all she could do for now was hope Katawa's hubris was leading him to his doom. Hopefully, he was severely underestimating his Darkscale brethren, which could mean death for them both, but she would accept that outcome if need be.

Katawa narrowed his gaze against her glare of malice, but then he leaned in and kissed her roughly. She pulled back instantly, turning her face away from him and spitting on the ground.

He laughed. "Don't act like you didn't miss that," he said, before continuing to drag her along.

Desert Rain wasn't about to dignify his comment with a response. She allowed it to feed her fury instead. She wished now that she had spat in his face instead of on the ground — except maybe he would've liked that.

Katawa scanned the gateway, tilting his head to the side. "And why am I not surprised that they haven't changed the gate guardian in all these years? My clan's become lazy."

"Guardian?" Desert Rain looked around, trying to see whoever it was Katawa saw.

Katawa knocked on one of the obsidian triangles. "Old Scyr, wake up and say hello to your old master."

With a soft rumble, the gate began to stir. The ground trembled as the archway extended upward, lifting out of the earth, and Desert Rain blanched as she saw that massive gateway was attached to segmented pillars of stone that grew from below in a long, wormlike body. What she thought had been obsidian doors designed to look like teeth were, in fact, actual teeth, and this giant stone leech curled from above to look down at them—although "look" was an assumption, since the creature did not have any eyes as far as Desert Rain could tell.

"These golems, so archaic," Katawa sighed. "This one should have been broken up for building stones years ago."

Old Scyr bellowed a deep, earthquaking roar at Katawa, its maw opening so wide, it could have swallowed the bastion behind it whole. Katawa, nonchalant as ever, stood patiently as the golem rushed towards him, mouth agape. Desert Rain tensed, preparing herself for consumption, accepting it if it meant it would end Katawa as well. But the moment that the golem came within an inch of Katawa, he simply reached out a hand and grabbed one of its teeth, channelling Distortion into it.

The golem immediately jerked its head back, squealing as its tooth turned to mushy goop and dripped down its front. It thrashed its head about, as pain appeared to be a new experience for it.

Desert Rain was too distracted by the golem to notice Katawa's hand coming at her. He picked her up by the back of her tunic and threw her, sending her through the air and straight at the golem's maw. She screamed as she watched those horrid teeth coming closer. Even with her wrists bound, she instinctively thrust out her hands before her, and a flash of Blueshine poured from her palms into the stone beast's face—or what little of it there was, as it was primarily mouth.

She landed against the golem's front teeth, but she realized the creature's body was no longer stone, but glass. After a few seconds, the glass dissolved into sand, and she plummeted in a swoosh of bluish powder. She landed softly enough, as the golem turned into a tall enough pile of sand to make a small dune. She rolled down the side of the pile, until she got stuck in a depression near the bottom.

Before she could wrestle her way to freedom, Katawa fished her out, taking hold of the whip again. Desert Rain coughed up grit, blinking some of the dust from her eyes.

"Well, that was fun," Katawa remarked, quite pleased. "I figured, why waste my magic when yours is so destructive? But turning things to sand, that's a new one."

He ruffled her hair with his fingers, shaking out the sand, but she pulled away from his touch. She realized now she should have let the golem eat her.

"Does it work on flesh and blood? I do like the thought that you could dissolve my dear brother's bones into my personal sandbox. But we'll get to that later. Come." Katawa tugged the whip again, and he steered Desert Rain around the sand pile, towards the now unguarded bastion.

With every step, Desert Rain could feel the wards of L'Teth Zurên penetrate her flesh to the bone, her body and resolve growing weaker. She closed her eyes, concentrating, her mental voice reaching out to the Lightscale. *Sir Luce! For Sages' sake, help me! What do I do?*

No response. Fear gripped her heart—did Katawa's control of the Lightscale sever her connection to Sir Luce? Or was Sir Luce too afraid to speak up, in case

Katawa sensed him? Could Sir Luce even do anything for her now? She wanted to cry, but she was too tired. She opened her eyes, lifting her head up. "We could've just stayed in the desert, you know."

Katawa paused. He turned to her.

She continued, even though her voice was soft from the exhaustion. "Would that have been so bad? If you just let all this go, all this revenge and madness. If we had lived out in the desert, away from the rest of the world, just us and our oasis. You could've learned to be happy with that, couldn't you?"

Katawa gave her a blank look. He seemed to be genuinely assessing her question. Several seconds passed before he gave her a pitiful smile. "Aw, Dezzy. You were so content with having and being nothing. But we were meant for so much more. And I'll make you understand that." He pulled hard on her again, like an impatient owner ordering their dawdling dog, and continued dragging her along.

Desert Rain knew trying to reason with him was foolish, but desperation was overtaking her. And now, she had no one. No friends, no guardians, no advisors—

Patience.

Desert Rain refrained from making any physical indication that she heard that familiar voice. But hearing it in her mind awakened her from her stupor of despair. *Grandma Luna? I've messed up so badly. What should I do?*

Patience, the calm, gentle voice repeated.

Patience? Desert Rain didn't have time for patience! But it was the one hope she had right now. The time would come. She had to wait...

A wide stairway of smokey quartz led up to the front doors of the bastion, two iron panels each with the

Darkscale insignia of the three currents of water over a tongue of fire branded into them. On each side of the doorway, there were statues of black jade, carved into the forms of draped hooded figures, twice as tall as Desert Rain—what were they? Monks, wraiths, reapers? They clearly didn't intimidate Katawa, as he spent the effort to push one over with one hand as if it weighed no more than a bamboo pole. The statue fell, shattering upon the stairway behind them.

Katawa placed a hand on one of the doors, and the metal warped beneath his fingers, withering into something like wet paper. The iron recoiled from his touch until it resulted in a hole about his size.

He tugged on the whip. "Ladies first."

Desert Rain stared at the hole, unable to help a slight shiver. She already felt like she was about to vomit; she didn't know if she could handle walking into this Wretched hellhole. "There's something inside that you want me to protect you from, isn't there?"

Katawa frowned, his eyes cold. "Forgive me for trying to have manners. Fact is, you're more welcome here than I."

Desert Rain remembered King Ragnor's words. She was heir to the Mother of the Wretched…did that designation apply to the Darkscale, too? It was too much to hope they would help her, but maybe they could be reasoned with, if Katawa could not be.

Inhaling and holding her breath, she tentatively stepped through the hole, into a room that she could only compare to a cavern. Hundreds of tiny iron lanterns glowing orange flames, barely casting any light on the space, hung on chains from the high ceiling like stalactites, and the room was so wide she couldn't see any walls yet—it was all bathed in shadow. The floor was shiny opal marble that looked like the cosmos, sparkling with silvery spots like stars. Dare she admit it, it was one of the most gorgeous floors Desert Rain had ever seen.

Despite the fact she couldn't see much beyond a few yards in front of her, she already sensed she and Katawa were not alone.

Katawa stepped in behind her, and he must have sensed the same thing. He called out, his voice echoing. "A surprise party? For me? Now, no need for that. Why don't we shine some light so we can all do proper introductions?"

The lanterns above abruptly switched to a collective deep-green glow. Emerald bonfires erupted from various holes around the edges of the room, which caused Desert Rain to jump back—Katawa wrapped an arm around her to still her. She realized the presence she had felt was encircling them, fifteen golden-robed figures standing in a half-circle around them. At first, she thought they were like the statues they saw outside, but these robed people all wore flat masks in the shape of crescent moons. The masks only had one eyehole for the left eye, which from that distance, Desert Rain could only see blackness in those eyeholes.

"Look, Dezzy! They knew I was bringing you," Katawa chuckled. "They got all dressed appropriately for you."

"Wh...why?" Desert Rain gasped.

Katawa leaned very close to her ear, whispering into it. "Because they fear you." He stood up straight and glanced around the half-circle. "No Ozran? Does my brother not wish to welcome me home?"

"You are not welcomed here, Twisted One," a deep voice sounded from one of the figures—it was hard to tell which, given that the acoustics of the room made sound reverberate everywhere.

"You all made that abundantly clear when you banished me to the furnace," Katawa snarled. He held up his end of the whip high over his head, which forced Desert Rain's arms up. "Do you know what this is? You know who *she* is, I have no doubt."

The masked figures were silent.

"Short answer: they're both *mine*," Katawa hissed, and pulled Desert Rain into his arms. "And the Darkscale is mine by right. Now, you may deliver the Darkscale to me willingly, or we can play scavenger hunt."

"We knew you would attempt to return," the deep voice echoed again. "Even with the Moonstone Dragoness's heir in your possession, you cannot take on the entire Darkscale clan. We will correct our previous mistake and you will not leave this place alive."

Katawa flashed such a terrible smile, it made Desert Rain's blood turn cold. "I have no intention of leaving. And neither will any of you. And if my brother wants to be a coward, I'll find him. You can't deny me my fate."

All the masked figures produced jars from their robes. Each jar had a different item within—one had a flashing yellow strand within, like a streak of lightning; another jar had some blobbish liquid that splashed around as if alive; and another had crackling green rocks. Desert Rain recognized some of these things from books on alchemy she'd read long ago, but many were items that Nobleland alchemists were banned from using.

"Honestly, this is what they lead with?" Katawa

shook his head. "Basic alchemic cantrips. They obviously are trying to avoid hurting you, Dez. See, I knew you'd be handy." He looked back up at the Darkscale. "None of you know how to put on a good show. Allow me!"

He knelt and touched a hand to the floor. The room became awash in the purplish hue of Distortion, crawling across the floor, up the walls, and turning the green bonfires into jagged sculptures of amethyst. The lights in the room extinguished, and everyone was plunged into darkness.

Desert Rain stumbled, straining for her eyes to adjust. She suddenly felt Katawa's end of the whip go slack. Had he dropped it? She got her fingers around the length of whip and concentrated. A golden light blazed into life as she summoned Wintermane's Whip to become Burning Talon's sword. Yes, she controlled the Lightscale again!

As she held it up to light the room, her heart dropped into her stomach. Fifteen bodies lay on the floor in a pool of greenish blood, all of them in contorted, unnatural poses like ragdolls. She couldn't even comprehend it—hadn't it only been a few seconds since the lights went out? How had Katawa done this so fast? What was even more disturbing was that the masks had fallen away from all the Darkscale alchemists, and Desert Rain could see…

Faceless. They were all faceless.

A sharp blow to the back of her head sent Desert Rain back into darkness.

CHAPTER TWENTY-TWO
A Helping Hand; A Devilish Dinner

A clattering noise awoke Desert Rain from her slumber.

She groaned as she sat up, rubbing her head to clear the brainfog. It took a few seconds, but she remembered. She immediately checked her pockets, her belt pouch, and looked around herself. She was lying on a floor mat, and the air was cold and dank. The windows around her had iron bars, yet she was not in a prison cell, at least not one that was designed to be such. It was a decently sized room, full of tables covered in various glass beakers, jars, and cauldrons. Strange equipment littered the room, their nature unknown to her, but they had wires, dials and bulbs that indicated advanced — notably forbidden — technology. Bookshelves lined the walls, stuffed with tomes and loose papers. It vaguely represented a classroom of the Syphurius spellcasters' school she had visited many ages ago, but this place reeked of misery and death.

Sages damn it! He took back the Lightscale, she realized, as she was left with nothing on her person except her clothes. She sat with her head in her hands, desperately trying to think. How long had she been out? Why had Katawa put her in this room? Did the Darkscale clan know she was here?

Her last question was answered by a tapping noise coming from a corner of the room. She looked around, spying a metal grate where the floor met the wall—it looked like a spot where water or chemicals would be dumped out. The tapping resumed, and it sounded more methodical than mere rats scurrying by. She cautiously crawled over to the grate and whispered, "Hello?"

A finger poked up through the grate. "You are the Moonstone Dragoness's soulkeeper, yes?"

Desert Rain didn't recognize the voice; it was that of a male, but small and raspy. "Yes, I'm Desert Rain. Who are you?"

More fingers poked up through the grate, and slowly, softly lifted it and slid it to the side. A hooded figure climbed out, his robe brown and covered in muck. "Forgive me, the passages below have not been kept in the cleanest conditions. But they will be suitable for our escape."

Desert Rain hesitated, unsure if this was friend or foe. "You are Darkscale?"

"Yes," the man replied, somewhat embarrassed, "which is the worst thing to be right now. I knew Katawa hid you away somewhere, and I have spent days trying to find your hiding spot."

"Wait, days? I've been knocked out for *days*?"

"Approximately three. I believe he used his imprinting abilities to keep you subdued." The figure pulled back his hood.

Desert Rain's jaw dropped, and she had to rein in her shock. "You...have no face!"

It was an astute enough observation; the stranger had a human-shaped head, light teal-colored skin, and impressions where ears, eyes, nose, and mouth should have been.

Somehow, without a proper mouth, the stranger

continued to speak. "Oh, yes, I apologize. That is something that bothers you Nobles, isn't it?"

Desert Rain gulped back her initial surprise. "I...I thought Katawa had done something to those Darkscale we ran into when we first arrived. I didn't realize that's normal for you."

"Yes, he dispatched our Alchemist Guard so fast, we were not ready. He has slaughtered so many of us in the last few days. I will tell more, but one moment..." The man reached down to his belt, which stored pouches, a handful of corked vials, and pocketbooks. He extracted small objects from different pouches. "Let's see...these two match... this is a good one... now did I bring my... ah yes, the human set."

Desert Rain realized, to her horror, that he had drawn out two dismembered eyes, a nose, and a set of teeth and gums. He casually popped each body part into his face, pressing them in as one might press a toy marble into clay. His face molded around each feature, forming lips around the teeth, eyelids around the eyeballs, until he had a mostly human façade. He then pulled out two round ears from his belt pouch and twisted them into the sides of his head. "There. Better?"

Desert Rain nodded, although her half-smile did not agree.

The man scrutinized Desert Rain's face. "Oh, right, I always forget." One more extraction from his belt, a handful of powder he dusted on top of his head and above his eyes. Dark blue hair sprung up from his scalp and brows, which helped to complete his visage, although there was still something uncanny about his face, like a ceramic doll. "Now, please follow me. I can help you."

"Why? You know I'm Hijn. I thought the Darkscale hated us."

The stranger slinked back into the grate hole. "Most, yes. But you are the soulkeeper of the Mother of the Wretched. And I don't believe you are in league with Katawa, otherwise he wouldn't have locked you up in this lab. You can still save those of us who are left."

Desert Rain wasn't sure if she could trust this guy, but what choice did she have? If days had gone by, who knew how much destruction Katawa had caused. "I'll do what I can. But why has Katawa kept me locked up and subdued? What is he waiting for?"

The stranger lowered his voice, a cheeky smile on his now-visible face. "Because he can't find the Darkscale! The device, I mean. And he can't fulfill his desires without it. Lucky for us, as the Darkscale Keeper, I know exactly where it is. And I will show you. Please, quickly."

Desert Rain followed the stranger into the hole, as vile smells hit her nose right away. The hole led into a dark passage that reminded her of a cobweb-encrusted crypt. The stranger took two small rods from his belt, striking them together and creating a green flame on the ends. He handed one rod to Desert Rain and then started leading her through the dark passage.

"Are we safe to speak here?" she whispered.

"In low voices. Ever since Katawa refreshed his imprint of you, his hearing has been omnipotent. But these walls are thick, and as you have equal auditory perception to him, hopefully you may hear him coming long before I."

Desert Rain grimaced — she hoped that wouldn't be the case in these cramped quarters. "You still haven't told me who you are."

"I am the first son of the Master Alchemist Suzorn Galfi, Scholar of the Shadow Tomes and Keeper of the Darkscale Balance." He paused, noting the confusion on Desert Rain's face. "Oh! You wanted my name. Ozran-Oculus Galfi."

"Wait, Ozran?" She had heard the name before and recognized it instantly. "You're Katawa's brother. The one he blames for sending him to the furnace."

Ozran sighed. "He blames me for much. His execution was out of my hands. I had no choice but to order it, to protect the clan. You've seen what his powers can do, what madness he wrought."

"You know he wants to kill you, right?"

Ozran stopped and turned to her, his torch-rod illuminating his face with an eerie glow. "He wants to kill all of us! And so far, he had murdered our Alchemy Guard, our practitioners, our scholars and our..." He swallowed hard, his face crinkled in despair. "Family. I am one of the few left. We have been hiding in secret pockets of L'Teth, and thankfully we always rearrange these hidden passages over the years so he has no idea where any of them lead now. He grows furious that he can't find me or the Darkscale Balance, and the Lightscale does nothing for him. It is useless in his hands. But you, you are of vital importance to his plans. We can stop him."

Desert Rain couldn't believe she was partnering with a Darkscale demon, but she was finding herself in league with the Wretched more and more lately. Apparently, being the heir to the Mother of the Wretched came with that obligation. "Listen, if I've been asleep for days, then my friend General Clova Flor and the Ahshi army may be on their way. I gave them one of your special compasses for detecting ancient magic, and hopefully it may lead them to either me or Katawa."

Ozran's lips formed a thin line. "Then I hope it is a large army. Katawa has already summoned his legions of Distorted to barricade the bastion. That was why none of us can leave the premises."

Desert Rain paled; was Clova, Kidran, and the elves walking right into an impending bloodbath? And what of Gabriel, Chiriku, Mac, and the Hijn? Hopefully, her friends had managed to free the Council, but how would they find her?

She followed Ozran through passage after passage, in a downward descent that sent them deeper into the underground. After what felt like hours, they came to what initially appeared to be a dead end. Ozran withdrew a talisman from around his neck, an iron pendant with the Darkscale symbol, and placed it on a specific brick in the wall. The bricks receded one by one, until it revealed a chamber lit by orbs glowing in swirls of red and gold.

In the middle of a room was an ornate, black-marble pedestal. And on that pedestal was...nothing.

Desert Rain looked at Ozran, expecting him to panic—surely, something was supposed to be on that pedestal? Had Katawa found the Darkscale Balance before them? But Ozran cooly walked over to the pedestal, leaning toward it and scrutinizing its surface. "Come, see," he said.

Desert Rain approached, squinting at whatever Ozran was seeing. Maybe an invisibility enchantment? But as she got closer, she saw that the pedestal was not, in fact, empty. Upon it was a tiny thimble, almost too small to fit a child's finger.

Desert Rain raised an eyebrow at Ozran. "And what exactly am I looking at?"

"You don't think we would leave the Darkscale looking as it really does, do you? Of course, we had to mask it, not just from Katawa, but in case any of your Luuvian Knighthood should happen to invade our bastion." He took out a pair of metal tweezers from his belt and gingerly picked up the thimble from its pedestal. "Remarkable, isn't it? The power to change the world, all in this little trinket."

"Um, doesn't it sort of give it away that it's important by putting it in a secret room on a fancy pedestal?" Desert Rain asked.

Ozran gave her a blank gaze. "As opposed to what? Keeping it in a sewing basket?"

"Fair enough." Desert Rain was about to touch it, but then drew back her hand. "Does it have a protective ward on it?"

"It is written that only one with the soul of a Sage of Perpetual Night can wield it, just as only an heir of a Sage of Celestial Light can awaken the Lightscale. Sadly, with my brother's dragon being the Death Walker, it makes him one of the rare few to wield it."

"*One* of the few? As in, there's another Hijn who could?"

Ozran gave Desert Rain a pointed look. "There is a Sage that not only possesses Celestial Light, but also is guardian of the Night. And I theorize that the Darkscale balance will not harm her."

Desert Rain took a second to process that. Katawa had even said it himself: *You're the Moon Hijn! The moon is tied to the night.* It stood to reason she should be able to at least touch the Darkscale, if not do something with it. It was worth the risk; the worst that could happen would be an electric shock, like the Lightscale did to anyone who shouldn't hold it. Then again, who knew what adverse effect the Darkscale could have on someone it deemed unworthy.

She held out her hand beneath the thimble, steeling herself. "Let's test your theory, then."

Ozran carefully, as if conducting a precise experiment, placed the thimble onto Desert Rain's palm. She felt a bit nauseated, feeling a heat in the thimble as if it had been sitting in the sun for a while, but it didn't repel her. If anything, she felt a strange sensation from the thimble, almost as if it was begrudgingly compliant.

Ozran smiled, fully satisfied with this outcome. "I knew you could hold it! Thank goodness your flesh didn't melt off like so many others did when they tried."

"Wait, there was a chance my *flesh* could've—"

"Never mind that now. This means, you might be able to activate the Equanume all by yourself!"

Desert Rain felt a lurch in her stomach. "And why would you want me to do that?"

Ozran grew estatic, almost hysterical, as he explained. "Don't you see? The Equanume is what allowed the Sages to transform Luuva Gros into what it is! The Great Manifestation! But it also holds so much more power than that."

"More power that literally changing the world?"

"Yes! They created the Equanume by pouring a fragment of their magic, their very souls, into it. That means, if the ancient texts are true, that the Equanume can *absorb essences*. Specifically, dragon essence. Do you understand?"

At first, Desert Rain assumed he was implying that the Equanume could destroy the Hijn, or at least the dragon souls within them, and she started to believe Ozran's motivations were far more sinister than she had thought. But then it dawned on her — he wasn't talking about all Hijn. Just one particular Hijn.

"Katawa! The Equanume could absorb the soul of Balthazin within him. Which would render him powerless and vulnerable to death," she realized.

"Exactly! If *you* activate the Equanume, he'll be finished!" Ozran laughed so brazenly, Desert Rain had to shush him from how loud he was. He quieted but couldn't stop giggling like an insane person.

"But…" Desert Rain studied the thimble in her hand. "Katawa has the Lightscale. If the Darkscale falls into his hands, and he somehow activates the Equanume, what happens then?"

Ozran's mad smile faded into a frown of horror. "I am positive my brother wishes to use the Equanume for its terraforming and cellular altering powers. He could use it to magnify his Distortion, literally twisting everything in Luuva Gros, and beyond, to his mad design."

Desert Rain shivered at the thought. An entire world poisoned by Distortion…every living thing, trapped in an existence of never-ending contortion and pain. Katawa would practically be — no, absolutely would be — a god.

"But he can't activate the Equanume on his own," Ozran pointed out. "He can only activate the magic of the Darkscale. He would need you, or another Hijn of Celestial Light, to awaken the Lightscale."

Desert Rain let out a sigh of relief. That was a

good point, there was no other Celestial—well, except for Guerda-Shalyr of the Sun, or Sir Luce who was the Star...who was currently inside the Lightscale...who Katawa was currently in possession of...

"Ozran, there's a Celestial Sage soul in the Lightscale right now! Can Katawa control him since he has the Lightscale? Could he use Veritas Lucen to activate the Equanume?" Desert Rain asked.

This small but significant detail made Ozran silent, his forehead wrinkled in thought as he contemplated the question. "I don't think it likely. He would have to convince the Sage to do so willingly, which I doubt he could distort a dragon's soul without drawing him out, which would in turn jeopardize the Lightscale's powers. That's the catch—the Equanume can only be activated if both dragon-soul parties are willing."

Desert Rain prayed that was true—it was highly unlikely that Katawa even knew Sir Luce was inside the Lightscale anyway. But then, that also meant Katawa was planning to convince her to awaken the Equanume with him—how in Luuva did he intend to do that?

"Ozran, you must see the problem here. If I can awaken the Equanume, which is a BIG *if*, then that's exactly what Katawa wants. I'd have to get Balthazin out of him before he overpowers me to get the Equanume. I have no idea how the Balance works! It could take me days, weeks, *years* to understand the Equanume!"

"I wish I had more encouraging advice to give on that note," Ozran replied, "But as I am not Hijn, and the clan has not had the pleasure to study one properly—not for lack of trying—that will have to be something you figure out on your own, with very little time."

"Not for lack of trying?" Desert Rain couldn't help

but acknowledge that fleeting bit of information.

Ozran suddenly looked sheepish. "I confess, I would've given *anything* to study that Swordmaster. I came close, too, as I had the pleasure of facing him in a confrontation on the border ages ago. Sadly, he escaped before the elixir I applied to his face could render him unconscious."

Desert Rain went rigid. The scars on Gabriel's face…

Ozran observed the redness brightening Desert Rain's face, pure crimson fury. "I suppose that's not something you wanted to hear, was it? I heard of his passing. Was the Swordmaster a friend of yours?"

Desert Rain's eyes became dark, and her voice dropped to a low, malicious tone. "Ozran, if Katawa doesn't kill you, I very well may."

The Wretched blanched, as if just realizing what Hijn he was with. He grinned awkwardly. "Well, if you must, make it fast. It will be better than whatever my brother would do to me."

Frantic scratching and scraping caught Desert Rain's ears. It was coming from the passageway behind them. "Do you hear that?"

Ozran was quiet but he shrugged. "What does it sound like?"

Desert Rain listened a moment longer — and could hear the scraping was accompanied by guttural growling and moaning. She almost couldn't reply as her breathing came to a halt. "Distorted," she wheezed.

"This way!" Ozran rasped, as he climbed onto the pedestal and reached up to the ceiling. He shifted a wooden panel, pushing it aside, revealing an exit. He scrambled up into it, and Desert Rain, after securing the thimble into her belt pouch, followed him and returned the panel to its place behind them.

The exit in the ceiling led to a rotted, but still functional, ladder, that the two of them ascended into darkness. Ozran cracked another light rod, sparking it into green light. After ascending a good way up, Desert Rain could hear far below that the room they had been in was now occupied, and a cacophony of enraged grunts and howls echoed behind them.

"Where does this go?" Desert Rain whispered, hoping the Distorted would not notice the panel and figure out their way of escape.

"The dining hall, I'm pretty sure. And from there, we can get to the armory where we can barricade ourselves in. There are others there already," Ozran said.

After climbing one ladder, they came to a small landing that supported another ladder, and after that, another landing with yet *another* ladder, and so on for however many levels, Desert Rain lost count. The ascent was so grueling, her arms and legs were burning by the time they got to the top of the final ladder. At the top was a trap door, locked from their side. Ozran removed a set of skeleton keys from one of his pouches and tried several before finding the correct key.

Ozran pushed up on the door an inch before something from above snatched him in its gnarled claws and lifted him out with a scream.

Desert Rain froze on the ladder. Someone knew they would come up this way — did they only expect Ozran, or her too? She waited to see if anyone would look down into the trap door. Ozran had become suddenly quiet up there. Everything had become suddenly, terrifyingly quiet.

She couldn't allow Ozran to be captured — *or could I? He's not exactly a good guy, after what he did to Skyhan,* came a passing thought. She shooed the thought away.

After her mind quieted, she heard a conversation — it wasn't directly over her. It sounded to be coming from the room above, but at a distant end of it.

"I don't know!" she heard Ozran plead. "I swear I haven't seen her! I was trying to secure the Darkscale but your creatures chased me away from its location before I could get it. If you let me go back, I'll bring it right to you — "

A bone-snapping crack, followed by a whimper, ended Ozran's sentence.

"Honestly, you're good for nothing, aren't you?" Katawa's voice paralyzed Desert Rain. "And you've become a terrible liar." A slight pause, and Katawa's voice raised. "Dezzy, I'm not going to drag you out, that's demeaning to both of us. Please join us. I'll even let your new friend breathe a little longer if you do."

She braced herself. She had the Darkscale; they each had a half of the Equanume. Not that she could afford to bargain, but maybe she could distract Katawa long enough for Ozran to sneak away. She took a deep breath and climbed out the trap door.

She was at the end of a long, elaborately set dining hall table, surrounded by intricately carved chairs. Candelabras with lit hunter-green candles accentuated the décor, and the floor was covered in plush, emerald carpet. The walls were adorned with light parsley paper with gold-leaf filigree, and even artwork — disturbing artwork of haunted faces that she could only guess were past Darkscale masters — lined the walls. This room could rival the banquet hall of any palace; it was, apparently, the one room that the Darkscale clan wanted to be decadent.

At the other end of the table, leaning back in a throne-like chair, his feet propped up on the tabletop, was Katawa. Around him were half a dozen hulking Distorted, and Ozran was hanging limply by his arm from one of the creature's crushing grip. Even from that distance, Desert Rain could see greenish blood trailing down his face from where his applied nose had been ripped off.

"Ah, there's the guest of honor!" Katawa exclaimed, clapping his hands. "I see you met my brother. And he put one of his nicer faces for you, both literally and figuratively speaking. Always hated that nose, though. Are you just going to linger way over there? Come here."

Desert Rain was tempted to comply so she could pick up a candelabra from the table and run it through his face. But she couldn't be hasty — she had to play this game right, now more than ever. She took her time walking over. "Your brother's a coward, Katawa. He's not worth your time. You want to talk to me. You've had your fun, just let him and whoever is left go."

Katawa raised his eyebrows, a wry smile drawing his lips back from his sharp teeth. "Oh, so noble to the end, Dezzy. Then again, I do like the idea of Ozran sticking around long enough to see my magnificent, new world, the one you and I will create together. Hmm, decisions, decisions. But we have time for that. Sit, you must be starving. I had dinner arranged. How long has it been since you had a decent meal?"

Desert Rain's gut cringed, but not from hunger. This could not be good.

As she approached, she saw three sets of plates and silverware had been arranged, one in front of Katawa and two on his right and left. The Distorted holding Ozran forcibly plopped him into one chair, and Ozran's arm hung lifeless at his side. He stared defeatedly down at the plate before him.

Behind Katawa was a pushcart with bowls of food—Desert Rain could now smell them, and it all reeked of charred meat. Her stomach flipped, despite her having not eaten in several days.

Katawa poured a chalice of deep red wine from a pitcher on the table. He held it up towards her, beckoningly. "At least drink something. You must be parched."

Desert Rain glared at him with all the hatred she could muster.

He tiled his head at her. "Cross my heart, or at least the spot where a heart should be, it's just wine. No funny business."

Damn it, she had to play nice for now, if anything to stall him in case the Ahshi army was on its way. She snatched the chalice and took a long enough sip to quench her thirst.

"Come now, sit," he said again, and Desert Rain yanked at the chair he gestured to before sitting down, glaring at him the whole time. "Now, your words the other day, about couldn't I have been happy living in the desert with you? It got me thinking. And I'd like tonight to be just like those old times again, when it was just us."

A Distorted brought over a bowl to Desert Rain and set it in front of her. Expecting something awful, she was surprised and suspicious to see it full of caramel cicadas, similar to the ones she used to make back at home.

"Not as good as yours, but I remembered the recipe. See, I pay attention," Katawa said. "And for me, you always cooked me that delicious desert rabbit." He paused as a plate of lean lapin meat was set before him. "But what to make for my brother? What would he like? I know! I think he should eat his words."

Ozran lifted his head, terror screaming in his eyes.

Katawa put his feet back on the floor and stood, leaning toward Ozran, his voice dripping with malice. "Which words, exactly? How about... 'you're nothing but an abomination, brother?' Or, 'you sealed your fate when you betrayed us, brother?' Any one of those?"

Two Distorted came over and held Ozran in a steel grip, one holding Ozran's head in place with a clawed hand. Ozran instinctively struggled but could not move an inch. One of the Distorted clutched the Wretched's face hard enough to force his jaw open. Katawa picked up a cutting knife from his place setting, twirling it in his hand. He reached into Ozran's open mouth and pinched his tongue between two fingers, drawing it out. "How about *all* your words? Every single word you ever let roll of your tongue."

"Katawa, stop!" Desert Rain ordered, standing up.

Katawa shot her a dirty look. "This is a family matter. You'll get your turn."

"What's the point of this? He's no threat to you —"

"Stop. Talking." Katawa's yellow eyes narrowed on her. "This is *my* moment."

"Let him go right now and I'll tell you where the Darkscale is." Dragons damn it, the words just popped out of her mouth.

Katawa froze, staring bewilderedly at her. His face

melted into scorn; he looked positively pissed. "You'd give me exactly what I want, for my brother? My *brother*, for Luuva's sake?? I'd expect this weakness for one of your friends, or those bastard Hijn that always treated you like garbage, but my brother?" He slammed the knife on the table and advanced on her. Desert Rain stood her ground, even though every nerve in her body begged her to run.

"I have worked so damned hard to free you of this bleeding heart," Katawa sneered. "I thought you having to face the cold, cruel world for once would solve that. But here you are, bargaining to save the scum of the earth! Do you even know what Ozran did to your precious Swordmaster? Before I killed him?"

Desert Rain stared at him steadily, unwaveringly.

Katawa's rage was temporarily tempered as he read the answer in Desert Rain's eyes. "Of course. Ozran, the eternal blabbermouth. I'm sure he couldn't help but rattle off his accomplishments to you. And even then, after he scarred your beloved, you still want to save this worm?"

Desert Rain was stoic in her response. "We aren't all slaves to vengeance like you."

The corner of Katawa's eye twitched. Then, he laughed. Deep, belly laughs, right in Desert Rain's face. Loud, long, horrible laughs.

"You do like to get under my skin, Dez," he said, wiping a tear from his eye. "But what pisses me off more is, I see your point. How do you get me to do that?"

Desert Rain must have looked surprised, because Katawa grinned at her reaction. "I have been a slave to my own failings, haven't I? I enjoy these games too much. And I get so wrapped up in the fun, that's when you get the upper hand on me. Here, I was going to cut out Ozran's tongue and make him eat it." He glanced at his brother, whose teal skin had paled to snow-mint. Katawa strolled back over to his side of the table to stand next to him, patting his shoulder. "But then you'd blast me in the face with Blueshine again, and then I'd have to thaw out, and then you get the Lightscale from me while I'm distracted, and it's all so tedious at this point. So, let's cut right to the chase."

In the most casual way, with no more thought than flicking away a gnat, Katawa picked up the knife again and cut Ozran's throat. Ozran gagged, a burbling in his throat choking him as blood ran down his front, and then he was still, his eyes glazed over. The Distorted released him, and Ozran dropped face first onto the table, lifeless.

Desert Rain managed not to scream, but a slight gasp escaped her lips.

"Don't feel bad for him. That was going to happen either way. You merely convinced me to make it quick." Katawa wiped the blood off his knife with a napkin before stabbing it into a piece of meat on his plate and bringing it to his mouth. He chewed and swallowed. "Now, you were saying that idiot gave you the Darkscale?"

CHAPTER TWENTY-THREE
The Battle of the Two Scales

Desert Rain's eyes lingered on Ozran's dead body for a few seconds as his blood dripped off the table onto the carpet. She turned back to Katawa and set her glower on him. "You knew I was with Ozran. You knew we'd come out that trap door. You must've already guessed that he showed me the Darkscale."

Katawa took a sip of wine from Desert Rain's chalice before replying. "It's not exactly a puzzle, Dez. I knew he'd crawl out of his rathole eventually, and once I found out you weren't where I left you, I pieced it all together. So, I have the Lightscale, you have the Darkscale, or at least you know where it is. The halves we currently possess are useless to us, but I gather you won't hand over the Darkscale to me at the drop of a hat. We seem to be at an impasse."

"Not really. The Lightscale may be useless to you, but I didn't need any special salve to hold the Darkscale. Speaking of which, I understand I've been unconscious for several days, so your special salve must be wearing off by now."

Katawa frowned at her statement. He chugged more wine until the chalice was empty. "I applaud you, Desert Rain. Biding your time, waiting for me to be unable to touch the Lightscale anymore. Meanwhile, you could have both halves in your possession." His frown slowly shifted to an odd grin. "The power of creation, in your hands, Dez! Oh, just think about it. This broken world, all these injustices, you could correct all the mistakes that the Sages brought on us. Who would treat you like you don't matter anymore? Who would treat *anyone* poorly if you command everyone be equal? No more wars, no more prejudice, no more unfair hierarchies. Only unity. Doesn't that sound lovely?"

Dear Guerda-Shalyr, did Katawa really believe he could sway her? "That's not what *you* want," she replied. "You're never putting the two halves together. You're never getting the Equanume."

Katawa set the chalice down and approached her. He looked deeply into her eyes. "You've lost so much. You've endured so much pain. You've dragged yourself all over this bloody land, trying to save people who don't even care about each other, let alone you. And how will they repay you, if you should succeed? You'll go back to your desert, and in time, they'll forget about you all over again. You'll end up alone again, Desert Rain. And that's the best scenario. More likely, everyone will argue that as Luuva Gros's Hijn guardian, you didn't move fast enough, didn't save enough people, allowed all this anguish to fall upon the people because the Hijn, well, they should be perfect, yes? They'll put the blame on the Hijn for even allowing this to happen—after all, I'm Hijn too, am I not? Luuva Gros is already doomed to tear itself apart, its system upended, its lies exposed. You can't return this world to the way it was. You won't even be a martyr, Dez. You'll be villainized, ostracized, remembered as the one who brought about Luuva's ruination. This land won't survive."

Desert Rain crossed her arms. "Are you done?"

Katawa put an arm around her—she jerked at his touch—and he led her over to a window. Down below, as far as she could see, the Distorted army circled the bastion—tens, maybe hundreds of thousands of Distorted, moving together like a dark, wavering ocean. The sight gripped her heart with dread—how many of Luuva Gros's people had Katawa turned? Who would be left?

"Look at them," Katawa said, gesturing out to the throng. "Can you even tell who is who? Who is human, elf, dwarf, Quetzalin, even Lejenous? All new worlds begin with agony, as does any birth. But the agony will subside, and what will remain is a world united by my vision, by my art. All one in the same. And they, everyone, will worship you, Dez. More than as some remnant of a dragoness that abandoned you, abandoned all of us. You will be a Creator, a Goddess. You asked me if I could be happy living in that desert? No, I couldn't be happy living in a blistering wasteland. But the thing I couldn't live without is you. You have been my greatest art, my finest creation. And look at you now! Your power, your strength, your will. You are not the Desert Rain I discovered in that burrow years ago. You are reborn!"

Desert Rain had another fleeting thought—*Katawa really missed out on the chance to be an orator, he's quite good at it*—and like before, she shooed it away. But she remembered Sir Luce's words: *The Lightscale cannot undo the Distortion. It is a component of balance, not a cure-all.*

The Lightscale by itself couldn't undo Katawa's darkness—it was a component of balance. She needed full balance to be restored. She needed to reunite the scales to make the Equanume, and she'd have to risk playing along with Katawa until she could do that. But she couldn't agree with him so readily...she had to dance this messy waltz first.

"There's no bringing Luuva Gros back to what it used to be, is there?" she asked, feigning melancholy. "It will always be broken, unless we do something."

"Now you understand," Katawa said, pulling her close to embrace her. "I know you see my art as gruesome, but you, you can perfect it. The Distortion can be so much more. It can bring about a whole new race, a new future! Our reformed world will be as much your design as mine. Whatever you desire."

She rested her head on his shoulder. "No more wars, or bloodshed? Just peace?"

"Unlike any you've ever even dreamed of."

She sighed. "I'm so tired, Katawa. So tired of fighting. I can't carry all this anymore, this weight. The harder I fight, the more people get hurt. I don't know if I believe in destiny, but at least the destiny you describe would relieve me of this futile battle." The sad thing was, she said this believably enough, because she felt it was partly true.

"I know you're tired. Soon, you can rest easy for eternity." He kissed the top of her head in that sweet way he once did, and then placed a finger under her chin to lift her gaze to his. "Let's save the world, shall we?"

*   *   *

L'Teth Zurên's throne room was a strange synthesis of lush opulence and mechanical madness — pillars lining the walls, high-arched stained glass windows, and the black marble floor gave the impression of a temple, but the metal spires encircled in wires and coils, cylindrical containment units filled with bioluminescent liquids, and a large metal sphere hanging overhead from which tubes and chains extended out, creating an ominous web across the room, indicated this was a playground of false gods.

Katawa led Desert Rain into this harrowing hall, and she suddenly felt small in such a vast chamber. She could imagine this throne room once having been filled with the entire Darkscale clan for ceremonies or initiations, but now the echoes of their footsteps filled its gloom.

Katawa was being unusually silent as he crossed the room, taking in every detail, every dusty drapery, every mysterious machine. After a minute, he stopped next to a particular spire, where there was a panel of buttons and levers. He flipped one lever, and the spire crackled to life, spitting a few sparks before an electric jolt flowed through it in waves of yellow. This reaction fed into the next spire, and the next, until the room was emanating a ballet of lightning around them. This ignited the liquid in the containment units, and they glowed with blobs of color like lava swimming in oil.

Katawa walked to the far end of the room, walking towards what Desert Rain thought, at first, was a grand musical organ or calliope. It was copper colored, as tall as the ceiling, with series of pointed vents along the top and flanked by two towers shaped like flaming beacons. Katawa stood directly before it, and Desert Rain, who had stopped several feet behind him, could see his shoulders rise in tension.

"Do you know what this is?" Katawa asked, his voice hollow like an open grave.

Desert Rain wasn't sure if he was directing the question at her, or to the ghosts of his mind. "How could

I?" she finally said.

His hand reached up to a chain hanging from the front of the organ. He pulled, and the front of the machine groaned as two jagged panels pulled apart, opening like a wolf's jaws. It opened into an abysmal darkness, a whoosh of ashen air emitting from it. Katawa glided to another part of the machine, where there was a bronze board of musical keys. When he pressed a few, no melodic tones came out, but a series of sighs, as if he was breathing life into the device.

The open mouth of the machine burst into hellfire, the heat spewing out and driving away the chill of the room instantly. Desert Rain stumbled away from it, taken aback by the roaring flames. She shielded her eyes from it, as Katawa stood before the fire. He turned around to face her, his eyes possessed by gleeful delirium.

"Now, do you know?" he asked again.

Desert Rain remembered his memory. The one she hadn't meant to see, back when she had found his lost memories in Syphurius. Even now, she visualized his pool of blood on the floor, in the spot she was standing... and Katawa's face anguished face reflecting in it, before numerous hands dragged him into a burning mouth.

"The furnace," she whispered.

"Where I rose from the ashes like a phoenix!" Katawa announced, raising his arms over his head. "And now, this very room, where I was tortured and defiled, I will ascend to my destiny. The fire of this furnace will perish as the Equanume flares into life—the old world dies so the new world can be born." He approached her, holding out his hand. "Now, my wondrous golden goddess, the Darkscale, please."

Desert Rain felt her insides twist tightly, as if

Distortion had already taken hold of her. She inhaled slowly. "An even trade, then? The Lightscale can't be used without my magic."

Katawa smile dipped slightly. "Let's not play games. You'll play your part. The Darkscale." His last word was punctuated with impatience.

Desert Rain breathed. *Patience.*

She reached into her belt pouch and drew out the thimble. As she expected, Katawa's reaction to seeing it was one of uncertainty—was she trying to fool him? But then his confusion subsided and was replaced by irritation. "My brother did love transmuting things. It was his specialty. What an insulting shape." He snatched the thimble from her, inspecting it. He placed it onto his pinky finger snuggly, and smirked. "I can already feel it begging to be released of its confinement. It knows its true master." He gave Desert Rain a sly glance. "It knows you too, Dezzy. It agrees with me, what I've known about you all along."

Desert Rain crinkled her nose mockingly. "And what's that?"

"There is darkness in your heart," he replied. "You can't help it. You are tied to the Night. You try desperately to fight it, but I promise, you will feel true freedom when you embrace it."

Desert Rain covertly scanned Katawa, trying to spy a pocket or a belt pouch where he might have hidden the Lightscale on his person. If he had managed to return it to whip form, it could be curled up in a small space. He was so in love with his own voice, maybe she could let him ramble on while she—

Katawa noticed her wandering eye. "Oh, looking for this?" He placed a hand on his chest, and to Desert

Rain's teeth-clenching horror, distorted a gap through his skin right above where his sternum was. He withdrew from *within himself* a foot-long black leather canister about an inch in diameter, which dripped with whatever in Luuva he was full of other than his ego.

"Ozran isn't the only one who can transmute," he explained, rubbing his open gap until it reclosed. "I just tucked the Lightscale away for safekeeping once the salve started to wear off."

Desert Rain swallowed back a bout of bile that rose in her throat. *You keep finding new ways to disgust me,* she thought.

"I apologize that I'll have the honor of reuniting the two halves," he said, his joyful anticipation rising in his voice, "but once that happens, the Equanume will be starved for our magic, like any newborn hungers. It will draw out Bellaluna's and Balthazin's magic on its own. You can just relax and enjoy our masterpiece blossom to life."

Desert Rain nearly choked. She took a step back. "Ozran said we had to both be willing to give our magic—"

A distorted tendril from Katawa's shoulder blade lashed out and coiled around her, pinning her arms to her sides as it coiled around her torso. It pulled her closer to him as she struggled against it.

"Ozran may have studied the old texts, but Balthazin told me everything about the Equanume himself. Besides, you *will* be willing, just as all the Hijn Council was willing to obey me."

He brought his finger close to her ear, and she could feel a slick ooze at his touch. Desert Rain felt a trickle of tar against her earlobe and she jerked her head away. *No, no! If that stuff gets in my head, he'll control my mind!*

Katawa grabbed her face and held her still. His voice dripped with delicious ruthlessness. "There's nowhere for you to go, no one to help you. You're mine, Desert Rain, and until I deem you should breathe your last breath, you're always going to be—"

Two blasts of a horn from outside cut him off. Before either of them could even piece together what that could mean, one of the stained-glass windows and the wall around it exploded in a flurry of glass, stone and smoke as a massive battle train barreled through it, with the ease of a bull at full speed running through fabric.

Both Katawa and Desert Rain stared flabbergasted at the train, as it came to a screeching halt in the middle of the room. From the engine's cab, a red-haired head poked out, looking around until his gaze landed on Desert Rain and Katawa.

"Are we interrupting somethin'?" Mac asked, grinning. "We can come back-kk later if you need, Dez."

Katawa's arms dropped to his sides, and his voice was unusually small. "What in the Eternal Deep—"

Desert Rain's prayer for a distraction had finally been answered, beautifully. She had enough maneuverability to get her long fingers around Katawa's tendril holding her, and Blueshine poured through her fingertips and rendered it brittle blue glass. She broke the restraints apart with a backwards jerk of her elbows, and Katawa had to shut his eyes against the splinters of glass that sprayed into his face. Desert Rain took advantage of his momentary blindness and in a swift motion, her hand was on Katawa's arm, the one with the Lightscale. A burst of Blueshine raced up his arm, transforming opaque flesh into transparent glass. With an upwards snap of her wrist, Desert Rain shattered his arm clean off his body, the sound of breaking glass music to her ears.

Katawa howled an elongated scream of both pain and shock. He staggered back from her as he surveyed the stump at his shoulder. In a sloppy, erratic movement with his remaining hand, he pulled and stretched at his stump with Distortion like taffy, producing a tentacle ending in a cluster of claws. The glare of hatred he gave Desert Rain could've killed her on the spot. "You black-hearted bitch," he growled.

Desert Rain clutched the canister, locking eyes with him. "You want your new world, Katawa? You're going to have to fight me for it."

"And us!" A gust of wind blew into the room with a mighty howl, and Chiriku, glorious golden feathers flowing, rode the wind to Desert Rain's side. She landed on the floor lightly, crossing her arms. "By the way, don't bother calling your beasts. They're enjoying a nice nap."

Katawa looked toward the giant hole in the wall that the train had bulldozed. His jaw dropped open as he saw snow — something the Inbetween never had — falling gently over the land outside. It was true; the cacophony of howls that they all should have been hearing from the Distorted congregation was dead silent.

Desert Rain smirked. Kidran's magic could really be a wonder.

Katawa curled his lip. "How did you fools even find this place? Only the Lightscale could find it!"

From the train disembarked two familiar Distorted and their smaller brother. Gank Vermin seemed much bolder in the company of friends. "BAD MAN CALL ALL DISTORTED TO HIM! MY BROTHERS

SAID YOU TOLD THEM WHERE TO GO, IN THEIR HEADS. THEY LED US TO YOU!"

"Also, wasn't hard to track you once I got back up in the air and saw all those Distorted heading in one direction," Chiriku added. "All we had to do was follow the stampede to your doorstep."

"Not to mention," came another voice, as Gabriel disembarked from the train, "We brought the entire Ahshi army with us. They're waiting right outside. You're the one who's surrounded now."

From beside Mac in the cab, Gothart cautiously popped up his shaggy head. "I'm here too…just thought you should know…holler if you need me…" He then popped out of sight again.

Katawa bared his teeth like a mad dog. "You all forget, I could order your precious Hijn Council to kill themselves with a single thought—"

"You won't be doing that." Stepping off the train, in dazzling jade and ivory splendor, Mage Skyhan descended to the floor next to Gabriel. She was still stained with Distortion ooze around her ears and eyes, but remarkably less so—more like some mud that would simply require a few baths to wash off.

Katawa looked positively gobsmacked, his eyes wide like a cornered animal. "How is that possible? Even your healing magic can't remove my Distortion!"

"No, not mine alone. But my dear friend Macapailius displayed a unique skill that gave me an idea." Mage Skyhan glanced back at Mac and smiled. "After watching our lizard friend shed your Distortion, I remembered that Luuvian lizards are immune to poison. After my healing magic examined him, it became apparent what your clan's experiments on him were for—to make him immune to any alchemic or magically induced plague, primarily of your variety. When they thought you were dead, they released him until he became needed."

Desert Rain looked at Mac, who grinned sheepishly at her and shrugged. She realized why the Darkscale had sent him to find Katawa—Mac would be the only one of their spies that was immune to Distortion.

Mage held up a hand, displaying a glass vial of red. "Because his biochemistry was altered by your clan's alchemy, his immunity is compatible with about every other race—consider him a universal donor. He was gracious enough to permit me to borrow some of his biochemistry for a bloodbind antidote, one that has allowed us to repel your poison and freed us of your control. And trust me, we all want a piece of you, Katawa."

"You've been done in by a lizard! Ha!" Mac called, gleefully honking the train's horn again.

Desert Rain's heart swelled. Here, Mac had worried that what the Darkscale had done to him was a curse—and now he had been the key to freeing the Hijn. Maybe fate wasn't a foolish concept after all.

Katawa's eyes darted from one foe to another, until locking eyes with Desert Rain. "You know I don't need my Distorted or even those useless Hijn. I'm more powerful than all of you combined. I'm going·to have our destiny fulfilled, Desert Rain, no matter how hard or how long you fight it!"

Desert Rain set her jaw. "Then fight, coward."

She tore open the top of the canister, and as if the Lightscale inside recognized her presence, a white beam sprouted forth, swirling out of the canister in a snaking spring of starlight, before wrapping around her in an illuminated cloak.

Katawa growled, a feral sound from the bowels of a nightmare. He held up his good hand, which still had the thimble on his finger, and clasped it into his palm. A veil of shadow, a fractured shard of midnight, wound around his fist, down his arm, up his shoulder and around his body. The Darkscale responded to him, his soul, his command—the thimble's façade fell away, and suddenly Katawa was enveloped in an armor that was something liquid, something air at the same time. It rippled around him like a whirlpool of the Eternal Deep itself. In his hand, a bastard sword materialized, one with a merlot-red blade that seemed solid one moment, then gelatinous like cooled blood at another. It dripped acid onto the floor and seethed with unbridled rancor.

This surge of power filled Katawa's eyes with wild delight. "You see, Desert Rain? The Darkscale knows that I am its—"

He did not get to finish as a warhammer, airborne on a rush of wind, flew from behind Chiriku and upper-cut him under the chin. The force of the blow propelled him up towards—and straight through—the ceiling, leaving nothing but a hole in its wake.

Everyone looked at Chiriku. The Quetzalin shrugged. "What? Did anyone want to hear whatever cliché villainy thing he was going to say?"

Desert Rain looked up at the ceiling, clenching her fists. She turned to Mage Skyhan. "The other Hijn, are they—"

"They will be all right," Mage confirmed. "The antidote is working for them, but they need more time to recover. They are with Clova and Kidran. We will all stand behind you, Desert Rain."

"Thank you, Mage," Desert Rain replied. "I'm going to try and get the Darkscale away from him. Wait here until I give you a signal."

"You can't go after him alone," Gabriel said, his face set with determination and concern.

Desert Rain went to him and embraced him, her light radiating even brighter as she did. "I couldn't have gotten this far without you," she said softly, "but what needs to be done, Bellaluna and I must do. If I fail, then you and Sir Luce need to use the Lightscale in my place."

Gabriel pulled away, grasping her arms like he wouldn't let her go. "Dez, I can't wield the Lightscale. I can't protect you. I'm not—"

"Yes, you *are* worthy. You always have been," she said, gently touching his face. "Skyhan didn't split you in two as your good and evil sides. I understand now. He split into his ideal self, and his flawed self. But it's only through accepting our flaws that we can heal and grow. I wish Skyhan had understood that you were what made him strong, because you were always his heart." She gave him a kiss on the cheek. "I've got to go, before Katawa gets away. Protect the others, I know you will." She then turned to Chiriku. "Chi, I need a lift."

The Quetzalin grinned. "You got it, Donkey Ears." A sweeping arc of her hands, and a flow of wind swept up Desert Rain, lifting her up and into the hole in the ceiling, up into darkness.

Desert Rain landed lightly on a landing, and she looked up into a long stretch of tower above her. She realized he must be in one of the steeples she had seen from the outside of the bastion, a lookout tower of sorts. There was a spiraling staircase leading upward, although it was narrow, a one-person-at-a-time ascension. The staircase was lit by small sconces, barely enough light to see twenty feet ahead of her.

She took a step on the staircase and noticed a slight jingling sound as she did so. Looking down at herself, she realized she was adorned in more than a shimmering cloak—from head to toe, she wore scale armor, overlapping plates of brilliant moonstone blue. Metal gauntlets covered her wrists, and even her boots were adapted for her prehensile toes, each toe protected by flexible scale. Touching her head, she found a helmet there, lightweight and designed with a crest like Bellaluna's.

We really are fighting together now, aren't we, Luna? Desert Rain thought.

Always, Bellaluna's voice answered back.

Desert Rain looked back up into the void of the tower. "Katawa, this game needs to end." She smirked. "Don't make me drag you down here, that's demeaning for both of us."

A blast of shadow, like an onyx fire, shot down from above, missing her by inches. She summoned Waterweaver's Trident and snuffed the fire out with a quick command of water sprayed from the prongs.

"My, you get sensitive when backed into a corner, don't you?" she said, ascending the stairs.

"And you've become far too arrogant," Katawa's voice dripped from above. Desert Rain couldn't see him, wherever he was hiding, so she summoned Burning Talon's sword. Yet its radiance was hardly an ember's glow in the surrounding darkness.

"The Darkscale has domain here," Katawa's voice echoed again. "You'll have to do better than your pathetic little sword."

That meant he could pop out of the dark at any time, and Desert Rain had little space to maneuver. She decided that defense might be the best plan, so she shifted the Lightscale into the gift from Zephyrsong's magic, a throwing shield that needed no strap as a breeze would return it to her should she throw it. She clasped Zephyrsong's Shield tightly, perking up her ears for the smallest of sounds.

She barely caught the sound of an incoming whoosh before she lifted the shield over her head, and a bone-rattling impact slammed into it. She nearly lost her footing, but the shield formed a protective wind around her, keeping her upright. The offensive force continued to push down on her, so she pushed back, her gale repelling the attack. She looked from behind her shield, and saw Katawa standing on the staircase a few yards ahead of her. He swung his bastard sword in an arc, and a rush of heat bombarded her in a flurry of crow-shaped wraiths. She held her ground behind her shield, although her stance on the stairs was tenuous. The wraiths shattered into dark splinters as they collided with the shield and her cloak, tinkling down the stairs behind her.

"Must we do this, Dez?" Katawa asked. "You already know even if you could best me, you won't. Cut me to ribbons, bash my face in, impale me. I'll always come back. Balthazin's magic was made for me." He tilted his head, glancing her up and down. "I'd much rather have such a formidable goddess at my side than needing to make you my pet. Distortion wouldn't suit you, so don't force my hand."

"No one's forcing you to do anything," she countered.

"Do you really believe I can stop now?" Anger rose in his tone. "I am so close to creating our new world. How dare you imply I can walk away from this?"

Desert Rain shifted Zephyrsong's shield into Silverheart, holding the hilt close to her heart. "I know you'd say you can't. But someone else still can. And I'm going to give him that chance."

Sir Luce, if you can hear me, she thought, *I'm about to beat the living daylights out of Katawa, so if you want to get your punches in, now's your chance. No pressure.*

Funnily enough, she believed she felt an odd pulse from the sword, and the only way she could describe it was pride.

Desert Rain launched herself at Katawa, her cloak uplifting her on a wave of iridescent moonlight. Even though Katawa had the higher ground, he found himself backing up the stairs as Desert Rain lunged and parried with unrivaled fury and focus. They came to a landing, and Katawa shifted his sword into a bizarre full-arm gauntlet with a head-sized drill on the end. Desert Rain blocked his thrust with Silverheart, but the whirring drill churned within inches of her face.

"Balthazin, I know you're in there," she tried to shout above the whirring. "I know you want to be free of Katawa's madness! I can help you!"

Katawa was stunned by Desert Rain's words. "What are you up to? Balthazin belongs to me! He can't hear you."

Desert Rain lifted a foot onto Katawa's stomach and kicked him away. He almost toppled off the landing but managed to keep his balance and leapt up the staircase.

"*You* can't hear *him*," Desert Rain corrected him.

"But I hear Bellaluna inside me. I hear Sir Luce. We Hijn have always been able to talk to our dragons. We just forgot how. But I'm betting Balthazin's been silent because you won't allow him to speak." She summoned Wintermane's Whip, lashing it out to wrap around Katawa's neck. Katawa grasped at it to free himself, but without his salve, it sent shocks of pain through his whole body.

Desert Rain spoke again, holding the whip steady. "Balthazin, I know what happened. You were worried that your powers within the Equanume could hurt Luuva Gros. That you needed to find an heir who could use the magic of a Death Walker to keep balance in the Eternal Deep. But you must see what destruction Katawa has brought, both to Luuva Gros and the Deep! You need to go back, Balthazin. You need to return to the spirits who need you."

Katawa shifted his weapon into a glove with curved blades on the fingertips, which he used to slice through the whip choking him. Desert Rain called the whip back before it could be seriously damaged, morphing it back into Silverheart.

"Shut up!" Katawa thundered, his pupils thinned to almost nothing in blind rage. "He can't leave me! Once a Sage is bound to a Hijn, they are joined forever!"

"The Sages believe they need vessels, Katawa." In a sweep of her arm, her cloak extended in a fluster of moonlight feathers, becoming wings. "But the truth is, they can forge their own destinies. As can we."

In a leap, she was in the air, and her prehensile toes clasped onto Katawa's shoulders, like an eagle snatching its prey. She soared higher into the tower, dangling him over the abyss below.

"Give me the Darkscale!" she ordered.

"Or what, you'll drop me?" Katawa's laughter reverberated through the tower. "Think I'll go splat? If I should fall, let us fall together."

His shadow armor suddenly engulfed them both, a vortex of night, blinding Desert Rain. She tried to raise Silverheart for light, but the weight on her body was too much. The Darkscale's force pulled and constricted around her, trying to crush her within her armor. Silverheart became too heavy to bear, and she felt it slip from her fingers. She wanted to scream, but the asphyxiation stifled her lungs. All she could hear was Katawa's insane laughter as darkness began to devour her alive.

Light exploded from the bottom of the tower in magnificent colors. It flooded the space, rising higher and higher in a tidal wave of brightness. Desert Rain found she could breathe again, as the Darkscale's magic waned in the overwhelming illumination.

Desert Rain collapsed on the stairway, and Katawa fell from her grip, tumbling down to the next landing. Once she regained her breathing, she looked down below towards the source of the light.

Swordmaster Skyhan stood at the bottom of the stairs. Wait...not Skyhan. The flowing silver hair was his, but not the facial scars, now blossoming in radiance as if his soul were aflame and shining through his skin.

"Desert Rain!" Gabriel called, holding Silverheart high over his head. His voice quivered, as if he was overflowing with relief and joy. "You were right, about me, about Skyhan, about everything. But you need to finish this!"

He flung Silverheart in a mighty arc, and up it

went on a stream of starlight. As Katawa rushed up the stairs at her, just as he reached out his tentacle claw to pour Distortion into her, Desert Rain caught Silverheart and spun around, burying the blade into the shadow armor, pushing until she heard flesh being punctured and bone cracking. Katawa gasped as Silverheart impaled him straight through his chest and out his back, his eyes bulging.

Desert Rain closed her eyes, concentrating on both the Darkscale and the Lightscale. At first, her ears were full of cacophonous screaming, whether it was the voices in her mind or otherwise. But then she heard something else. It wasn't Sir Luce, or Bellaluna, yet she knew the voice.

I hear you.

"Balthazin, Bellaluna is waiting for you!" Desert Rain said. "I know the Equanume needs both a Celestial and a Night Sage's souls to work. But it's more than that. It's the balance of souls, but also of hearts. Both you and Bellaluna's hearts were broken that same day the Equanume was, and now they can be healed. If it is your wills, I release you both."

An overpowering chaos, light and darkness spinning out of control, enveloping everything and sent both Katawa and Desert Rain spiraling out of the world.

CHAPTER TWENTY-FOUR
Goodbyes

Her armor was gone. The Lightscale and the Darkscale were gone. Everything was gone, although she remained. Desert Rain felt peace unlike any she had ever known. She floated, not caring where the current carried her, not caring when the journey might end.

She knew where she was. The Eternal Deep. At least it was cool here, like taking a never-ending drink of clean water without drowning. At least her death was relaxing.

Not yet.

Desert Rain blinked her eyes open. Normally, she might have been terrified of the massive dragon standing before her, with scales of the deepest night shimmering with subtle stardust, but she wasn't afraid. His topaz eyes were kind.

A gentle nudge in Desert Rain's back compelled her to turn around. She smiled, holding back tears as Bellaluna's green eyes shimmered with love.

"Oh, my Desiree," she said, wrapping an arm around her in a warm embrace. "It's so good to see you."

"You too, Luna. But…if I'm not in the Eternal Deep, then where are we?" Desert Rain took a good look around and couldn't find the words to define their location. It was ocean, desert, forest, mountain, everywhere all at once in a kaleidoscopic display. Where they were, it was a sense of feeling whole.

Bellaluna basked in the colors and sensations.

"This is the Equanume," she replied.

"Oh? I thought the Equanume was a machine. The Machine of Ancient Magic."

"Yes, in the way nature is a machine—many moving parts that all come together in a seamless symphony." Bellaluna strolled with Desert Rain among the ever-shifting imagery. "The Equanume is balance itself. Something we Sages designed by combining our magic into one, to keep things in order, to balance our essences with the land. But we should have trusted the land to find a natural balance with us, even if it took time. And I believe that's something you, and your people, can do. You can find balance together. You must show them how."

Desert Rain nodded. "And we have to accept that the balance might tip sometimes, and we have to set it right."

"Exactly." Bellaluna embraced her again. "I will miss you so dearly. Are you sure you want to let me go?"

"I need to, Luna." Desert Rain held her close, burying her face in the dragon's neck. "You need to be with Balthazin. You taught me so much, but you have a path as much as I do. It's time for you both to rest. I'll miss you, and I'll never forget you."

Bellaluna nodded. She touched her nose to the moonstones on Desert Rain's forehead. "A part of me will always be with you, even though the Blueshine will fade away. But you have a power so much greater than mine, and I know you'll continue to use it for the greater good."

Desert Rain paused, knowing what it meant for Bellaluna's soul to leave her. "I guess I'll be seeing you again someday. I mean, how quickly are the years going to catch up with me, now that I — "

You have plenty of time, Balthazin assured her. **Thank you.**

The two dragons drifted away, swirling into a royal blue void, and Desert Rain swore she heard music coming from somewhere, almost like a fanfare welcoming lost loved ones home.

*   *   *

There was a heartbeat. Her own.

She gasped as she woke up. Close to her, holding her head in his arms, Gabriel's silver-blue eyes stared into hers.

His stoic façade cracked as his smile grew from ear to ear. "Dez! Thank the Divine Beasts." He embraced her, laughing in relief.

"Gabe…" Desert Rain was drained, and now every ache and pain from battle was rioting through her body. "They're gone. Bellaluna and Balthazin…they're gone."

Gabriel held her, brushing her hair from her face. He paused. "Your moonstones…"

Desert Rain reached up and felt her forehead. Her moonstones were gone. And yet, she felt surprisingly at peace with that. She looked at her fingers, still long and golden, and she could feel one last twinge of magic at the tips. One last gift from Bellaluna before she left.

Gabriel looked over his shoulder. "So, if Balthazin is gone, what do we do with him?"

He helped Desert Rain to sit up. She now saw they were back in the throne room, and on each side of her was Silverheart with the Hollow Eye, and the Darkscale, which had lost its glamour and now resembled a labradorite scepter topped with an orb inside which a small galaxy swirled. She was surrounded by all her friends, collectively overjoyed. Chiriku swooped in for a hug, and Mac was bouncing around like a kid at play. But Desert Rain couldn't acknowledge their victory yet, as Gabriel pointed across the room to a prone body.

Katawa slowly pushed himself up onto his hands and knees. Desert Rain was stunned how different he looked—he had retained his imprint of her to a degree, long ears and human shape, but now she saw some of his natural features too, ones that were not combined with Balthazin's draconic aspects. He looked skeletal, emaciated, and his eyes were sunken. His skin was pocked with ages-old scarring, from all the times he had reshaped himself with Distortion—it all caught up to him now.

Katawa turned to see her and her companions. His voice was weak, almost elderly. "Dez...you hate me so much, you rid us both of our power. I knew you were a fool, but..." He coughed and blood trickled from his lips. He curled into a ball, writhing. "Mortality. We both have it now. You've doomed yourself as well as me."

Desert Rain stood and walked over to him. She no longer felt anything for him—not hate, not pity, nothing. "Mortality is only a curse if you waste your life, Katawa."

He lunged and grabbed her foot. She didn't bother to move. She knew Distortion was his power, not Balthazin's, but he was so certain he knew how it worked. The last glint of malicious glee left his eye as he saw his touch did nothing. "Why...why can't I..."

"Didn't you once tell me that all the Distortion does is reveal people for what they truly are? Twisted on the inside?" She sat back on her haunches, coming down to his level. "That only works if you make people believe they're broken. I know what I am, as do my friends. You can't twist me, or anyone, anymore. And together, we're going to reverse everything you did. Your new world is over."

"We could've been gods!" he hissed, pushing himself up again. "Now you're not even Hijn. You're nothing."

"Really? Because all of them—" She gestured to the others. "They've all fought with me. They stood beside me. I'm everything because of them. It's your side of the room that's empty."

Katawa glared at her. "So, what now? Just going to keep gloating? Lock me away? Throw me in that damned furnace? Or let all your comrades tear me to pieces?"

"I vote for the last option," Chiriku piped up.

Desert Rain shook her head. "We've all been through enough pain. The cycle needs to end. I give you mercy, Katawa."

Katawa's eyes softened, and he gave her an innocent smile. "Mercy? Oh, Dezzy...the grace of a goddess. You know, the more I think about what we once had, the more I believe I could be happy if we returned to the desert—"

Desert Rain touched a finger to his forehead, and with the last, tiny remnant of Blueshine she had left, sent a jolt of it through his skull and into his brain. His expression froze, and after a few moments, blue-green sand began to seep from his mouth, his nose, his ears, and from around his horror-stricken eyes.

"Balthazin has returned to guard the Eternal

Deep, but I don't think he'll want to let you in," Desert Rain said softly. "So, the question is, where are you about to go?"

Katawa's eyes widened one last time, taking in that final thought, before he collapsed to the floor with one last exhale of sand.

Desert Rain stood up tall, even though her strength flagged. A warm hand on her shoulder filled her with soothing relief, and she looked at Mage Skyhan.

"You're going to need a bit of healing," Mage said with a smile, "so this won't hurt quite so much.'

"So what won't—"

The flood of embraces fell in around her, from Mac, Chiriku, Gabriel, and even more arms than she had first thought were present—including the irritated goat who said, "Can we PLEASE go home now?"

EPILOGUE

ONE YEAR LATER.

Desert Rain inhaled the aromas of the flora assortment of the flower stall. She held back a sneeze; as usual, she wasn't used to this pungent variety of flowers. Clova was like a child in a candy shop — she was enamored with a new breed of hydrangea that the florist had developed, a deep blue with twinkling golden spots.

A trumpet sounded, alerted them to the time.

"Clova, they're starting!" Desert Rain said, making her final selection of prickly poppy plants — they would look lovely in the Oasis — and placing them tenderly in her basket. She and Clova traded goods with the florist before heading towards the academy.

The new Knighthood of Luuva Academy had opened a few months ago, but already had a robust student body of eager young men and women. It was a stone's throw from the main square, the perfect spot for the townspeople to gather to witness the latest recruits standing at attention on the Academy's pavilion lawn. Desert Rain and Clova found a spot by the square's fountain, which had recently been rebuilt with a new statue in the center: a circle of figures, human, elven, dwarven, Featherin (a new classification that Falcolin and Quetzalin had agreed to try as a gender-neutral term, for now), Yopeis, Cindrean, Coastfolk, and to initial consternation by some higher-ups, a Lizard — although its representation there was more than well deserved, and always had been.

Desert Rain cast a glance among the line of new recruits, noting that some of the older ones in their twenties had slight marks and scars on their faces, the scars of Distortion. It was both a pain in her heart that they had been transformed, but also a touch of joy that all of Mage Skyhan's work for the past year had been successful. Mage, Desert Rain, Gabriel and Clova had worked together with the most unexpected of sources to learn more of Mac's unique Distortion-immune abilities — the alchemists of Darkscale, or those who were left, at any rate. They had discovered the remaining Darkscale clan hiding in a barricaded room of L'Teth Zurên shortly after Katawa's demise, and after negotiations — which included the Darkscale retaining possession of the Darkscale balance, having their brightest alchemists admitted to Syphurius's spellcasting school, and a peace treaty between the Darkscale and the Knighthood, they worked in tandem with the Noble Races to create a potion that they spent months administering to those affected by Distortion.

V'Tanna had been especially helpful in distribution, as she was able to use her magic to spread miles of rain infused with the remedy across Luuva Gros, even in the Inbetween. All the Hijn Council had worked above and beyond to ensure all their regions were supplied with the remedy, although it wasn't a perfect cure-all. Initially, while the remedy was a Sage-send to free the Distorted of their pain, the physical effects had not worn off immediately. However, without Katawa's presence to control the Distortion, and with time and healing in both the physical and emotional senses, bodies began to revert to their natural state. While purplish scars remained, the people of Luuva Gros had been reborn anew — not through the Equanume, but through compassion, community, and heart.

And Mac, having been the bearer of the key to its renewal, opened new doors for all Lejenous. Even now, Desert Rain spotted clusters of Bayou folk standing in the crowd, no longer being shunned by the Nobles. Sadly, the Vermin Brothers weren't among them, but she knew upon Gimch and Goude's healing from the Distortion, all three brothers had built a new ship to go exploring the seas around City Cindrea for the summer months. Desert Rain had been there to wish them well on their voyage. She had even received one letter from Gank, as he liked the idea of having a pen pal. It was too bad his writing was illegible scribbles, but Desert Rain believed she understood he was writing with delighted excitement.

A cold splash hit her and Clova on the back, as something fell into the fountain. They both turned to see Mac, dressed in the light blue tunic and black trousers of a squire, lying in the clear, sparkling waters. His scaly red face looked up at them with a grin.

Desert Rain reached in a pulled him out of the fountain. "Mac, what are you doing? Initiation is going to start any minute!"

Mac squeezed the water from his tunic. "I was-ss runnin' late-ttk, so Chi said she'd help me get-ttk here on time, but she ain't-ttk too good at controlling her windspeed yet-ttk."

A gust of breeze announced the Wind Hijn's arrival, as the yellow-feathered Quetzalin dropped down from the air beside them. "You said fast, Mac, so I brought you fast!"

Mac gave her a smirk. "Eh, never ask-kk a chicken

to take-kk you anywhere. They're so bad at directions, they don't-ttk even know why they cross the road."

That remark earned Mac a swift push of wind which landed him back in the fountain. Desert Rain pulled him back out, stifling her laughter, before leading him through the crowd. "No time for playing around, Mac! Get up there, it's time!"

Mac fell in line with the other recruits, and Chiriku settled down next to Desert Rain and Clova on the fountain edge. The timing couldn't have been better, for as soon as Mac was in the formation, the front doors of the Academy opened. Out walked, in perfect cadence, a V-shape formation of nine Knights, and at the front was Gabriel, his armor and silver hair shining in the sunlight. No helmet, no hat, his scarred face was held high and proud.

No one was prouder of him than Desert Rain. Because Gabriel was by all accounts the Swordmaster, even if he was the half most people were unfamiliar with, so he was still a member of the Knighthood. His founding and leadership of the Academy was nothing short of incredible. He didn't train the new knights alone; even now, he drew forth Silverheart, which every squire at the Academy had trained with. Sir Luce had been as invaluable a mentor as Gabriel, and it was well known that the two were inseparable. Desert Rain also knew, from personal observation, that Gabriel and Sir Luce spent hours every evening talking, learning and working together with a renewed trust. The original Swordmaster Skyhan was gone, but his spirit lived on through them.

Sir Gabriel went to each recruit, presenting them with Silverheart one at a time. As each squire held the sword, there was a moment of silent conversation between student and sword, and then Silverheart would glimmer with a glow, indicating Sir Luce's and Gabriel's approval. Once Silverheart was handed to Mac, who took the sword with some trepidation in his eyes, he held it for a long time, before a confused look crossed his face.

"Uh, Gabe? Sir Luce says I should order some leeches or something? Do you know what that means?" Mac asked sheepishly.

Gabriel laughed lightly. "Sir Luce and I discussed it. What he said was, we would like to establish an Order of the Legion, with you at the lead. Would you be up to this task?"

Mac's eyes went wide with surprise. "The Legion? What's that?"

"We hope to eradicate the word 'lejenous' from the Luuvian vernacular. It will take time and talks between the Bayou folk and the Nobles, but perhaps a better word we could propose would be the Legion. To mean brotherhood, community. Does that sit well with you?"

The lizard man's eyes brightened. "That would suit-ttk me just-ttk fine, Sir Gabe."

The crowd erupted in applause and cheers as the newest Knights of Luuva presented themselves. Desert Rain was so caught up in the moment, she almost didn't notice the tap on her shoulder from Chiriku. Once she did, the Quetzalin gestured to a thin man standing nearby — she could tell from the gray skin and green eyes he was Bloodburn, although he didn't wear the blackened leather and armor of a soldier. He was dressed in a green smock under a wheat-colored vest and matching leggings, perhaps a notary. He also wore a hatted hood that curved at the top in a crescent shape.

"Madam Desert...Rain," the Bloodburn notary said, although his glance at her was skeptical. Desert Rain couldn't blame him—she looked a little different every time he saw her, as her ears became shorter and rounder, her skin less golden, and her eyes now matched in their rich brownness. Not that the Bloodburn were unfamiliar with changing their appearances, but it must have seemed like a joke to him that Desert Rain was gradually changing more and more human-looking.

"His Majesty King Ragnor sends his regards, and wanted your advice on his latest proposal to the Syphurian govenors," the notary continued, presenting her with a scroll.

Desert Rain took the scroll, nodding to the notary. "Tell his Majesty I would be more than happy to discuss this with him. Perhaps by week's end, when I've had time to review this?"

The notary gave her a quick bow and then was off through the crowd. Some people gave him glances, but seeing a Bloodburn representative was becoming more familiar to them, especially with King Ragnor having established trade business with Syphurius.

Clova watched the notary walk away. "So, how is King Ragnor these days?"

"Oh, quite well," Desert Rain said, tucking the scroll among her purchased wares. "We've met a few times about business and creating relations with some of the Noble Cities. Even though Luna's not with me anymore, I guess he still trusts me."

"Weird," Chiriku said, spinning a small vortex on her fingertips. "Hey, how did he and the Bloodburn escape Katawa, anyway? You never told me."

"They way he tells it, Ragnor said Katawa had

thrown them down a chasm and left them for dead, or to starve to death," Desert Rain said. "But he said a group of people from the Taigalands found them and pulled them out, as if they knew they were down there and needed help."

Chiriku raised her eyebrows. "The winter gryphons?"

"My best guess. Perhaps the gryphons want a new Court to partner with. We still have no idea if any of the Secret Sacroth survived, but Kidran's been scouting around up north trying to find anyone who might be hiding underground."

Clova breathed in the crisp air. "So much still needs to be repaired between our people. But at least everyone is willing to take steps. I never thought I'd see the day that there would be partnership between the Nobles, the Legion, and the Courts of the Wret—wait, is it Moon Blessed now?"

Desert Rain smiled. "Moonborn. Believe me, I didn't propose it, but the Darkscale and Bloodburn both agreed to it and added it to the treaty.'

"The Courts of the Moonborn. Yes, that sounds more elegant," Clova agreed.

As the crowd dissipated, with many staying to congratulate individual knights, Desert Rain, Clova and Chiriku went to Mac to give him hugs and best wishes. Desert Rain noticed Gabriel had already slipped away, as was his habit—despite his reborn confidence, he kept to himself most of the time.

"Emily is waiting for me to bring her these cookies," Desert Rain said, checking on the package of savory sweets in her basket. "Thank Guerda for his infinite patience, but I'm sure she's getting feisty. Shall we go?"

"Actually," Mac said, while scratching the back of his head. "I was hoping Chi could show me where that-ttk new tea shop is around here? I was-ss thinking of getting' something to drink-kk before I get Kurl from the stables and get-tkk going."

Chiriku gave him a pointed look. "Where are you and Kurl off to? I thought your wandering merchant days are over."

"They are," Mac said. "Just-tkk, that I've been savin' up money, and I got-tkk me one of those nice townhouses here in Syphurius-ss. So, I've got-tkk some things to move that-tkk I need Kurl for."

"I thought you already have all your stuff in the Academy barracks."

Mac's red scales, somehow, blushed a deeper red. "I meant-tkk your stuff…from your grandfather's old place to my townhouse, if you…want-tkk to."

Chiriku stared at him silently. She frowned at him. "Macapailius Lizard, are you asking me, the Wondrous Wind Hijn of Luuva Gros, to move into your little townhouse with you?"

The lizard's awkward smile withered into a flat line.

The Quetzalin grinned. "Because that would be really nice."

Desert Rain didn't know how long she was wistfully smiling at Mac and Chi, as the two took each other by the hand and started walking away, before Clova nudged her. "Shall we leave the two lovebirds — uh, lovebird and love-lizard — alone?"

Desert Rain nodded. "For now." With that, she drew out the Hollow Eye, which she wore habitually under her tunic collar, and with a thought, she and Clova blinked out of Syphurius.

*   *   *

The Oasis was a marvel of floral beauty. Desert Rain planted the last prickly poppy in one of the flower beds, while Clova tended another part of the garden. Guerda-Shalyr's flock drank from the watering hole and lazed about in the shade of the palm trees, including Gothart, who, despite having been allowed to retain his humanoid shape, spent most of his time like any other goat. His days were spent lying on cushions and munching away happily on figs and dates that grew in the Oasis. Sure, there was always bickering between him and Guerda when the shaman wanted the goat to work, but Desert Rain could always appease Gothart with a nice shiny reward from Ulomin or Syphurius for him cleaning her burrow.

Emily splashed in the waters, dancing among the droplets as they rained around her. Desert Rain had no idea what future laid in store for a young goddess, but Emily was growing up with care and kindness, so she didn't worry. Perhaps Emily would take her place on the Hijn Council when she was ready. Even though Desert Rain would always be a member of the Council—even Fierno Ginso had been treating her amicably for the past year—she was essentially human again, even though traces of Luna still lingered. But somehow, being legal council for King Ragnor, the liaison for the Darkscale, and the co-guardian for the Lightscale with Gabriel was plenty of responsibility for her.

"Hey, look!" Emily pointed off to the distance.

"We have a guest!"

Desert Rain stood up and saw a figure approaching on a strongback. She figured it must be Mac and Kurl, and she wondered why the lizard was coming to see her. Given that the knighting ceremony had been four days ago, he must have left Syphurius that same day and hoofed it quickly to get here.

Yes, the strongback was Kurl, but the rider wasn't Mac. Desert Rain spotted the silver hair reflecting the sunlight as Gabriel came within proper eyeshot.

Clova smiled. She gestured to the goddess playing in the water. "Emily, would you mind helping me and Grandfather make some dinner? It looks like we'll have one more place to set tonight."

"But I want to see—" Emily paused, looking over at Desert Rain, and then at Clova, before mouthing "ooh" in understanding. "Okay, how about cactus cake tonight? I love making cakes!"

Clova laughed. "We can't have cake every night, but let's see what Grandfather Guerda might have cooking." She guided Emily over to the front entrance of the burrow, waving to Gabriel as he and Kurl approached. Jubis greeted them at the door, yipping as he normally did, now that his Distortion scars had diminished to one twisted paw and a crook in his muzzle.

Gabriel dismounted Kurl, who gratefully drank from the watering hole. The Knight walked to Desert Rain, and for a minute, neither of them spoke a word.

Eventually, Desert Rain cleared her throat. "How was the journey?"

Gabriel gazed into her eyes with a depth that made Desert Rain hold her breath. "Kurl is well acquainted with the route. Mac was kind enough to lend him to me for a while."

"Ah." Again, a moment of silence. "You've come a long way. Is there something you need?"

"Yes." The answer was quick, but there was no explanation. He didn't need to give one.

She smiled at him. "I'm glad you came."

"Me too." Gabriel didn't break eye contact with her.

Desert Rain tried again. "Is there a reason you...?"

Gabriel blinked, as if waking up from a reverie. "Oh, yes. I wanted you to know that the Hijn Council never had an official welcome for Chiriku as the new Hijn. So, we were planning a celebration, and we'd like to discuss how, and where, and all that. Plus, I'd like to know how your diplomacy meetings with King Ragnor are going, if he's mentioned anything about the border agreements with the Inbetween and Luuva —"

"Here." Desert Rain removed a flash that hung at her waist and offered it to him. "Drink first."

"Thank you." He took a long swig from the flask.

"Would you like to help me plant?" Desert Rain interrupted him. "I find it very meditative."

Gabriel hesitated at the question. "Oh, sure. I guess that was rude of me to launch into all those political matters first thing."

"I think it's your habit to do that." She knelt next to her flower bed. She handed him a hand shovel and pointed to small plants in pots. "These can go right in a row here."

For a few minutes, she and Gabriel planted in silence. A light warm breeze played with their hair.

"Do you still play music?" Gabriel suddenly

asked.

Desert Rain looked down at her fingers, which were no longer long, but the normal length for a human. Her feet had lost their prehensile nature, and she was still caught off guard to find toes when she looked down. "I do, but not as well. I had to relearn with shorter fingers. But Emily likes to hear me play."

Gabriel patted a plant into the soil. "It's strange to see you change so much over the year. I confess, I'll miss that green eye of yours. The fire in it when you were angry, or brave. Although your eyes now are so..." He cut himself off.

Desert Rain hid her grin. "The only constant is change. By the way, I like that you grew your hair longer instead of that crop you used to have."

Gabriel patted his hair. "Not exactly knight regulation length." He paused. "What does this mean for you now, that you're not Hijn anymore? I mean, do you live like a normal human now?"

Desert Rain shrugged. "I'm guessing. I just picked up where I left off, from before I met Luna. I didn't instantly become an old lady, so I guess I'll age normally from here. And yes, I think a normal life sounds nice."

Gabriel reflected on this. "You know, I'm technically not Hijn either."

Desert Rain looked at him.

"I mean, Sir Luce is in Silverheart. So even though we speak to each other, and I can wield the sword, I don't have his soul or magic within me. I guess I'm a normal human too."

"Normal doesn't seem the proper adjective for you," Desert Rain replied. "But, yes, I suppose that's true."

"So, we'll both grow old."

"Yes. Does that scare you?"

"Not really."

Desert Rain placed another plant in the ground. "I think it means, for us, time is far more precious."

"Yes. And there is still so much to do."

"Later. For now, we just breathe."

Gabriel nodded.

Twilight washed over the desert, and Desert Rain and Gabriel barely noticed by the time Emily called out to them for dinner. Even then, the two lingered in the Oasis, lingered in the glow of the gentle moon against the evening sky, lingered in that one moment where everything was at it should be.

THE END

A native of Riverside, Illinois, A.R. Cook is the author of the young adult fantasy series *The Scholar and the Sphinx*. She also has short stories published in the anthology "The Kress Project" from the Georgia Museum of Art, and the *World of Mirstone* anthologies. Her short film *B.L.I.S.S.*, directed by her husband David, won the Audience Choice Award at the 2022 Great Lakes International Film Festival.

Visit http://scholarandsphinx.wix.com/arcook to learn more.